# PASSION'S CAPTIVE...

Something in the sheer excitement of risk, of deception and intrigue, ignited in Sophy an ecstasy she had never dreamed of knowing. She had never before felt so beautiful, so alive, but she knew well that the secret passion she shared with Edmund Sutton was one that would flare quickly, then die.

She paid little heed to her handsome lover's promises of marriage and undying devotion, and when he did abandon her she tried to erase him from her heart, to grasp her chance of happiness with the one man who truly loved her . . . to endure the memory of a rapture that still beckoned her to be its captive. . . .

# BELOVED SINNER

(formerly titled *The Dresden Finch*)

*Jessica Stirling*

A DELL BOOK

Published by
DELL PUBLISHING CO., INC.
1 Dag Hammarskjold Plaza
New York, N.Y. 10017

Originally published under the title *The Dresden Finch*
Copyright © 1976 by Jessica Stirling

Dell ® TM 681510, Dell Publishing Co., Inc.

ISBN: 0-440-12116-7

Reprinted by arrangement with
Delacorte Press

Printed in Canada

First Dell printing—June 1978

# BOOK ONE

*The Captain of Hussars*

# One

Sophy Richmond resisted the temptation to reach out and slap her stepmother's bland, smiling face. Agatha would like nothing better than to taunt her into a display of temper and retaliation. Sophy vowed that she would not give the woman that satisfaction. She had given enough as it was.

"Surely there are other rooms in the house that would be suitable for your children?" Sophy said, mildly.

"None as suitable as this, I fear," said Agatha, in mock apology. "Together with the box room and the small sewing room on the corridor they will make an ideal nursery suite."

Sophy tucked her fists into the folds of her gown. Agatha, the smug cat, was thoroughly enjoying the latest encounter in the battle between them, especially as her clever stratagem had given her the upper hand. Anger and frustration brought a flush to the girl's cheeks. Agatha's smile widened into a grin.

Hastily Sophy edged from the open door into the room —*her* room, already spoiled by the woman's interference, now about to be stolen from her.

Carefully she steered the hoops of her gray moire skirt round the spindle tables that Agatha had brought from her previous home in Chiswick, on the outskirts of London. According to Agatha every item was a masterpiece of contemporary domestic fashion. If that was the case, then

Sophy preferred the fine old styles in which the mansion had recently abounded to the trash of the eighteen-fifties.

The tables' ugliness and their uselessness were emphasized by scores of lumpy ornaments, pinchbeck boxes and mottoes encased in flowery scrolls. Blue velvet curtains shrouded the handsome casement, looped by ropes of crude gilt thread. Heavily beaded cushions, hard as boulders, lorded it over the dainty antique chairs—all part and parcel of her stepmother's scheme to set her mark indelibly upon the household.

Agatha would not be content until she had ruined two centuries of comfortable traditionalism and refurbished Huffton in accordance with her suburban notions of taste. The solid old Yorkshire mansion already groaned with her bric-a-brac and, through the medium of warehouse catalogues, more arrived by carrier from Manchester and Birmingham each week.

The rooms in which Sophy had passed the best part of her twenty years were already tainted by gaudy clutter; the girl's protestations had been firmly overruled. The final step in gradual dispossession had not been wholly unexpected.

Ever since the day, six months ago, when Agatha had swept into Huffton House as Thomas Richmond's bride she had shown herself to be opinionated, brash and utterly devoid of refinement. She was confident in her own ability and in her beauty, and not in the least reticent on the subject of motherhood. As a demonstration of her fertility she had presented her late lamented husband, a gentleman not much younger than Thomas, with three male heirs in as many years. The three small sons were sniveling, podgy little specimens, less in need of discipline and castor oil than frequent doses of affection. Their pallid little lives were presently dominated by Nurse Simpkins, an exact replica of Agatha, though plainer in appearance.

For the first three months of her reign Agatha had merely been unpleasant, worming and burrowing her way into a position of authority in the household. In recent weeks, however, she had shown signs of becoming dangerous.

"In the unlikely event of my agreeing to give up my rooms," said Sophy, "where do you suggest I sleep?"

"I've given the matter a great deal of thought," said Agatha sweetly. "You, my dear, are also one of my children now, you know."

Sophy winced: there couldn't be much more than ten years between them, though Agatha was evasive about her age.

"Where?"

"I thought," said Agatha, "that you would be most comfortable in the large corner room overlooking the garden. I appreciate that you have not yet come to love your little brothers as you should. In the corner room you would have seclusion and . . ."

"The corner room is Mother's sitting room!" Sophy exploded. "Father would never countenance such an outrageous suggestion. All my mother's treasures are there, her favorite pieces, cherished and untouched for fifteen years. Father loves to go there, to sit alone and remember her."

Agatha pursed her lips. "Oh, really! On how many evenings of late have you found him there?"

There was no answer to that question. The truth was undeniable: since he had met, wooed, won and wed his Chiswick Venus—all in the space of a month's sojourn in London—Thomas Richmond's character had changed radically. He no longer seemed to take pride in the mansion, with its handsome paneling and hand-carved furnishings produced by Yorkshire's most skilled craftsmen and collected with care over the past three generations. He no longer spoke fondly of his youth, of Elizabeth, Sophy's mother, their happy marriage and mutual love of Huffton and its surrounding dales. As Agatha had tacitly pointed out, in marrying her, Thomas had buried the past, its pleasures as well as its sorrows.

Since his remarriage, it was Thomas Richmond's custom

now to loiter for only an hour after dinner, absently scanning business correspondence, then to bid Sophy and her governess, Miss Frampton, a gruff goodnight and hasten impatiently to the master bedroom where his new wife awaited his arrival.

As Thomas Richmond was now fifty-six years of age and had been a widower for close on sixteen years, Sophy found his tactless eagerness quite disgusting. She did not altogether blame her father: by certain standards of taste, Agatha was an attractive woman. Wide eyes, a full mouth and a generous figure were her natural assets. She had taught herself to capitalize on them by dressing well and paying much attention to her coiffure. In addition, she flattered Thomas, and seemed to exude an appetite to match her husband's; she was forever whispering naughtily in his ear or brushing him with her long expert fingers as if she found him irresistible. The effect on the widower was powerful enough to counteract the shock of inheriting three small stepsons and even seemed to blind him to the despoilation of his much-loved mansion.

"Do you really understand me, Sophy?" Agatha inquired. "I must constantly remind myself of your tender years and the fact that your knowledge of the world, and the male sex, are respectably limited."

"Not quite so limited as you imagine, Agatha."

"Nonsense! You're an innocent fool."

"And you," Sophy retorted, "are a trollop."

"Guard your tongue, child."

"May I remind you that I'm twenty years of age," said Sophy, "old enough to realize that you married my father only to provide comfort and status for you and your sons. But *your* kind, Agatha, cannot be content . . ."

"My kind?"

"Now that you have stamped everything with your appalling taste, I think you are looking for a way to be rid of me."

The flinty rage which caused Agatha's features to harden for a moment relaxed into a complacent smile once more.

"Indeed, I am," she admitted.

"But I mean to stop you," Sophy declared. "My father may be infatuated with you, but he cannot have lost all sense of fairness. He will uphold my position as his daughter."

"Are you sure of that?" Agatha's eyes glittered. "Thomas will do what I want him to do, because I have what he needs most. It's simple human arithmetic, my dear. He can no longer live without me."

"Agatha you . . . you *disgust* me."

Sophy swung towards the door. Trollop she had called her stepmother and a trollop Agatha was—but it was less the woman's blatant sensuality that caused Sophy's anxiety than the vivid pictures that rose in her own imagination. In one way she could not blame Agatha, though her understanding in no degree cooled her loathing. Sophy too longed to have a husband of her own. By supplanting her as mistress of Huffton House, Sophy knew that Agatha had seriously decreased her chances of finding a husband of her own class and station among the Yorkshire gentry.

The Richmond family fortunes might be based on wool and, far back in its languid history, there were probably all sorts of vulgarians and rogues, but Sophy had been brought up to believe in privilege and had been sufficiently protected from the crassness of moneymaking to develop a certain snobbishness in that respect. All that too had been wiped out by Agatha.

"I shall speak to my father," Sophy said.

Agatha laughed throatily. "Do that, child," she said, "and perhaps you will learn then that the woman who makes a man king in her bedroom is the ruler of the rest of the house."

It was unfortunate for Sophy that her father's habits.

had changed so much. Before the advent of Agatha she could have been sure of a patient and sympathetic ear for her problems. As matters stood now, however, she had trouble acquiring even a few moments of her father's time in privacy.

Since the focus of his emotional life had shifted, Thomas Richmond's business had also suffered neglect. The honorable gains of the small landowner, backed by investment in several well-established companies, had always supported his modest claim to be a gentleman and had provided a satisfactory standard of living. Agatha, however, had extravagant notions and a keen interest in increasing the inheritance which would fall to her in due course. She had "advised" her husband to exploit his capital and seek faster and larger profits by speculating. There was no danger of bankruptcy, of course, for the tenant farms on Huffton estate were leased by good, honest men; but the stock market was skittish and lively and, at an age when most men were content to ride slow horses, Thomas Richmond found himself in the saddle of a willful colt. He was obliged to work harder, think faster, and make his presence felt in areas of business that, previously, he had regarded as beneath his dignity.

Though, for a time, the dual challenges of a sensual young wife and a nimble market awakened youthful vigor in him, the effort of sustaining the attack wearied him, made him short-tempered with everyone and everything— except his loving bride.

By lurking in the hall, Sophy finally waylaid her father in his library. The long, narrow room had lost its contemplative atmosphere in recent weeks. The table that had once held only a copy of the family Bible and a favorite book of poems was littered now with newspapers, journals and cloth-bound volumes of reports on all sorts of esoteric subjects.

The struggle to keep abreast of changing times kept Thomas Richmond on his feet. He read with fierce concentration, shuffling round the table, scratching for facts which would help him understand the geography of the mid-nineteenth century and plot his route through its economic shoals to a safe harbor, a harbor that became more and more of a mirage as Agatha's greedy ambition increased in ratio to her husband's success.

Caught off guard, pebble-lens spectacles propped on his nose, shoulders stooped like a heron's, Thomas Richmond showed the burden of his years, his cares and his appetites.

When his daughter entered, he was mumbling over the latest report of Her Majesty's Inspectors of Factories, trying to determine what the suggested innovations meant and how they might affect his annual dividends. Mastering of the terminology was difficult enough to make his brain clack like a shuttle and his eyes flicker and vibrate like a loom of red thread. His coat was tossed on the brown leather reading chair. The lamps were no longer neatly arranged but ranked, dangerously, down the length of the table, though spring sunlight still glimmered in the garden outside. A year ago, if she had broached him thus, Sophy's father would have welcomed her intrusion, would have put his book aside and walked with her in the soft twilight under the elms and larches to the ridge of Huffton Pike.

Tonight, he rounded on her, snarling.

"Do you not know that I'm not to be disturbed?"

Sophy realized then, with a sinking heart, that Agatha would win not only the skirmish but the war. Because she had not taken time to marshal her arguments, and had not, on this occasion, discussed the matter with her governess, Miss Frampton, she found herself tongue-tied and nervous, quite unable to give him a pointed answer when he sourly demanded, "Well? What is it you want?"

"My . . . my room . . ."

"Yes." He pulled off his spectacles and tossed them on

to the table, kneading the bridge of his nose with finger and thumb. "Yes, I have heard of your selfishness."

"*My* selfishness?"

"Agatha informs me that you are unwilling to cooperate in finding accommodation for your brothers."

"They are *not* my brothers."

Thomas Richmond scowled and thrust out his jaw. His face had once been handsome, smooth-planed and firm. Now, Sophy noticed, the skin was grayish, sagged under his throat and puffed about the eye sockets. He had spilled brandy upon his ruffed shirtfront. A decanter and a glass were hidden by the nook of the hearth.

"Do not quibble with me," her father told her. "You are spoiled. I see that now. I've failed to make a lady out of you. I've overindulged you. I suppose, as Agatha says, I can expect no other reward."

Sophy wavered between rage and pity.

"Reward, Father?"

"Ingratitude."

"I'm not ungrateful. I love you."

"Then you might show it."

"But . . . but how?"

"By accepting Agatha; by doing as she says in all things."

"I . . . I . . . Very well, Father, if that is your wish," said Sophy, humbly. "The children may have my rooms."

"Put them and that nurse into the wing. More convenient; more private."

"Did Agatha also inform you that she wishes me to occupy Mother's room?"

Thomas Richmond had the decency to hesitate. At first Sophy thought that he was giving the proposal very careful consideration, then she heard the sound of the clock chiming in the recesses of the hallway. On the library mantelshelf the domed monstrosity Agatha had given him as a dowry gift whirred and cheeped out nine wiry notes. The man darted round and stared at the clock, his eyes squeezed half-shut in a strange display of avidity and apprehension. He fished a half-hunter from his vest pocket and consulted it, then, gathering himself, lifted his coat and, while buttoning it on, squinted at his daughter as if she was a bumbling servant.

"Father, do *you* wish me to occupy the sitting room?"

"Agatha . . ."

"*You*—you say it."

"Yes."

"And Mother's things?"

"We will . . . put them in the cellar."

Sophy felt tears start into her eyes. She turned her head away. He was still squinting at her, not curiously but with brusque impatience. It was as if he had been possessed of some demon, a succubus, which had drained him of all decency and respect.

"And when Agatha decides that she must have the corner room for . . . for a music salon, what then?" Sophy said. "Will I be put in the cellar too?"

"That is *enough*, damn you! *Enough!*" He caught her by the elbow and without a shred of gentleness, steered her towards the door. "I'm sick to death of your petty squabbling over domestic affairs. I've no time for such trivialities; no time, d'ye hear, girl? Leave me alone."

Only a grain of pity, and the memory of the man she had once loved, prevented Sophy from screaming abuse at this stranger. In addition, she realized that she and Agatha were, after all, not really poles apart. The true difference between them was that Agatha was frankly selfish and wore no disguise unless it suited her immediate purpose. Agatha was also the winner, the conqueror.

Controlling herself, Sophy announced her surrender to the inevitable. Instead of breaking from him, she secured his arm, holding him and checking his forward progress. The clocks finished their accounting. The silence in the old house was broken only by the faint and far-off wailing of the smallest of her stepbrothers. It reminded her, sadly, of the night her infant brother had died, only weeks after his birth. She had heard her mother's cry of anguish hanging in the air and, even at the age of five, had instinctively understood the equation of death and loss.

The man listened too. Perhaps the same memory haunted him. He had buried two baby sons and his wife in the years of his prime, had redeemed from his first marriage only a daughter.

Looking up into his face, Sophy said, "Do you mean that, Father?"

"Hm? What?"

"Do you wish me to leave you alone?"

The moment was gone, lost, broken like the petals of a delicate flower.

"Yes," the man snapped. "Leave me. It's time I was in bed."

Sophy's eyes were dry now, her voice calm, almost casual. "In two weeks," she said, "I will be out of your house for good."

"What's that?" He was startled, jolted briefly by this totally unexpected announcement. "Now, now: all because of a silly quarrel over a room?"

"My . . my brothers need you, Father. They need you more than I do."

Bewilderment furrowed his brow.

"Do they? But . . . ?"

"I suggest you look after them as you once looked after me."

"Sophy?" He could not find the strength to ask forgiveness; nor could he quite bring himself to reject the opportunity she had offered him to be rid of the encumbrance of endless female conflict.

"Where will you . . . ah, go, Sophy?"

"To Switzerland."

"Switzerland! You cannot travel abroad, alone."

"Alone? I'm alone here now, except for Miss Frampton. Besides, the Redfords are spending the summer near Lucerne, and have invited me to join them for the season. I told you of it weeks ago, but you appear to have forgotten. Do I have your permission, Father?"

"Will you . . . come back?"

She had given him enough. She had softened the blow, had tried to rouse him to an understanding of his new responsibilities. None of it had penetrated the armor of his infatuation and his Agatha-inspired ambition. His gentleness had melted into weakness. Eventually Agatha would rub him down like an inferior grindstone, wear him away to nothing.

Suddenly Sophy felt strong, like Agatha, and, like Agatha, quite capable of manipulating her own destiny.

"No, Father," she said, with a trace of contempt. "I will not come back."

Turning, she left him alone in the room. As she walked across the hallway and ascended the staircase, she still showed the gracefulness of a girl, but her bearing now was sedate, assured and womanly.

That evening, Agatha Richmond had to wait for her husband's arrival in the master bedroom. She had intended to castigate him for his tardiness and withhold, for a little, the treasures he so avidly desired. But Thomas Richmond's eyes were red with weeping, and Agatha, more astute than affectionate, gave him comfort in lieu of loving and much good advice on the subject of his daughter's future.

Where Eunice Frampton had come from and what course her early career had followed, Sophy could not be sure. The governess was not so much evasive about her background as inventive. In the years during which she had been Sophy's teacher, companion and unofficial lady's maid, the woman had concocted such a mosaic of adventures for herself that, had she been a hundred instead of forty, she could hardly have crammed them in. With the waning of childish impressionability, Sophy had mischievously indulged her mentor, encouraging her flights of fancy, all the while believing that Miss Frampton's origins were staid and dull rather than mysterious and colorful.

In a sense it was Miss Frampton who finally gave Sophy the courage to carry out her threat to leave Huffton House. Without the governess to act as chaperone and maid Sophy could hardly reach London on her own. Huffton and the Yorkshire community had been her home, protecting her like a little turtle in its green and gold shell.

Agatha, however, primed to seize every stray advantage, took up the challenge Sophy had thrown at her father and confirmed it by dismissing Miss Frampton as redundant. Agatha also briefed the family lawyer to come to certain generous financial arrangements to ensure that Sophy, and her governess, would be well enough provided for to make the outward trip in comfortable style. To all of this, Thomas Richmond gave bemused agreement and his signature when required. It did not occur to him that Agatha now had Sophy's purse strings in *her* hands, and could, if it came to that, exercise a modicum of control over her stepdaughter no matter how far from home she wandered.

So, whether she wished to change her mind or not, Sophy found herself pushed towards a rapid departure from the mansion which had been her home for all of her young life.

Eight days after the confrontation in the library, Sophy stood on the shallow step in front of the house with luggage piled around her, watching the groom load up the coach that would take her, and Miss Frampton, into Middlesborough and the beginning of their long journey across Europe.

A breeze was striding over the dales, bringing the breath of the English summer morning. An ache of homesickness caught Sophy unaware. She paused, not to savor

her last close view of home but to exorcise it as swiftly
as possible from her mind.

The tableau on the step was motionless. The figures
might have been wax—Agatha, smugly smiling, Thomas
Richmond, gloomy and embarrassed, the three small boys
ranked in front of the gigantic nurse; all posed, mannered,
and anxious to step back into their own lives.

It would have been natural for Sophy to kiss her father
and even to make the gesture of kissing her stepmother.
But, whatever else she was, Sophy was no emotional
hypocrite. She did nothing, simply stared at them for a
moment, then, to their surprise, hoisted herself into the
hired coach and instructed Miss Frampton to close the
door.

The coach rolled off down the steep driveway.

Sophy looked neither left nor right. She stared straight
past Miss Frampton's ear at the buttoning of the leather
bench, waiting for the pain to increase to anguish. But,
oddly, it did not. All her sorrow and loss had been dissi-
pated during the months since her father's return from
London by the shock of realizing that the woman with
him was not a new domestic but his wife, and that she,
Sophy Richmond, had no place in his life or his house
any longer. Today, this moment, was an inevitable ending.
She left Huffton to strangers, her inheritance to Agatha,
and her hours of childhood happiness for three anonymous
little stepbrothers to discover if they could.

Ahead of her lay Europe.

Stiffly, she lifted the handkerchief in her hand and blew
her nose.

To bridge the minutes before the coach finally left the
Richmond estate, Miss Frampton said, "Switzerland is a
beautiful country, so I've heard, thronged with the most
fashionable people in Europe at this season of the year,
including gentlemen."

Sophy smiled politely.

She understood the subtle meaning in her governess's remark. Switzerland was no mere avenue of escape. The Redfords were bound to be the center of a group of interesting males and she was pretty, well-bred and of thoroughly marriageable age, even if she no longer had a dowry.

Flight did not become her. She saw her departure as a quest, a quest for a husband and a home of her own, a husband wealthy enough to make dear Agatha turn jade with envy and compensate in double measure for the love and security that the trollop had stolen away.

# Two

According to the guidebook, Switzerland was reputed to be Europe's most exhilarating country. Sophy was willing to take Mr. Baedeker's word for it. Personally she found no thrill in views of precipitous mountains dripping with ice and could not for the life of her detect a trace of *lapis lazuli* in the waters of the lakes. In company, however, she uttered such appropriate cooing sounds of awe and admiration that nobody in the Redford crowd guessed how much it all bored her.

The Schneegarten chalet hotel stood in a private forest high above the lake, ten miles from the town of Lucerne, a white-painted, wooden building, with bright green shutters pierced by heart-shaped peepholes, and jutting eaves carved with birds, bells, chalices and flowers. All in all, it was far too picturesque and wholesome to impress Sophy, and its appearance hardly compensated for the discomforts of communal living, and being a victim of boring Sir Arthur, a prey to Lady Patricia's matchmaking pranks, and a pet to all the children who thronged the lawns and salons. What galled Sophy most of all was the fact that she had committed herself in advance to staying for the summer. She regretted her decision more and more as the days glided past and nothing in the way of diversion appeared on the narrow horizon of Schneegarten society.

For the past twenty years, Lady Patricia Redford, a

close friend of Sophy's mother, had taken a keen, if distant, interest in her daughter. There had been intermittent communication between Huffton House and the Redfords' Ulster estate. Stephen and Walter Redford had spent one November hunting with the Middlesborough pack. The boys were obsessed with riding, sailing, shooting and fishing and not at all with the pursuit of the fair sex. Sophy could not imagine Sir Arthur's heirs following his footsteps into Parliament and imprisoning themselves in London for half a year at a stretch.

Considerate hosts, the Redfords offered their guests the usual choice of healthy entertainment. With as much bonhomie as she could muster, Sophy was obliged to take part in picnics, boating expeditions and kindred open-air activities. When she discovered that the Redfords' card of visitors was unlikely to include any of Sir Arthur's influential acquaintances, her disappointment made it difficult for her to sustain the pose of a carefree young maiden.

The guests were a dismally dull collection, too young, too stupid or too impoverished to be entered on Sophy's list of prospective mates.

There was Albert, a friend of Walter's, a student of Divinity at Oxford; Frank, a chum of Stephen's, bent on a military career; George, a taciturn youth striving to master German grammar and simultaneously grow his first moustache; Herr Waller, a pompous young vintner who stayed only three nights and proclaimed himself a misogynist; and there was Laurence Flaherty, nicknamed "The Flea," who stalked about the chalet in a bathing costume and was purportedly earmarked for Angela, youngest female Redford, who was too naive to notice the blemishes in her hero's character. In addition there were sundry cousins, male and female, so disgustingly similar that Sophy did not even try to recall their names and addressed them all, when necessary, as "my dear." It was typical of the Irish crew to go to the expense of leasing an entire hotel, and its staff, for three months, and then to do nothing worthwhile with it.

In the evenings, after an early dinner, a little attempt at sophisticated entertainment was provided—some dancing, singing and frivolous games. Lady Patricia conversed with Sophy, and Sir Arthur, when he noticed her at all, bumbled on about the state of agriculture, as if she were interested in *that*. But the guests soon began to yawn, and by nine, or shortly after, Sophy would find herself alone in the salon staring disconsolately across the furniture at Miss Frampton who, with a needlessly discreet flicker of her fan, would indicate that it was time to retire too. Mercifully, Sophy had padded her luggage with assorted novels and whiled away the hours by reading of the exploits of sundry suffering heroines who, lucky little ducks, never had a spare moment to be bored and whose problems seemed to Sophy so much more fascinating than the reality in which she had planted herself.

For ten days her tedium found no relief and devolved into a sulky lethargy that, had Miss Frampton not kept her up to the mark, might have lapsed eventually into truculence.

Close to the middle of June, however, diversion at last presented itself in the form of a trading acquaintance of Sir Arthur's, a gentleman whose enigmatic manner intrigued Sophy far more than his worth as a potential suitor.

Sophy had voluntarily confined herself to the salon that morning, for the sun was very hot. She first saw the man flitting like a ghost across the recess between the salon and the dining room. There was nothing ethereal about his appearance: He wore an impeccably formal suit and carried a fat leather portmanteau. Sophy quickly changed her seat—she had the salon to herself—and peeped into the closetlike room Sir Arthur used as a sanctum and which was recognized as being out of bounds to the guests.

The stranger was seated on the edge of an armchair, portmanteau balanced on his knees. She rated him at once as being in his forties and, if her reading of his complexion was right, put him down as foreign.

It was his stillness which impressed her most. He was squat and broad-shouldered, and the lapels of his coat and dove-gray vest could not hide the depth of his chest. She could hear Sir Arthur's rumbling, unflurried voice, the tone he used when discussing serious matters, quite different from his usual hearty booming. She did not linger too long in case her host caught her eavesdropping. Besides, she could not decipher the conversation and, after a moment, the study door was quietly closed from the inside.

Throughout the remainder of the morning, Sophy loitered in the salon. Her fortitude was not rewarded and Sir Arthur and his associate remained in private conference over luncheon. At last Sophy's patience flagged and she retired to her room for a short *siesta*. Shortly after three she resumed her vigil. But her intriguing bird had flown. It was not until dinner that he made his first public appearance.

Sophy was extra careful with her *toilette* that night, draping herself in a dress of emerald satin which showed off her bosom rather daringly. She had no interest in impressing anyone in that house; the maneuver was self-oriented, designed to draw the stranger's attention. Whether or not she cultivated him, she would make sure that he noticed her.

Covertly, she studied him across the dining table. He sat on Sir Arthur's right, too far down the table to engage in casual conversation. Perhaps he was not so old as she had first imagined. His swarthy complexion made it difficult to gauge his age. He was reserved, but not shy, articulate, but not communicative. He did not seem to give her more than a passing glance. For all that, Sophy was impressed by the watchfulness in his dark, slumbrous eyes.

In the brief *soirée* which followed dinner, she looked around for him, only to discover that he and Sir Arthur had gone into seclusion once more. She did not dare risk seeming forward by pumping any of the Redfords for information. Tomorrow, however, she would persuade Miss Frampton to make a few inquiries, simply for the novelty and because she felt him to be as out of place in that gay and youthful company as she was herself.

That evening she learned only two things about the stranger. He was a merchant from Brittany and his name was Leon de Nerval.

A trader and a Breton peasant: Agatha would laugh her to scorn.

The clank of the ewer wakened Sophy and she raised her head from the pillow to watch Miss Frampton decant warm water into the basin. Daylight was searingly bright, the scene beyond the bedroom window, with its mountains, streams and tiny chalets, so changeless that it might have been etched on the glass.

"Good morning, Sophy."

"Good morning, Miss Frampton."

Eunice Frampton, like Alpine scenery, was also changeless and hard-edged. In twenty years' time, Sophy thought, the governess would probably look exactly as she was now, neither old nor young, neither in fashion nor out of it. As a concession to her voluntary duties as a lady's maid, Miss Frampton wore fresh picot edging on her black dress and covered her skirts with a spotless white apron.

"Did you sleep well, Sophy?"

This dialogue between them was a morning ritual.

"Very well, Miss Frampton. And you?"

"Undisturbed, thank you, my dear."

Sophy swung her legs out of bed, toes groping for the slippers by the bedside. She stretched, unbuttoned the top of her nightgown and, passing to the washstand, dabbed her hands and face with a moist sponge. Meanwhile, Miss Frampton had turned down the bed and was rearranging the dresses which the Irish maid had sprawled out on the long box. She handled the garments with that ease and gentle confidence gamekeepers display in handling small animals. Toweling her face carefully—dabbing not rubbing —Sophy inspected the dresses critically.

"Not the foulard, Miss Frampton. The new yellow muslin, if you please."

"I thought you were preserving it for a special occasion, Sophy."

"Today is a special occasion."

"It is?"

"The picnic."

"But there is invariably a picnic arranged."

"And I feel like looking my best: the yellow muslin."

Miss Frampton gave no sign of curiosity: Sophy and the woman were close enough to share confidences without words.

A half hour later, Sophy was accoutered in the muslin dress and its proper accessories. The governess kneeled to put the finishing touches to the hem. Looking up, Miss Frampton said, "If you will excuse me, Sophy, I believe I will stay in the chalet today."

"Are you unwell?"

"No," the woman said. "But I do not wish to . . . to hover over you."

"What will you do?"

"Perhaps I will take lunch with the servants."

"Really?"

"Their conversation can be most informative, particularly about newly arrived guests."

"Ah!" said Sophy. "You'll enjoy that more than sitting in a field, I'm sure."

"I really don't know where they acquire their knowledge," Miss Frampton said. "But it is usually accurate, and profuse."

"Good," said Sophy. She kissed the woman on the cheek, then left the bedroom and sailed downstairs for breakfast.

The Flea and his diminutive companion were seated at a side table delving into grilled kidneys and buttermilk. They were dressed for the day's outing. The Flea carried a bundle of personal belongings on his knee wrapped in buckram and rope like a footpad's bedroll, and seemed ready to spring into action as soon as the first wagon arrived. A couple were playing backgammon on a board by the window and, through the window, Sophy could see other guests propped on the fringes of the lawn, the girls like foundered sailboats in their frothy summer dresses. She greeted them pleasantly, wiggling her fingers, then helped herself to a sliver of bacon, a grilled chop and an egg, all taken from the griddle over the charcoal trench-fire that acted as a servery in this quaint old room.

"Miss Richmond, is it not?"

Leon de Nerval's voice was deep, mellow and as English as that of a Bond Street shopkeeper. There was only a slight trace of a French accent. Sophy blushed. It was an easy feat, done automatically as a sign of delicate propriety on first meeting a stranger of the opposite sex. The fact that the stranger was almost old enough to be her father, and a foreigner to boot, did not deter the winsome functioning of her tissues. She was encumbered by her breakfast plate, and he was burdened by a fluted silver coffee pot: she could not offer her hand.

"Yes," she said.

"I am Leon de Nerval, Miss Richmond. Will you share this fresh pot of coffee with me—unless, of course, you would prefer a dish of tea?"

His eyes were too dark to give much hint of his thoughts or motives. It might have been courteous coin-

cidence that had brought them to the servery together—
yet he had known her name.

"Coffee will suit perfectly, thank you," Sophy said.

Polished manners and an easy grace enabled de Nerval
to usher Sophy to a seat at the long table and even to
draw out the chair for her, without releasing his grip on
the heavy pot. Like a palace butler, he attended to the
placement of her cutlery and cruet, plate, saucer and cup.
He had blunt hands, tufted with black hair. Though he had
on the same formal coat he had worn the previous day, he
had exchanged his hard collar for one of soft, pointed linen
filled with a fulsome silk cravat.

"We did not have an opportunity to meet last night,"
he said.

"That . . . that was unfortunate," said Sophy, a shade
startled by his directness. "I'm glad that you have made
amends this morning."

He took the setting opposite her. Apparently he had
eaten earlier, or perhaps he did not eat breakfast at all.
He drank cup after cup of black, unsweetened coffee, while
Sophy toyed with her food. He was not reticent now, and
put many questions to her about herself and her background, the deep pleasant voice with its lack of insistence
removing the sting of impropriety. A younger man in the
same situation, Sophy knew, would have sparred away at
desultory small talk for hours before daring to display any
interest in her at all. She answered his questions readily
enough, though guarding the true state of her family connections, of which she was needlessly ashamed.

De Nerval said, "I gather that you are one of the Richmonds of Huffton?"

Flattered, Sophy said, "That's correct, M. de Nerval."

"I've done business, indirectly, with your father."

"Wool business?"

"Indeed, in quantity, by the marked bale."

"From which market?"

"Hardacre."

"You visit the North.then?"

"I have done. Normally I buy through an agent; a Mr. Aylmer, from Liverpool."

The name meant nothing to her; Sophy finished her chop.

De Nerval said, "The wholesale price is remarkably cheap for a Yorkshire grain, and the wool is quite suitable for weaving military fabrics."

"I see," said Sophy. "You are a regimental supplier?"

"I do supply regiments." De Nerval laughed softly. "British regiments, and Russian, and the new peacocks of France. I've even sold goods to the Lords of the Atlas Mountains, though not often and exclusively on the barter system."

Could he be telling her that he was wealthy? Sophy placed her knife and fork on the empty plate and allowed de Nerval to pour coffee for her.

"One of the best pieces of exchange I've made this year," he said, "I effected only this morning."

"Oh?"

"With Master Paul Redford, no less."

"And what did he have that was worth a price?"

"For payment of a shilling, young Master Paul has guaranteed that I will sit beside you in the fifth carriage."

Sophy blinked.

"I've never spent a more profitable shilling," de Nerval said.

"Sir, I'm not at all sure . . ."

"Have you encountered a person of my race before?" he asked.

"Of course," Sophy lied.

"Among your father's friends?"

"He has no such . . . I mean, no, not in Middlesborough."

"Have you ever met a real merchant before?"

"Only wool men."

"Then," said de Nerval, "if you have no objection to my company on today's picnic, it will prove enlightening for both of us, Miss Richmond. Perhaps I may introduce you to the finer points of my profession."

"That will be most interesting," said Sophy, adding, "but what can you possibly hope to learn from me in return?"

"One can learn so many things from a beautiful woman," de Nerval answered. "The only secret you will be permitted to keep is how you achieve such beauty."

"Thank you," Sophy said.

She knew then, for sure, that she had just become the target of an unexpectedly strenuous wooer.

"Did you really bribe the lad to put you next to me?"

"A whole shilling," de Nerval replied. "Paul Redford will be as shrewd a trader as his father when he grows up."

"More shrewd," said Sophy. "I think he made the best of this bargain."

"I must be the judge of that," de Nerval said, rising. "Come, Miss Richmond. I hear the carriages drawing up outside."

Without reluctance, Sophy took the merchant's arm and allowed him to escort her through the hall and out into the bright morning sunshine.

Once, the workers in her father's factory had been treated to a picnic in a meadow some miles from the town. Sophy had gone with him to see the workers off on their jaunt, and the spectacle had strangely impressed her at the time: familiar folk changed by Sunday clothes, laughing and jostling on the wagons under gaudy flags and plaited evergreens. Sophy had envied the tenants and laborers their fun and, in that long-ago moment, had wished that there were no barriers to prevent an owner's daughter sharing the pleasures of the peasant classes. Since then, however, she had come to respect, almost to revere, those very barriers and to uphold them at all cost as her protection against the rigors of masculine authoritarianism and to maintain whatever power a woman had in her own circle of society.

Seated in the open Swiss carriage as it lumbered down the pathway of the hotel, she was reminded of that day in her childhood and, turning, raised her hand in a gesture of farewell to Miss Frampton. The sight of the governess standing by the steps, growing smaller and smaller as the wagon progressed, filled Sophy with vague apprehension.

Once clear of the hotel and onto the loamy forest roads which climbed gradually into the foothills, however, she relaxed and absorbed herself in de Nerval's conversation. In spite of his threat to educate her in nationalism and brokerage, he made no further reference to these subjects and contented himself with pointing out the mountains, the Pilatus and the Rigi, which towered over the lake. Albert, the divine, made several observations on the connection between altitude and weather, and de Nerval joined with the girls in congratulating the young man on his knowledge. But something in the Breton's manner, something that was not quite patronizing, gave her the impression that Leon de Nerval was more knowledgeable on more subjects than the whole company put together.

About noon, the small strong horses brought the carriage-wagons to the gate of a high meadow in which a vanguard of six favored servants had already spread out an assortment of cushions, rugs, parasols and checkered tablecloths. By that time, de Nerval had slipped into addressing his companion as "Miss Sophy," an informality to which Sophy did not object. The meadow was fanned by snowy breezes from the ice-field that hung only a few thousand feet above them, glittering yet benign in the sunlight. Within minutes of arrival, the Redford boys had organized a game of bat and ball into which everyone,

Sophy and de Nerval included, was incorporated, the players pausing in relays to rest among the flowers or refresh themselves with glasses of *limonade gazeuse*. After the game, there were races, in which Sophy did not participate, and then luncheon was served out of the huge wicker hampers.

Though the picnic was not much different from previous excursions, Sophy found herself caught up in the enjoyment of it and less guarded in her relationship to de Nerval than she would have been in an English setting. The food was the best she had ever tasted; Alpine trout, Chamois venison cooked in butter, crumbly goatsmilk cheese, and a dessert of wild strawberries washed in iced wine and frosted with sugar. When the feast was over, there was not one soul with the energy or inclination to do more than lie on the grass and be lazy.

Resting under a parasol, Sophy found de Nerval's talk so interesting and entertaining that she forgot the passage of time. He did not discuss any of the topics with which older men are inclined to bore young women, and, before she was really aware of what was happening, Sophy was involved in argument over the merits of certain contemporary novelists, a subject upon which Leon was well informed.

Whatever topic might have engaged them when literature was worn out, Sophy did not discover. The arrival of two young Bavarians, on a walking tour of the Alps, caused a diversion. Blond and wiry, their scanty clothing seemed hardly suitable for the present terrain, let alone for barren passes and peaks. The taller of the pair had a zither slung across his shoulder, an incongruous piece of equipment for a mountaineer.

"What little gear they possess will be hidden away somewhere until they are ready to use it," de Nerval explained.

"What do they intend to do?"

"Scale the mountains."

"Those mountains?"

"The Rigi is only a little carbuncle to them. I imagine they will be after bigger conquests."

"Are they mad?"

"Most people think them mad," said de Nerval. "But if they were English gentlemen with mutton-chop whiskers, tweeds, and compasses in their buttonholes, then they would be hailed as heroes."

"You sound like a cynic, M. de Nerval."

"Perhaps I am, a little. The Bavarians have so little money, and so much ambition. . . ."

"Ambition, to risk their very lives just to reach the summit of a mountain?"

"That's the essence of ambition," de Nerval said. "It's a quiet thing, not accompanied by fanfares of trumpets, symbol of a style of life, of a whole philosophy. The Teutonic races are rife with it."

"Why do they come here, to our picnic?"

"In the hope that we will ask them to sing. They will then pass round a hat and rely on our generosity to support them for another week's climbing. In our passive way, we will help them come one step nearer to their destiny."

"And do you approve of that?"

"Wholeheartedly," said de Nerval. "To have an objective in life and to take all possible steps to attain it is admirable. If I would find any fault with them it's in the haphazard manner of their preparations. Still, there's probably no help for that, and it's better to attack life ill-equipped than to wait for conditions to be perfect."

"Are you making a general analogy?"

"I do believe I am," said de Nerval. "But see, Sir Arthur has asked them to entertain us with a song or two."

At that moment the younger of the boys began to sing. His clear, supple voice was perfectly audible across the meadow, and seemed to summon an echo from the ravines of the mountain above and to borrow the precipices' strength and grandeur. De Nerval whispered a translation of the German lyrics.

> *"Farewell, ye green meadows: farewell sunny shore.*
> *The herdsman must leave you, the summer is o'er."*

It was strange that the song should be so sad, not joyful and arrogant and sensual as the boys were. But as they sang and played, their handsome faces altered and Sophy saw in them a mournful wistfulness which made their quest, for whatever end, seem all the more touching and, paradoxically, seductive. When the last note of the last verse had vibrated away, on the touch of a zither string, there was a pause among the picnickers, a silence intensified by the faint, far-off tinkling of cowbells in the valley and the rushing wind in the pinetops—then came an outburst of appreciative applause. It seemed to Sophy that the song still hung in the air, poignant and lonely.

"Why must they sing so sadly?" she asked.

"It's appropriate," said de Nerval; "a tune set to the Herdsman's speech from Schiller's *Wilhelm Tell*. The sentiment is guaranteed to evoke sympathy in the listeners, and make us wonder if the young men really are saying their farewells."

"So that we will be more generous with our purses?"

De Nerval laughed, ruefully, "Do you feel moved enough to be generous?"

"I do," said Sophy.

"I see we have learned much from the young Bavarians."

"I'll think about that," said Sophy. "And them."

"Do you find them attractive?" asked de Nerval abruptly.

Sophy glanced at him, but he was serious, and intent upon her answer. "Of course I do," she said. "But I find many types of men attractive, not only blond striplings with sweet voices."

"You haven't yet caught sight of *your* mountain, however."

"I'm not sure I understand you," said Sophy.

"No matter." De Nerval pushed himself to his feet and, reaching into his coat pocket, went forward into the crowd which had gathered round the mountaineers.

Sophy watched, full of a strange unrest. She envied them their male confidence and that element of youth which, when freed from inhibition, would tilt brazenly at any sort of fate. One of the students slapped his leg in glee at a remark by de Nerval as the coin discreetly changed hands. The boy's blond hair shone almost white in the sun. There was something in the bare brown arms and smooth neck which made her want to touch him, to cull some of his incredible, subtle strength. She was conscious of an appetite within her, a hunger which she had experienced several times before, but never to this degree. She sat forward, hugging her elbows into her lap, her face shaded by the brim of her hat, half afraid that de Nerval would read her private thoughts.

The trader returned, and seated himself on the rug by Sophy's side. He was quiet, thoughtful, as if he too had gained unexpectedly from the contact with the youths.

"What will they do now?" Sophy asked.

De Nerval sighed and lay back on his elbows. "Go down into the woods, find a quiet spot to count their haul and chuckle over the stupidity of the English who are so vulnerable to sentimentality."

"Is that all that it is—sentimentality?"

"No," said de Nerval. "But the Bavarians do not yet know the true value of what they possess."

"Heaven help us if they ever find out."

"Oh, they will," said de Nerval. "But by that time it will be gone, quite irrecoverably gone, and they will be condemned to pass the rest of their lives under the shadow of regret for its loss."

"A Bavarian trait?"

"No," de Nerval said. "Unfortunately, it happens to all of us, regardless of sex, race, creed or country."

"I hope it never happens to me."

De Nerval did not answer.

Though dawn came early, it was not yet light when the rumble of the chaise's wheels over the log bridge at the driveway's entrance wakened Sophy. She had gone to bed tired for once, and had slept well if not deeply. A gleam of moonlight patched the floor of her room and laid a silvery screen across the sloping ceiling. On it Sophy imagined a shadowgraph of coal-black horses and black-cloaked men, figments of some cheap, sensational novel which had lodged in her mind. She confused it with the memory of the mountaineers, thinking that even now they might be storming into the chalet to rob and pillage and rape. The vision was ridiculous, totally at odds with the nature of the blond Bavarians. Besides, there was nothing particularly frightening in the chaffering of the horses in the drive.

Rising, she drew a robe over her night garments and tucked her feet into her slippers. Encouraged by the sound of voices, she crossed to the broad window and peered out into the night. The landscape was as she had never seen it before, etched by moonlight, more grand and more sinister, with all the tranquility glazed from the lake and the massive blue-black brows of the mountains.

In the yard below, the hired chaise from St. Hertog waited, the coachman stowing a modest bag into the interior. Even as she watched, Leon de Nerval walked from under the eaves, carrying his portmanteau. The driver nodded, growled a word or two, then hurried round the conveyance and climbed into his seat. De Nerval hesitated, glanced up at the chalet's façade, then stepped up into the coach. Making hardly a sound, the chaise rolled off. It was as silent as a cortège, as if the hoofs were muffled and the wheels felted.

Sophy shivered. For an instant she was prepared to invent a secret occupation for de Nerval, but truth intervened. Clearly, he had left at such an ungodly hour only to catch a dawn connection at Lucerne. He was off across Europe to buy, sell or barter some valuable commodity, to engage in transactions no more romantic than the shifting of tallow from Marseilles or seacoal to Cologne, activities not so different from her father's after all.

Sophy slipped back into bed again, settled herself, and stared at the screen of moonlight on the ceiling. She was restlessly confused and disappointed that de Nerval should have left so suddenly without giving her a hint of good-bye.

It was probably typical of that kind of man—reticent, forthright, and utterly selfish. At least he had provided her with *some* diversion. She promised herself that she would sustain the energy her contact with the trader had generated and break away from the round of fruitless pastimes that the Redfords offered. Tomorrow she would persuade Miss Frampton to accompany her into Lucerne. There, in the town, she would surely find some sort of society to keep her from becoming bored again.

As she drifted into sleep, however, her mood became more melancholy, and she seemed to hear again the mountaineers' refrain, carried by the strong, supple, sensual voice: *"The herdsman must leave you, the summer is o'er."*

Did de Nerval consider himself her herdsman? The notion was laughable. The summer had not yielded up a husband, nor a lover. It was not destined to be Leon de Nerval, of that she was sure. Only a prolonged association, a campaign like a siege, could have warmed her heart towards a Breton peasant, no matter how witty he was and how much his assertive attentions flattered her. In any case, he was gone—without so much as a word. If ever she encountered him again, she would be much less familiar in her treatment of him, teach him that she was not some Continental *demoiselle* to be patronized and teased for the exercise.

All in all, it was best that he had left when he did. He was not the man to become an acceptable husband to take home to England, nor even a lover to lessen the tedium of the long summer days.

She sighed, perhaps with relief, and fell asleep.

A handful of hours later, de Nerval was forgotten; everything was forgotten, as Sophy's summer and, indeed, her life, climbed dizzily towards a zenith which nobody, least of all the girl, could have predicted in advance.

# Three

Lucerne was crowded with tourists on that hot June day. To Sophy's chagrin, Miss Frampton resisted sightseeing, and would have preferred to spend the afternoon seated in one of the lakeside gardens. Sophy, however, was anxious to seize the advantage of her first trip to the canton and, armed with a guidebook, dragged her governess round several ancient churches, over a quaint bridge and through a government building designed in the likeness of a Roman palazzo. From Miss Frampton's viewpoint, the best service given by the guidebook was to direct them at length to the Krone Gardens where tea could be obtained.

"I've never been more ready for refreshment," puffed Miss Frampton, easing herself onto a wrought-iron chair. "You've exhausted me utterly, Sophy. Sometimes you forget my age."

"Come now, Miss Frampton, you are not so old."

"I feel it," the woman complained. "I do feel it, in this heat."

The edge of Sophy's enthusiasm had also worn off. She was irritated by the aimless hubbub of the crowds. While the gardens were certainly attractive, the promenade of people proved familiar enough to be dull. There was nothing here that she could not have seen in Leamington, a town that attracted a greater proportion of the real *haut monde* than Lucerne, by the looks of it. The throng was quite vulgar—parents hauling wailing children, middle-aged husbands grousing at their dowdy wives, spinsters and widows bickering with their sad-eyed paid companions.

Sophy sighed and bit into a pink-iced cake.

She wished that Leon de Nerval had not departed in such a hurry. She would have welcomed his company today. No doubt she would have found his comments on the passersby amusing and instructive and his flattery a relief from the limp conversational snippets exchanged between women.

Under her dress her body glowed, not uncomfortably, but with vibrant restlessness. She looked up over the shrubs and flouncing bonnets to the placid flanks of the mountains that, under a heat haze, made her realize today was no day at all for a town, and that she longed for other, more sensual pleasures. Manners should be discarded like velvet in the ripeness of summer. Sensuality should hold sway. Her body seemed to demand simple physical satisfactions.

She reached for her teacup and washed down the sticky sponge. The tea, though fresh, did not taste English. Too much of "England" on the one hand, and not enough on the other.

Soft laughter directed her gaze to a nearby table. It was occupied by a young couple who, at first glance, seemed no different from a dozen other couples in the vicinity. For all that, Sophy sensed a special aura about their relationship that suggested they might be on honeymoon. She would not honeymoon in midsummer. Such a ritual demanded an autumnal setting, with long, dark, misty nights to contain the intimacy of the bedroom and draw the loving couple closer together. She would insist on a honeymoon in October, a month spent in three or four of Europe's grandest hotels. She would dance, promenade, and ride out, eat magnificent dinners, drink champagne, and spend the nights locked in her husband's arms, coaxing his ardor time after time until he was besotted with love, and belonged to her in soul as well as body. With a sudden shock she realized that she was thinking as Agatha must have thought.

"Isn't it pleasant to see young people so happy?"

"Yes, Miss Frampton," Sophy replied. "I believe they are recently married."

"Setting out on the voyage of life together, full of faith and love." Miss Frampton was prone to stilted eloquence. "Ah, but the little brides seem younger all the time."

Sophy had not considered this aspect. Discreet study confirmed the truth of the governess's remark. They were children, a boy and girl, not yet twenty by the look of them. Wistful desperation engulfed Sophy for a moment. She assuaged it immediately by salvering a wedge of cream-filled layer cake from the third tier of the stand, and doing some skillful surgical work on the pastry with her fork. The cream was thick and eggy and did not comfort her much.

She would be less restless back at the chalet where she could at least recline in comfort and, in the coolness of the salon, amuse herself by educating little Angela Redford in the finer points of coquetry. Lucerne had thrown up no diversion worthy of the name, no antidote to her discontent. Yesterday had been more pleasant, up in the clean high meadow with the trader to humor her and stretch her wits that little bit.

"M. de Nerval left this morning, Sophy—did you know?" said Miss Frampton.

"Of course I knew."

"I understand his habits are rather strange, that he is given to slipping away at night while good honest folk are still fast asleep."

"Perhaps early rising has helped him make his fortune," said Sophy.

Miss Frampton leaned forward eagerly. "Oh, so you heard, too, did you?"

"I heard nothing."

"He *is* wealthy; very, very wealthy."

"Servants' gossip?"

"It's sound money, too, not disbursed capital. Most of it is banked in England; though there's no saying how a man like that may scatter his holdings. I heard, however, that he professes to have scruples about finance, and will not engage in certain kinds of trading. Does that not seem strange?"

"What sort of scruples?"

"Apparently he's not a lender."

"I doubt if Sir Arthur would have any truck with such a person."

"The gentry put more business in the way of traders than anybody, my dear. Believe me: I've had experience—not personally, of course—of such matters."

"M. de Nerval buys and sells things, that's all; rather like Father."

"What else did he tell you, Sophy?"

"Not much."

"I believe that he also has considerable influence."

"With whom?"

"Heads of state, politicians," said Miss Frampton, vaguely. "Doesn't he give you the impression of a man well used to power?"

"Money *is* power," Sophy retorted. "In any case, even if he were Prince Albert's valet and keeper of the Royal Mint, he's still a peasant and nobody at home would approve of him."

"Yorkshire is full of traders, my dear, but that's hardly the point. Do *you* approve of him?"

"I'm . . . really not sure."

"Do you *want* to marry, Sophy?"

"Naturally," said Sophy. "I didn't travel to Switzerland simply to admire the scenery. If I'd known how unrewarding the Redford *ménage* would be . . ."

"Leon de Nerval could buy and sell the Redfords and their whole *ménage* a hundred times over," said Miss Frampton, quietly. "You've never met a man so placed before. In addition, it must be obvious, even to you, my dear Sophy, that Leon de Nerval is *taken* with you."

"Perhaps."

"He must be encouraged."

"How can I encourage him when I don't know where he's gone, or if I'll ever cast eyes on him again?"

"I have the premonition that he'll turn up again."

"When that day comes, I'll consider the matter."

"Sophy, don't you understand? De Nerval can offer you much, much more than a paltry family inheritance, especially one that is already half nibbled away by that harl . . . I mean by your stepmother."

"Father is not exactly poor."

"Your father has a wife now, and three stepsons. Who is to say that he will not spawn sons of his own."

Sophy was startled by that suggestion. She pushed away the cake uneaten. "Do you think me skittish and vacillating?"

"Don't be naive, my dear."

"Miss Frampton, you forget yourself."

Sophy's protest died. The governess had spoken the truth. There was no life, no future at Huffton House. She had known it long before she left, had known too that she would never go back, at least not until she could return in triumph, flaunting wealth, position and a husband. Why, then, was she hesitating about encouraging a wealthy, urbane gentleman who could grant her the life-style she believed she craved?

She could not decide if she could ever bring herself to love Leon de Nerval. But that was an irrelevancy. Chalked against him was his quiet manner—which might mask slyness—and the fact that he was physically so unprepossessing. No, perhaps not unhandsome—just different, so unlike the tall Yorkshiremen who had peopled her dreams.

She said, "I'm not sure that I want a man like M. de Nerval."

"You are young," said Miss Frampton, with that faint air of patronage which so irked Sophy.

"I *am* young," said Sophy, "and I'm pretty enough to attract almost any man."

"A dangerous philosophy, and rather vain, don't you think?"

"Any man I want."

"And what kind of man *do* you want?"

Still annoyed, Sophy scanned the gardens.

The sun gleamed on the crockery and melted the edges of the layer cake.

"One like that," she said.

The soldier was the most handsome male she had ever seen. His appearance at that precise moment seemed not just fortuitous but fatal. The uniform might have been designed with just such a figure in mind. The broad chest of the blue tunic blazed with gold braid, ribbed from the waist to the hooked collar and fanning out, like an eagle's wings, to the shoulders. Another band of gilt braid furrowed the outside leg of the Prussian-blue trousers. A pelisse of dark fur lined with scarlet was slung from one epaulette. The flat-topped busby, held like a trophy in the crook of his arm, was decorated with a plume of white cock-tail feathers. White gloves and blackly polished boots completed the portrait.

Suddenly losing the thread of her argument, Sophy watched the officer approach. In no detail was he less than perfect. Tall, with fair waved hair and an impudent moustache, his blue eyes shone with good humor from a tanned and regular face.

At the very sight of him, Sophy's diffuse dissatisfactions coalesced into a single bright, hard spot, like a diamond.

Her heart thumped in her breast and one hand gripped the other tightly beneath the level of the table.

"Yes, he's certainly a dashing specimen," Miss Frampton conceded, glancing round. "So that is your idea of a suitable husband?"

"Per . . . haps," said Sophy, defensively.

"Is he a dragoon?" asked Miss Frampton.

"A dragoon, or a hussar," said Sophy.

The officer had seated himself at a table not ten yards away, in direct view of Sophy.

Smiling, Miss Frampton said, "Not a husband, Sophy, surely?"

Sophy did not deign to answer. She was engaged in private speculation, watching the hussar closely as he ordered tea. It was brought to him in a trice by two serving girls, both Swiss misses agog at the honor of waiting upon such a personage. Sophy's trancelike state was tainted by dejection. In five or ten minutes, when he had finished his tea, he would pay his bill and swagger off into the crowd, ending the sweet, impossible period of opportunity, and the weird excitement which his presence brought her. She could not help but stare at him, stare so hard that her eyes ached.

"You're being rude, Sophy."

"I don't care."

"Sophy!"

"Oh, be quiet."

"You're behaving like some little street gel."

"Miss Frampton," said Sophy firmly, "why don't you take this opportunity to write a *carte postale* to your sister?"

Miss Frampton hesitated. In nine years of service, she had learned when to humor her charge and when to defy her. What considerations she now gave to Sophy's blatant breach of decorum the girl never found out. It was sufficient that the governess meekly nodded and, rummaging in her reticule, fished out the leather wallet which contained her writing kit, a miniature pen and a tiny vial of violet ink. She fussed with nib and cork and then, in the crabbed script of an inveterate writer of postcards, obediently busied herself with the composition of a message on the back of a colored card.

At that moment, it was unclear who was the principal opportunist—the girl, the governess or the hussar.

Calmly, efficiently, the soldier decanted tea. He drank two cups and ate three slices of bread and butter spread with black cherry jam, chewing with appetite and a crisp martial rhythm, as if he could hear the beat of drum and fife in his ears. His manners were best-drawing-room; he did not smudge his moustache with jam, a hazard which had brought about the downfall of many an elegant dandy at the tea hour.

The hussar appeared to devote full attention to plate and cup and it took Sophy several minutes to realize that he was giving her as thorough a scrutiny as she was giving him. Recognition of his returned interest caused her to tremble a little and the stout guidebook slipped from her lap onto the flagstones. The trivial incident threw her into unusual confusion and to cover her clumsiness she brushed crumbs from her skirts with her gloves before stooping to retrieve the book.

The short scarlet cloak swung across her vision.

"Please, allow me."

He was so close that, as he bent to pick up the guidebook, she could feel his breath on her brow. He put the volume directly into her hands. She grasped it as if it was the Grail, staring up, too surprised to give him thanks. Lowering his eyes, he smiled and with a bow returned to his seat at the adjacent table.

Now the fellow made no pretense at all. He looked over at her unflinchingly, unashamedly—and nodded?

Only then did Sophy notice the piece of paper which had been folded into the pages of the guidebook, a *billet doux* which he must have scribbled by sleight-of-hand, since she had not noticed him writing it.

"How fortunate for you, Sophy," the governess said.

"What?"

"To have such a close view of your . . . hero."

"Yes."

"What is that?"

"My . . . my marker, Miss Frampton."

"Ah!"

The governess released her end of the conversation and resumed work on her postcard, crouched over it as if it were a secret cipher.

Sophy lowered the guidebook, plucked out the folded paper and read: "*The Swan Pond. Please.*" The last word had been underlined several times.

She looked up at the hussar. She felt very calm now, like a person who, after thrashing about in treacherous waters, has discovered that it is easier to float than struggle against the currents. The hussar was waiting, frowning. His lips formed the question: "Will you?"

Sophy nodded.

Miss Frampton hummed a jaunty air to herself, content in the throes of composition, thinking, perhaps, of how much pleasure the card would give to her dear sister Cora in distant Cornwall.

Sophy nodded again, emphatically.

The hussar rose, paid his bill and threaded his way through the crowded tables towards the lake.

Dropping the note into the book, Sophy snapped the volume shut.

"I think," she said, evenly, "I will buy a souvenir."

"By all means," said Miss Frampton. "The stall is just around the corner. Do you wish me to accompany you?"

"It's not necessary."

"As you wish," said the governess. "Take care in making your choice."

"I will," Sophy promised.

Displaying no undue haste, Sophy sailed round the corner of the tea-garden and down the long wall under gay canvas awnings. She felt no sense of urgency, only of mischief, the power that conscious wickedness brings. Impulses were put into humans to remind them of their right of choice, and she had *chosen* to meet with the hussar.

It was not her first adventure. Though still a virgin, she had flirted outrageously and daringly with several young men in Middlesborough and York. Finishing school had provided an education in other accomplishments besides music and deportment. Her senses quickened as she caught sight of the soldier.

Swans rippled the pond, fluting the water like glass under the strong sunlight. The flimsy booths of the trinket sellers framed him. He looked larger than life among them, hands on hips, his chest broad under the gilded wings.

"I wasn't sure you would come," he said.

He touched her arm and, with a gentle movement, drew her into the partition between the booths.

"I gave you a promise," Sophy said.

"And your aunt?"

"My governess," said Sophy, "is busy writing postcards."

His gloved hand remained lightly on her forearm. She did not ask him to remove it.

"I must introduce myself," he said. "I am Captain Edmund Sutton, of the Seventh Hussars."

"I am Sophy Richmond."

"You are English?"

"Do I not look English?"

"More English than . . . than the Queen herself."

"I'm not used to receiving notes from strange gentlemen," Sophy said, enunciating as clearly as if she were translating the text of a French novel.

"Yet you responded?"

"Yes," said Sophy. "I'm intrigued to learn *when* you wrote the little note. I didn't see you do it."

"I confess," Sutton said, "that I wrote it before I took my seat at the table."

"Before?"

"I've been following you most of the afternoon."

"Really, Captain, is that how you spend your days?"

"No," Sutton said. "But on this occasion I could not help myself. From the moment I saw you crossing that fake Roman palazzo, I was anxious to meet and talk with you."

"Even if it meant being imprudent?"

"For that I apologize. I could think of no other means of making contact. Please do not be offended."

"I'm not offended, Captain Sutton. But I'm still curious as to why you followed *me*."

He was suddenly serious, no longer brusque. "Because you are the most beautiful woman I have ever encountered, in any country."

"I am also too experienced to succumb to such an outrageous lie."

"No lie, Sophy, I swear," the hussar said. "Are you staying in Lucerne?"

"No, in a private hotel near St. Hertog."

"I must see you again."

"Very well," Sophy answered, without hesitation.

"Tomorrow?"

"That's rather sudden, isn't it?"

"I may be recalled to England at any time, Sophy. Tomorrow, please."

"Where?"

"Here."

"For what purpose?"

"To get to know one another better, to enjoy each other's company while we can. We'll sail on the lake, on a steamer. Please say that you'll come."

The urgency in his voice so matched her own that she gave herself up to the joyous realization that she had this handsome fellow already snared and that a whirlwind relationship could only be to her advantage. It was, she supposed, a star-crossed encounter. The romantic in her, though dominated by waywardness, was stimulated. She gave no thought at all to the practicalities of embarking on an affair while still a guest at the Schneegarten; that would be part of the adventure.

"Sophy, please?"

"Here, then, at this exact spot."

"Alone?"

"If I can."

"When?"

"Ten o'clock."

"I'll live for tomorrow."

With a last tightening of his fingers on her arm, he was gone. He had released her for her own good. Perhaps, she thought, he had sisters at home and knew how modesty bound them like caged songbirds with threads around their wings.

But that, she realized, was too fanciful an explanation of his behavior. It did not account for her response to his outrageous advances. He was playing the same game as she was, seeking diversion, the excitement of a flirtation in this bland foreign town.

Sophy strolled from between the booths. Children clustered round the sweetmeat stall; the swans upon the surface of the pond were gracefully regal. She hardly noticed any of these things, for she was filled with malicious anticipation at the enormity of her impending deceit. She saw it as a natural extension of her conversation with Miss Frampton, a positive acknowledgment that her future was *not* linked to Huffton House, Agatha and her father. Perhaps her agreement to meet the hussar could be construed as a blow for freedom.

Hurrying a little, she bought a postcard and, holding it like a ticket, moved quickly back towards the tea-garden. She did not have to go that far. Miss Frampton waited by the corner under the awnings, her bonnet neatly tied, her gloves tight over her long, bony fingers, the reticule pinched primly at her waist.

"I thought I had lost you," she said.

"Not just yet, Miss Frampton."

"I thought you might have gone in pursuit of that hussar."

"How ridiculous!"

"If only *he* were staying with the Redfords, how diverting that would be for you."

"But he is not," said Sophy, closely.

Miss Frampton took her arm, saying chattily, "My sister, Edith, was once engaged to a young lieutenant. Delafield was his name, as I recall. He died, horribly, in a mishap with a gun-carriage on Chatham Fields."

"How awful!" said Sophy dutifully.

The woman and the girl steered towards the stone archway which led to the transport hiring office at the tail of the old town. As they passed through the arch, Sophy's eye caught a flash of gilt between the trees at the park's rotunda. She was treated to a last glimpse of the bold Captain Sutton, tall, gallant, arrogant, but somehow rather forlorn, standing among children and waddling spinsters, watching her departure.

"On consideration," said Miss Frampton, "I believe you are right. There's nothing *quite* so attractive as a military man in all the glory of dress uniform."

"Not even a wealthy merchant?" said Sophy.

Miss Frampton laughed.

"Some women endeavor to have both, you know."

"Really!" Sophy said. "I hope you don't mean that I should?"

"Of course not, my dear," Miss Frampton said. "You're far too sensible for that."

In the week that followed her first meeting with the hussar, Sophy's wiles were tested to the full. With the guile of a master cracksman and the low cunning of a saboteur, she devised so many ways to escape the confines of the Schneegarten and concocted so many convincing lies that she was in danger of becoming *blasé*.

If the Redfords were at all suspicious, they were too polite to mention it. Besides, Miss Frampton gave needed support by tacitly providing alibis to cover Sophy's long absences, though there was no open acknowledgment that the governess knew exactly what her pupil did during her truancies.

Deception and intrigue provided almost as much entertainment as her affair with Sutton. For sure, she was no longer bored. In fact, she had never before felt so beautiful, so *engagé*, and so alive. Sutton's flattery was patently insincere. No matter how ably he masked them, his intentions were obvious. Sophy had no illusions on that score. The more the amorous captain embroidered his declarations of undying devotion, the more certain Sophy became that he was inflamed with the sort of passion which would flare up quickly, then burn out. Consequently, she paid little heed to his extravagant promises and the plans he wove for their future together. To appease him, to hold him off until she was prepared, she acted the role of ingénue, shivering like a rabbit mesmerized by a ferret or, for variation, becoming as winsome as a china shepherdess, teasing him with her apparent naïveté.

Four days out of seven had been spent in his company. So far, she had made the steamer trip from Lucerne to Fluelen with him, and had as a memento an appropriate bauble: two tiny figures encased in a glass dome, the male in blue uniform, the female in yellow crinoline, a gold-paper star pasted to a scrap of turquoise sky above, a chemical blizzard lying dormant round their ankles.

She had also trudged halfway up a glacier in a long straggling line of tourists, gasped at the sight of the huge serpentine mass of ice, streaked and hued like a thousand rainbows, coiling down into the valley, and blushed at Edmund's ardent announcement that, "I came to Switzerland for this sight, Sophy, but I did not expect to meet someone whose beauty makes Nature pale into insignificance. If this were the Egyptian desert or the Russian steppes, and you were by my side, Sophy, I would feel that I was in Eden."

She had ridden in a raffish two-wheeler on narrow tracks through dense pine forests, urging her hussar to whip the horses to greater and greater speeds until it seemed that she was flying through the lavender twilight like an owl, the lake at last like *lapis lazuli* and the mountain peaks tipped with vermilion. She had clung to him then and kissed him, crushing her breasts against him as the chaise swept round corners and he wrestled with the reins of the expensive team and could not brake them in time to take advantage of her momentary ardor.

She had drunk spiced wine and eaten herb cheese in an isolated café like a wooden music box in the foothills above town, whispered nonsense back at him when he pandered to her vanity with loving phrases and stroked her arms and shoulders and slunk his arm about her waist to cup her breasts.

At length, she had inched herself to the point where she could no longer resist the only thing he had left to offer.

She craved its consummation almost as much as the captain, and, for a quarter of an hour, surrendered her caution and let him kiss her and fondle her body until the tether of her authority was so badly frayed that she might have given way to him there and then had it not been late and the place too close to the back gate of the

Schneegarten estate. So she had torn herself from his arms, startled by her own emotions, and he had cried out pitifully, "Oh God, Sophy! Tell me when." And she had answered with more coolness than she felt, "The day after tomorrow, Edmund. Meet me here at eight in the morning." He had uttered a gruff, throaty grunt and turned away before she could gloat at his distress.

She had scampered off past the line of uncut timber which marked the chalet property, down the stony path past the huts where the saws and snowplows were stored, had reached the hotel by the scullery yard and sneaked up to her bedroom by the back stairs.

She changed rapidly and appeared "with the soup" at the dining table as though she had spent the whole afternoon resting quietly in her room.


Sweeping from the narrow valleys of the north, the *Fohn* died out before morning and left a thin, chill drizzle of raincloud down upon the mountains. The private chaise had a tarred black hood and bib, however, and the couple were snug and dry inside. Edmund looked raffish in warm dress blue which, though lacking the gilt trimmings of his ceremonial, was still a handsome uniform. Never before had Sophy so admired a man's appearance. Everything about the hussar was so perfectly in proportion and so masculine.

She greeted him with a kiss; but at first the soldier was subdued, almost gloomy. She realized that his mind was not on her or her promise. Saying that he would show her the Switzerland that the tourists neglected—peasant country—he drove the chaise at a leisurely pace through quiet rain-soaked forests away from the Schneegarten.

"What's wrong, my love?" she asked.

"Mars and Venus are ill bedfellows, Sophy."

"Have you been recalled to your regiment?"

"No, but I fear that my leave will have to end soon."

"How soon?"

"I cannot say with accuracy. There's much talk in the Vandler this morning. Russia is threatening Turkey apparently, and the French and British fleets are on their way to unite in the Dardanelles."

"What does it mean, Edmund?"

The captain shrugged. "Perhaps nothing."

"And perhaps war?"

Edmund nodded.

"And what of us then?" said Sophy.

He glanced sharply at her. "I'm not my own man, my darling; I'm a soldier."

"Don't soldiers' ladies travel with them?"

"Yes, but there would be no time, don't you see?"

"Does it take long?"

"There are so many things to be done."

"But not today, Edmund?" she said. "There's only one thing to be done today."

The captain laughed. He had read the meaning of her remarks at last. He clicked his tongue, shook the reins and harried the little horses on towards an unknown destination.

In view of the weather, he suggested a return to Lucerne. But Sophy, knowing that the Redfords would descend on the town in force today, persuaded him that she was not sugar candy and would not melt in the rain. She wanted to be alone with him, unafraid of discovery. Besides, she felt that what he had in mind would be a room in a pension, in the Vandler itself, and that setting was not for her.

Trim little wooden villages dropped behind them, and the tracks were narrow. The rain was not heavy enough to cause much mud, however, and the ground was firm under the wheels. They ate an early luncheon in a drovers' tavern, a low stout-walled building, immaculately clean, and sat for an hour or more by the log fire and drank

mulled wine and talked. The conversation largely concerned Sutton's past campaigns, regimental feats of arms,
and victories, exciting enough if innocuous.

For all that, Sophy's restlessness, increased by the
warmth and the wine, reached an almost unappeasable
stage over the meal. She realized that she did not inhabit
her body like a lodger, but that she owned it, all of it; that
her body *was* her. The pleasures of such a self-orientated
philosophy were heady, spiced by guilts, linked at root to
the power she craved over men.

Now, in a situation which was in itself compromising,
she found that her instincts contradicted everything that
her intelligence told her to do. Edmund Sutton's seductive
cunning appealed to her. The very factors that a sensible
girl would have considered most against surrender were
those which made the strongest attraction for Sophy. She
was sure he did not love her or so admire her virtues that
he wished to burden himself with her as a wife. She did not
blame him for picking her out as the target of a potential
conquest. She was ready to admit that she was all of these
things, and more. To be like her stepmother, she must
learn what it was that made men a woman's slave. If only
Edmund could have read the most secret parts of her
mind, he would have known that his intention was her
intention too.

In the early afternoon, they drove on, upwards, the track
shedding the last of the farms and communes, the rain mist
thickening. Over her traveling dress, Edmund had spread
a rug. She leaned hard against him, to feel his tension as a
match to her own.

"Where are we going?" she asked.

"To the end of the world," he said, so leadenly that
the phrase sounded pompous.

They could see little now through the fine rain which
sifted down from the mountains. They were in a world of
shadows created by rain and ghostlike scarves of mist. Even

the fat cattle which browsed on pocket pastures seemed insubstantial, the clanking iron tongues of the cowbells as muted and mysterious as goblin music. The rain hung like a web across the track, and the pines were enormously tall, lofting up into chalky cloud.

The pace of the horses became more and more plodding. Finally Edmund checked them to a halt.

"I think we must turn," he said.

"But why?"

"In case we become lost."

"I'm lost now," said Sophy.

"If the rain were less heavy," Edmund said, "I would suggest that we walk a little way."

"This is not English rain," said Sophy. "It reminds me of the tales of the Norse gods which my governess used to read to me in the nursery."

"You won't find Asgard here, Sophy."

"Can you be sure?" She folded back the rug. "Let's walk, then, and see."

The captain unhooked the proofed bib and helped her down. Sophy felt like a figment of the mist, strangely light, as if the slightest stirring of the air would move her and set her drifting. She walked ahead of him, not sure of what she would find, but sure enough that there would be some dwelling, some shelter which her conniving Captain Sutton, like the good soldier he was, had spied out in advance. It was not chance that had brought him here. There was a path faintly marked through the grass, but nothing else to be seen except the sparse trunks of the conifers and, when she glanced behind her, nothing in her wake except Edmund.

The hut loomed ahead.

Rain had wet the nap of her garments and made the edgings limp. She looked down at the lace nervously, then up at the low, isolated building. It had the stump of a tower at one end, like a miniature chapel. Its fabric told her that its purpose was not spiritual. It was little more than a rough box of dry stone, timbered with unbarked pines. The flat thatch roof was coated with moss, the door bleached stone-gray. It was more primitive than any hut she had seen in England, yet it drew her like a magical cavern. She knew that this place was destined to be the final sanctuary to contain herself and her lover and keep the world well out.

Never had she imagined that she would be alone in such a place as this, vulnerable to insensate mischief and her desire for ultimate freedom. Thinking fleetingly of the Redfords and her fellow guests back at the chalet, she imagined them in the mists, like watchers, silent in their condemnation.

She did not need persuasion or instruction. She opened the latch on the door and stepped inside out of the rain. It was a small room, much smaller than it appeared from the outside. The narrow window gave only enough light to let them see the candle stump on its iron bracket on the smoke-blackened wall above the hearth.

There was a rough wooden bench and a table, a kettle and pot on one side of the fire, a few logs and a bale of hay on the other.

Sophy brushed the rain from her face. Without turning, she heard Edmund enter and drop the latch.

"Whose place is this?"

"A goatherder's," said Edmund.

"Will he return?"

"He comes here only in spring and autumn."

"You are sure he will not . . . ?"

"No."

"Light the fire, Edmund."

Standing, she watched him kneel before the hearth. He twisted straw, lit it with a match, fed twigs onto the pyre, then logs, and, in the course of several minutes, coaxed the fire to burn up bright and warm. He did not speak, or look at her, but gave his full concentration to the matter in hand.

Sophy hesitated. Thoughts of an opulent bedroom in a grand hotel strayed fitfully across her mind. Sutton's back was broad and his muscular thighs strained against the leggings of the uniform. His cheek was flushed with the flickering fire in the half-darkened room.

Already she was too deeply committed to pull back. He could do as he wished with her. All she needed was the touch of his hands, a certain brutal roughness to match their surroundings.

She was trembling.

He turned now.

Flames licked into the dry dead wood. The pungent goatish odor of the hut was cleansed by pine scents. Edmund did not rise. Squatting, knees spread, he tilted his face inquisitively up at her.

"Come closer, Sophy."

She took a pace towards him.

"Come to me, Sophy."

There was no staying him, no reticence in her.

The hussar was fully cognizant of her need for him. Reaching, he caught her skirts in his fists and pulled her against his thighs, nuzzling his face against her bodice. Sophy gasped. At the last moment, she struggled a little to be free. But Edmund Sutton had trapped her. There was no seriousness in her attempted retreat. He clenched his arms about her and drew her close against his chest. His hands moved, stroking the skirts against her flanks. Shifting, he molded and shaped the material smoothly against her calves and his fingers hitched and furled her undergarments until he touched her nakedness.

Sophy winced. The fingers stole caressingly higher and higher. She was as limp as a doll against him, her breast resting against his cheek, her arms slack across his shoulders.

"Sophy, I must have you," he said, thickly. "I must have you now."

"Yes," she said. "Yes: now."

"You're so . . . beautiful."

"Yes."

Cradling her in his arms, he rose and swung her gently to the clover straw which carpeted the floor.

"Wait, Edmund," she pleaded, fumbling with tapes, hooks, buttons.

But the hussar was afraid that she would reject him, even at this last moment. He pinned her with his forearm while he peeled off his tunic. Ignoring her protests, he straddled her, ripped her bodice apart and bared her breasts.

Sophy winced again as his hands closed on her, then, responding to his touch, she clasped him about the waist and made him her prisoner.

Pinpricks of firelight reflected in his eyes gave him a demonic and wrathful look. His breath rasped harshly in his throat as he devoured her breasts with his hands. Dropping, he bridged her with his knees. Beneath him, Sophy kicked and wriggled, not to dislodge him, only to be rid of the impediment of her skirts. Relieved, she felt the fire's warmth on her nakedness.

Edmund was too importunate to draw back. Head pressed against the straw, Sophy squeezed her eyes shut. She was momentarily frightened by the ferocity of his demands and by memories of tales she had heard of the searing pain of first entry. But the pain proved nothing, sudden, sharp, rapidly flooding away on a wave of pleasure.

Pleasure mounted swiftly into trembling ecstasy. She hoisted herself to meet him, flowering, slackening, flowering once more, her passion welling into a cry of intense relief. The captain loomed over her, brow sweat-beaded, features contorted. His power poured into her. He shouted out; a long, low masculine sound which, by its strangeness, brought Sophy to a third flowering and left her spent.

His weight went from her. Perspiration dewed her body. She could hear the crackle of the logs, even the faint, soft fingers of rain brushing the thatch. She felt his breath upon her mouth and the touch of his lips as he kissed her.

She opened her eyes.

"Sophy, my love," he murmured.

She experienced no guilt, no depression, no fear. A kind of vanity and joyfulness filled her. Stretching out her hand, she grasped her hussar by the neck and brought his mouth down to her breast.

"Edmund," she said. "Again."

To her chagrin, the captain laughed out loud.

The first course of dinner had been cleared before Sophy made her entrance into the dining salon. Heads lifted, eyes seemed to fix upon her knowingly, and she imagined that rumors were passing from mouth to mouth between the tables—ugly, petty accusations. Fists clenched, she forced herself to remain serene. After all, there was no visible outward mark of her changed state. She had intended them to stare at her, had selected the rich plum-colored gown specifically to achieve that end. Its boldness matched her mood. Let them goggle. The Redford crowd were as colorless as newts. In social or moral matters she was not under their jurisdiction.

The gown bolstered her vanity, its décolletage showing off her breasts, the black bobble trimming adding maturity.

Lady Patricia leaned forward from the high table, teasingly wagged her fork and passed a remark about Sophy spending all afternoon at her dressing table. The pleasantry raised laughter. Sophy laughed too, then, bowing, moved on towards a vacant chair at a table by the window bay.

As she walked towards it, she caught a glimpse of her

reflection in an ornamental mirror, saw no girl now but the portrait of a beautiful woman with a wanton assurance in the tilt of her head. The image vanished, but the confidence it imparted stayed with her.

She smiled almost contemptuously at Stephen Redford as he hurried to draw out a chair for her. At last he had really noticed her. Was she that much changed by her newfound womanhood, or was it the swelling breast that attracted him? She seated herself in a swirl of plum-colored skirts, and raised her hand to summon the immediate attention of a serving boy.

"Did you pass a pleasant afternoon, Sophy?" Stephen asked.

"Wonderful, thank you."

"In spite of the rain?"

"Because of the rain," Sophy said.

"We were in Lucerne all afternoon, and did not see you," said Walter Redford.

"Perhaps because I wasn't there," said Sophy, leaning forward to expose just a little more of her bosom, confuse the young men at the table and divert their minds from the conversation.

Somewhere deep inside herself, Sophy felt a glow of triumph, as if an intangible membrane had suddenly snapped. She was superior now to these children, familiar with their prized male secret. She had outstripped every woman she knew; including Agatha, perhaps. She had not been afraid; indeed, there had been nothing to fear. Old wives' tales of pain and humiliation were very farfetched. She had much still to learn, of course, but Sutton would teach her. He had promised as much. She doubted if he would decamp for England for a while yet, even if the Tsar of Russia rode his troops into London.

"Wine, Sophy?"

"The red, please, Stephen."

She watched the glass fill until the liquid reached the

brim. She sipped it carefully then, turning on impulse, found that Miss Frampton, far across the salon, was studying her. The governess smiled enigmatically and raised her glass in a toast.

Though she did not quite understand the meaning of the gesture, Sophy returned it and, lifting her glass, drank deeply of the full red wine.

Their affair no longer required time-consuming preliminaries or the pretense of a relationship without the physical act. Oddly, it was Sophy and not Sutton in whom the passionate fires burned most brightly. The soldier was not slow to seize advantage of her ardor. Even he, however, was not quite prepared for the generous flood of sensuality which Sophy Richmond released on him.

It was much easier to slip away from the Schneegarten for a couple of hours than for a whole day, and Sophy conducted herself, over the next ten days, with a gaiety which caught the Redfords off guard, restored her reputation for good spirits among them and gave her a cloak for her secret rendezvous with Sutton.

Sutton was happy to be at her beck and call. He spent many hours lurking in the woods by the deserted back gate of the Schneegarten estate waiting for her, and if she were less than prompt, did not complain.

They made love a dozen times in that ten-day span, in deserted huts, on flowery banks under the pines, even in the hooded chaise when no more convenient spot could be found. One dismally wet afternoon was spent, by arrangement, in the double bed in an upstairs room of a none-too-respectable inn in a hamlet an hour's drive west of Lucerne.

More than Sophy's passion was satisfied. She also assuaged her curiosity in regard to the male anatomy, with a frankness which made even the soldier blush and protest. By the week's end, he called her—only half in jest—a harlot at heart, adding the rider that harlots often made the best of wives.

Sophy was no longer taken in by his mentions of marriage, which became vaguer and more infrequent as their lovemaking became less inhibited. She was shrewd enough to realize that, though Sutton made an ideal lover, she did not love him in the accepted sense of the word and would no more want him for a husband than she would want Herr Waller, or Flea Flaherty. There was no more sentimental discussion of Mars and Venus, or of parting, and it soon occurred to Sophy that she might be lucky enough to have the exquisite pleasure of dismissing Captain Sutton with a broken heart, rather than the other way round. Something in that fancy appealed to her.

But that part of it was not to happen. One afternoon, shortly after four o'clock, she arrived at the woodland gate only a half hour late for a meeting with the hussar —and found that he was not in attendance. He had either left or had not come at all. She lingered for an hour, then returned, a little crestfallen, to dress for dinner in the chalet.

She was not unduly concerned at his absence, however; a number of minor accidents could have kept him from her. Next afternoon, punctually, she again slipped away to the back gate, only to be disappointed once more. After a third visit, and a third disappointment, she gave up that line, and waited, not quite patiently, to be contacted.

By Saturday, she realized that she had been thrown over, abandoned, without so much as a letter to give a reason or an excuse. According to Sir Arthur the situation in regard to the war had not changed much, though, when pressed, he admitted that letters from London indicated that England was marshaling her forces as a precautionary measure.

Quickly, Sophy fell back into the simple pattern of life at the Schneegarten, boating, riding, playing tiresome games with bat and ball and cards. She resisted for a full week, then, seizing the opportunity of a ride on the mail wagon, traveled down to Lucerne and sought out the Vandler, the pension in which Sutton had lodged.

To her surprise it was in the lowest quarter of Lucerne. The trinket-vendor from whom she asked directions gave her a curious look as he pointed out the way.

Vandler's pension was a mean, narrow-fronted building packed between a stable and a public laundry. Two wings of a wooden door were flung wide to the wall. A few flies droned listlessly in and out like permanent guests. The stink from the stables permeated the foyer and more flies hovered round the broken lampwheel above the reception desk. The walls were peeling. The varnish on the box-sided staircase was scraped and scarred by luggage and spurs, the felt lining on the stairs themselves worn through to the tread.

Holding a cambric handkerchief delicately to her nose, Sophy advanced cautiously to the desk and addressed the one-eyed, middle-aged scarecrow of a man who appeared to be in attendance.

She asked him, in French, if he spoke English.

He answered, in tortured English, that he did not.

She asked him, in French, if Captain Edmund Sutton, an English gentleman, was still in residence.

The proprietor grinned foxily, showing a mouthful of decayed teeth. A tongue that seemed as pointed as a viper's licked his nether lip speculatively.

"Captain Sutton. Please inform him that a lady wishes to speak with him," ordered Sophy, lapsing into English as a sign that she was not some common trull to be ogled and sneered at. She was, her haughty tone indicated, not only a lady, but an *English* lady.

The man made a great show of pondering the question, while eying Sophy's figure with unabashed interest. Finally, she slammed her fist on the desktop, making the dried and suppurating inkwell leap up in its socket.

"Captain Sutton is an English officer," she declared.

"Ah, yah!" said the proprietor, inspired. "Capitan Sootun."

"Where is he?"

"Departed: gone."

"Did he," asked Sophy, with a shade more patience, "take his baggage with him?"

The man smirked, swallowed the insult that obviously crossed his mind, and nodded. "Every steek ov eet."

"Thank you," Sophy said. "How long since he left?"

The man held up his grimy hand, counting with his fingers. "Foar daze."

"Thank you," said Sophy again, and turned to go.

"Ma'mselle?"

She glanced round.

"Mizz Richmond?"

"I am Miss Richmond."

From beneath the ledge of the desk, the man drew out a letter. He laid it on the desk edge and made her return for it. She looked at it, tempted not to accept it—but vanity was stronger than pride. Finally she lifted it and slid it quickly into the sleeve of her dress. She turned again and prepared to sweep out with a few remnants of dignity remaining.

The doorway, however, was barred by another soldier, not so young, nor nearly so prepossessing as her hussar. The uniform told her that this fellow was not a dragoon but an infantry lieutenant. His face was flushed and his eyes had a sly glint in them. A faint astringent odor of spirits emanated from him.

"You," he said, without introduction, "can only be the lovely Sophy that ol' Edmund kep' ravin' out about. I know all about *you*, my liddle pigeon."

The lieutenant swayed back on his heels, staring down his nose at her as if he were inspecting some nag which was up for auction. "Hum! Didn't lie, did he? We all thought he was exaggeratin' your charms, my luv, but he didn't do ye justice."

"I'll thank you to let me pass," said Sophy, stonily.

"But ol' Edmund's gone, trotted off back to swerve his Queen and Country, though I'd say he'd been swervin' his country well enough here."

Frightened and thoroughly humiliated, Sophy looked in vain around the foyer for another clear exit to the street. Over the box-rail of the stairs peered two other faces, puffed, blowsy male faces, with impudent eyes and lecherous simpering smiles plucking out their lips horribly.

"Landlord?" Sophy said.

The scarecrow feigned deafness, leaned on his elbows and watched the little drama with a scornful grin.

"Never mind, pretty," the lieutenant went on, stepping closer and reaching out to touch her arm. "Willy'll take good care of ye now."

Sophy had the presence of mind not to retreat before him. Her cheeks were scalding with shame and she was close to tears, but her fury at being spurned *and* discussed like a dancing-palace trollop held her to the spot. Even when his fingers brushed her shoulder and the heel of his palm lay against the crown of her breast, she did not flinch. She even managed to flutter her eyes a little and break the vestige of an inviting smile onto her lips.

"A wonderfully developed little filly, ol' Edmund said you were, my darlin', with an appetite for all sorts of cunning sports. Come upstairs with me and I'll be teachin' you a few extra tricks that ol' Sutton never learned. I'll have you standin' on your head with delight before you can say 'knife.' "

She hit him with her fist. She prodded the blow straight at him, aiming up at the wide nostrils between the swell of his moustaches, driving as hard as she could, rocking backwards on her heels with the impact.

The lieutenant yelled. Blood gushed at once from his nose, his hands fluttering to cover the injury.

In an instant, Sophy was past him and, skirts caught in both hands, ran frantically along the short stinking street and across a cobbled square, through flower and vegetable stalls back into the main area of the town where there were decent Englishmen and women to protect her should she be pursued by her victim.

She slowed only when the dome of the Krone teahouse came into view, pausing under the first awning to dab her brow and compose herself as best she could.

Fear and shame had gone out of her, discharged in the blow she'd delivered in the doorway of the Vandler. Anger at Sutton remained. She thought of him lounging in the dining room, a cigar clenched between his teeth, a bumper of rum in his fist and her name on his filthy tongue. She could well imagine the ribald, obscene laughter which would greet each added detail of Sutton's account of his trysts with the foolish English virgin who had fallen to him like a ripe peach.

At the edge of the Swan Pond, she tore up his letter. Disregarding the mildly curious glances of the passersby, she scattered the fragments, unopened and unread, onto the rippling water. It was not a romantic affectation, only a convenient means of being rid of the hateful, deceitful communication and, symbolically, of the last shred of regret at Captain Edmund Sutton's sneak-thief departure out of her life.

Miss Frampton sat by the rose trellis, at a table for two. She had eaten four slices of bread and butter and two almond pastries and had thoughtfully ordered a fresh pot of tea only minutes before Sophy came into the gardens in search of a restorative before her return to St. Hertog.

When Sophy first caught sight of her governess, the woman, writing a postcard, appeared to be oblivious to all around her. Oddly, Sophy felt no surprise at finding her governess there. She did not hesitate for an instant before wending between the tables and seating herself on the waiting chair, as if they had come to the town together and had met here by prior arrangement.

Miss Frampton licked the end of her bone pen and continued with her composition.

"The tea is newly infused, Sophy."

Sophy poured, applied milk and sugar, and drank thankfully.

"Are you upset?" asked Miss Frampton, casually.

"Why should I be upset?"

"The hussar has gone, I take it?"

Still Sophy felt no panic. It seemed the most natural thing in the world for Eunice Frampton to be a party to her guarded secret.

"Was it so easy to guess?" Sophy said, sipping, and looking at the roses and the butterflies which flitted along them.

"I felt it was incumbent upon me," said Miss Frampton, still penning news to her sister, "to guard your welfare, and your reputation."

"I'm grateful to you for that. But why didn't you try to stop me?"

"You forget, Sophy, I too was young once."

"Did *you* have a . . . ?"

At last, Miss Frampton looked up, her expression softer than Sophy had ever seen it. "A lover? My dear child, I wasn't pretty enough to bag a hussar."

"Miss Frampton, did you see my . . . my soldier?"

"Only once: a most handsome gentleman, so suited to the uniform."

"He treated me shabbily," Sophy glumly confessed.

"And how did *you* treat him?"

"No, Miss Frampton, you mustn't ask me that. I've no wish ever to talk of it, or to hear his name mentioned again."

"I take it, then, that it is over?"

"Yes: finally."

"Good!" Miss Frampton said. "I hoped it would end as suddenly as it began, that you would not make a fool of yourself by falling in love."

"With a mere Captain of Hussars!" Sophy sneered. "I have more breeding than that, I think."

"And you have proved it," Miss Frampton said, patting the girl's hand understandingly. "Now, drink up your tea or we shall miss the chaise back to the village."

"Miss Frampton . . ."

"Hush now, Sophy! I want no share of your secrets, please. Let's say no more about it, shall we? No more."

"Agreed," Sophy said, and smiled fondly at the woman across the table.

# Four

"I'm pregnant," said Sophy, without a trace of emotion.

She sat on the edge of the bed looking down at her body as if it had betrayed her. Rain dashed on the glass of the chalet window and cast freckled shadows across the girl's nightgown and the rumpled sheets.

Miss Frampton turned from the window, her arms still raised to the pinafore curtains. In that odd position, she asked, "Are you sure, Sophy?"

"No, I'm not sure—but the signs . . ."

"How long?"

"Six or seven weeks."

"Nausea?"

"Intermittently. I thought it was the food."

Miss Frampton, showing no more distress than if her charge had announced the onset of a head cold, crossed the room and, standing directly before the girl, caught her chin in bony fingers and tipped her head this way and that, examining her expertly.

Sophy looked drawn and her color, in spite of the dusting of sun on her skin, was ashen.

In rapid fire, Miss Frampton rapped out a dozen intimate questions which Sophy answered with equal honesty and lack of embarrassment.

Miss Frampton sighed.

"Am I right?" said Sophy. "Am I . . . with child?"

Miss Frampton sighed again.

Seating herself on the bed, she took Sophy's hands in her own. "Yes, it would seem so," she said. "On the other hand, one can never be absolutely certain until a medical practitioner . . ."

"No," Sophy cried. "Oh, no! How can we summon a doctor here? The Redfords . . ."

"Be calm, my dear," said Miss Frampton, sharply. "I wouldn't dream of involving the Redfords in what is, after all, a highly private matter. We will return to England."

"Go . . . home?"

"Do you wish to go home?"

Sophy wept, not loudly but copiously. "I . . . can't go home: not now, not like this. Agatha would . . ."

"Agatha may be the least of your problems, Sophy."

Miss Frampton got to her feet and stood before the window looking silently out over the drizzled autumnal landscape.

Recognizing the woman's posture, Sophy blew her nose on a handkerchief and waited for the pronouncement, the "sensible" plan which would surely come from her governess.

At length, Miss Frampton said, "If we returned to Huffton, I would certainly be sent packing at once, and you would be alone with your stepmother. What would then transpire is doubtful, to say the best of it." She paused and scanned the dismal view once more for several long minutes. "I have a little money saved . . ."

"Money?"

"We must live, you know."

"We?"

Miss Frampton glanced round. "Unless you wish it, I've no intention of abandoning you."

Sophy rushed from the bed and flung herself into the woman's arms. "Oh, no, dear Miss Frampton: I can't do without you. I can't face it alone."

The governess patted the girl's shoulder absently. She

was still rapt in thought. "With your allowance and my severance monies and the little I have saved, I believe we might be able to afford a modest house of our own, in London."

"I can't . . . can't take your money."

"Too proud, Sophy?" There was derision in her tone, a trace of it at least.

Sophy shook her head. "No, no; but . . . but what will you do?"

Miss Frampton gave a curt throaty chuckle. "I will do what I did before I came into your father's employ: I will muddle along somehow."

"And the child?"

"Leave all that to me."

"When will we go?"

"Tomorrow."

"But the Redfords don't leave for another two weeks."

"The season's over," said the woman. "I will make an excuse, and we will depart for London tomorrow."

"London?"

"I have . . . acquaintances there," the governess said; "acquaintances who will help us through the difficult months ahead."

"A doctor?"

"Yes, Sophy, a gentleman we can trust."

The girl would have shied away from the conversation in any other setting. A hotel lounge, an inn bedroom, even a swaying railway carriage would have provided too intimate a setting for the subject, and Sophy, weakened by her condition and reduced in her resolve, would have taken refuge from the sordid truth in tears and near-hysteria.

Now that Switzerland was behind them and the protection of the Redford *ménage* finally shed, she found herself confronted by a future of great and terrifying uncertainty. The stigma of unwanted, unwed motherhood had been implanted into her from infancy, and she regarded her changing functions as a detestable, public advertisement of the sinful act which had caused them. She shrank from the most casual gaze, quailed before servants, cowered in corners of waiting rooms all across Europe under the impression that every man was smirking at her and every woman condemning her. Even Miss Frampton could not coax her from such nervous and debilitating fantasies.

On the boat, however, it was different.

There was privacy there, a peculiar sense of unbelonging. Though the gangplanks had been crammed with returning tourists and the sternholds were bulging with luggage, the long, narrow steamship seemed to absorb and disperse its human cargo, above and below decks, and the bright, brisk sea and wide horizons gave Sophy her first hours of consoling seclusion in over a week.

Nobody would see her body, wrapped under countless tartan traveling rugs and squeezed down into the ash and canvas chair out of the wind in the nook between the funnel and the rear of the first-class lounge. Gay bunting clipped overhead and the gulls—were they French or English, the girl wondered—screamed and hovered, clean and strong, above the wires and ropes and polished brass rails. The funnel was red, the paintwork white, and the sea a thousand shifting shades of green.

Sophy was free of nausea. The stiff, salt breeze seemed to scour away her unease. Surreptitiously she placed her hands on her stomach under cover of the rugs.

Miss Frampton, who had the constitution of a Greenland explorer, had acquired a jug of broth and a crisp loaf from the dining salon. She decanted the thick savory liquid into two large cups, broke the loaf in half and urged Sophy to partake of refreshment.

Suddenly Sophy found that she had an appetite. She was not just hungry, but ravenous. Struggling from her wraps, she held the cup in one hand and the loaf in the

other and ate with as much greed as a seagull—and only
marginally more manners.

Miss Frampton did not chide the girl for her lack of
refinement. Instead she smiled to see this healthy hunger
manifest itself: another sign that Sophy was, indeed, in the
early weeks of pregnancy.

Calais had dropped back into a faint blue undulating
haze. The Channel roadstead was busy with shipping, from
huge naval warships to the tiniest of fishing smacks, a
fresco of sails and funnels and pennants of brown smoke.

Sophy polished off the soup, popped the bread into her
mouth and, chewing, sank back.

Miss Frampton passed over a clean cambric handkerchief and Sophy wiped her mouth and fingers with it. The
couple, fed and comfortable in spite of the long, shudder-
ing roll of the waves in mid-Channel, sat back and contem-
plated the coast of France receding by the moment into
total invisibility.

Miss Frampton said, "If things are with you as we
suspect, my dear, have you thought what you will do?"

"Yes."

"And what have you decided?"

"I must seek out and marry Edmund Sutton."

Miss Frampton sat up like a wooden jackanapes jerked
out of its toy box. She stared at Sophy in total disbelief.

"Marry . . . marry a soldier?"

"He's a captain, you know."

"And a scoundrel," Miss Frampton snapped. She
glanced round at neighboring passengers, then drew her
chair closer to Sophy, leaning half across the girl. "This
. . . this hussar is not for you. He treated you shabbily,
Sophy. He took advantage of you and then abandoned
you. You said yourself that he was worthless."

"He is the father of my child."

Miss Frampton's jaw thrust out like that of a cornered
fox. Harshly, she said, "As a lover, Sophy, he may have

been all that you dreamed of, but his behavior indicated that he would bring you nothing but heartbreak and suffering as a husband."

"My child will need a father."

With a shade more control, Miss Frampton said, "A drunken, lecherous, never-at-home barracks rat?"

"You mustn't call him that."

"In six months, England may be at war. Your gallant captain will be in some far-off land, and you will be a soldier's wife imprisoned in some Cripplegate slum."

"I will go with him."

"Don't be such a fool, Sophy! You can't travel in the wake of an army with your belly . . . I mean, in your condition."

"Then I shall join him later."

"With a suckling infant? Think of it—the discomforts, the disease, the dangers."

"What else can I do," said Sophy, offhandedly.

"Saints!" exclaimed Miss Frampton. "You *want* to marry this painted tin soldier, don't you?"

"It *is* a solution to my problem. At least I'll have a husband, a name and a father for my baby."

"And a lifetime's misery in store."

"You can't be sure of that."

"*Pshaw!*"

Miss Frampton threw herself back into the chair, hands clenched in her lap, jaw muscles knotted with temper. Never had Sophy seen her governess in such a royal bad mood. Realizing that she still needed the woman's help, she offered a flag of truce.

Reaching out, she took Miss Frampton's hand. "What do *you* advise?"

"Oh, marry your hussar by all means."

"No, seriously, dear Miss Frampton: what other course is open to me?"

"My sister, now departed, had a liaison with a soldier once . . ."

"And he was killed in an accident?"

"Yes, but he left my sister in motherhood—three months gone. Perhaps he would have married her; she thought so."

"What did she do?"

"She went into seclusion, was delivered of the child, and . . ."

Miss Frampton studied the anatomy of a herring gull perched on the rim over the salon canopy.

"What did your sister do?" Sophy asked, with keen interest now.

"Put the little infant to a good home."

"Oh no!"

Abruptly Miss Frampton was leaning across her, cupping her hands in her own bony fingers. She spoke with an impassioned intensity, almost pleadingly. "It costs a little money, that's all. London is full of loving folk who have no babes of their own to raise and cherish and be a stave to them in later life."

"I couldn't do it."

"Would it not be better than to watch your infant starve?"

"I will . . ."

"Can you, selfishly, deny the boy or little girl a chance to share in a real family life? Condemn your unborn child to . . ."

"I will marry Edmund Sutton."

Miss Frampton snapped her teeth shut on her argument, clicking them. Her eyes blazed with thwarted rage.

"Very well, Sophy. Do as you wish."

"I meant no offense to your sister, Miss Frampton."

"It's too late for her: she has gone to her Maker."

"And her child?"

Indicating with a wave of her hand that the subject was too painful, Miss Frampton adjusted her bonnet to keep the bright, fragile sunlight out of her face, lay back and closed her eyes.

Panic filled Sophy; the comfort of the crossing was gone.

"Miss Frampton. Miss Frampton?"

One eye opened, squinting, obsidian. "What is it?"

"Will you still help me?"

"Help you?"

"To . . . to . . . to find Edmund."

A smile flickered across the governess's lips, fixed and not reassuring. "Of course, my dear," she said. "I promise I won't abandon you; not until you see fit to send me away."

Sophy sighed with relief.

"That day will never come," she said, and, leaning on her elbow, kissed the governess tenderly on her gaunt cheek.

Miss Frampton's smile remained fixed.


The house in Pelican Lane was hardly prepossessing, a long "thump downstairs" from the quaint splendor of a private chalet hotel. But it was better by far than the sinister lodginghouse in which Sophy and her governess spent their first week in London. This incursion into the vast areas of the capital that lay beyond the fashionable stores and theaters of the West End was a revelation to Sophy. Until that time, her experiences of the city had been confined to a half dozen educational visits and shopping expeditions, based in quiet, modest hotels near the Green Park. Though she had not then gone blind through the streets, she had effectively blotted from her consciousness the glimpses of squalor and poverty that impinged upon her enjoyment and sense of lighthearted adventure.

London now, though, was no adventure. Pelican Lane was not Knightsbridge nor Grosvenor Square, but a clutter of ramshackle houses, shops, taverns and warehouses, within sight—just—of the crust of St. Paul's, within earshot of the zoological rumpus of traffic charging up and down Ludgate Hill.

The lodginghouse too had been in that general region.

On Miss Frampton's instructions, Sophy had kept strictly to her room there, leaving it only to partake of breakfast and an evening meal in the dining room.

She had sat alone by the window, staring through the streaky glass at the life of London ebbing and flowing below. She had filled her ears with vendors' cries and dog yelps and the Chase-me-Charlie shrieks of twilight women.

Shabby but not altogether a slum, the lodginghouse was on the fringe of the nighttown. Strange, soft, muffled sounds of laughter, punctuated with occasional oaths, told Sophy that the owner, a widow woman who seemed to be a model of unctuous propriety, had more irons in the fire than the care and feeding of respectable ladies at modest prices.

The brawling, bustling street and thoroughfare's junction kept her mind from dwelling too much on her own predicament.

On the third day Miss Frampton returned from one of her prolonged absences accompanied by a small, shrunken man of indeterminate age. He was dressed in a fashion which suggested that he too had once been *up* and had but recently *come down*. He sported a rusty moustache, full frock coat and an incongruous beaver hat, though the weather was still too warm for such a top-piece. His name, so Miss Frampton said, was Sclater, a member of the medical profession, and a Scotsman.

Sclater's eyes betrayed not the slightest hint of human interest in Sophy. The man's utter indifference, and the ritual nature of his examination, enabled her to go through the undignified business without complaint and to answer his curt, gruff questions without reticence. By the end of it all, she was as indifferent to his pronouncement as the doctor himself.

Wrapping his tube round his forearm like a washerwife's rope, he said, "Aye, you're carryin' a bairn. Nine or ten weeks gone. Just time enough."

"Time enough for what, sir?" asked Sophy, pausing in the process of hooking her bodice.

She glanced from the doctor to Miss Frampton, who was frowning and shaking her head at the man.

Sclater frowned too, then shrugged.

He stuffed the tube in his pocket and, without another word, went into the passageway at the top of the third-floor landing.

Miss Frampton followed him, closing the door. Sophy, her heart pounding, listened against the door, heard the dry mutter of voices. The sense of the words was lost, though, swallowed up in the rumble of a dray on the cobbles outside. Before that thunder had passed, Miss Frampton returned.

Sophy said, "Who *is* that man?"

"Dr. Sclater: I told you."

"Is he really a doctor?"

Miss Frampton hesitated. "Of course, my dear."

"What did he mean by saying 'time enough'?"

"A medical expression to do with providing for your welfare in the months to come. While we remain in London, Dr. Sclater will attend you."

"Can we not find . . . ?"

"In addition to being highly discreet, Sophy," said Miss Frampton, snappishly, "the good doctor is also inexpensive."

Sophy accepted that argument. Her monthly allowance, paid over the counter of Jaspers', a merchant banker in Bread Street, was sufficient to keep her in moderate comfort. To take on the lease of a house of her own, however, stretched the sum thin. Already, she thought, she might be in Miss Frampton's debt, financially as well as morally.

As if to prevent Sophy asking further questions, the governess said, "I have found you a house."

"Oh, where?" said Sophy, eagerly.

"Not far from here. Pelican Lane. It comes furnished, with a resident maid."

"A maid?" cried Sophy, in delighted astonishment.

"Now, my dear, don't build up your dreams. The maid is no more than a drudge. You'll see little enough of her. I will undertake most of the domestic chores in the public part of the house."

"How large is it?"

"Four rooms."

"Is that . . . ?" Sophy bit off the complaint.

"Two upstairs, two down, and kitchens."

"When do we take up occupancy?"

"Tomorrow."

As September waned towards October and gas lamps, sparsely scattered down Cheapside and Leadenhall, came alight early, Sophy was thoroughly homesick for the moors and dales of Yorkshire. In Huffton the trees would be turning russet, the harvests of the tillage on her father's tenants' land would be taken in, fields lying cropped and golden in the late sunshine.

In Pelican Lane there was precious little sunshine. By night, beyond the roofs and towering warehouses, the sky was lit by the vivid limelights of laborers in the railway cutting by the Eastern Counties station. That electrical glow seemed more natural to London than the tarnished sunshine which hung in the smoke haze during the hours of the day.

Number Four Pelican Lane was one of four old dwellings tacked on to the end of a line of store sheds and black brick warehouses; a *cul-de-sac* chopped off by a red brick wall topped, probably at some distance, by slate roofs and a sad, sick chestnut tree.

The ground-floor rooms were long but narrow—indeed the whole house was like a pencil box put on end—and furnished with solemn masculine opulence. In contrast, the upstairs bedrooms were garish, overornate and utterly vulgar. Agatha would have felt quite at home in them. For some reason the public rooms downstairs reminded Sophy of those scarred disreputable bachelors whom one saw sometimes in Middlesborough.

The large double bed was comfortable enough, though stuffy, since the brocade drapes which covered the windows were ring-locked to prevent them opening more than a foot or so. She would have slept with the window sash lifted, but she was afraid of cutthroats and burglars.

The maid was a pinched, sickly Shropshire girl, younger than Sophy. She did her work, laboring at the kitchen furnishings, from dawn until dusk, and slept—and probably snored, thought Sophy—in a cubbyhole behind the laundry room. Her name was Rosemary. Sophy saw her only a half dozen times in all in her six weeks' sojourn in Pelican Lane.

Shortly after her arrival in the house, within a day in fact, Sophy was stricken with a feverish chill that brought a return of her nausea. Dr. Sclater called each evening, provided medicines and, strangely, a certain comfort by his taciturn declarations, repeated twice like a litany: "Ach, you'll be fine; you'll be fine, lass."

It was the first week in October before Sophy recovered enough to engage Miss Frampton in prolonged conversation and bring to the fore those points that had troubled her during the nightmarish days of her fever.

The first session of questioning, while she still lay propped in bed as weak as the watered wine Miss Frampton had given her to wash down her draught, was an attempt to take hold of the situation. Sophy was not unaware that her governess had "protected" her from concern by making all the arrangements necessary for her lengthy seclusion. But facets of the dealing had thrown up a perplexing degree of mystery.

"Why, Miss Frampton, must we incur the expense of taking on a house of our own?"

"Surely, this is better than living in a common lodging?"

"Without doubt," said Sophy. "But it is considerably more expensive."

"A decent hotel would not have you, at least not when your condition became apparent."

"How long will we stay here?"

"That . . . that depends."

"On what?"

Miss Frampton sidestepped that particular question.

She said, "Dr. Sclater is not concerned. He says you are a strong, healthy young woman and will bear with ease."

"In March?"

"Yes."

Sophy bit her lip, and toyed with the ears of the embroidered counterpane, a seething Oriental arabesque of silk and cheap gilt threads.

"For how long have we leased this house?"

"By the month," said Miss Frampton.

"To whom does it belong?"

"A gentleman, I believe."

"Who sleeps in a bedroom like this? Where is the gentleman?"

"Abroad."

"Do you know him?"

"I discovered the house through a leasing agent. Sophy, why do you ask me these questions? Don't you trust me?"

"I trust you implicitly, dear Miss Frampton. I'm curious, that's all."

Miss Frampton removed the wineglass from the bed-table and poured Sophy another generous dash from the decanter.

"Come to the point, Sophy," she said.

"You seem to know your way about London."

"I spent several years here, residing with a family not

a half mile from this house. The district has come down a little since then, of course."

"Were you a governess even then?"

"After a fashion," murmured Miss Frampton. "Yes, I looked after four children."

"Does my father know where I am?"

"No: I thought it best to inform him that we were traveling. Jaspers' is a reputable enough accommodation address."

Sophy nodded. She had had a horror of waking one evening to be confronted by a gloating Agatha.

Suddenly she felt much less inclined to push forward with her questioning. It was not, she convinced herself, that she doubted Miss Frampton, merely that so many of the woman's stories had come into focus since the beginning of the summer. The woman's competence seemed now like the fruit of vast and varied experience of life at several levels.

Evaluating Miss Frampton's strengths and weaknesses, if any, would be important soon—very soon.

The following morning, though still weak, Sophy rose, dressed herself and wavered downstairs.

Miss Frampton was in the dining room, seated in a padded high-backed chair at the head of the elongated table, eating breakfast. Rosemary was in the room too, her features puffy and stained with tears.

Miss Frampton looked up in surprise.

"How good to see you downstairs, my dear," she said. "Is it wise to be up so early, however?"

Sophy reached a chair and sank gratefully down on it. The servant was staring at her with a mixture of curiosity and fear. Miss Frampton dismissed the child with a wave of her hand, and turned her attention to the plate of beef and scrambled eggs before her.

"Are you hungry, Sophy?"

"As a hawk."

Smiling, Miss Frampton lifted the lids on several silver dishes and prepared an ample breakfast for the girl.

The women ate, chatting throughout. Sophy experienced a sense of lost companionship that almost made her regret the necessity of crossing her governess and probably incurring her wrath.

Still, there was no help for it.

After the teapot had been emptied and the toast rack cleared, Sophy said, "Miss Frampton, I am extremely indebted to you for all that you have done for me."

"It is my duty to look after you."

"No, your kindnesses have gone far beyond duty."

Miss Frampton bowed her thanks for the compliment. Sophy said, "May I now take advantage of your kindness and your familiarity with the city and ask you to find Captain Sutton?"

"I thought," said Miss Frampton evenly, "that you had discarded that foolish idea."

"Not discarded," said Sophy, "merely put aside. I am, without doubt, carrying Edmund's child, and, if your good doctor is to be believed, I will be delivered of it in March. Miss Frampton, I need a husband and a father for my baby."

The woman tapped her teaspoon on the edge of her saucer, lips pursed. "Sophy, in my opinion, you are squandering your youth and beauty, your life, on this gesture."

"Learn where the Regimental Headquarters of the Seventh Hussars is located," said Sophy, with great firmness, "so that we might inform Captain Sutton that we are in London. You will tell him no more than that, please, but will invite him to dine here at his earliest convenience."

"And what if he laughs at your invitation, as well he might?"

"Insist."

"He will think that he has a fine fool on his hook."

· "Let him think what he likes," said Sophy. "He will learn differently when he meets me again."

Miss Frampton tutted under her breath, making it very obvious that she thoroughly disapproved of Sophy's determination to reinvolve herself with Sutton. It seemed ironic to the girl that such a pillar of moral rectitude as Miss Frampton had always appeared to be should, at this juncture, show herself in favor of a liberal, if not depraved, approach to birth out of wedlock. Most other women would have howled for justice and a wedding ring even if the groom had been an ogre.

Marriage to Edmund would not be so awful. He must have some financial resources, or else he would not have been traveling abroad, even if he could not afford better lodging than Vandler's. Vandler's Pension! The sordid incident there had diminished in Sophy's mind. She recalled the letter she had impetuously torn up and, with that flair for self-deception that tribulation increased, almost managed to convince herself it had contained a declaration of undying devotion.

She got to her feet.

She was no longer a humble girl, a pupil.

"Do as I say, please, Miss Frampton."

"It is your decision, my dear," Miss Frampton said.

"And I will stand by it, I assure you."

An hour later the governess left Pelican Lane with the express purpose of tracking down Sophy's errant hussar.

Dusk came early that evening, swooping over London on cloudy wings, drawing a swift merciless gloom over the house in Pelican Lane. After luncheon, a miserable cold collation, Sophy had spent the afternoon in bed. But sleep would not come to her and she consoled herself by eating a whole tub of candied fruits which Rosemary had fetched from a confectioners in Beech Street. Sophy's mind was in a turmoil of expectation; every thud and thump in the street seemed to be a signal that Miss Frampton had returned. Her fanciful imagination created melodramatic welcomes and tearful reunions between herself and Captain Sutton. The romantic aura of the affair had, oddly, not decreased as the reality of an illegitimate infant in her womb become daily more apparent. Patience, however, was not part of the dream. The afternoon dwindled into evening and the evening into night and every hour became long and more unendurable.

Rosemary dared to knock on her new mistress's door and inquire if there would be two or one for dinner, and what was wanted. Sophy occupied herself for half an hour picking a menu for a candlelit supper which she hoped to share with Edmund. In the end, however, she gave orders for a meat pie and vegetables, and a simple suet pudding, a filling repast which might do something to appease her ever-increasing appetite.

At eight, she descended the stairs, took her place in the dining room and began on the mutton broth. At half past eight, just as Rosemary was struggling up from the kitchen with the pie, the governess let herself into the hallway with her key.

Sophy was at the door in an instant.

Miss Frampton, divesting herself of her overcoat and hat, endeavored to prop them on Rosemary's left arm as if the girl were a music-hall juggler.

"Is that dinner?" said Miss Frampton, nodding at the pie.

"Yes, do you wish soup?" asked Sophy.

"No, I will begin with the savory."

"Another place for Miss Frampton, Rosemary."

Sniffling at the confusion, Rosemary placed the pie dish on the stairs, disposed of the woman's hat and coat, then vanished below stairs again.

Miss Frampton carried the pie in state into the dining room and, without any preliminary, set it and herself down, salvered a steaming wedge from the dish and, using Sophy's plate and cutlery, began to eat.

Standing behind one of the chairs, leaning on it to support her trembling limbs, Sophy said, "Well, what did you discover?"

"What a dreadful day," said Miss Frampton, forking food into her mouth avidly. "I'm utterly exhausted."

"Did you find Edmund?"

"Not exactly."

Sophy's patience snapped. She leaned forward and beat her fist on the table, making the dishes ring and clatter.

"Not exactly? What does *that* mean?"

Miss Frampton glanced at the girl. Sophy saw a soft sort of pity in her eyes. At that moment, Rosemary barged into the room bearing a tray of plates and cutlery. Clumsily the servant set out a place on the governess's right, nervously eying the woman as if in expectation of a clip on the ear for tardiness.

Holding herself in control, Sophy waited until the domestic had completed her task and was moving towards the door.

"Miss Frampton, what . . . ?" she began.

The governess interrupted her. "Rosemary, is there brandy in the house?"

"Yes, mum; in the cellar closet."

"Bring a glass, a large glass—then you may leave us in private."

"But the puddin' . . . ?"

"Eat it yourself," said Miss Frampton. "Now fetch the brandy; and be quick about it."

Rosemary left. The governess finished her meal, adding potatoes and cabbage to a second slice of pie and putting that helping away in the short time it took the servant to reappear with the liquor.

"Give the glass to Miss Sophy."

Rosemary did so.

"Now go."

Rosemary went.

Weakly, Sophy slid into the chair. She was in need of the brandy and sipped the fiery liquid gladly while Miss Frampton wiped her lips on a napkin and, with her elbows on the table, disgorged the sorry story of her afternoon's odyssey.

Sophy had already guessed that the news would be grave.

"Your soldier shipped out with his regiment three days ago, Sophy," Miss Frampton said. "The regiment's quartered near Folkstone and may already have embarked for the Crimea. As you can imagine, the clerks in Regimental Headquarters were not generous with their information. Indeed, they treated me at first like some sort of Muscovite spy."

"But . . . but Edmund has gone?"

"Yes," said Miss Frampton, cautiously. "And it is perhaps a blessing in disguise."

"How *dare* you say . . ."

"Edmund Sutton is a married man."

Sophy swallowed the brandy, all of it. The rim of the glass was like a razor and seemed to cut into her lips. Tears welled up and blurred her vision and she could feel the liquid scalding her throat and breast.

She gasped and dropped the glass upon the table.

Miss Frampton was at her side, hugging her.

"I'm so sorry, my dear. I understand. I . . ."

Sophy thrust her away, rising, swaying, shouting: "You have been palmed off with misinformation. Couldn't you even do a simple errand for me without error? All you had to say was that you required information regarding Captain Edmund Sutton, serving officer . . . and bring . . . me . . . the answer. That is *all* you had to do. *No.* I *don't* believe it. I *won't* believe it . . ."

"Sophy, you will do yourself serious injury."

"*Leave me alone.* He *couldn't* do this to me."

"It is done," said Miss Frampton, sharply. "It's over, Sophy."

"Oh, God!" Sophy cried and, weeping, flung herself down upon the musty rug. "Damn him; damn him! *Why* did he have to pick *me?*"

Miss Frampton knelt by her side, stroking her hair soothingly—all to no effect. She said, "You picked him, Sophy. The error, if any, was your own."

"*Don't say that.*"

"The truth it is that hurts the most."

"Leave me; leave me."

Thrashing on the floor, Sophy buried her head in her arms.

Even Miss Frampton's composure was disturbed by the sight of the girl's wild emotion. She continued to stroke and soothe her, wordlessly, until the first spasm of rage and anguish had spent itself and Sophy limply allowed her governess to draw her into her arms and, rocking and crooning, comfort her as if she were a child again.

"What shall I do? What can I do?" Sophy moaned.

"Listen, Sophy; listen to me, my dear," the woman said, gently. "You must be certain in your mind that I have told you the truth. Captain Sutton is married. His wife lives with his parents, and his two children, in Hampshire."

"Two *children?* Oh, God!"

"He has been married some eight years. I have it on good authority that your hussar is not a model husband, though he does keep up a pretense of supporting a home and family. The . . . ah, holiday in Switzerland was not his first foray abroad. A . . . 'hunting trip' the clerk called it. Women, apparently, are Captain Sutton's natural prey."

"How did you discover this?"

"Not to put too fine a point on it," said Miss Frampton, "I bribed a clerk in the paymaster's office. It's the truth, Sophy, I swear."

Sophy sobbed for another minute in her governess's arms, then allowed the woman to help her to her feet and settle her on a chair.

Miss Frampton knelt in front of her, hands clasping Sophy's wrists. "To be honest, Sophy, I suspected some such turn of events."

"Why did you not warn me?"

"Would you have listened?"

Sheepishly, Sophy shook her head.

Miss Frampton went on, "I have a proposal. Will you listen to me now?"

"Yes."

"In order to protect you from scandal, it's necessary that *nobody* knows that you have . . . given yourself to a man."

"But . . ."

"Hush, now; listen to me."

"Yes, Miss Frampton."

"My dear sister Cora has a cottage in Cornwall, some thirty miles from Penzance. The situation is very isolated; my sister prefers to live the life of a recluse. I have taken the liberty of writing to inform her of your situation. She suggests that we reside with her until your child is born."

"But Cornwall is so far away."

"Precisely."

"Can we not stay here?"

"I do not think that is advisable. We can be traced here. Your stepmother, or your father, could find us. Do you wish to run that risk?"

"No," Sophy admitted reluctantly.

Miss Frampton got to her feet. She seemed to tower over Sophy, as if the young woman had shrunk again to the stature of a little girl.

Sophy remembered the woman's strength, her decisiveness, and the awe in which she had held her during the early years of their association. She had thought that sort of feeling was past, gone with the French lessons and the Latin grammar and the dreary hours of piano practice and embroidery. Now it all came flooding back.

"Your situation is desperate, Sophy. The happiness of the rest of your life may depend on what you choose to do during the course of the next few weeks. Make no mistake, you are carrying a soldier's bastard."

Sophy flinched and would have wept again if the governess's fingers had not closed upon her head and tilted her face up, forcing her gaze to lock with the woman's.

"Think of the future, my dear. Do not be afraid. You may still find the happiness that you crave. But, for the time being, you must heed my advice and do as I say—even if it seems harsh and cruel."

"I'll accompany you to Cornwall," Sophy conceded.

"Good! Now, you will write and inform your father that you will be wintering in Cornwall—no need to be specific —and ask him to forward through Jaspers' office the sum of one hundred pounds . . ."

"One hundred pounds!" Sophy exclaimed.

"One hundred pounds against your allowance. Assure him that you will make no more demands on him. Give him that promise in writing. Agatha will seize the opportunity to cut you off and your father will comply, I'm sure."

"But what will happen to me when the hundred pounds is all gone?"

"Trust me, Sophy."

"I don't *want* to beg from that household."

"You must."

"Cut myself off?" said Sophy. "What . . . ?"

"Regard it as an investment in your future. Agatha would do—indeed, *will* do so."

"Miss Frampton," said Sophy, perceptively. "Exactly what do you intend me to do?"

"Find yourself a husband," Miss Frampton said; "a wealthy husband."

"And my child?"

Miss Frampton shook her head. "I will find a loving home for it."

"I can't; no, *I can't do it.*"

"Then there is no help for you, Sophy; none at all."

"But to farm out my baby . . . how can I?"

"You must trust me; and be very strong."

Sophy wept.

"Think, Sophy. Think most carefully, and decide what you want from life."

A husband.

By morning, after an endless night, Sophy had agreed to Miss Frampton's plan—and stepped, without further persuasion, into the governess's subtle trap.

# Five

When the matter of her immediate future was settled, Sophy slipped into a pattern of moods which ranged through minor emotional scales, touching neither joy nor despair. She behaved as if she was constantly bored. The truth was that, robbed of impulsiveness and her capacity to dream grandly, she had simply become compliant.

The weather that October matched her mental state; not cold, not warm, not sunny, not wet. Bland gray cloud capped the city like a saucepan lid, changing its weight hardly at all as morning melted into noon and afternoon congealed again into dusk.

The larger, more fashionable West End stores already exhibited their Christmas gowns, the only indication that the neutral spell must inevitably end in a misery of frost and ice in which the holiday stood, like a radiant gate, in the distance.

By Christmas, Sophy knew she would be swollen and ugly. Thinking of that prospect, she was gladdened by the governess's persuasions and her own compliance. Cornwall, however bleak, was the best place to hide oneself away, to conceal the unwholesome evidence of indiscretion and the damning fact that she was a woman who could not even snare a husband in the wake of loving. She would, perhaps, have dropped the next half year completely from her consciousness, as some prisoners are known to do on sentencing, if Miss Frampton had not taken her firmly in hand and insisted on frequent shopping trips, with all the respectable trimmings.

Bond Street, Oxford Street, St. James'—they still had the power to excite Sophy and, spending freely, almost foolishly, Miss Frampton accoutered her charge with as many elegant fripperies as appealed to her. Sophy would not risk a fitting, however; the only gown she agreed to purchase was bought off-the-peg, measured over her chemise. Novels, too, a whole carton of them bought from secondhand stalls along the Soho lanes, fed Sophy's long-term ambitions with descriptions of the *haut monde* and perils and travails successfully overcome by scheming and good fortune.

Now, it seemed, there was no hurry to quit the city. The Pelican Lane lease would expire on the last day of the month. On the morning of November first, the couple would, after putting much of their baggage in store in honest premises in Goodge Street, depart for Penzance.

During their shopping expeditions, Sophy's eye was reluctantly caught by babyware displays, cribs, cots, shawls and frilly miniature frocks, all the paraphernalia which little heirs and heiresses-to-be would need for their layette. On these occasions, the girl would be brought up sharply, a pang of sorrow cutting into her prevailing mood—and Miss Frampton would chatter more loudly of the splash Sophy would make next summer in Eastbourne or whichever spa they decided to grace with their presence, and hurry her along.

Gradually, surely, Sophy learned to consider herself as a woman in cold storage, not as a mother-to-be, but as a debutante in bondage. She did not, ever, train herself to hate the evolving mite in her womb. She simply came to regard it as an awkward tenant whose lease would expire in March, who would fly by night and leave her once more free and self-possessed.

By the middle of the month, the tenant was spreading

evidently under her night attire. Miss Frampton tailored her crinoline dresses to disguise the thickening, however, and none of it showed, even to a keen eye.

As October entered its final week, and the time for departure neared, Miss Frampton became peculiarly agitated. It could not be because of money.

As the governess had predicted, Thomas Richmond had sought his wife's advice and had received the diplomatic answer that Sophy must have her cash. A bill of hand had been dispatched to Jaspers' that same day. Sophy's letter —declaring the hundred pounds to be an ultimate claim against her paternal allowance—was discreetly whisked off into the locked deed box in the bottom of Agatha's wardrobe. Sophy had her working capital; Agatha had her waiver, legal in any court of law; and Thomas Richmond had the satisfaction of a charitable salving of his somewhat inflamed conscience in the matter of his only daughter's welfare.

Four days of the month remained. Miss Frampton had left Sophy at home several times of late, going out alone in her best garments to conduct certain small items of "business" too involved to explain to the girl. Dr. Sclater made what was to be his last call, pronounced Sophy fit for motherhood and, with an unexpected burst of warmth, predicted that the infant would be a bouncing boy.

Sophy had the suspicion that something serious was troubling her governess. The woman was restless, pacing the drawing room, rising from the dining table to peer out into the hall, starting at the slightest sound by the front door. When tentatively questioned, she poo-pooed the very idea and laughed at Sophy's flight of fancy. Nothing was wrong, she said.

One day remained: Thursday, the last of October—All Hallow's Eve, to those of superstitious bent. Miss Frampton, surrendering the enigmatic imp which tormented her, had given way to unusual snappishness and fits of pique. In Sophy's sight, and to the girl's amazement, the governess soundly boxed Rosemary's ears for spilling consommé at luncheon, a few speckled drops only on the tablecloth. Sophy, who had never seen Miss Frampton so raw and nervous before, was frightened by the inexplicable display.

The baggage was packed, laid ready by the kitchen door to be collected next morning by the storeman's menial. The standing account at Jaspers' had been cleared, the cash, in five pound notes, sewn into Miss Frampton's stays, save for the sum necessary to pay the fares to Cornwall. There was, that long, neutral afternoon, nothing to do and nothing to be done. Sophy would have welcomed a final cab ride up to Regent Street to take tea in Maddeley's or walk through the Piccadilly arcades. But Miss Frampton would have none of it. It was not until the early evening that the woman at last gave in to the girl's whining and, wrapped warmly against the chill night air, accompanied her on a stroll along the pavements as far as Finsbury Square and back again.

Rosemary, breathlessly, opened the door at the sound of the key.

"A genn'lemun, miss," she stammered. "I . . . put . . . 'im in . . . t' parlor."

Miss Frampton's face brightened. She beamed as if the visitation was from the Prince himself. In an instant her surliness was gone, and briskness returned.

"Thank you, Rosemary, my dear. Will you bring the best nutty sherry and three glasses to the drawing room immediately?" she said loudly; then, in a sibilant undertone, "and do up your hair, for Heaven's sake, girl."

"Who is it?" asked Sophy, apprehensively. "Who knows that we live here?"

Miss Frampton did not answer.

She steered Sophy rapidly across the hall, so that, no matter how she twisted herself, the girl could not make out the identity of the man who stood by the drawing-room fire.

"Upstairs," Miss Frampton commanded, *sotto voce*.

"Change into the new gown which you will find in the closet. Change everything. And arrange your hair too. Wear the jewels you'll find in the box in the top drawer of the dressing table." Pushing the girl on, Miss Frampton tore off her overcoat and hat and tossed them down the dark corridor towards the kitchen stairs. "Make sure that you are perfect, Sophy. Do you hear—*perfect*."

"But . . . ?"

"Do as I say."

Astonished and afraid, Sophy pulled herself upstairs.

Below in the hall, Miss Frampton fussed and primped before the armorial mirror, then, fixing on her warmest smile, sailed into the drawing room.

Sophy craned over the balustrade, straining her ears.

Just before the door closed she heard Miss Frampton say, "Ah, good evening. How clever of you to run us to earth. It's *so* good to see you again, M. de Nerval. Sophy *will* be thrilled."

Sophy was dismayed.


Leon de Nerval had not changed at all. Indeed, they might have been facing each other across the breakfast table in the Schneegarten hotel, so natural did their meeting seem on the surface. He stood by the fire, sipping the glass of wine which Miss Frampton had poured for him, watching Sophy enter the drawing room.

As her governess had instructed, she had put on her new gown and made herself as beautiful as time allowed. She tried to walk elegantly, not waddle—though Miss Frampton said that the graceless gait was all in her imagination.

Leon de Nerval quickly put down his glass. Miss Frampton was seated behind him on the black leather couch, hands folded primly in her lap.

For an instant, Sophy was confused. By now she had guessed that Eunice Frampton was somehow responsible for bringing de Nerval here. She could deduce the reason, too, but she did not yet know de Nerval's degree of duplicity in the arrangement. For example, was he acquainted with her condition and did he therefore regard her as an easy prey?

No. She rejected that idea.

The trader's suit was elegantly cut, more English formal than Continental. The hard, shiny-white collar contrasted with his swarthy complexion and tanned skin.

"Miss Sophy," he said; "even more beautiful than I had remembered you."

"Thank you, M. de Nerval." Sophy offered her hand, which he kissed. "And you, are you still employing nefarious practices to get what you want?"

His momentary bewilderment indicated that he was probably not in league with Miss Frampton. He grinned. "You refer, I think, to my bribery of Master Redford."

"I do, sir."

"This time, Sophy, it cost me a half crown to a clerk in Jaspers' merchant bank, though not as bribery but in gratitude; he had already given me your forwarding address."

"But," said Sophy, glancing past the man at her governess, "how did you know that Jaspers' were in charge of my account?"

Miss Frampton said, "I thought it proper to inform Lady Redford where you might be reached—and Jaspers' . . ."

"Ah, yes, of course," Sophy interrupted. "I'd quite forgotten."

"I returned to the Schneegarten, you know," said de Nerval. "I missed you by a week."

"How unfortunate," said Sophy, stiltedly.

"Will you dine with us, sir?" asked Miss Frampton.

"I had hoped," said de Nerval, "that you would do me the honor of taking supper with me."

"Most civil of you, M. de Nerval," said Miss Frampton. "But we are leaving for Cornwall in the morning and we have much packing still to be done."

De Nerval made no attempt to hide his disappointment.

Rising, Miss Frampton touched his arm sympathetically.

"I do not flatter myself, sir, that you long overmuch for *my* company. Sophy, I'm sure, would be happy to take supper with you. She will be quite safe with you without a chaperone."

The governess's ruse appeared too obvious. Sophy made fluttering protests, but Leon de Nerval would have none of them. His eagerness overcame her anxieties. Finally she agreed.

It took her only ten minutes to make herself ready, then she accompanied the Breton out into Pelican Lane, leaving Miss Frampton, smiling warmly, behind.

For a moment, looking up at the limelit sky behind the brick wall of the *cul-de-sac* and the faint yellowish cloud and hearing the bustle of the vulgar street ahead, Sophy felt like a tiny snail that had been winkled from its protective shell. How, for instance, would Leon de Nerval react to finding them living in such a shabby quarter of London?

As if reading her thoughts, de Nerval took her arm and, breathing deeply through his nose, declared, "I adore the sounds and smells of the city."

"I prefer the countryside," said Sophy.

They were walking along the pavement towards Ludgate, in search of a hackney rank. De Nerval seemed quite at home on foot, brushing past pedestrians, threading a way for his companion through crowds at busy crossings.

"Strange," he said. "I did not think that you quite fitted in with the Redfords' circle."

"Why not, sir?"

"I think you belong here, in London—or possibly Paris."

"Are you making fun of me?"

"Of course not, Sophy. I'm perfectly serious." He waved his free arm in the most expansive gesture Sophy had yet seen him make. His self-containment appeared to have been banished by the vigor of the city. "This is where progress is to be found."

"And squalor?"

"That will be cured in time," de Nerval said. "You cannot have progress without turmoil. The English countryside is asleep, wrapped in its traditional blanket. But here—as you can see—men and women are awake to every opportunity. Here one must compete for the prizes life has to offer."

Agatha, thought Sophy, was a Londoner. She said, "That may be all very well for a gentleman, M. de Nerval . . ."

"Leon."

"Very well: Leon, it may be all very well for you, but women cannot compete in that way."

"Nonsense!" De Nerval smiled at her, arm tight in her elbow. He had developed that slight swaying motion which educated fellows had, of necessity, acquired to cope with their female companions' bell-like skirts. Sophy crooked her arm a little higher to make it more comfortable for him. "Look how the urchins make way for you."

It was true. The sprawling, brawling children who romped about outside the lit shop doors and in the mouths of the broad lanes, who clambered over handcarts and ducked under the belly-belts of the drovers' nags, they *did* seem to make way for her, pulling back to give clearway for the couple.

"That is because I am with you," Sophy said.

"That is because you are a lady, and emanate an aura of successful prosperity."

"*Pshaw!*" Sophy exclaimed, borrowing Miss Frampton's word. "May we, please, defray all further conversation until we are seated?"

"You must learn," said de Nerval, bawling now to make himself heard over the deafening drone of traffic on the hill, "you must learn to argue standing up, sitting, even *running* if you have no other choice. Indeed, several of my most lucrative negotiations have been made at the double. *Par example!*"

He released her and, inserting two fingers into the corner of his lips, blew a piercing whistle which not only caught the attention of the hackney cab driver who had innocently turned out of his stable in Cheapside but startled every horse within a quarter of a mile.

The driver brought his conveyance to the curb, and de Nerval, who had obviously enjoyed giving vent to his feelings, helped Sophy into it. He instructed the driver as to their destination, then joined the girl within the leather-and-tarpaulin vault.

He sat back.

"Now," he said, "to return to our debate: do you really believe that righteousness breeds riches?"

Sophy realized that she would need to be nimble-witted to keep abreast of Leon de Nerval. Somehow she had expected a more paternal and sophisticated introduction to the evening out. He had changed in the London environment, away from Alpine meadows. He still looked purposeful and almost severe, but there was a boyish quality to his mischievous love of discussion, and Sophy could see behind it a desire to crystallize their relationship, probe into her mind and discover not only what she thought but also what she felt. She was on guard now. Briefly her predicament and departure for Cornwall were forgotten. She felt keenly alive for the first time in many weeks.

She said, "I don't wholly subscribe to that glib adage."

"I don't subscribe to it at all," de Nerval told her. "Long ago I learned the difference between righteousness and honesty, and between riches and wealth."

"The former I understand," said Sophy; "the latter is too subtle for me, I'm afraid."

"Riches are but trappings, a public show. Any rogue with an income of twenty pounds per annum can put on a pantomime of riches. Wealth, however, is a private matter; the satisfaction of knowing that all one's books balance and that one's credit will be honored with eagerness in any large clearinghouse in Europe."

Was he boasting? Was he hoping that she would show an inordinate interest in his "wealth"? Sophy resisted the bait. He was watching her, dark, slumbrous eyes glinting in the flicker of the gaslight that penetrated the cab window.

She said, "I am more interested in your opinion of the fittingness of competition in respect of the female sex."

"Ah, you make it sound so serious, Sophy, like a lecture in the Royal Soho."

"You will never find me among the Bloomers," Sophy quickly retorted, making her companion laugh. "But tell me, sir, how do you philosophize on success?"

"A woman competes; she seeks a husband, position, the status of marriage and family."

"Humdrum humbug!"

"Do you think so? There is true power, authority and an unmatched form of success in a compatible marriage."

"Are you saying that we should not compete with our masters, only with other females of the species?"

"You should not compete with men," de Nerval said.

"I see! We are not your equals . . ."

"You should not compete with men, because you women will always win. We are no match for you."

Agatha and her wiles came again unbidden to Sophy's mind's eye. She could see her stepmother purring like a tabby cat and rubbing her ringlets softly against Thomas Richmond's cheek as she passed him wine at table. Then, in an instant, Thomas Richmond had been replaced by Leon de Nerval. Would *he* succumb to such obvious blandishments? Somehow, Sophy doubted it. Yet he must have an Achilles heel. Had he not confessed as much, tacitly acknowledging that he too was susceptible to feminine charm?

Once more, uncannily, de Nerval might have read her thoughts.

"Your father, I believe, married for a second time quite recently?"

The statement was unexpected. The change of mood, let alone the shift in direction, caught Sophy unaware.

"How did you . . . ?"

"My agent told me of it."

"My father has been a widower for many years," the girl said defensively.

"And you," said de Nerval gently, "are 'traveling'?"

"How far is it to the supper rooms?"

"Not far," he answered, then went remorselessly on, "Is there, by chance, a connection between your father's marriage and the fact that you are, to use a contemporary phrase, 'touring'?"

"I think," said Sophy, "that that is none of your concern, sir. For your information, I believe that my father deserves such . . . happiness as he can find."

"At your expense?"

"He has many new responsibilities. I am grown now, and wish to see something of life outside of Yorkshire."

De Nerval nodded, and let the subject go, at least as far as Sophy was involved.

"Twenty-eight years ago, I too went traveling for the first time. I was a little younger than you, Sophy, and I did not have the protection of a governess. I traveled, on foot, from St. Pol-de-Léon to the town of Brest, the very first occasion I had been away from my home village. Almost a dozen years of life had been spent looking at the same horizon, the same faces, the same squat church steeple against the sea."

"Why did you leave?"

"I had nothing to keep me," de Nerval said. "My mother died that autumn, twenty-eight years and one week ago to be precise."

"And your father?"

"I never knew him. He was a deckhand from a Dutch

trader. He came from the sea like a cock-salmon and returned to the sea, leaving a child and a churched wife behind. Oh, he did the honorable thing and married his '*paramour*.' My mother would talk of him wonderingly sometimes, as if he had been Neptune. She had many sisters, *Maman*. We lived with three of them, her mother and grandmother, in a tiny farm cottage. The women all looked like me—small and dark and ugly. They spoke seldom, and then only in a *patois* which bore little resemblance to our beautiful French language. I think they communicated in a vocabulary of about three hundred words. When my mother died and I was faced with staying alone with these silent women, I took myself off."

"To become a merchant?"

"Not so easily, Sophy, nor so simply. Brest—ah, I remember that evening: the smell of the town, the hubbub, all the matelots chattering in the taverns. I was suddenly made aware of the variety life had to offer." De Nerval paused, then went on with less obvious enthusiasm. "After Brest, I went to Cherbourg, then to Le Havre. I made my first visit to England on a sea-coal barge. I was sick all the crossing. But it taught me much, that I did not have the stomach to be a sailor for one thing. Paris taught me even more valuable lessons. Have you ever been to Paris?"

"Never."

"Perhaps I'll take you there . . ." De Nerval stopped and made a soft apologetic sound, as if he had been caught in the web of an illusion, an impossible dream. "Meantime, I will concentrate on trying to get us both as far as Portman Square."

Rapping on the lid of the coach, he attracted the driver's attention and requested more speed. The injunction, and the exchange of a discreet shilling, had its effect. A few minutes later, de Nerval helped Sophy to alight in front of the black-and-gilt-painted frontage of Colyer's French

Rooms. Assisted by a couple of front-gate footmen, he ushered her past the wrought-iron defenses which encroached on the pavement, through the forbidding doors into the foyer of London's most exclusive restaurant.

Though Sophy feigned a proper indifference—as if she dined in similar surroundings every night of her life—she was awed by the lavish décor and the suave attentions bestowed upon Leon de Nerval, and, equally, upon herself, by the staff.

Crowned by four magnificent chandeliers, the supper room was still large enough to shade discreet tables in discreet corners. It was to one of these that Leon led her. The wall hangings were of rich, scarlet flock, though not vulgar or in any way suggestive of an improper atmosphere. The value of the silverware alone, Sophy calculated, would have secured lease on Pelican Lane for a full year.

She decided, at length, to be frank with de Nerval and seek his advice on ordering from the astonishing eight-page menu.

Leon's pronunciation, together with explanations of the artistry which went into the preparation of each dish, acted on Sophy's appetite. Encouraged by her host, she spooned and carved her way through Purée of Artichokes, Cutlets à la Provençale, a wild duck in herb jelly, Beignet soufflé, and four small cheesecakes. Quantities of wine washed down the supper. The conversation, as seemed only fitting, revolved on food.

Leon de Nerval ate more sparingly than the girl; yet he seemed to take pleasure in her appetite, to encourage and stimulate it and, in rapid French, to intercede on her behalf with the waiters and little lacquered trayboys who toured hopefully with platters of special miniature delicacies, savory and sweet. Any conspicuous tightening of her crinoline cords could now be excused by the acceptable vice of gluttony.

Without doubt, he treated her only to the best that this establishment, itself the best in the city, had to offer. For that, Sophy, who could be open without being gauche, thanked him most profusely.

When the inevitable pot of coffee stood before de Nerval and he had asked her permission to light a small cigar—such a thing being "done" in a French establishment—the Breton once more reined the conversation round to personal matters.

Sophy had been mellow and somewhat sleepy at that point. Abruptly, she was alert, bringing her full attention to bear on the Breton's leading questions.

"You will not return to Huffton, will you?"

"As Miss Frampton has informed you, we leave tomorrow to winter in Cornwall."

"At the home of your governess's sister?"

"Yes."

"You rely much on Miss Frampton, do you not?"

"She has been very kind and attentive and a tower of strength to me."

"It was she, I take it, who secured the lease of the house you stay in, in Pelican Lane?"

"Yes. I was slightly indisposed just after our return to England."

De Nerval made a puzzling sound in his throat.

"Is something wrong?" asked Sophy.

"Do you know who the owner of that *maison* happens to be?"

"The transaction was, I believe, effected through an agent."

De Nerval nodded.

After a pause, Sophy could not help but ask, "Do *you* know who the owner is?"

The Breton blew smoke, clouding and obscuring his face. "No," he said curtly. "Tell me, Sophy, are you enthusiastic about Cornwall?"

"It is warmer than London, and I have not been in the best of health. The sea air and solitude will do me good."

"Would not Virginia do just as well?"

"Virginia?"

"And Carolina, too."

"Tobacco and cotton," said Sophy, promptly.

"I am leaving in a week's time for the Americas." De Nerval leaned back, cigarlette angled between finger and thumb. "Come with me?"

"M. de Nerval! How improper of you to . . ."

"As my wife."

There was no ardor in his voice. He did not insist. In fact, he posed the question as casually as he might suggest a stroll round Regent's Park.

Sophy could not believe her ears.

"I do not think that marriage is a subject for—for jest, Leon."

De Nerval took a deep breath, poured another cup of coffee for himself and more of the sweet wine for Sophy, then leaned back and studied her once more.

"I am serious, Sophy," he said. "Marry me and travel to the Americas with me."

"I . . . I don't know whether to be insulted or . . ."

"I would prefer you to give me an answer."

Her heart was thudding. The wine seemed suddenly to have gone to her head, making her senses spin. The chandeliers were a thousand times brighter than they had been a moment ago, radiant with a spectrum of rainbow colors. Blood rushed to her cheeks.

"You want *me* to marry *you*," she stammered.

"Is it so unthinkable?"

"No, not at all; not . . ." Sophy took control of her tongue. "We hardly know each other, Leon. After all, we've spent only a dozen hours in each other's company."

"In some countries, civilized countries," de Nerval said, "the bride and groom first meet at the altar rail."

"I do not believe in arranged marriages."

"Come, Sophy." Leon stubbed out his cigar and pushed away the coffee cup. Leaning, he took her hands in his. "Give me an answer."

"I can't, Leon," the girl said. "I'm flattered, and touched, but . . . No, I cannot marry you."

"So I must go to America alone?"

"Unless you can find another girl to become your wife."

"That's cruel, Sophy," Leon said. "I'm not in search of a wife, or a traveling companion. I wish to marry *you*."

"But we hardly . . ."

"I know you well enough, Sophy. Besides, I've been in love with you since the first moment I saw you."

Sophy retreated at the mention of love. She sensed that it was wrong of her to tint her performance with a jocularity that, she realized, only made it seem like scorn. "Is my face so pretty, then? I'll wager you've met a hundred women more beautiful than I am, Leon; did you propose to them too?"

The Breton bit his lip, then answered: "Yes, I have, in many years of traveling, encountered women of ravishing beauty. But I have never been seriously in love before, Sophy."

"And you believe yourself to be in love with me?"

"I know it."

"But why, Leon?"

"I want you to be my wife, Sophy." He sounded irritated by her interrogations. She could hardly blame him.

"I don't love you, Leon."

"What does that matter?"

"It matters very much to me."

"I will be gone," he said carefully, "for five or six months. May I visit you again in the spring?"

"In the hope that I'll change my mind?"

"Of course."

"Then . . ." Sophy hesitated: the spring, that period of release. "By all means, Leon, you may visit me again in the spring."

De Nerval smiled. "Thank you," he said, not without a touch of sarcasm. "May I also write to you during the winter?"

"By all means."

He nodded.

"I did not mean to sound ungrateful, Leon," Sophy said. "You took me completely by surprise, that's all."

De Nerval shrugged, his indifference feigned.

"Perhaps," said Sophy, "you will meet some fine American lady, a plantation *belle*, and will feel impelled to marry her instead of me."

Leon did not treat the remark as flippant.

"When I was a very young man in Paris," he said, "serving my apprentice years with a certain M. Veron, I imagined that one day I would marry his daughter. That was the arrangement between us. When I grew old enough and rich enough to consider taking a wife, I found that, after all, I could not embark upon a lie. I could not marry Celeste Veron."

"Was she ugly?"

"No, she was pretty," said de Nerval. "But I simply did not love her."

"What did you do?"

"I left Paris."

"Jilted her?"

"No," said Leon. "I told her my reason. She understood. Her father was less understanding, of course; I lost a very dear friend in him from that day forth."

"You have never felt inclined to marry?"

"Frequently," said de Nerval, honestly. "But I buried myself in my work. I concerned myself with the acquisition of wealth."

"And now you are in search of a suitable wife."

"Sophy!" he said, sternly. "It is not your suitability that attracts me. I . . . I don't know *what* it is. All I can say is that you are the first woman I have ever met that I can, in honesty, marry."

Sophy hesitated, then, rising, said, "It's late, Leon. Will you be good enough to take me home?"

\* \* \*

They said little in the carriage as it rumbled over the cobbles through the quiet streets. Gas lamps hissed above the thoroughfares, the moon slung low above them like a gaseous competitor, vague and yellow in the sky. Leon did not attempt to make love to her, or speculate on what might come to them in that nebulous future on the far side of winter. He held her hand, that was all. Sophy, in turn, rested her head against his shoulder.

When they reached the mouth of Pelican Lane, Leon told the driver to wait and, still seated in the cab, turned to Sophy once more.

From the pocket of his overcoat, he took out a small packet wrapped in layers of gossamer-fine paper.

"A remembrance," he said. "Take it."

Unwrapping the packet, Sophy saw that the gift was a tiny china bird, graceful and delicate and softly colored. Her finger stroked the blush-pink curve of the breast.

"Oh, Leon, it's quite exquisite."

"It's a finch: a Dresden finch. When I saw it in the porcelain-seller's window, I could not resist it. Now I want you to have it and, when I write to you—as I promise I shall—you may look at the finch and remember that I love you."

Sophy was touched.

She felt awed by Leon de Nerval's declarations, and more than a little ashamed of her own duplicity. Would it have been better to tell him the whole, sordid story and watch him recoil in disgust from her? She would lose him then, be rid of him.

In all respects, he was a perfect husband for her. He had charm, wit, perception—and wealth. Agatha would weep with jealous rage if her stepdaughter turned up at Huffton with such a catch as Leon de Nerval. It no longer seemed terribly important that he had once been a Breton peasant, or that his money came from vulgar, and probably shady, trading. That he was almost twice her own age mattered not at all.

What did matter, and what made Sophy feel incredibly dishonest, was the plain fact that she did not love him. He did not repulse her, but he did not ignite that singular spark as Edmund Sutton had done. At that moment of parting, she could not bring herself to lie to Leon, to offer him endearments and kisses and all the other signals of willingness.

She held the finch to the light, admiring it.

Leon de Nerval could offer her a lifetime filled with such fine and expensive toys, such appealing treasures. What could she offer him in return—a soiled chastity and a soldier's brat: no more.

"I will do as you say, Leon," she told him, wrapping the finch in its paper nest.

"And give me some reason to hope, Sophy?"

"We'll see," she said. "We'll see what happens in the spring."

Miss Frampton had put out the lamps and sat before the mirror in her bedroom, clad in the plain shift which she wore as a night garment. Buttoned high to her throat and spread out like a nun's habit, it revealed no curve of her figure at all. She had released her hair, filing the pins neatly in a cork card on the dressing-table top. Her hair, gray-streaked and lusterless, hung to her shoulders save for one long coiling strand that draped almost to her waist.

Sophy pushed open the door.

The girl was flushed with the effects of food and wine and the excitement of her evening with de Nerval, caught too in the midstream of happiness and anxiety. Her confusion manifested itself in irascibility.

"You look radiant, Sophy," said Miss Frampton, turning.

"You arranged it, did you not?"

"Arranged . . . ?"

"You lured him here?"

"Nothing of the kind, my dear. I merely left a tiny

trail which any intelligent gentleman might follow—if he so desired. Apparently, M. de Nerval did desire. What did he say? Where did he take you?"

"He took me to a French restaurant," Sophy retorted, "*and* he proposed marriage."

Even Miss Frampton was surprised.

"Marriage? But . . . but when?"

"Immediately. He wanted me to accompany him to the Americas."

"How wonderful for you, Sophy."

"I refused."

Miss Frampton, wary, asked, "In what manner did you refuse?"

"I told him I would not be hurried."

"Sound; very sound."

"He has asked permission to call upon me again—in the spring."

Miss Frampton's smile hooked up the corners of her mouth. She looked smug and fatuous as she rose to embrace her protegée.

"Most astute, Sophy. May I congratulate you most . . ."

Sophy pulled away.

"It's just as you planned, isn't it? Tuck me away. Be rid of the encumbrance and then blossom forth with a suitor all ready to . . . to *take* me."

"I would prefer a more delicate phrase," said the governess. "But, if you insist on being blunt—yes, that is approximately what I had planned. I didn't, of course, foresee that dear M. de Nerval would pop the question with such alacrity or disregard for the decencies; nor that he would be traveling so far afield all winter." The smile became even broader as the full implications penetrated Miss Frampton's brain. "But that is *perfect*: *utterly perfect*. It absolves us from the need to . . . to stave him off for six months. With luck, you will be delivered and fully recovered before he makes his return."

"How cold you are, Miss Frampton."

"Cold? I help you; I advise you; I salvage you from the mess you would otherwise have made of your life, and you accuse me of being cold. I find your attitude remarkable, Sophy, and . . ."

"What do you hope to gain from my marriage to M. de Nerval?" Sophy interrupted.

"One thing only," said Miss Frampton. "I wish to secure tenure as your housekeeper in whichever part of the world your husband elects to settle."

"He isn't my husband yet."

"Sophy, Sophy!" The governess made another ineffectual grab at her pupil. "Can't you understand that I've been both teacher and—dare I presume to say—mother to you for nine years. Nine years of happiness. I want it to continue. You are all the family I have—except for my sister. You are, if you will pardon my frankness, as close to my heart as my daughter would be if God had seen fit to grant me the blessing. You are *all* I have."

Sophy paused, drawing closer to the woman.

She allowed herself to be enveloped in her arms, in that peculiar dry odor which was Miss Frampton's choice of perfume; a musky, lemony scent.

Miss Frampton hugged her.

"In a year, Sophy, when this nightmare is over and on its way to being forgotten, you may find it in your heart to thank me."

"Perhaps," said Sophy. Her weariness was catching up with her. She was full of strange regret that Leon was leaving for the Americas and that she would be separated from him not only by the Atlantic but by the Frampton sisters and the unwanted burden of Edmund Sutton's child.

She found that she was weeping soft tears of self-pity. Because she had no other friend in the world, she clung to Miss Frampton until she felt relieved and comforted.

"There now, my dear," the governess said, tenderly, "it will all be over before summer comes again. You'll see,

Sophy. We'll all be happy. You, your loving husband, and, if you'll allow it, myself. We'll have a grand mansion, a fine, high style of living and this episode will be put behind us forever."

"Yes," said Sophy, meekly. "Oh, yes, Miss Frampton." It was what she wanted to believe.

A thin drizzle glazed the cathedral dome, transformed every surrounding stick, stone and slate to anthracite. Even the horses seemed dunned by the rain, and plodded sluggishly through it like amphibians on a lava beach. Cloud formed a pelmet over the south bank, and a great black hollow to the west, cupping the railway station. Rain ran rivulets, like fissures, down the window of the coach which carried Sophy, Miss Frampton and a meager quantity of luggage out of Pelican Lane and, by muddy side streets, into the thoroughfare of High Holborn.

Gentlemen whose incomes depended on the vagaries of weather stared gloomily from the steamed windows of coffee shops and chophouses, mariners by proxy. Urchins, beggars and honest street arabs hung about under porticos and eaves and streaming arches cowled in sacks like monks or turbaned in brown paper like so many Moslem miners. Mad broomboys plied a good trade at crossings, sploshing gaily and parting the "windsor soup" to allow their clients leeway through the mud. There was profit for some in the rain—the umbrella-sellers, sweepers, casual Hercules and Mercuries, toting parcels or delivering messages. But, by and large, London's bustle was considerably stilled by the heavy, ceaseless drizzle.

Seated under a tartan traveling rug, Sophy leaned her brow on the cold glass of the coach window and watched the city, floating on mud, ebb away from her.

She experienced no excitement at the prospect of Cornwall. Indeed, she would rather by far have been traveling home to Huffton House, to beard the lioness in her den and, at least, have the comforts of Yorkshire round her in the difficult season ahead. But such a move was not only impractical but impossible—as Miss Frampton had patiently, and frequently, explained.

Sophy consoled herself, guarded against an excess of melancholy, by conjuring up visions of warm, mahogany rooms, bright fires with brass fenders, tea trolleys set with china plates piled high with cakes and hot buttered muffins. In her imagination, she built and furnished a luxurious nest and peopled it with callers, gay and amusing ladies, just the right sort of circle to entertain on wet winter afternoons. She pictured herself as a young matron, kind but firm with her servants, supervising the setting of dinner, with many silver plates and beautiful crystals. She saw herself in a whole array of Vanity Fair dresses and gowns welcoming husband home from his city office. Her imagination balked at giving features to the man; Leon de Nerval, however, was the lay model for this figment of wish-fulfillment.

Leon de Nerval, already willing, already intent upon the bait with which Miss Frampton—and she—had set the trap. Thinking of the trader, Sophy slipped her hand into the proofed reticule she carried in her lap and touched the smooth shape of the Dresden finch. Through tissue wrappings, she caressed it with her fingertips, felt her misery change and subtly alter into mellow speculation.

The glass bauble with its star, snowstorm and Lilliputian lovers, the memento Edmund Sutton had bought for her in Fluelen on the shores of Lake Lucerne—it was not in her possession. It was packed away with other discarded souvenirs in a trunk in a dank Goodge Street warehouse.

Such nostalgic trinkets would have no place in the Framptons' cottage in Cornwall.

The Dresden finch, embodiment of all her dreams, was different. Wherever she went from now on, it would go with her, always ready at hand to comfort her through the lonely months ahead.

# BOOK TWO

*The Breton Trader*

# Six

Cornwall was not at all as Sophy had imagined it. Inhospitable rocks and barren moorland enclosed and confined her as effectively as prison walls. In spring and summer, perhaps, it would be a place of wild beauty gentled by warm winds and currents. But in that raw November month, harsh rain scythed constantly from the sea. "Clean weather" Cora Frampton called it. She saw the climate in the round: winter as a natural scouring of the summer's bounteous larders, much more invigorating than London's iron frosts and fogs or northern England's snows.

To Sophy, however, the weather was but a fitting handmaiden to the bleak location. At least, in Yorkshire, the dales were dark and weighty and took their annual blizzards manfully. Here, round Rose Cottage in Penarvah, the land was an arrangement of serrated tors and tartar-yellow ridges, honed sharp by incessant storms. Even in the hinterland, no corner was free of the ocean's thunder. Gales boomed daily round Cora Frampton's cottage, ripped trellises and skeletal vines from the walls, plucked the beech hedge to tatters twig by twig and scattered the leaves in a willful whispering dance across the bleached handkerchief of lawn. Two cats, one earth-brown, the other gray as flint, personified the spirit of the place. They were lithe, handsome and restless, feral in their manners and sly beyond the instincts of their kind. Cora regarded the toms as special pets and wasted a goodly portion of each day trying to prove the point. She crooned and cried for them to come to her, lured them with milk and mackerel heads and sought to capture them, to hug and lavish unwanted affection on them. The cats would not yield. They were more than commonly aloof. Vicious and cruel, they found countless ways of procuring tasty scraps without relinquishing one iota of their independence. Scratched hands were all that Cora got in payment for her attentions. Her patience and determination, however, remained unimpaired, and all winter long the garden rang to her unctuous calls of *Puss* and her fingers and skirts smelled of fish.

Cora Frampton was not so tall, not so gaunt, not so sallow as her sister—and not so young. Though only five years separated Eunice from Cora, in demeanor the elder might have been the mother of the family. Even in the isolation of her "Cornish retreat," as she termed it, Cora had perfected a façade of maternal concern and sympathetic wisdom which was at odds, Sophy soon discovered, with the spinsterish vinegar which flowed in her veins.

Cora's smile was plumper but no less brittle, her eyes brighter but no less inscrutable, and her voice more candied but no less imperious, than Eunice's. She was undisputed ruler of the quarter acre of bought ground on which Rose Cottage stood and, by extension, of all the surrounding miles of nothingness as far as the craggy headland cliffs.

Neighbors were sparse. A tenant farm lay two miles inland. A hamlet of four sunken cots clung to a cuticle of sand under the brow of the cove. During attendance at the local church Sophy encountered only a dozen women and men, all leathery, sullen, and suspicious of the Framptons. The vicar was an ancient wheezing pole of a man with a shock of white hair like a thistle in seed. His welcome was hardly effusive; obviously he did not care for strangers in his parish. By early December, Sophy's condition had become so obvious that even Sabbath worship was dropped for decency's sake.

Only one man ever entered the cottage door, and he was no Cornishman. Unlike Sclater, Dr. Summerhays was bright and brimful of chatter. All that he said, however, was inconsequential and added not a farthing's worth of real information to Sophy's meager stock of data on the history and circumstances of the Frampton sisters.

Summerhays had a high-pitched, droning sort of voice and a fondling touch which quite repulsed her. His toper's nose was as red and pointed as a carrot. Sophy guessed that he was a Londoner, closer to seventy than sixty. Though they fed him cakes and Madeira wine after his weekly examination of their charge, the Framptons professed ignorance about "their friend's" age and origins and, as on so many topics, sheared off Sophy's questions politely but firmly.

The sisters never discussed personal matters in the girl's hearing. Except for exchanges of endearments and trivial pleasantries concerning tea, fish, flour, eggs and the weather, they said very little to each other and not much more to Sophy. In the night, however, after she had retired to her tiny attic bedroom, the sound of voices rose from the kitchen below, animated murmurings spinning out all the conversations that had been stored through years of separation. Exactly what the sisters discussed, Sophy could not quite make out. Once, when she crept from bed to the head of the stairs, their alert ears picked up the sound, conversation chopped off in midsentence, and Miss Frampton loudly inquired if Sophy was unwell. After that Sophy made no attempt to eavesdrop. She was often forced to lie in acute torment, teased by the murmurings and occasional exclamations which floated through the warped floorboards.

In a sense, she accepted her role as prisoner—at least for the age which carried November into December and drew the year over Christmas into January. Leon de Nerval's letters brought the sole relief to her oppressive isolation. Though she looked forward to his regular twice-monthly communications, she did not enjoy the strain of composing replies. In contrast to de Nerval's long and interesting accounts of his travels in America, Sophy's "duty" letters were invariably curt and devoid of wit. They did not, she felt, reflect her character in the least—yet, being products of a grand deception, perhaps they reflected her character better than she knew, being dull and stilted. Naturally, the one topic which came more and more to obsess her could not be mentioned. She covered the shame at the core of her epistles with guarded hints of affection, though, in fact, she felt no increase in warmth towards the trader. She appreciated his letters only as relief from the monotony of the daily round of sleeping, walking and eating which was her own particular limbo as the new year began.

At the end of January her patience was exhausted, and her nerves, ground raw by a ceaseless gale, snapped. It happened suddenly at the end of the tea ritual, taken early in the afternoon. The delicate clink of china cups seemed so horribly at odds with the animal power of the roaring wind which strode from the sea and shook the cottage. The gale was so strong and lusty that it reduced the tissue sighings of the gowns and the polite monosyllabic exchanges of the three "ladies" to mousy chirpings. Staring through the rungs of the wicker cakestand, Sophy suddenly saw herself as a fat female mouse doomed to paddle forever round a wicker mill, her features becoming more rodent-like as the weeks passed and her eyes turning pink. She looked at her trembling fingers on the edge of the saucer and imagined them as paws, tiny scrawny claws. The sponge cake in her mouth turned to sawdust. She expelled it, disgustingly, onto her plate; then, as the sisters exchanged that all-too-familiar glance of cold sympathy, she hurled the teacup across the dining recess and watched it splash against the miniature cabinet and break on the tiled floor below.

Eunice Frampton did not reprimand her charge. Cora did not even bother to follow the flight of the cup. The sisters did nothing, said nothing, merely swished their skirts aside in a uniform gesture and fixed their eyes on Sophy. The girl thrust herself away from the table and, like a cumbersome moth, fluttered and flapped about the confined space, from window to door to window, calling angrily, "I must get out. I must get out. Anywhere, anywhere away from here."

It was not, Sophy later appreciated, madness, only a willful subterfuge to alleviate the crushing boredom of endless days of waiting. She carried it, not without design, as far as she dared, crying, "I want to see *people*, to look into *shops*, and to walk on a *pavement* again."

"Not wise," murmured Miss Frampton. "It is too near your time."

"Then," Sophy shouted, with ridiculous overemphasis, "perhaps you will not object if I walk on the clifftop— *alone.*"

Cora balked at this, made to rise, her face twisted with temper and anxiety. Eunice prevented her sister's intervention.

Even as Sophy snatched her coat from a cupboard and flung open the door to the yard, she heard her governess say, "Let her go."

"But, sister . . . ?"

"I know her. Let her go, I say."

So even that act of defiance was somehow stamped with Miss Frampton's strange blessing, just as her affair with Edmund had been similarly approved all those long months ago.

Sophy did not, of course, walk upon the cliff. She got no closer to the dangerous edge than a knoll a half mile west of Rose Cottage. From there she could see the gale's manifestations, streaming currents of dun-colored winter grass on the breast of the moor pastures and beyond it the sea.

Great snakes of foam wriggled across its surface. Massive waves broke on the rocks of Penarvah Head, booming and growling, sucking back into steep troughs to rise up again to gray-green peaks and break once more— endlessly.

A small boat beat under the protection of the harbor cove. Fascinated and terrified by the sight of that distant seascape, Sophy strained her eyes to follow the craft's erratic course towards an anchorage. What had called the fisherman out in such a spell of weather, she could not, in her ignorance, imagine. For the space of five minutes, she watched the boat. She was briefly caught up in its perils, lifted from herself; then, as it weaved out of sight under the whaleback hill, an overwhelming passion of loneliness drove her to stumble back through the rain and humbly let herself into the cottage once more.

The Framptons sat exactly where she had left them.

She hung up the soaking coat and, not meeting their eyes, returned to her place at table.

Cora poured fresh tea for her and she sipped it to wash the taste of salt from her lips. Her heart was pounding. She could feel a weight pressing within her, and the tenderness of her breasts as if the gale had mauled her like a rough lover.

But she was utterly contained now, numb almost.

"Motherhood," said Cora, in her most matronly tone, "is *such* a trial."

"*Such* a trial," said Eunice. "Is it not, my dear?"

"Yes," Sophy answered, leadenly.

Apparently, Edmund Sutton's son shared something of his father's impetuosity. Like a good hussar, he charged into the world regardless of vicissitudes and hazards in the early evening of the ninth day of March.

Strong, gusty winds raked cloud across the Atlantic and broomed up the first outriders of an early dusk. Rain pattered intermittently on the windowpane. Sophy clung to that sound in her minutes of consciousness and clarity during the five-hour labor.

At this climax to the long winter, the Frampton sisters proved admirable nurses. In conjunction with the good Dr. Summerhays—who, it seemed, treated birth as an astonishing triumph of nature over medicine—the sisters pampered and calmed Sophy and gave her confidence in her innate ability to endure the pain.

With considerable wiliness, Eunice clasped her hand tightly, spoke not of happy days to come but of the injustices of the past. She brought up the subject of Agatha and stayed on that topic as long as poor Sophy could concentrate.

In the last hour, however, Sophy stood alone against the pain, obedient to Summerhays's wheedling suggestions that she give the poor mite some assistance, responsive only to his stream of mild commands.

Out of the pain, she recalled the shape of the doctor's nose in silhouette against the grainy glass of the window, and Miss Frampton's hands, like staghorn hooks, offering themselves as urging posts. In that miasma of perspiration and discomfort, she recalled a feverish vision of Edmund standing by the crystal waterfall of the Swiss glacier, hand on his hip and short cloak spread, his hat in his other hand, cheering her—a ridiculous image, but one so vivid that she even cried out to him a moment before her son entered the world and gave her relief. An ecstatic sensation of freedom swallowed her as she felt the baby lifted away. His droning wail, echoing in the cramped bedroom, flooded her with pride and love.

Flopping backwards, she sought to lift herself on her hands and saw, for an instant only, the infant's pink face and minute fists within the swaddling shawl as Summerhays transferred him into Eunice Frampton's arms. Sophy keened and groped to take ownership of her baby, to possess it. Three faces peered at her, without joy or tenderness, each marked by a frown. She saw Miss Frampton shake her head, then turn away, drawing the shawl out of sight.

Sophy screamed louder and struggled. Only the doctor's hands upon her shoulders prevented her fighting her way from the bed.

"Now," Summerhays said, very gently, "you will do yourself no good, Miss Richmond; no good."

"My . . . my baby?" Sophy sobbed.

"A fine little bantam, healthy and strong," Summerhays informed her.

Cora Frampton handed the doctor a wineglass, which he held to Sophy's lips.

"A . . . boy?"

"Drink this."

Parched, Sophy allowed the man to tilt her head and infiltrate the liquid into her mouth. It was bitter and honeyed at once, burning a little as it touched her lips. She flinched and tried to reject it, but the doctor's insistence was easier to accept than rebuff.

Sophy drank.

Rain pattered on the window. Wind gusted loudly over the thatch and marched across the chimney head. She could still hear her son wailing faintly, very faintly and distantly.

Languor stole over her, at once welcome and hateful. She had no will to shake it off. Her lips and throat prickled with the effects of the medicine. Summerhays smiled warmly, seated on the bed by her side, holding her hand in his.

Sophy's eyes fluttered and closed. She felt now as if the mattress was a drift of warm snow into which she sank like a snowflake. Edmund Sutton stood by the brink of the glacier; then, enveloped in a soft blanket of mist, faded. The ribbon of the glacier melted swiftly and poured silently over her, warm too and comforting. And she slept.

Sophy Richmond, the mother of an infant son, slept undisturbed through that evening and night and far into the morning of the following day.

When she awoke, she suffered at first a period of prolonged disorientation, drawn far out of herself by the effects of the drugged and exhausted slumber. Only when she moved and an ache gripped her did the memory of the momentous event come flooding back. It brought her upright in the bed, regardless of her spinning head and blurred vision.

The ache dispersed into vague areas of pain. Binding cramped her, flannel and linen wrapped round her tender breasts.

Still confused, she called out into the empty bedroom.

Instantly, Miss Frampton, her governess, entered.

The woman was dressed in a Highland cloak of somber material and wore high boots. She looked oddly soft this morning, though there was no evidence of a lessening of determination in her dealings with Sophy.

"Where is my . . . my baby?"

"Warm and snug by the fire downstairs."

Eunice Frampton stripped off one of her gloves, lifted Sophy's wrist and expertly checked her pulse against a large ticking watch from a fretwork stand on the table.

"Good," Miss Frampton declared, nodding. "Cora is preparing soup for you, Sophy. According to Dr. Summerhays you will be strong enough to be up and about in three days."

"I want my baby."

"Cora will sit with you. There is a letter from M. de Nerv . . ."

Realization clutched at Sophy's intelligence—the traveling cloak, the boots, the news that *Cora* would look after her.

"*No*," she screamed. "*No*."

Fierce longing engulfed her, a desire to wrap up her

child and hold him, to tear off the painful binder and give him her breast.

"Sophy," said Miss Frampton sternly. "It is all arranged."

"I want *him*; I want *him*. He's *mine*."

She scrambled onto her knees and, hands clasping the governess's wrist, pleaded and begged dazedly. Her loosed hair hung lankly across her brow. She shivered and trembled like a crone with the instinctive urge to reclaim the child that had already been lost to her. "He's too tiny. Cannot be moved. He will die."

"Nonsense, Sophy. He will come to no harm, I assure you. I have engaged a wet nurse—a healthy girl—from Penzance. She has been staying with Dr. Summerhays this past week."

"Another woman!"

"Her milk is plentiful and . . ."

"*No!*"

Miss Frampton struck her, a neat stinging slap across the cheek. It was shock rather than the force of the blow that drove Sophy back against the pillows. She gaped in horror at the governess.

"Please let me see him."

"Certainly not."

"He's mine."

"He is Sutton's child, born out of wedlock."

"Mine."

"A bastard, Sophy; d'you hear me?"

"I want him," the girl moaned.

"He will be well cared for."

"And never know me."

"You should have been more sentimental and less carnal nine months ago, Sophy," the woman said. Her features were angular, planed into an almost geometric design within the half-folded capuchin hood of the cloak. "You had no thought then for consequences; you considered only your own immediate pleasure and satisfaction. You have paid the price."

"Is *this* the price?"

Miss Frampton ignored that maudlin question. She consulted the watch that ticked obediently and loudly in her hand. "I have a train to catch. I must leave you."

"How will he . . . ?"

"He is fully fed and well protected against the elements. A little boiled water will meet his requirements until we reach the city. A wet nurse has been engaged in London too."

"Oh, God!" Sophy moaned. She turned her face into the pillow, pressing hard as if to smother herself and thus be released from the frightful anguish that racked her heart and closed her brain to any other thoughts but the agony of loss and sorrow.

Miss Frampton stooped over her, brushing her hair with a fingertip. "I know it is not easy, my dear. I am no monster. But it must be done now. It would be a thousand times harder on you, if you . . . When you are married, you will have a dozen babies if you wish. Now, stop it. Stop sniveling and look at me."

The authority in the woman's voice touched deep into Sophy's girlish self, stirring the habit of obedience. She lifted her face just enough to look into the governess's face. Her intelligence told her that what Miss Frampton said was true, that the arrangement must stand. But she had not bargained for the rage of instincts that warred against the "logical" solution. She only knew that she wanted her baby in her arms.

"I will tell you this, Sophy," said Miss Frampton; "the woman who will look after the infant is a mother herself. She is clean and loving and respectable and will raise him as one of her family."

"Yes," Sophy whispered.

"Now, gather your strength and put the past out of mind. In a year or two, though you may not believe it now, you will thank me."

"Yes."

Miss Frampton moved away. The watch, returned to its stand, ticked less loudly, though it was still audible in the quietness of the bedroom.

Sophy found herself straining every sense to catch some evidence of her baby, some last banal sound to stand as a memento of the child she had borne and lost. But there was nothing, nothing at all.

The door closed.

Sophy sat up. A faint pearly glint of sunlight replaced yesterday's gray rain upon the window glass. A gull croaked on the roof close overhead.

She felt hollow, like a tree smitten and burned out by fire, dead.

In her mind, Miss Frampton's final words coiled and raveled bitterly. She had been given no last choice. She *must* do as she had been bidden, follow that vile and heartless course that she had agreed upon in her . . . her former existence. In a year or two the pain of this day might have eased away, but it would not be forgotten. Nor would she, Sophy resolved, ever find it in her heart to thank Miss Frampton for making her a mother without a child.

No achievement would ever compensate for the grossness of such disloyalty. She knew that, come what may, she could never be truly happy again.

Though she sat in that position, motionless, for an hour, she caught no sound to tell her at what precise moment her child left the cottage and began his long journey to London, out of her life forever.

# Seven

Tobacco Street was not so very far from Pelican Lane. It lay east into the hinterland of lading docks, timber yards and railway cuts that scarred the hoof of the Isle of Dogs. Eunice Frampton still had a few stray taproots sunk in this area, for her family had had its origins in the river loop between the Pool of London and Blackwall Reach—in no one house, though, shifting on as domestic circumstances improved in ratio to her father's unscrupulousness.

In his heyday Daniel Frampton had been known as the sharpest chandler between Shoreditch and the sea. He kept a sober mind and nimble wits while battalions of his pals, partners and victims, succumbing to grog and the law, wound up in Newgate, the Fleet or, mysteriously, in the muddy brown bosom of Old Father Thames himself. Daniel Frampton was shrewd enough not to encumber himself with much family responsibility. Having spawned only a boatscrew of daughters, he sold them out for schooling and left his fat wife free to rattle the dice for sons. No sons appeared, however, before the poor woman surrendered to cholera in the spring of '28.

By that time, all the girls, including the littlest, were thoroughly dispersed, and Daniel's hold on them quickly slackened. He died, in penury and unmourned, after being clubbed by a footpad on the Barking Road one November night; not even Eunice, who still lodged in the vicinity, bothered to claim the corpse from the authorities. Kate

Dreyer owned Eunice and Cora. She reared and schooled them well by her own odd curriculum. Common trulling was not to be the fate of Kate's adopted lassies. She fitted them for profitable service to the commercial lords who owned mansions in the district and were, in many varied ways, "exploitable." By the time that Kate Dreyer coughed her way out of the world, Eunice and Cora were well set in their separate "respectable" careers and knew how best to milk their employers and trade on trust as once their father had traded on gullibility.

Returning to Limehouse that dismal March night, Eunice Frampton felt as if she were returning home. The effluvia of the Reach and the marshes drifted like fog over the cluttered rooftops, bringing a certain mild nostalgia to the unsentimental woman. Before the hackney wallowed through the narrows of Tobacco Street and halted in the stretch beyond the jughandle, however, the governess was once again engulfed in practicalities, though her attitude was one of pleasurable anticipation at the conclusion of the bargain she had struck by post and by a gutter courier of casual acquaintance. Whatever she had done in connection with the annexation of Sophy's future, she had done through the friends of friends, not directly. No man, trained in deduction or otherwise, could hope to unspool the cords that tied Eunice Frampton to Sophy's unchristened child. Even so, so strong had been the memory of her youth that, as she alighted from the cab and peered up and down the stunted street, she half expected to see her father lolling at the corner under the chandlers' storm lantern, or to have the low plank door of the narrow house open on a tableau of Kate Dreyer and a band of her young villains.

Silent as a little plucked pullet, the infant was a barely discernible bulge on Miss Frampton's arm, hidden entirely by her cloak. The linctus that Dr. Summerhays had provided and that Eunice had administered in a dose of boiled water, had had its effect. The precise measurement, upon which the doctor had insisted, had put the babe neatly to sleep without, as far as the woman could discern, noticeably affecting his pallor or rate of respiration.

"Be ye sure this is place ye want, missus?" The driver bent down from his stance, frowning at boarded windows and pitted timber walls.

"Certain, thank you." The governess handed up the fare and a small bonus, then remained motionless on the broken walk until the driver shrugged his shoulders and jingled his horse on up the hunchbacked street out of sight round the chandlers' corner.

Only then did Eunice Frampton scan the dwellings, counting down from the black slit of a passageway, her given landmark, until she discovered an arch and a scrap-wood door across which was scrawled in rusty red lead—HORNER: BOTTLES. She pushed open the door. There, not more than a yard before her, was another door, narrower, lower but more solid than the first. On it was stippled in a firmer hand—KNOCK.

A dumpy black iron bottle strung from a hook by a ragged length of hemp made a stifled clacking sound when lifted and dropped, as if the house were a gigantic fishbox slotted on end between its more solid neighbors.

The noise roused children and the children cried, some with intelligible demands for attention and others, more feebly, with fractious whimperings and wailings.

A voice boomed out and there was silence within the house, a stealthy, listening kind of silence that carried suspicion and a strange overlay of threat. Eunice Frampton could imagine the waxworks within, the man with fist raised, the children cowering, even the tiniest already impressed by the force of discipline and authority.

She smiled her approval, and knocked again.

The portion of the woman's face that appeared in the crack was lit from beneath by a candle stump crammed into an empty pickle jar. The light cast the shadows of her slablike cheeks upwards, masking her eye sockets with a dark harlequin and pointing up her tousled hair like coal-oil flame. She was, as Miss Frampton had already been informed, a woman in the prime of life, radiating dogmatic robustness.

"Mistress Horner, I believe?"

"Whatcher want?"

"I have called in connection with the . . . ah, advertisement."

The prearranged code was not simple enough, apparently; Mistress Horner was, for a moment, bemused.

"Wha' 'vertisement?"

She was still scowling when a hand descended on her cheek and pushed her to one side. The door opened further. The bulk of the proprietor filled the closet hall, jammed hard against his spouse's buttocks, jostling with her for space.

"Willum 'orner at yer service, ma'am."

"Good evening, Mr. Horner," said Miss Frampton, smoothly. She was tired, damp, and, though the baby's weight was negligible, inclined to cramp in the left arm. She let none of her vexation at the slow progress of the charade show, however. "My advertisement in the window of the Bow Gardens Victuallers; my agent in the area, a Mr. Flannigan, informs me that . . ."

Horner, too, was impatient with the ritual. He nodded and, reaching out a hand, scooped and ushered Miss Frampton through the closet into a larger closet at the rear of it.

This, she surmised, would be the master parlor. It contained a pine table, a hammocklike chair repaired with rope and scuffed corduroy, and a handsome ebony-faced cabinet crammed with half-empty liquor bottles. The furnishings tilted towards a half wall in which was set an ornate grate with a pyre of sea-coke smoldering in its belly. The half wall was matched by another door, broad as that of a cattle barn, canted open on stringy hinges. Involuntarily Miss Frampton looked down into the main apartment of the Horners' "suite," a basement sunk three or four feet below the level of the street.

The governess did not care to study the scene for long and was considerably relieved when Horner, with casual alacrity, closed and latched the door. It was quite some hours, however, before she rid herself of the memory of that place, floored with filthy matted straw, lit by a solitary tallow and the angry glare of the fire cavity under a brick oven. Among the eight or ten bony faces that had peered out of the gloom at her was a tow-headed boy of about eight who stood against the light. He wore only a torn shirt and his sticklike legs were scarred and thatched with burns. In his fist was a raw mess of vegetable, perhaps a potato, which he applied to his mouth with furtive truculence. By his ankles was a younger child, a girl, clawing mutely for her share of his supper, unable, it seemed, to raise herself properly from the straw.

William Horner clapped his hands and chaffed them vigorously.

"The advertisement, Miss . . . ?"

"My name is of no consequence. Mr. Flannigan will be kept informed of my whereabouts and will, likewise, keep me informed of the . . . ah, progress of this transaction throughout the years."

"Like that, is it," muttered Horner's wife.

"I wouldn't want ter be spied upon, ma'am," Horner put in, with deference.

"Understand this," said Miss Frampton, finally discarding all pretense, "I am putting this child into your *care*, sir." She drew the baby gently from under her cloak. "I do not intend that he shall languish and, shall we say, pine away to his grave. It is possible that, at some future date, I *may* have reason to take him from your care, Mr. Horner."

"Gotcher," said Horner.

With one coarse finger he touched back the swaddle of the shawl and beamed down upon the slumbering infant.

"Ain't 'e a treat, though. Ain't 'e a proper liddle manni-kin. Look'ee 'ere, Violot."

Violet Horner looked and uttered appropriate sounds of approbation and affection, though her glum expression belied all enthusiasm.

"Take 'im, then," Horner hissed.

Violet relieved Miss Frampton of the burden.

Though she had not previously noticed it, a corner of the parlor was curtained off with a drape of faded sail-cloth. She was shown it now, as Horner, with a proud flourish, drew back the curtain and revealed a perfect miniature shrine to bountiful motherhood.

On a shelf stood a wax candle in a fluted glass unit casting clear yellow light on a broad mattress quilted warmly with scarlet blankets and clean if threadbare sheets. In the center of the bed sat a plump girl, no older than seventeen, clad in a lace jacket that amply exposed her heavy breasts. She grinned at Miss Frampton and widened her empty china-blue eyes, reaching up her bare arms to accept the baby.

"Lost 'er own, poor fing," Horner explained. "Lost the liddle wight ter the croup at five weeks."

The girl now enfolded herself in some more comfortable world, secure and isolated with the new arrival to add to her previous charges who lay, contentedly enough, Miss Frampton supposed, in a box drawer by the bedside; two pink sleeping faces. The girl crooned a stuttering tune and, as she unwrapped her father's latest gift, seemed no longer fey but innocent.

"How much?" Miss Frampton asked.

"Mr. Flannigan said you were a generous lady."

"I am generous, Mrs. Horner, but I am not a fool," replied Miss Frampton. "Nursing and 'adoption' fees are worth forty pounds, no more."

"Here now," said Violet Horner. "We takes the orphan inter the bosom of our fam'bly and offers ter give it all the loving kindness we bestows on our own offsprings back there, an' you comes through wif a paltry forty janes . . ."

"Stow it, Vi," Horner snarled then, smiling again, addressed himself to the diplomatic bartering, which ended in a satisfactory arrangement.

"Forty-five pounds cash down," said Miss Frampton. "For that payment you will undertake to keep the child in good health . . ."

"Barrin' acts o' Gawd," put in Horner.

"Barring acts of God," agreed Miss Frampton. "You will keep him in good health until such time as I may require him again."

"How long?"

"I cannot be sure if I will ever require him again."

Horner suppressed his smile and nodded.

"But, understand this, Mr. Horner, while I may not ever wish to see the boy again, and certainly have no interest in his welfare, I will dispatch Mr. Flannigan or some other agent to check with you once yearly and, provided the child is well, to pay you a further five pounds."

"A knew you was a generous lady," said Horner.

It was a fools' bargain, and Eunice Frampton knew it. Flannigan, a fuddled drunk, would not be able to tell one child from another and she would only have his word for it that Sophy's son was still in the Horners' care. The alternative was to visit the place herself—but that was dangerous and, in a sense, unnecessary. The five-pound promise would keep the Horners up to the mark, at least for a year or two and, barring the inevitable "acts of God" that the man had raised, the infant should at least grow if not exactly thrive. That five pounds per annum was an insurance, less to protect the babe than to quiet her own dormant conscience. It was highly improbable that she would ever "require" to redeem the child—but, as Kate

Dreyer had taught her, it was wise policy to hold one's options open where possible.

She offered Horner her gloved hand.

He shook it.

The "adoption" pact was sealed.

Eunice Frampton paid out forty-five sovereigns from the fifty she had in her purse. Any more evidence of wealth might have given Horner ideas, though she had a second reserve in a pouch on the hip of her stays, another twenty gold pieces.

Horner counted the cash, wrapped it in a strip of brown paper and tucked it into the pocket of his vest.

"Any further 'doptions, ma'am," he said, "an' we'd be delighted to put up the sank'tory of . . ."

"Good night, Mr. Horner."

She did not ask for one last glance behind the sailcloth. She could hear the girl crooning still and—unless she imagined it—the first faint fretful cries of the baby wakening hungry from his prolonged sleep. She went quickly to the inner door, opened it and billowed into the closet-shaped hall. Horner did the honors, graciously opening the outer and street doors for her. She was on the point of stepping onto the narrow walk when the touch of his hand stayed her.

"A thought," he said; "what about a name? 'As 'is nibs got one?"

"No," said Eunice Frampton. "No name."

"Well?"

"Call him . . . anything you like," she said with a shrug, and a moment later glided out into Tobacco Street and was soon lost in the sour river fog.

William Horner snorted in wry amusement. Another one with no handle, forty-odd janes'worth of helpless anonymity to do just as he liked with. Nobody in the world to care what became of the brat.

Shaking his head at the profitable folly of the human race, he went inside and locked the door behind him.

The clifftop and the sea were no longer hostile to her. She would have welcomed a closer union with them, to be lured by one and swallowed up by the other, sucked away out of all discovery for eternity. It was no more than she deserved. Shame and grief were like fevers in her, subtle diseases that made no show upon her features but wasted her from within.

In all things, Sophy was meekly obedient to the Framptons and to Summerhays. She struggled from bed when the doctor gave her leave to do so. She ate the broth and fish and drank the fresh milk that he recommended for her health, and she went through degrading ordeals devised by Cora Frampton to remove as rapidly and thoroughly as possible all evidence of motherhood. Dutifully she anointed her skin with oils and astringents, and took off her milk, in spite of the ache in her breasts and in her heart at this daily ritual. Her only escape was to the clifftop, to the very brink, and her only helpmeet was the sea.

Even the Dresden finch, which had been a talisman of some comfort during the dreary and frustrating months of pregnancy, had no power now to restore her interest in living out a future that had cost so high a price. The pretty ornament stood on her night table, ignored, meaningless, the toy of a stranger, the trophy of a younger girl who had once lodged in her body and who had gone now as totally and as suddenly as the baby to which she had given life.

Sophy Richmond was no longer a girl, no longer capable of dreaming, of sustaining herself on the selfish promises of the future. It did not occur to Sophy that redemption of her son was remotely possible: that plot did not gather in her mind and give her the power to lift herself from the quagmire of despair into which she sank during the three weeks after the birth. The Framptons understood enough of the change to treat her with caution—and it made no matter to her now; she realized, uncaringly, that she was most firmly in their power.

Strength returned to her limbs soon enough, and her wasted frame filled out. By the first of April's easy days, when the sea was kind and the gulls dressed in new and whiter plumage, Sophy looked, outwardly, as well as she had ever. Indeed, Miss Frampton might have been tempted to congratulate her on acquiring that ladylike reserve that had never been a point of her character. Though some of the grace was gone, the governess felt that Sophy had matured and that her quietness and reserve would only serve to make her more desirable in Leon de Nerval's eyes.

At that period, their correspondence had spluttered out. The last letter from the trader had come from a miserable outpost on the edge of the American plains where, so he explained to Sophy, he had discovered that the buffalo was a singularly unpleasant animal and fit for very little as a source of meat, bone, and leather by European standards. In spite of Eunice Frampton's pressure, Sophy never did reply to that communication, and steadfastly refused to pen even a card of acknowledgement to her admirer. It seemed that Leon de Nerval too was to be condemned, locked away with everything and everyone, into that volume that had closed with the loss of her son and that she, Sophy, would never deign to open again.

From Huffton, from Thomas Richmond, there had been no word at all during the course of the long winter. Though Sophy often found herself remembering her childhood and her happy days in her father's care, even that route was blocked by the phantom of her hatred for Agatha, a mere remembered emotion, not vivid, not now cathartic.

No word was ever spoken in regard to Eunice's visit to London and no reference ever made to the baby. It was as if the infant had been magically reabsorbed, coaxed back into that darkness from which his life had come, like a tin-miner's lantern brought to a tunnel mouth and then withdrawn.

Sophy was given no hint that Miss Frampton's three-day sojourn in the capital had largely been taken up with finding exactly the right sort of accommodation, and that another prison was being prepared for her in a tall and not unfashionable building in Harwood Square, not a hundred yards from the junction of Bond Street and Wensley Street; nor did she feel any quickening of excitement when the signs pointed to the fact that release from Rose Cottage, and the long winter, was imminent.

The Framptons, Eunice in particular, were more alert and active now, and Summerhays's calls had been reduced to one each week.

Such phrases as, "We must do something about your clothes, Sophy," and "Be a little more careful of your complexion, my dear," impinged upon her melancholy sufficiently to tell her that her governess intended to sweep her up again and return her to London, or Manchester, or Timbuctoo, for that matter; and Sophy could not bring herself to care.

Only a fleeting curiosity, and vanity, made any inroads into her lackluster state. Once or twice in that stretch of six weeks, she found herself arrested by the sight of her own face, and her unclad body, in the mirror in the bedroom. Then she would study the changes, searching for more signs than there were of her delivery. But she found none and, indeed, was reluctantly forced to admit to herself that her face had filled out just enough to restore her beauty. Her figure too, with the exercise of walking and the remedial massages that Cora supervised, had lost little of its shape. When her milk was gone, she would be as she had been before—in outward appearance at least.

It did not, she reprimanded herself, concern her—but it did: the interest in her looks was the first symptom of healing.

When, towards the end of April, Miss Frampton told her

that she must pack her belongings, Sophy was tempted to ask where they were going and what they would do. The very fact that she had to stifle the question and feign indifference now, indicated that Miss Frampton, as usual, had timed her next move to perfection.

On a fresh April day, with the sea booming at the foot of the headland, Sophy and Eunice Frampton left Rose Cottage and set out on the return to London.

If the property in Pelican Lane had been eccentrically appointed, Number Three Harwood Square was a model of all that a modest *pied-à-terre* should be. It was situated in a good quarter of the town, in a quiet enclave of similar houses all of whose windows were discreetly curtained like the eyes of chaste spinsters. The carriages that came and went—none after ten at night—were of the old school, solid, trim, and unostentatious, horsed by animals as well groomed and staid as their owners.

The apartment's interior appointments were light and not too imposing, and the walls and woodwork had been recently decorated with fresh paper and paint.

On arrival, Sophy found that all her stored luggage had been brought from its warehouse, and the trunks and boxes carried upstairs to her bedroom at the rear.

A servant had been engaged, a mild-mannered, reticent woman who, it transpired, had a distant acquaintance with Cora Frampton. In addition to Miss Wellington, as the servant liked to be called, there was a daily scullion and an occasional cook. All in all, Sophy thought, if she chose to die of shame, at least she would do so in style and comfort.

The cost of the half-year lease, according to Miss Frampton, was "very reasonable." Sophy did not inquire further into expenditure, nor face up to the fact that her hundred pounds must surely have dwindled to little or nothing over the last seven months. It did not, of course, occur to her that Miss Frampton would have had to pay a sizable emolument to have the baby adopted; Sophy still blanked all thought of her lost child from her waking mind, though her subconscious remained enmeshed by confused emotional sufferings.

Four days after their installation in Harwood Square, Miss Frampton took Sophy on a shopping expedition, wending only a few hundred yards round the west corner of the square to a small but exclusive seamstress's establishment in whose curtained alcove Sophy was duly measured and chalked up from ankle to collar, and the relevant figures recorded in Miss de Beer's green ledger. Later that same day, Miss Wellington was dispatched by hackney cab, custodian of a collection of Sophy's gowns and dresses, to have them altered to the last half inch.

To her astonishment, Sophy found that she had much enjoyed the excursion and could not solemnize it with cold, silent anguish at the past year's tragedies. Miss Frampton's direct efficiency was having its effect at last. Only in the hour of sallow spring twilight did real, uninspired melancholy assert itself in full measure now. The pool of regret was shrinking within her, contained only by a frail loyalty to her baby. She saw how sharp the governess had been in removing the infant unseen, untouched. The recollection of her glimpse of a tiny wrinkled pink face was too slight to bear the weight of so much self-recrimination. In spite of her chagrin at the shallowness of her emotions, Sophy could not delay the recovery of her spirits and interest in living.

The final chapter in that heavy second volume of her life came to an abrupt end on the evening of her sixth day in Harwood Square.

According to Miss Frampton the celebration was strictly for its own sake, an excuse for dressing up, eating well and drinking a drop too much wine. Two of the altered gowns had come back that afternoon from Miss de Beer's;

the fitting and primping assumed a party atmosphere, with the girl and the woman rediscovering a sense of companionship that Sophy had thought gone forever. It was not contrition or forgiveness so much as habit that brought them together, nor were they as close as they had been before the Swiss summer. Some gratitude for Miss Frampton's stewardship was due, however, and Sophy, grudgingly, gave it during the afternoon among the gowns and feminine accessories that had been carefully unpacked from the trunks.

The suggestion that they both dress for dinner, send out for the cook and generally "do themselves proud" at eight that night in the sanctuary of their own—rented—dining room was readily accepted by the girl.

Left alone, Sophy robed herself with care and sang quaint tunes as she toiled at her coiffure. It occurred to her that perhaps Miss Frampton required a demonstration of her resilience and restoration, a signal that she was ready once more to step into society. But Sophy, though she toyed with the prospect, could not bring herself to a commitment one way or the other.

In her chamber at the rear of the house, she did not hear the muffled clang of the doorbell. She did not hear Miss Wellington cross the hall to answer it; did not hear anything to prepare her for the shock of suddenly confronting Leon de Nerval once more.

All she heard was Miss Frampton's knock upon the bedroom door and the glib announcement that dinner would be served in five minutes.

Sophy gathered her dress, gave a last dab to her hair, studied herself in the cheval glass and was smugly pleased at what she saw.

Sweeping along the corridor, she turned onto the top step of the flight of broad oak stairs that descended directly into the front hallway. She failed to notice that the candles were all new and that the two globe mantles that gave gaslight to the landing were turned up full. She had lifted her skirts an inch or two to come down the staircase, holding the silks in her left hand, her right hand stretched out to the banister and her body lifted just a little. In that pose, she paused, staring down at the figure who waited below, motionless and awe-struck.

Dressed in the full bloom of an evening suit, black silk waistcoat bulging with the breadth of his chest, Leon de Nerval smiled and said only one word.

"Sophy!"

It was the manner of speech, and the small sigh, like relief, that he uttered that disconcerted her, that and the look in his eyes, a frankness she had never before associated with him.

Immediately, their previous meetings, their letters, their relationship came flooding back to her, all the emotions associated with it. A confused torrent of joy and heartache swept over her and made her momentarily faint. She had the presence of mind to remain there, hand on the rail, until she was steady again, and then, very slowly and gracefully, to go down to where he waited.

His hand reached for hers. She felt his strong fingers clasp and tighten round her arm—and the comfort of that steadying grasp broke her.

Before she could prevent herself, she had cast off all poise, courtesy, and reserve and, flinging herself into his arms, wept away the sorrows of the past half year.

Dinner was over, the drawing room curtains closed, a small fire lit in the grate, and the liquor tray and recharged pot of coffee set on the side table. Leon was leaning against the mantelshelf, like some lord of the manor, relaxed now and thoroughly caught up in the tales that Sophy had drawn for him after that initial period of tongue-tied awkwardness had diminished. She had been more embarrassed than Leon by her outburst and vastly grateful to him for his unforced comfort. There in the hallway, he had hugged and consoled her, assured her that he loved her more deeply than ever and would not lose her again.

During the course of the dinner, discreetly served by Miss Wellington, Leon had indicated that he had heard of her illness—Sophy started—and that he understood just how debilitating to the nerves influenza could be. Apparently, though Sophy did not press for information, the kind Miss Frampton had written to him to explain Sophy's silence and had, by a letter to his New York agents, set up this meeting far in advance. Leon's efforts to keep the appointment were amusing enough to set the sourest member of the Travellers' Club grinning and guffawing at his mishaps along the route.

Passing on, Leon spoke then of his trading ventures, his encounters with redskinned Indians and pioneers and, in primitive townships in the southern states, with men of such wealth and power that they would put their aloof English counterparts to shame. He spoke of the drive and energy of the founding states and the bravado of men, and women too, who risked their very lives to grasp the branch of success and achievement. He catalogued the riches that had only just been tapped on that fascinating diverse continent. Glad of the excuse to recover herself, Sophy encouraged the trader and soon found herself thoroughly engrossed in his witty accounts. He had brought her several trophies, an alligator hide, a buffalo skin, a wonderful feather headdress and many other smaller gifts. That part of his baggage, he assured her, he had guarded like crown jewels, though some of his personal effects had gone down with a shoal-wrecked riverboat on the broad Mississippi.

Sophy did not inquire as to what he had gained, other than adventure, from the trip; that would have seemed like mercenary prying. By way of conclusion, however, Leon volunteered the information that he had established several lucrative trade contracts with plantation owners in Virginia and North Carolina to supply his subsidiary companies with maize and corn in addition to other raw materials. He also hinted that he had struck a bargain for a gunpowder concession, though he had still to solve the problem of transportation to England.

"Gunpowder?" said Sophy, in surprise.

"For the feeding of England's beloved Brown Bess."

"And what is that—a horse?"

Leon laughed. "A musket, an antique smoothbore musket."

"Soldiers," said Sophy, suddenly grave.

"As it's forty years since your country went seriously to war," said Leon, "I believe that the regiments have quite some catching up to do—and much revictualing."

"You are trading on war?"

"I am a supplier of raw materials to the British Army—piecemeal," said Leon. "War will be officially declared within the week; then we will see how times have changed, I'll be bound."

"You sound . . . pleased?"

"Should I not be pleased? Every patriotic Englishman is clamoring for war, and the officers, flamboyant and effete alike, are straining at the leash to be allowed first cut at the Russians."

Sophy nodded; her ears no longer really heard what Leon said. She was thinking now of Edmund Sutton, who had purchased himself a commission, and all that went with it, and would now be far away from home in some unhealthy climate, laughing and joking with his fellow officers. She wondered if he ever thought of her. If he did, it was most probable that he presented her as the butt of a good jest. She could accept that now, all his deceits and arrogant exploitations.

For months she had been cut off from, and totally disinterested in, news of the progress of the unpleasantness in the Balkans. It surprised her to learn that England was not already at war, for the few rumors that had impinged upon her consciousness during the winter had seemed to indicate that conflict was at hand. If Miss Frampton's news was as accurate as Sophy believed it to be, Edmund had been gone from home for months now. Would he fight, she thought, in that fine, handsome uniform? Thousands of soldiers in such a gaudy livery would be a grand sight to see, a spectacle to stir the heart.

Suddenly, she found herself weeping again, though she did not understand the cause of her tears. In a moment, Leon was on the sofa by her side, arm about her shoulders.

"Sophy, darling, what's wrong? Are you unwell again?"

"No," she answered. "No, it . . . it was the talk of war."

"But war is . . . ?" Leon hesitated. In some strange way she had embarrassed him. Could it be that he was not wholly at ease to be trading in men's lives? Stuff and humbug! Soldiers adored combat. When they had no enemy to fight, and no oppressor to subdue, they fought, and even killed, each other. She knew that much. For all that, there was a troubled oppression in her at the thought of her hussar embroiled in killing.

"What is war, then, Leon?"

He bit his lip. "A fact of life, I suppose."

She knew that to be true, but it did not ease her bout of depression. For a fleeting, and nightmarish, instant she saw her son, in Edmund's image, riding by his father's side amidst the smoke, blood and death of a battlefield.

"Sophy, you look dreadfully pale."

"The influenza . . ." the girl said, leaning on the trader's shoulder for comfort. He put his arm gently around her and together they stared into the flickering flames of the fire in the grate, saying nothing.

"No more talk of war, then," Leon murmured at length. He gave her another minute to recover her composure then, still gently, turned her face towards him. "My little finch," he said. "If you wish I will cancel my contract for the exchange of gunpowder."

"I know nothing of that," said Sophy, taken aback. "I cannot interfere with your livelihood."

"Cotton to clothe them, corn to feed them, and tobacco to keep them content—but not, I think, gunpowder. No, not that," said Leon de Nerval. "You are right, dearest."

"Leon, I have no . . ."

He put his hand against her lips to silence her.

"Sophy, I'm in sore need of a conscience."

"Leon?" she began to protest again, lips brushing his palm.

"No, hear me out," he insisted. "I want you for my wife. I propose that you become my wife, Sophy, if you will. The world is shrinking, and yet I feel more alone than I have ever done." He laughed ruefully at the confession. "Since meeting you, I'm lonely. There's only one cure."

"Leon, I . . . I am not myself."

"Marry me," he said, with tender authority, "and become mine."

In a whisper, Sophy heard herself say, "*Yes.*"

# Eight

Spring had caught up with Yorkshire. The dales were shot through with the new green growths, the great elms and oaks on the borders of Thomas Richmond's estate sprinkled with unfolding leaves, bright and frivolous in the warm breezes of late afternoon. In the surrounding fields were fat lambs, noisily nuzzling ewes heavy with coarse winter wool. A small herd of dairy cows browsed over hay troughs and picked hopefully along the bottom of the dykes for the first of succulent weed-shoots and herbs that they liked so much and that, according to local tradition, gave their milk its aromatic flavor.

Huffton House stood, just as she had remembered it, warm and solid against the bosom of the hill, bathed in slanting sunlight. Nothing, outwardly, appeared to have changed since the days of her childhood, yet her quick eyes were soon to pick out stray signs of neglect in the fabric of the outbuildings, and notice such small items as a wooden hobbyhorse, an iron hoop and a miniature painted wheelbarrow with broken shafts, upon the lawn—the toys of other childhoods, not her own.

Leon, aware of the mingled emotions in her, said nothing, holding her hand in his, as the coach made the long curve of the drive and braked to a halt before the shallow steps of the reception door.

Suddenly Sophy was apprehensive, nervous as to their welcome and the impression that Leon would make upon her father—yes, and upon Agatha. Though she had changed much, some of that former jealousy remained in her, bitterness towards her stepmother; that scheming usurper who, so Miss Frampton surmised, would go through the family's income as a woodworm goes through an old damp timber. It was to exorcise that petty animosity that Sophy had agreed to come to Huffton at all. And because Leon, who had insisted on formal proceedings, was to ask her father's permission to take his daughter in matrimony.

"What if Father says no?" Sophy had asked, only half teasing.

"Then I must look for another wife."

"Oh, Leon!" she had said. "I mean it. What will we do if Father refuses?"

"Is it likely?"

"I . . . I don't know."

"We'll marry in spite of him," Leon had answered. "He has no hold on you now, Sophy. Even if he had, I would wrap you in a Persian shawl, stow you aboard a barge with silken sails and whisk you off on the trade winds to Araby to live with you forever in a marble palace."

"That, sir," Sophy had said, "sounds most impractical. Besides, an inner berth in a Persian shawl would make me sneeze, I'm sure."

"Very well, then," Leon had told her, "I would take a leaf from Robert Browning's book and elope with you to Italy."

"And encourage me to write sonnets?"

"Perhaps," Leon had said; "but I would rather encourage you to have babies—three or four little girls as pretty as their mother, and a son for me."

Sophy had cut off the whimsical conversation abruptly. Through the coach window, in the open door of Huffton House was seen a figure waiting upon the top step, a stooped, wizened old man she did not at first identify as her father. A pang of alarm and sorrow went through her, turning at once to love. But the memory of her departure from this place, of her father's casual dismissal, was still too strong. Instead she put on the air of a lady and went slowly through the procedure of stepping down from the conveyance on Leon's arm, delaying the eventual moment when she must approach the steps, kiss that scowling, withered cheek, and introduce the man who would soon become her husband.

Why was it so desperately important that her father approve of Leon de Nerval? Agatha was the enemy, the object of the mannered attack. It was Agatha who must not only approve, but actually covet, Leon.

Sophy negotiated her bell-like skirts up the steps and took her father's hand. It was as dry and brittle as a beggar's kindling, yet the flesh of his cheek, when she brushed it with her lips, was soft and moist, like a fungus. Her sense of shock, and pity, deepened.

"So," Thomas Richmond said, "you've come home, have you?"

He was looking past her, eyes glaucous, sanguine, surveying the stocky figure of Leon de Nerval, who had politely remained on the bottom step.

"Father," said Sophy, "may I introduce you to M. Leon de Nerval? As you know from my letter, M. de Nerval and I intend to marry."

Thomas Richmond grunted, mumbling something inaudible as he beckoned Leon to approach. Sophy was ignored, neglected. She glanced round; there was no sign of Agatha, or any of the servants. The hall lay empty, hollow. She could smell cabbage and a strong fish odor and, listening carefully, a fractious whimpering far off in the deep recesses of the house.

Thomas Richmond's first words, as he shook Leon's hand, were, "Not English, sir, are you?"

That pointed, and inexcusable, insult set the tone for

the visit. A flush rose to Sophy's cheeks and anger at her father and all the rustic suspicion which he emanated claimed her, steeling her against sympathy for the worn-out and ailing old man, in his run-down mansion.

"No, sir," Leon answered, making light of it, "I am as French as frogs' legs."

"Aye, you've the look," Thomas Richmond muttered, then, dropping Leon's hand—almost tossing it aside—he turned on his heel and went on into the house without another word, leaving Sophy and her fiancé to follow if they wished.

Sophy and Leon walked together in the twilight on the path by the rear of the meadows. Sophy was full of apologies for her father's behavior, but Leon did not appear to take the insult to heart. To Sophy, Huffton was no longer home. She had been in so many different lodgings in the past year that she had hoped to find a new direction by returning to her place of birth. But Agatha's vulgar hand was everywhere in evidence, garish and grubby. The troupe of servants who had replaced the elderly retainers were products of the city like their mistress. In a remarkably short time, it seemed, Agatha had defied the sanctity of four generations and had claimed the house as her own.

So far, Agatha had not deigned to make an appearance. She had conveyed her apologies and excused herself by indicating that the children required her attention. After dispensing a meager glass of wine to his guest, Thomas Richmond had also excused himself and retreated to his study, leaving a surly young maid servant to escort Leon and Sophy to their rooms on the upper floor.

Sophy wept a little on the bed. She might have so far forgotten her new role as to seek out Agatha and rage at her for the gross discourtesy and the slur upon the family. Leon, however, had slipped a note below her door inviting her to walk with him and show him the estate. Sophy had been relieved to quit the suffocating atmosphere of the house.

Leon said, "Do stop apologizing, Sophy."

"Such bad manners are inexcusable."

"I understand why they are suspicious of me. You forget that I come from stock not too dissimilar to your own, though further down in the compost of society. It gives me genuine pleasure to be here at all, no matter the reception."

"But why?"

"Because this is where you were born." Leon paused, leaned on a dyke and nodded at the grazing sheep. "Besides, where in all England could one see such a fine strain?"

"My grandfather was a husbandman of some repute," said Sophy, rather proudly. "My father, however, was too busy in his other ventures to continue the experiment."

"Your father is not a well man, Sophy."

"No," said the girl, sadly. "He has aged terribly in the past year. I . . . I fear for him, Leon."

Leon nodded again, agreeing. "He is no longer your father, Sophy. Is that what you mean?"

"Yes."

"We grow up, and often we grow wiser than our partners and our parents."

"I still love him, Leon—though I no longer like or respect him."

"Then love will have to be enough. I suspect that he loves you too."

"No, he loves only . . . only my stepmother."

Leon leaned his back upon the low wall and took her hands in his own. Behind him twilight had thickened upon the pasture. The flocks were folding, clustering, moving down to the circular pens under the elms, lambs and ewes bleating and baaing softly.

"Sophy, you once asked me why I loved you," the trader said, quietly. "Few women would have dared ask that question honestly. They would have fished with it for compliments, not for the truth. I am not one with English society; my origins must always set me apart. More important, though, is the fact that I have lived my life as *I* willed it, giving and taking nothing from man or woman—nothing, that is, that could not be totaled in *sous*, *gulden* or sovereigns. Last summer, before I visited Arthur Redford, I came to realize that I wanted more from life than the illusory consolations of money. I do not spurn wealth, understand, nor do I regret any transaction I have profitably arranged; but I saw, gradually, that my discontent stemmed from that loneliness that creeps insidiously into a man when youth is over. I decided that I must marry; that I must seek out a wife, settle, raise a family."

"Are you saying, Leon, that you picked me only to . . ."

"No, *not* in cold blood, my darling," said Leon, smiling. "I am saying that I set out to discover a suitable wife as I might have set out to uncover a cache of gemstones. Soon after we met, however, I knew that I had not taken account of love. There is no way to explain, no way to put that emotion down in terms of profit and loss. It simply happened, and once it *had* happened I was no longer lonely. Life once more had savor for me. Oh, I was uncertain and unsure, plagued by all the fevers that silly swains fall heir to—but I loved you, and that was compensation a hundredfold for the normal aches of the heart."

"Why do you tell me this now?" Sophy asked.

Leon hesitated. "Because, I do not think that you love me."

"No, Leon. I do love you," Sophy blurted out, in alarm.

The trader smiled, and cocked his head. "But I will make you love me, Sophy; oh, not by force or by demand. In time, you will no longer be puzzled by my feelings for you. You will not bind them up with the crêpe and satin of romance. You will appreciate that true love is not delicate, fragile like . . . like that little Dresden finch I gave you. The feelings I have for you are strong, supple, and will survive any insult or accident."

"Are you saying, Leon, that I must trust you?"

"Trust my love, Sophy."

"I do," the girl said quickly, though the soft passion of his speech had put her in doubt. Did she truly love this Breton trader, or was she using him as a substitute for that lost love that had lain closer to her than life itself? Was de Nerval only plain purchase in exchange for her child?

The emotions were too complex. She could not bring herself to explore them here and now, not in this place. How, she wondered, would her stepmother have reacted if a man had made such a speech to her? An admission of love would, for Agatha, signal an exploitable weakness in the man.

Involuntarily Sophy glanced up at the house, a dull silhouette against the paling sky now that the sun had gone. She thought of her father and, though she did not comprehend the meaning of what Leon had told her, it made her understand Thomas Richmond just a little more. Perhaps that was what Leon had intended, that and no more.

She kissed him on the brow, then led him back, without another word, to dress for dinner and presentation to Agatha, who, Sophy began to realize, had long ago equated love with passion and passion, in its most clumsy form, with power.

It would have been so easy for her to have fallen into that same trap; indeed, she had done so. But that was over now and she had been greatly fortunate to have found such a man as Leon de Nerval.

For the first time, she felt a certain relief at being unencumbered by a fatherless baby.

Sophy chose a gown of heavy cream silk, skirt laid in tiers of ruched flounces, each edged, like the deep neckline, with a fall of fine lace. The gown was regal and looked even more costly than it had been. Shortly after purchase, Sophy had earmarked it as the one she would wear to dinner with her stepmother. She was not disappointed in the effect it made. She could feel Agatha's scrutiny from the moment she stepped into the dining room. Leon, too, had accoutered himself in that rich, formal evening dress he wore so well and that gave him, Sophy thought, the dignity of a royal consort.

Disengaging herself from de Nerval's arm, Sophy wafted forward and dutifully pecked the air three inches from Agatha's cheek.

"Why, Sophy," said Agatha, magnanimously, "how grand you look."

"How kind you are, Stepmother. Allow me to introduce my fiancé, M. Leon de Nerval."

"Ah yes, the French . . . 'gentleman' of whom we have heard so much."

Leon and Agatha sized each other up; Sophy could detect no true emotion on either face. Agatha, it seemed, had already decided that de Nerval was too cosmopolitan to succumb to a gushing performance and therefore contented herself with pretending that she was a thoroughbred lady and played out the predinner ritual with an air of condescending autocracy. Leon, Sophy thought, would see straight through such a transparent manner and would be secretly amused by it. Agatha's dress probably cost as much, if not more, than her own. But it was vulgar, too youthful in style and cut for a matron, and showed too much bosom.

Dinner, and the subsequent charade of a sociable evening that followed, were marred by continual skirmishes between Thomas and Agatha Richmond. It was all too obvious that the embarrassingly avid hunger of the aging estate owner for his Chiswick Venus had decayed rapidly. The relationship now was that of a domineering mother and a surly, recalcitrant child. It was clear too that Thomas

Richmond had lost his status in the business world. He was all at sea with Leon's questions as to the state of the English wool market and its dependent manufactures.

If Sophy had feared that Agatha would probe into her doings during the previous summer, ask pointed questions concerning Switzerland, London and Cornwall, she was relieved by Agatha's total indifference as to how Sophy had spent her year.

Desultory conversation limped on throughout the meal, which was served with bad grace by truculent servants, including one snobbish horse-faced butler hired from Manchester especially for the event. Agatha was powerless to impress Sophy's fiancé and, after a few flurries intended to exhibit her "sophistication," fell back into the fortress of motherhood and waxed eloquent and at length upon the virtues of her offspring. It was not until the men had repaired to the study, primed with decanters and a dusty box of cigars, to allow Leon to put a formal declaration of his intentions to her father, that Agatha and Sophy, for a few lively minutes, drew daggers.

From her seat on a flounced, overstuffed round-chair by the hearth in the drawing room, Agatha poured coffee, offered seedy-looking sweetmeats and—daringly—a glass of arsenic-colored liquor. Sophy accepted only coffee and, settling on an adjacent sofa, watched her stepmother delicately sip liquor from a thumb-shaped glass. It was gratifying to note that nature had etched hard lines and ineradicable wrinkles on Agatha's features and that her complexion was varnished with cosmetical preparations. Her hands and wrists were fat and the exposed flesh of her bosom quivered within its whaleboned balcony.

Perhaps Sophy smiled; perhaps Agatha only sensed her stepdaughter's derision.

Agatha said, "So you are to be married; and to a *foreigner*. Well, I suppose it's fortunate that you managed to find a husband at all."

"Leon is French; hardly 'a foreigner' as you mean it."

"*Breton* French, according to Mr. Aylmer of Liverpool who seems to know your prospective husband *rather* well."

"Ah," said Sophy. "I'm glad that you were sufficiently interested in my welfare to inquire into the status of my husband-to-be."

"*Breton* French," Agatha went on. "Peasant stock with the dirt hardly washed out from under his fingernails. I have even seen his name mentioned here and there in the journals; *not* in a flattering context, I may add."

"But the journals are English, are they not?"

"I do not insult my intelligence by reading *foreign* trash."

"In a foreign language you would have difficulty in reading anything, Agatha," said Sophy, sweetly. "However, as you have bothered to investigate my fiancé so thoroughly, you will know also that he has many talents and skills and is renowned, if not liked, for his business acumen."

"Business acumen!" scoffed Agatha. "Lack of scruples, more like."

Sophy was in no doubt now that her stepmother was feverish with jealousy. Her cockney accent was making itself apparent again, as it always did when the woman was on the verge of a tantrum.

It should have been a moment of triumph for Sophy. But, oddly, she felt nothing, and conducted the rest of the combat without venom or arrogance, almost indifferently.

Agatha's cherished secrets, from which had originated much of her power, were secrets no longer. Sophy understood the nature of male passion and even the arcane freemasonry of childbirth. Deep, deep down, she still envied Agatha, but the source of her envy now had shifted to the three little boys in their nursery upstairs.

She sought to put that thought out of her mind and, with Agatha's assistance, succeeded.

Sophy heard herself say, "Leon's acumen rests on his ability to tell at a glance the true from the false. He is an honest man, Agatha, not easily taken in by cheapness and vulgarity."

"How is it then that he failed to see through you?" Agatha demanded, belligerently. "After all, you left home with the express intention of *snaring* yourself a husband, *any* sort of husband. I question, yes, I really *do* question, Sophy, if your methods of . . . of *trapping* M. de Nerval were honorable. After all, it's well known that French peasants consider 'an association' with an English lady as something of a masculine coup."

"You speak, I take it, from experience," said Sophy, casually.

"How dare you!"

"What 'honor' is there in your relationship with my father? After a year of marriage, he has degenerated into an old man."

"Illness did that. I've had to nurse him constantly, I'll have you know."

"Illness—or misery," said Sophy; "what, Agatha, is the difference?"

"You have no *right* to talk to me in that manner."

"I have every right. I am his daughter, his flesh and blood."

"And hope to inherit your *share*, no doubt."

"Inherit?" Sophy was genuinely puzzled, then the implications of the woman's unguarded remark broke down her apathy. "Do you mean that he is like to die? Has the physician . . . ?"

"He won't *consult* a physician."

"You are his wife; you must make him."

"He's too stubborn. In any case, Sophy, I lied to you. It's not illness, but *drink* that has pulled your father down."

By offering some frank truths in a pretense of concern and honesty, Agatha hoped to draw the talk away from that revealing word "inherit."

Sophy said, "Don't you care if he dies?"

"I am his wife; he is the only father my sons have; I buried one husband already, and have no wish to bury another," Agatha blustered, pouting.

"The truth, Agatha."

Silence. The ugly ormolu clock on the drawing-room mantel clucked, and, from the pastures outside, a lamb, lost in the flock, bleated pathetically for its mother. Agatha opened her lips, then closed them again firmly.

Rising, Sophy said calmly, "Do you *want* him to die?"

In a low, hissing tone, Agatha said, "You will wish your Breton dead, too, in time, miss. I promise you that. Marry for *money*, and you will soon come to crave . . . love. *Love*, do you understand me?"

Sophy felt a chill clutch at her heart. It was as if Agatha had seen down into her, had sensed uncertainty in her match with de Nerval. Perhaps she had deluded herself as to the meaning of her feelings for him. It seemed now as if Agatha might have done the same and been less conniving than Sophy had imagined.

"Do you suppose," Agatha went on, "that *I* have what I want?"

Sophy shook her head.

"Only *half* of what I want," said Agatha. "I want . . . I *need* loving."

"To command," said Sophy. "Is that what you mean?"

"Discard all this stuff and pretense," Agatha told her. She reached out and grasped the girl's hand. "You are marrying this Breton for his *money*, and you will pay for it in the bedroom."

"Agatha!"

"Pay for it first by what is *done* to you, and then, in rapid time, by what he *cannot* do."

Sophy drew her hand away. She had been contaminated enough by this woman, wrongly impressed by the values of the whore. In honesty, she could not blame Agatha for *all* that had happened to her, yet an important part of the tragedy of the hussar must be laid at her stepmother's door.

In a former time, a previous incarnation it now seemed, Sophy would have lost her temper, stormed and raged and hurled recriminations like spears at this woman. But she saw Agatha now as a product of a dying era, her materialism as a philosophy that would not stand long against the winds of change that age and a new generation would bring under the bright new banners of emancipation.

There was no sincerity in her shocked exclamation, and the girl gave up the last pretense.

"I may not love my Breton trader," she said, "but I *will* keep my bargain to him—because, Agatha, I know that he loves me; and that is enough for any decent woman."

As Agatha struggled to her feet, determined to climax the scene of ruthless confession, Sophy turned towards the door and, fortuitously, was saved from further self-revelations by Leon's cheerful arrival.

The trader burst happily through the doors, flinging them back, his arms wide.

There was no play-acting in his joy. It was as if he had come here as a raw, unsophisticated lad to beg for her hand in marriage and was overwhelmed by her father's kindness in generously granting it.

"We may be married, Sophy," he cried, prancing forward and sweeping her into his arms. "We may be married just as soon as we wish. Is that not grand news?"

Sophy searched his face for a hint of irony or deceit—and found none.

Laughing, she allowed him to whirl her about the drawing room in an impromptu polka without noticing that Agatha, in tears, had fled.

* * *

It was long after midnight. Huffton House languished in an uncommon silence on all its lower floors. Upstairs the maids and the nurse snored, and the smallest of the step-sons whimpered fitfully in his sleep. Agatha Richmond, who had closeted herself in her own boudoir, tossed and turned, with muffled groans, caught in a discontented dream. Snug in the guest bedroom, Leon slept well, for he, with all his perspicacity, had failed to notice all the colors of the cloth from which his bride's youth had been woven and which, that very evening, had been ripped from its frame and destroyed.

As a concession to de Nerval's desire to do properly by the affair, Thomas Richmond had made a brief appearance before the couple. He had come no further from his musty hermitage than the door, however. Keeping his daughter and her fiancé in the hallway, he had given a grudging bow, announced that Leon's credentials had satisfied him and that Sophy "if she wished" might marry the fellow. Then, before she could thank him, her father had inched back into his gloomy chamber and had drawn the doors behind him, shutting out all further discussion of the pre-cise form the event would take. The gesture clearly signi-fied that he no longer cared, that the pair were free to make what arrangements they wished—provided he was in no way involved.

At that moment, Sophy had been close to tears. Only Leon's kindliness, sympathy and obvious pleasure at the prospect of having her for a wife, kept her from slipping into melancholy.

Leon did not allow her a moment, through the last hours of that long day, to brood upon the careless cruelty of the house, or of the fact that he, Leon de Nerval, was all she had in the world to call her own.

But Sophy, though she put on a casual manner as she wished her fiancé goodnight, was too restless to undress and go to bed. She too had been allocated a guest bed-room, a narrow, chilly room at the end of a long corridor.

In it she experienced no nostalgic harmony with the house in which she had spent most of her life. True to her threat, Agatha had taken over Sophy's suite of rooms and had planned their refurbishment as a nursery. Out of apathy, and a scarcity of ready cash, however, the plan had foundered and the rooms had stood stripped and grimy for six months.

For an hour or more, Sophy sat at her dressing table— a small antique from her great-grandmother's collection and now discarded as lumber—and watched the candle drip and flicker in its wooden clasp.

The fly-specked glass reflected the girl's beautiful face, but she covered her brow with her hand to discourage the mirror image's accusing scrutiny.

At length, taking the candle, she left the room in the east wing and made her way softly along the dark corridors, each nook and alcove familiar from childhood games. Not in a dozen years had she experienced recollections of her early life with such aching vividness, the drifting, dreamy security of parental love in a house that held no terrors.

The corner room remained untouched. Agatha had not, after all, found it necessary to eradicate that sanctuary and pleasant shrine to her predecessor; she had demolished the past by other more subtle means.

Stealthily Sophy opened the door.

Though night shrouded the garden, the broad, diamond-paned windows admitted light from the sky, starlight strengthened by hints of the quarter moon. The unoiled hinge creaked and the door opened sluggishly, releasing that faint odor of lavender and thyme from the sachets with which Thomas had once sweetened the air of the unused sitting room. Gilded furniture, tarnished and peeling, looked dainty and new in the pale glow of the candle flame, curves and chosen patterns falling into place in the dim portrait of a place where once there was contentment and a feeling for the changeless appeal of finely made things.

Stepping noiselessly into the room, Sophy made herself a part of that portrait, its focal point, and, unwittingly, pierced the crust which capped her father's heart. For a moment, she brought the old man his youth again, before pride and bitter sorrow closed round defensively.

Startled, she heard him sob—once, deeply—and then his hoarse demand to know what she wanted, what she sought in this part of the mansion.

Without knowing why, she answered, "Peace, father; that's all," and heard the long, indrawn raucous suck of breath.

She could not see him yet, not until the clink of a bottle against the rim of a glass drew her attention to the recesses of a porter's chair that stood, bleached and cracked, with its back to the windows.

She came a pace or two into the room, closed the door behind her. The extended candle shed a sliver of light upon her father. He sat low in the chair, far under the cowling, thin shanks splayed out, the squat black brandy bottle in his lap. He had loosened his waistcoat and collar and dragged down the knot of his tie, and lay huddled and disheveled as any piece of human flotsam along the walls of the Marshalsea prison.

Tenderness, and pity, caught Sophy for an instant. But there was no place for them now, not even in this room full of memories. Though he did not say it, she knew that she had struck him as a ghost of her mother; the rich stuff of the gown, the oval of her face, melting into a phantom of forgotten love in the wan circle of candlelight.

"I did not mean to disturb you," she said, firmly.

"Peace?" he said, bitterly. "You seek peace here? Better seek peace with your trader, Sophy. There's no peace, and no money, here now."

"Are you . . . in debt, Father?"

He laughed, curtly. "Think to buy me out, do you?"

"No, Father."

"Nay, lady, I'm not in debt—not yet. It's a donkey race now, though, to see whether death or the bailiff will reach me first."

Sophy could not separate his disillusionment from melodrama. Was he speaking the plain truth, or did he simply curry sympathy for the foolishness that had brought him to ruin?

Cautiously, she said, "We are concerned about your health, Papa."

"*You* are concerned? Why should you be concerned. *Agatha*—her I can understand. *She* is concerned; concerned I don't go fast enough." He craned forward, gaunt jaw thrust out, eyes red-rimmed. He tapped himself upon the chest with the base of the bottle. "*I'm* not concerned. I've done all I could for you. Hear? All I can do, I've done. For her, too."

"Leon and I . . ."

"Live your own lives; let Agatha and me live ours."

Sophy made one last bid to infiltrate his lachrymose despair. "Do your little stepsons not love you, Father, as I used to do? Don't you make them laugh as you . . ."

"No time," he snorted. "The laughter's all gone, past, finished. I don't even remember it."

"Then why are you here, in *this* room, on this particular night?"

He hesitated. Fleeting emotions touched his mouth and eyes, then set hard again.

He laughed curtly, barbarously.

"To drink in peace, thank you," he said.

And it was over, forever.

Dawn filled the eastern sky above the dales. Flocks browsed on the dew-glistening grass and birds trilled in the trees and hazy hedgerows. A bull calf lowed drowsily and tagged to his mother's flanks in hope of breakfast.

In the disused sitting room overlooking the wild garden, Thomas Richmond slumped in sleep, bottle and glass, sticky and empty, dropped on the carpet by his ankles.

Upstairs, the three sons of the household lay awake but mouse-quiet, not daring to rouse dreaded Nurse Simpkins before her appointed hour of six. The dawn hour would be an eternity for them.

A scullion, who had spent the night on sacks in the hayloft with her lover, slunk into the kitchen by the still-room corridor. To her dismay, she found that the stove had been stoked without cleaning and that some thieving glutton had boiled coffee in the pantry pot and taken it away. The girl scuttled off to hide in her cot and let some other soul take the blame.

Dressed in a traveling pelisse, her bonnet already pinned in place, Sophy knocked upon the guest-room door and, at Leon's bidding, carried in the tin tray with the pot and breakfast cup upon it.

Leon, dressed in a brown robe, was shaving by the window.

If he was surprised to be waited upon by his fiancée at this ungodly hour, he gave no sign of it.

Sophy put down the tray, poured coffee into the cup and handed it to him.

"Leon," she said. "I wish to leave—now."

His dark slumbrous eyes betrayed no hint of curiosity, though the visit had been arranged to cover two days.

"Very well, Sophy." He drank coffee with one hand and toweled soap from his cheeks with the other. "There is a train, I believe, at eight-thirty from Manchester station."

Not then, and not later, did her Breton trader ask her reason for quitting Huffton House without a word of fare-well to her father or his vulgar wife.

All he said was, "I take it that I may make arrangements to marry, without consultation?"

"As you wish, Leon," Sophy said. "And as quickly as possible."

Leon de Nerval kissed her on the mouth, and reached hastily for his shirt.

# Nine

On the first day of September, Leon de Nerval and Sophy Richmond were married by the vicar of the church of St. Gage in the parish of Marylebone, in which borough the happy couple would set up home

The bride wore a blue taffeta dress and modish little bonnet, the groom a checkered jacket, side-swept trousers and a blossom cravat which, he claimed, made him look more like a Bohemian artist than a businessman; it would not do to appear at such a happy and momentous ceremony in his "working togs," now would it? Sophy agreed. In fact, Sophy agreed to most things Leon said, meekly accepting the leadership of her lord and master in all matters pertaining to their nuptials.

Later, on reflection, Sophy could not determine just when she had made her stand on Miss Frampton's future, or what special argument she had used to persuade the reluctant Leon to employ the governess as housekeeper of the de Nervals' brand-new home in Damaris Square. She could not even recall that Leon had actually refused her request that Miss Frampton, that dear and good friend, be "taken care of" in this way, though she seemed to recollect that he had been hesitant about giving consent.

In any event, Sophy wanted—needed—the governess. In other circumstances, she might have been more inclined to break cleanly with her former life, to pay off Miss

Frampton with a generous emolument, and find her other employment. But, as things stood, the presence of Eunice Frampton allowed Sophy the illusion that she still had not "lost" her child.

It was no conscious plot, no long-term scheme. Sophy hid it from her intelligence by preaching "loyalty" and extolling, as much for her own benefit as Leon's, the advantages of having such a competent woman, such a trustworthy friend, in charge of household management until she, Sophy, could find her feet and assume her domestic duties according to the manual. If she had been truly honest with herself, Sophy would have admitted that she sought to appease the governess who, by her knowledge, had fettered herself to Sophy for as long as she wished.

Leon, for whatever reason, concurred, and Eunice Frampton, as was her way, duly shouldered the burden of paying off the lease on the Harwood Square property, seeing to the transfer of Sophy's belongings, to the discharge and reengaging of suitable domestic staff—acceding to the master's wishes, of course—and in general making herself invaluable in all departments.

It was, however, highly questionable if Leon de Nerval, for all his sharpness of observation, marked the governess's ambition quite so high, or read the true meaning of the hold she had on his intended. Certainly, even the worldly trader would have been shocked if he had been permitted to eavesdrop on the last conversation that the governess and her charge had, on the night before the wedding, in the girl's boudoir at the Harwood Square address.

"But he will know; he will *know*."

"Nonsense, Sophy," Miss Frampton had assured her. "The application will take care of that."

"But I'm not . . . I mean, I've given birth to a child."

"You have been using the preparation, haven't you?"

"Of course, but . . ."

"The fact of your virginity is unimportant. Many girls

damage themselves intimately while horse-riding. Your trader will not even consider . . ."

"My breasts . . . ?"

"Tender, that is all. He will respect your body, my dear, be assured of that. Unless I misjudge the gentleman he will not be brutal."

"And the marks?"

"Mercifully, the oil has made them almost invisible," the governess had said. "Care, caution and, ah, modesty will take care of the rest of it. Do you understand?"

Sophy had nodded.

The woman's advice was sound—yet Sophy wished with all her heart that she might go to the marriage bed carrying only natural tremors and maidenly fears to mix with her excitement. Being a country girl she had never held the prospect of loving in horror. Only the shadow of discovery made her nervous in the days before the quiet service and its subsequent celebrations.

It was for that reason that Sophy did not accede to Leon's suggestion that members of the Redford family be invited to the wedding as guests of the bride. The Redfords, that Swiss summer's mingling of joy and sorrow, delight and despair, were best put totally behind her, thrust safely into the past. She feared that one of the Redfords might drop an injudicious remark or, in some unimaginable manner, expose her guilty secret on the very steps of the altar.

She made excuses for not inviting them, feeble excuses. Leon did not press the point. He assured her that it did not matter to him; nor would it matter to his side of the aisle if the bride came alone to the church. He had, he declared, good friends enough to share.

Miss Frampton did not think it fitting that she should act as maid of honor. This pleasant duty fell to the sister of Leon's friend and London accountant, David Lloyd, a jovial young Welshman who, in his turn, ably supported the groom.

Eunice Frampton was the bride's only representative. No acknowledgment, no gift, and no visit came in reply to Sophy's written invitation to her father, stepmother and brothers. Huffton House greeted the news of her wedding with resolute silence. It was no more than the girl had anticipated, though the hurt still stung her heart as she glanced at the empty pews on the left side of the tiny church; ten rows of rush seats with only Miss Frampton, rather somberly dressed for a wedding, standing tall among them.

Leon's friends had marshaled their support. Sophy had never met them before, with the exception of David and Gwen Lloyd, and was rather startled at the variety of types and races who filled the right side of the aisle. Jews as well as Gentiles sang the hymn to the bride, even one handsome and elegant gentleman whose tint and hawklike nose suggested that he might be from the East. Three dozen men, shaken out of the city for the occasion, turned up, and three women whose contribution to Leon's business could only be surmised.

The wedding breakfast—an early luncheon, in effect—was taken in Colyer's French Rooms. The significance of this gesture was duly announced to the guests who, to a man, raised a nicely ribald cheer that shook the silk screen partitions round the three long tables and made the waiters smile.

All in all, the wedding and reception were just as Sophy had dreamed—except that she did not take great pleasure in them. Along the way, somehow the dream had altered, transformed itself from a vain, peacock parade into a public display of the permanence of marriage. In the vicar's droning sermon, in the after-luncheon speeches, in the guests' congratulatory messages, Sophy read the hidden ironies. She wished only that the day might pass and that she might survive the deceptions of the wedding night as swiftly as possible and set around her screens of habit to protect her from losing all that she had gained.

In the early evening, alone in the liveried carriage, Leon and Sophy drove back, as man and wife, to the elegant new mansion in Damaris Square, there to change, collect personal luggage and set off to catch the night packet to France.

Damaris Square: a stone's throw from Wimpole Street in which the Barretts lived, grieving for their talented and willful daughter. The de Nerval home was one of a short row of Georgian terrace houses, complete with tiny balconies and black-painted ironwork around the doorway and servants' steps. The three servants who had already been hired stood in the hallway and scattered rose petals on the bride as the groom lifted her and, staggering under the weight of her skirts, carried her across the threshold and into the drawing room where, closing the door with his heel, he set her gently down.

He kissed her, with passion. "Now, Madame de Nerval, tell me—are you happy?"

"Yes, Leon; yes, I'm happy," said Sophy, weeping.

All around her were the treasures of her new home, elegant furnishings, rich carpets, freshly painted cornices, the imposing fireplace with its jut of whorled black marble. And there were Leon's promises that she would spend her first weeks as mistress of his mansion "filling in" the spaces with ornaments of her own choosing so that the imprint of her taste would be upon the house too and make it more fittingly "their home." Silver markets, crystal bazaars, the arcades of china merchants, stockists of the best imported brocades and linens, she would become familiar with them all that autumn. She would spend his money, as much as she wished, and finish the feathering of their nest in grand style.

Though she wept still, Leon swept her into a waltz and, with boyish impatience, kissed her again and again until the bride was too breathless to do more than collapse upon the ottoman and let her bonnet fall from her head to lie like a discarded posy upon the carpet.

On one knee, in a pose formal but not mocking, Leon lifted her hands and kissed them.

"Do you remember, little finch, the man who skulked shyly round the Schneegarten . . ."

"In . . . in a dove-gray vest," put in Sophy.

"The man who had no thought for anything but business . . ."

"But took time to serve me coffee like . . . like a butler."

"Well, my love, that man has gone. He was aged before his time, a surly bachelor, an ogre, and a fool."

"He is the man I . . ." Sophy hesitated. "He is the man I fell in love with, Leon."

"You will love the other Leon more, Sophy, I promise you."

She threw herself into his arms, weeping again. She had everything that she had ever dreamed of in the years before her departure from the shelter of her father's house. She was the wife of a rich man, with a home of her own, rooms brimful of fine, expensive things—and tomorrow she would be in Paris with her husband.

She clung to Leon, laughing at her tears. She might even have forgotten her modesty completely and encouraged her own mounting passion if, at that inauspicious moment, a discreet knocking on the drawing-room door had not brought an end to their privacy.

Sighing, Leon pushed himself to his feet.

"Who is it?"

The door opened a little, and a familiar voice said, "If Madam wishes to prepare at leisure for her journey, might I suggest that she come now, as the hour is already late."

Sophy bit her lip and exchanged a glance of resignation with her husband; then giggled in a muffled tone at the high-sounding formality of the housekeeper's announcement.

"Very well, Miss Frampton," she answered, adding without conviction, "thank you."

\* \* \*

Paris was home to Leon de Nerval. His love for that gay, bustling city almost equaled his love for his new English wife. Not for the de Nervals a trudge round lofty museums, conducted tours through galleries thronged with gaping visitors or pilgrimages from one dull historical monument to another, like wooden ducks on a string. Being a true Englishwoman, instilled with the notion that culture must be taken neat, Sophy would not have objected to joining the sightseeing herds. It took her only half a day, however, to fall in on Leon's quick heels and throw herself wholeheartedly into the wild, wicked and unending spree that was Paris in season at the beginning of the Second Empire.

The Hôtel du Roi Soleil was as resplendently baroque as its name suggested. Built to accommodate a favored mistress of the Bourbon overlord, its trappings represented the zenith of regal opulence. Most magnificent of all the palatial mansions along the Champs-Élysées, it was destined to remain the great original never to be overshadowed by the grandiose pastiches that sprang up in the Empire.

Wealth was all that guests required to partake of the Hôtel du Roi Soleil's sybaritic pleasures.

Its principal salon was cathedral-length. A dozen tall windows spilled soft light across a ceiling upon which the famous painter Lalamarchard had depicted the Sun God —pagan not political—as a majestically naked Apollo dipped in flowery clouds and surrounded by flocks of nymphs. Curving along the outer lips of the oval dome were a dozen giant goddesses whose elongated limbs twined a fleshy wreath around their lord.

Such treasures studded the hotel's many suites, chambers and salons; hangings of Lyons damask, mantels of alabaster, staircases of unflawed marble all lit by glittering chandeliers and massive bronze lusters. Every individual suite had its share of ornate luxury. The de Nervals' private bathroom housed an onyx tub lined with silvered bronze and embroidered with delicately erotic intaglios. Their bed chamber was a tabernacle of rare woods inlaid with ivory studs, and the canopied bed was as huge and as utterly voluptuous as a sultan's barge from a magical tale in the Arabian Nights adventures.

When, in the first flush of awe, Sophy was callow enough to mention the expense, Leon merely grinned and made a throwaway gesture as if to indicate that money, at that period, had no other purpose than to provide his wife with comfort and pleasure.

The choice of the most exquisitely extravagant hotel in Paris, however, seemed a little at odds with the staid image that Sophy had cherished of Leon throughout the Cornish months. Another side to the man she had married was revealed, adding a facet to his character that made him seem mysterious and deliciously sinister.

Marriage, the wedding ring, protected her from any possibility of scandal. She was in a perfect position to revel in the depravity of the world of vaudeville theaters, pleasure gardens, opera *bals* and discreet "boating" restaurants on the Seine. Sophy could, in fact, pretend that she was sister to the *grandes cocottes*—without endangering her reputation.

Each night, heady with wine and excitement, Leon helped her keep up this pretense. There was such an ardent quality to his lovemaking that Sophy suspected that, at some time in the past, he had been instructed by one or another of the superb women whom he pointed out to her, in the company of noted writers or artists, on the Boulevard des Italiens, at the tables outside Tortini's café or during the five-o'clock drive along the Bois de Boulogne.

Sophy did not care. She adored the pampering, the petting and all the sensual indiscretions. Most of all, she basked in her husband's unmasked ardor in the darkened bedroom of the hotel.

Undoubtedly Miss Frampton would have been shocked,

the Redfords distressed; and her former Yorkshire friends, pillars of social hypocrisy, would have disowned her on the spot for such "un-English" behavior. But they were far away. Yorkshire, Cornwall, London were the dream places now—Paris, and Leon, the reality.

At the end of a week, Leon suggested that they travel on to Baden-Baden to catch the sting in the tail of the season there. Sophy would have none of it. In Paris she felt free and uninhibited, rid, at last, of all guilts and anxieties. Even rumors of the Crimean campaign—which hardly featured as a topic in the chatter of the *boulevardiers*—struck no more than a faintly disquieting chord.

"We will stay in Paris, Leon," she declared.

"Forever, Sophy?"

She laughed and pressed herself against him under the silken sheets. "If you wish."

"And I would go each day to the Paris Bourse and haggle like a real Breton peasant?"

"And we would live in a house in St. Germain, and entertain notorious people."

"What if I fell in love with one of these notorious ones?"

"I would make sure that you did not," said Sophy, sliding against him until her limbs were entwined with his. Outside accordions sounded, faintly, squeezing out a last quadrille for the late-night lovers under the Chinese lanterns.

"How?"

"Like this, my darling."

"Ah!" Leon said. "It is you who would have lovers, a horde of them, prostrate at your feet. No, finch, we will not live in France."

"Don't talk."

"How can I when you hold me so?"

Three weeks, and the month of September, swirled past. Sophy's explorations of the nether world of the French capital kept pace in daring with Leon's, and eventually outstripped them.

They even visited the Closerie des Lilas, sat at a table in the groves watching the *biches* and their whiskered clients drinking, smoking, and taunting each other until the heat of the September night seemed palpably to emanate from that cloistered alcove. Plucking a cigar from Leon's case, Sophy lit it and, struggling not to cough, puffed out smoke like the girl opposite. So perfectly did she emulate the *fille*'s throaty, suggestive laughter that Leon took her off at once, pretending to be dismayed at the performance but secretly burning to have her alone in the Arabian bed in the huge wooden cavern of their hotel bedroom.

Satiety did not overtake Sophy. She did not suffer the fatigue that, by the end of the month, had slowed Leon's enthusiasm for Parisian frolics and had even, on occasion, caused him to fall asleep as soon as he turned between the sheets. He dared to drowse through a rowdy performance of *La Dame aux Camélias* at the Vaudeville, head nodding against the flock-papered side of the box until his snores competed with the languishing dialogue of poor Marguerite, and Sophy, sniffing tearfully, nudged him impatiently and caused him to wake with a start.

But Leon had no intention of allowing his honeymoon to end on a low-key note. He had saved his biggest surprise for the day before their departure for England.

The first Sophy knew of it was at breakfast in the Hôtel du Roi Soleil's suntrap salon, a long glass arcade filled with exotic plants and palms among which the cream-lacquered tables and wickerwork chairs were discreetly tucked away. Here, in a truly civilized country, breakfast was served silently and discreetly until eleven of the morning to allow the guests to catch up on their sleep.

Sophy buttered a crusty breadroll and spread a dab of peach jelly upon it. She drank coffee and ate the roll as hungrily as a Huffton milkmaid, with almost as little regard for the refinements of good manners. Palms protected the couple, and Leon too demolished his full "English" breakfast with relish, wiping his plate with a pinch of bread and popping it into his mouth with a gratified sigh.

He smiled at his wife and asked, "What do you plan for today, my love?"

Sophy shook her head. She felt it should be something wildly momentous, but could think of nothing that she had not already done.

"I think," Leon said, frowning now, "that we should apply ourselves to the serious purchase of a ballgown, Sophy."

"Together?" said Sophy.

"In Paris, a woman dresses to please her gentleman, not to please herself," said Leon. "Consequently, it is not uncommon for gentlemen to venture into the exalted haunts of high fashion to give advice on the selection of material and the suitability of style."

"That," said Sophy, "is quite remarkable. Do you gentlemen not object?"

"The gentlemen thoroughly enjoy it, I assure you."

"And the ladies?"

"Naturally; they have the pleasure of a captive audience," said Leon. "Shall we purchase a ballgown for you, my love?"

"To take back to England, do you mean? Will the alterations be completed in time?"

"Paris is the city of seamstresses. For a few extra francs the needles will dart like dragonflies and the scissors clip like woodpeckers' beaks and, as if you had waved a wand, your gown will be fitted around you."

"Then," said Sophy, "let us purchase a ballgown."

"I . . . ah, I have a reason, you see." From his inner pocket Leon produced at this moment an ornate envelope emblazoned with a crest that even Sophy recognized.

Eyes round with wonder, fingers trembling, Sophy accepted the envelope, opened it with her knife, and slid out the embossed and engraved invitation card. Their names were printed in scarlet: Madame and Monsieur Léon de Nerval. A screed of French, in gilt italic, followed and then, in vibrant, shiny blue letters the names of their hosts.

"Of course," Leon said, "if you have other plans, my darling, we can always send our formal regrets."

"Is it true, Leon? Leon, is it?"

"Quite authentic, I assure you."

"The Emperor Napoleon and the Empress Eugénie," gasped Sophy. She stared very hard at the card as if to seek out deception. "I . . . I . . . I can hardly believe it."

"It *may* be a hoax," said Leon. "Shall we dawdle along at nine this evening and find out?"

"You tease! You wicked tease!" Sophy cried, and flung her arms around her husband's neck, almost dragging him down into the pot of peach jelly.

If ever Sophy would be beautiful and entrancing, then this was the night when all the elements converged to make her so. The gown Leon helped her choose was of pewter glacé silk, with an overskirt of palest mauve caught up around the hem with clusters of satin ribbon nipped into filigree bows. The bodice was trimmed with a deep lace fiche, draped into the tiniest of cap sleeves to exhibit her powdered shoulders and upper bosom. A ribbon fanchon sprinkled with flowers encircled her smooth coif and a simple fan-shaped pearl clasp completed the ensemble.

"*Alors, m'sieur.*" The maid fractionally adjusted one bow on the skirt then retreated past Leon, still crouched, leaving Sophy in the center of the dressing room, alone.

In the romantic novels she had so avidly devoured in the past Sophy had thrilled to compliments delivered by fine gentlemen to beautiful women. Now she was herself the object, the beautiful, the loved one, and knew that the strangest miracle of all had been accomplished by the magical power of her husband's money and influence. He had given her, at this hour, the greatest treasure of all: he had made her *feel* beautiful and loved.

His compliments were not hollow nor vapid. They came from the depths of his heart.

"Little finch," he said, "you are ravishing. When I am old, and you are no longer quite the flower of youth, this is the moment I will cherish, the portrait that I will carry with me, untarnished, forever."

He kissed her, his hands barely touching her, then with a crooked grin—as if embarrassed at his own emotions— he stepped away, saying, "So, please instruct the maid to fetch your cloak before you have second thoughts about allowing such a dull and very plain fellow to accompany you into royal company."

Gravely, Sophy told him, "There is no other man in Paris, in all the world, Leon, whose company I would prefer, now and always."

Leon cleared his throat.

"Come," he said. "It won't do to keep Napoleon waiting. The war has made him scratchy enough, so I'm told."

The ball marked the end of the exiled summer season. More, perhaps, it represented Napoleon's promise to his court and his followers that the Crimean campaign would not last long and that a *belle époque* would surely come upon France very soon, and with it an ordered and agreeable way of life. The social festivals, the banquets and balls and opera evenings, demonstrated the willingness of the Emperor and Empress to keep alight the candles of gaiety even in the pervading gloom of Europe at war. There was keen rivalry for entrée to those functions that they graciously inaugurated or even consented to attend.

Titillated by such snippets of information relayed by a quizzical Leon, Sophy spent the journey from the hotel to the mansion-house on the Parisian outskirts in a glow of anticipation.

The grand mansion was set far back from a private road

approached through stone-pillared gates set in high rough
stone walls. The lawns and tree-lined walks were silvered
by moonlight, which mingled at length upon the swooping
tiers of shorn grass with golden light from the open doors
and windows and torchlit terraces: the perfect setting for
the dream through which Sophy moved faultlessly and with
a grace that she had never before attributed to herself.

As in a dream there seemed to be no awkwardness and
no impediment. She surrendered her cloak in the vast
hallway and, her hand on Leon's arm, flowed on through
marbled pillars and a high scrolled arch into the glittering
ballroom with its throng of guests, shimmering sea-green
floor and alcoves of Italian porcelain banked high with
scented blooms. She could see the golden gleam of the
instruments of the orchestra on the dais behind the fluted
railing, and the white gloves of the musicians. The women
were all beautifully elegant, and the men, several in gaudy
uniforms, formed a suitably aristocratic retinue.

Sophy did not lack partners. After the first polka with
Leon she found herself, to her utter astonishment, the
center of an admiring circle of attractive men, young and
more mature, who vied with each other to command her
attention. Dance after dance, her feet barely touching the
floor, she reveled in the magical quality of the evening. But
she did not altogether close her mind to the knowledge that
Leon had engineered the invitation deliberately, to show
her, as modestly as possible, that his status in this noble
company was high and that, beneath his sober manner, his
power and influence lifted him from the ruck of very plain,
dull businessmen. She knew that she was beautiful and that
that was one reason why she was given so much attention;
but her native shrewdness told her too that being Leon's
wife was no handicap and, indeed, in this country, would
have won her a lofty place in society.

A distinguished British ambassador, a peer of the realm,
confirmed Sophy's growing recognition. Propelling her

stolidly through one of the more stately dances, Lord Denzill growled her husband's praises. "Fine man. Cracking good chap, yuh know. All grateful to him. Imperial Majesty told me so himself, no less, last week. Not won without supplies, wars ain't, yuh know. Saw it all coming, your husband did. Hum! Laid us all in stock. Hum! Know the Redfords, do yuh? Hum?"

Sophy admitted to knowing the Redfords, then, with a faint pall cast upon her happiness, navigated the conversation away from the area of mutual acquaintances.

When that dance was over, Sophy sought Leon. She slid her hand into the crook of his arm.

"I had no idea that you were so famous!" she said.

He looked at her out of the sides of his brown eyes, more rueful now than amused. "They need me," he said. "I am famous because I am needed, that's all."

She might have asked for a full explanation but it was neither the time nor the place. In addition, at that moment the host and hostess entered from the long private salon and the diplomatic dinner party that, for a handful of elder statesmen and their wives, had preceded the ball.

A buzz of excitement filled the ballroom, the sound gathered immediately into the strains of the royal anthem as a furrow in the phalanx of guests spread and opened until the whole center of the floor was cleared for the entrance of Napoleon III and his Empress, Eugénie.

Napoleon was not tall, but had a fine soldierly bearing accented by his commander's livery. He suited the martial accouterment and somehow formed a symbolic contrast with the Empress, an exquisite figure, diadem sparkling in her rich auburn hair, her body sheathed in a gown of sheer ivory satin.

With all the wonder of a child, Sophy watched the couple's sedate promenade down the length of the ballroom, coming closer and closer to the place near the dais where she waited, mutely, by Leon's side.

When she heard Leon present her as his wife and the Emperor's rather amused reply—in a French phrase that she did not fully understand—she felt as if her heart would explode with pride and joy. In halting English, Napoleon spoke with her, asking if she had enjoyed her first visit to France, and complimenting her on selecting a Breton husband.

"Bretons," the Emperor said, "are notoriously faithful."

Sophy murmured a reply, then glanced down in amazement at Napoleon's hand. It was extended towards her in a gesture that was both invitation and command.

The Empress was engaged in conversation on the far side of the room.

Prompted by a discreet nudge from Leon, Sophy offered her arms to Napoleon who, it seemed, had actually invited her to be his first partner of the evening and to sail out into the emptiness of the ballroom floor.

Stiffly at first, certain that she would trip and fall at his feet, she followed his graceful lead as the orchestra struck into the opening bars of a waltz.

It lasted all of four minutes; four minutes as the partner of one of the most powerful and glamorous figures in Europe, and then, with great diplomacy, the third Napoleon excused himself and moved on to favor other ladies.

Leon cut in, hardly losing step, sweeping her discreetly from the periphery of the dancers out into the swirling gowns once more.

Though he pretended otherwise, even Leon de Nerval was impressed by the Emperor's gesture.

"You see, Sophy," he said. "You *are* the most beautiful woman here."

And, for the rest of that fantastical night, Sophy believed it to be true.

The following noon, with the coming of the rain to mark the very end of the month, the de Nervals, laden with boxes and trunks far in excess of those with which they had arrived, left the Hôtel du Roi Soleil and entrained for Calais and their home in Damaris Square, London.

Midmorning in Damaris Square: Sophy, alone almost for the first time since her wedding eve seven weeks ago, sat in a stiff new day dress in the pristine morning room on the ground floor of her mansion, listening wistfully to the sounds of the city going about its business outside.

Church and clock bells chimed. The sedate clopping of carriage horses' hoofs on the cobbles came and went in a rhythm that reminded the girl of nodding funeral plumes on a cortège parade. The catsmeatman's cry was a profound eulogy, taking up where the newsboy's soprano call had left off.

Many stealthy noises filled the house: the muted clack of a dustpan snapping up invisible dust; the whispered *hush* of a horsehair brush; the tickle of a feather bouquet in the fretwork of the hall balustrades; the tap of maids' slippers on the parquet; and, once, a muffled guffaw from Miller, the Boots, who, though barely fourteen, stood six feet tall and had the irrepressible booming laugh of a docker in his cups.

Miller the Boots, Vera the scullion, Miss Harkness the cook, maids Priss and Queenie—the squad selected and presided over by Miss Frampton "with the mistress's approval." In time there would be a butler and possibly a footman, too, but the size of the house hardly justified it, in spite of the unwritten laws that linked acquisition of staff to income and not to convenience. In fact, Miss Frampton's choice of domestics seemed admirable and the month had gone past without a single hitch. For all that, there was something so obsequious about maids, cook, and scullion that Sophy did not feel bolstered by them but rather usurped. Even Miller, in spite of his open features, had a sly glint in his blue eyes that Sophy found disconcerting. She did not, for once, confide her apprehensions to

Leon who, in the easy manner he had acquired of late, left such matters entirely to his wife's pleasure.

Now, however, Sophy would have been glad of a *confidante* among the domestics, someone to whom she could talk, gossip even, about the war. Miss Frampton, with her flair for role-playing, had opted out of companionship; Sophy, too, no longer felt close to the woman, though she relied on her efficiency and positiveness during her early days as mistress of her own household, and more than ever upon her advice in purely practical affairs.

That late-October morning Miss Frampton had been, if anything, a shade too attentive to her mistress's welfare and, shortly after Leon's departure for the city, had brought a neatly folded bundle of newspapers and journals and, without a word, had placed them on the sewing table by Sophy's hand.

"What is this, Miss Frampton?"

"The newspapers, madam."

"Madam? I do wish you'd go back to calling me Sophy."

"It sets a bad example for the maids."

"When we are alone?"

Miss Frampton unbent a little, her hard features softening. "We will always be friends, Sophy, I hope."

"Of course."

There was no sincerity in the exchange, on either side. Sophy lifted a copy of the *Times* and glanced at the block of microscopic black print. "Is there something in particular to interest me this morning?"

"No, mad . . . no, Sophy," the governess said. "But you have been cut off from the events of the world for so long that I felt you should . . . acquaint yourself with . . ."

"But why?"

"M. de Nerval will undoubtedly wish to converse with you on topics of the day, the war in particular."

"M. de Nerval will . . ." Sophy cut off the retort.

"During the course of the dinner party next Tuesday," said Miss Frampton, "the talk will undoubtedly be of the war. Surely, Sophy, you do not wish to seem vague and ill-informed in front of guests."

"No, I . . ." Holding the newspaper at arm's length, Sophy scanned the text. It concerned itself with a critical discussion of a battle—the Alma, wherever that was—and seemed to be involved with gains and losses like one of Leon's stock reports. Her eyes round, Sophy stared up at the governess. "Is it . . . *him*?"

"Who?" said Miss Frampton, pretending to be puzzled. "Captain Sutton?"

Miss Frampton smiled. "Oh, no, Sophy; how fanciful of you to imagine that your former . . . friend would be involved in the first real battle of the war. I've no doubt that the bold Captain Sutton is ensconced well behind the lines playing lotto with the French or, shall we say, gracing the tents of the Turkish ladies who, I believe, have already installed themselves as comforters of the weary in advance of the gallant Miss Nightingale and her thirty-eight nurses."

"Thank you, Miss Frampton," said Sophy, evenly.

The woman hesitated.

Sophy said, "That will be all."

Miss Frampton bowed, like a crow pecking, and left the morning room.

Outside, the sun at last banished the midmorning mist and the cries of the vendors were louder, more confused.

Sophy lifted the journal at the top of the bundle and spread it on her lap. A savage engraving glared up at her, men and horses and an ugly black cannon moiling among rocks. The Alma, she learned, was a river in the South West Crimean Peninsula. There was a map, and another engraving showing wounded men propped outside a tent: Frenchmen. On the right of the tent, on a stake, was a hand-painted inscription—*Café Tortoni*. She had a vivid picture of the Parisian café, and crowds of painted women and indolent whiskered men on the pavement of the boulevard indifferent to their countrymen's fate.

Connections and heartaching ironies confused Sophy's mind. She looked down from the paper at the stuff of her new green day dress and at her tiny, hand-lasted shoes peeping out from under her skirt. She looked round at the room, polished, shining, immaculate, rich and secure.

She turned another page, and saw the horseman. The sketcher had caught him in the moment of his fall, the gray charger's legs warped and contorted and the hussar flailing backwards in a blizzard of ball-shrapnel. She closed her eyes and tugged the paper and slapped the page down and looked, instead, at the décor of Her Majesty's Private Drawing Room in the Palace of Saint Cloud—neat, regular, ordered, opulent and peopled by overdressed puppets.

But the portrait of the cavalry officer gripped her and obsessed her imagination. She returned to it and sat, for many minutes, with the journal open at that place.

Then, silently, she wept, and not, this time, for herself.

# Ten

The purpose of the dinner party was to formally introduce the Lloyds to the new Madame de Nerval. Though David and Gwen Lloyd had served important functions at the wedding, Sophy had hardly exchanged more than a dozen words with the Welsh couple and was curious as to the extent of the friendship that existed between them and her husband. It was soon apparent that the Lloyds knew her husband better than she did. In the half hour before Miss Frampton called dinner, Sophy was inclined to be jealous of their intimate rapport with Leon, to feel excluded from their familiar badinage.

David Lloyd, for example, declared that he was glad that Leon had "gone off the marriage market at last" as Gwen had been inclined to wed him herself just out of sympathy for his bachelor plight.

"Wouldn't have stood for that, no indeed," the Welshman announced, sipping brandy and lime juice. He was a big, bluff, stoop-shouldered man of thirty-five, a dozen years older than his sister. He had a plump stomach that protruded from the band of his nankeen trousers and showed an acre of shirt frill under the wings of his waistcoat. His jacket was of brilliant azure blue, cut in mastermariner style, with huge flared cuffs and brass buttons as large as *louis d'ors*. An Albert on a gold cable leashed his chest. His sand-colored hair had thinned away from his brow and crinkled over his ears. In a tricorn hat he might have modeled for an Admiral of the Fleet, though his sea-faring experience, so he said, was limited to once falling off the dock steps at Wapping and having to swim for it. "Goodness, no, couldn't have that. Fraternal advice prevailed, glad to say. Couldn't countenance a crass French peasant as a brother-in-law. Bad enough being employed by one. But *related* to one—phew!"

Gwen Lloyd was slender, pert, and fashionable though not ostentatious in her manner of dress.

Sophy said, "Have . . . have you known Leon long, Miss Lloyd?"

"Too long, I say," David interposed. "Since that night we all shared a bed. What a way to start a relationship."

Leon laughed. "And you, Lloyd, have been nudging me in the ribs ever since, you great green leek."

"Shared a . . . a bed?" gasped Sophy. "All three of you?"

"Three pilchards on a plate," said David.

Sophy inspected the couple closely. She had witnessed so many forms of depravity in Paris that she was sensitive to certain eccentricities in Leon's past that may not have been revealed to her before.

As if reading her thoughts, Gwen tapped her brother's shin with her fan and chided him to mind his tongue.

To Sophy she said, "It's not what it seems, Sophy—may I call you Sophy?—and the adventure was innocent enough. We met years ago as passengers on a Dover coach on a wild winter's night, when the railway was closed. The coach overturned near Ashford and we were, it seemed, in peril of our lives from cold and hunger."

"So the bold Frog and I," David put in, "waded through the drifts, found a farmstead and persuaded the worthy farmer to take us in and give us rough lodging. The drivers put up in the barn; Leon, my sister and I were graciously given the alcove bed in the kitchen."

"We did not, under the circumstances," Leon added, "disrobe."

"Nor did we sleep," said Gwen, "with you and David arguing all night about the grain trade."

"Out of that meeting," Leon concluded, "sprang the first de Nerval office in London, managed—though I can't think what came over me—by this lumpkin."

Putting on an arrogant expression, David sprung open his Albert and held it forward so that its ticking filled the room. "For every second that passes, m'lord," he said, "another ha'penny drops into the de Nerval coffers somewhere in the world."

"No thanks to you," Leon said.

Tugging his forelock, or what there was of it, David Lloyd said, "I only counts 'em, master."

The bantering, argumentative conversation between the men continued throughout dinner. David and his sister were vastly interested in Sophy's impressions of Paris and not in the least shocked by the range of her experiences in the *demi-monde*. Gwen Lloyd, though she had traveled much in the low countries, had not been to Paris.

"I shall just have to buy you a husband to take you there," David said. "But not some reprobate who will drag you through the stews as part of your *éducation sensuelle*."

"I enjoyed every moment of it," said Sophy, defending her husband.

"Don't listen to my brother, I beg you," Gwen said. "He talks far too much and says very little of consequence."

"This I will say," David declared, lifting his wine glass; "how our Frog ever managed to secure himself such a beautiful wife is quite beyond my comprehension. Madame de Nerval—Sophy—may I offer a toast to a lady of incomparable charm, and bid you welcome to the enclaves of the House of de Nerval."

Still discomfited, Sophy blushed.

Comfortably supplied with port, brandy, and walnuts, the two men remained in the dining room to smoke their cigars, drink, and wail with laughter at those jokes that, however outrageous, still fell within the bounds of social propriety. Whatever their failings, however strong their friendship, David and Leon were gentlemen and did not discuss matters that would have offended the ladies.

In turn, the ladies retired to the drawing room to drink coffee. Sophy had acquired the habit of coffee-drinking from her husband, and now found tea little to her liking. She was apprehensive about Gwen Lloyd, still faintly suspicious that the relationship between her husband and this attractive girl had not been innocent.

Gwen Lloyd brought the matter into the open at once.

"Leon," she said, dropping a sugar lump into her cup, "was too close a friend to us ever to be considered as a husband."

"In Yorkshire," said Sophy, rather primly, "it is customary for good friends to marry."

"I did not love Leon—not in that way," Gwen confessed, disarmingly. "I always regarded him as a second brother."

"I see," said Sophy.

"I hope *we* shall be good friends, Sophy."

"I'm sure we shall." Sophy smiled. "You must tell me more about my husband. You see, I do not know him well. Does that sound strange?"

"It's not strange in the least," Gwen said. "My father once told me that after thirty years of marriage, the discovery had not gone out of his relationship with my mother."

Sophy remembered her own father and how he had talked of Elizabeth, her mother.

Gwen said, "What a pretty ornament."

Rising, Sophy took the Dresden finch from its place on the mantelshelf and gave it to Gwen to admire. "My first gift from Leon."

"Leon has never been happier," Gwen confided. "Whatever you may believe of him, Sophy, he has never been a social gentleman. No doubt he has seen much of life in his time. But this house, this home you have built together, and a loving wife, those are all that Leon really cares about. I suspect that all his struggles and successes have been for the purpose of achieving just such ends."

"I too suspected it, Gwen," said Sophy, gratefully. "But it is comforting to have it confirmed by such an old friend."

In the weeks that followed, the de Nervals and the Lloyds saw much of each other, dining in Damaris Square or in the Lloyds' house in Hampstead. On two afternoons each week, Gwen and Sophy met and ventured out into the shopping arcades or to take tea in one of the London cafés. There were visits to the theater and ballet, to the latest art exhibitions and educational lectures. In addition to a husband, Sophy found that she had acquired the nucleus of a circle of true and loyal friends.

It was all the more ironic then that Gwen Lloyd should be responsible for sparking off the chain of events that brought Sophy to the brink of despair and all but destroyed her marriage.

Perhaps it was the widening of Sophy's social sphere and the consequent lessening of her dependence on her former governess that spurred Eunice Frampton to hasten on with the scheme that had evolved in her mind as far back as the previous summer. Perhaps it was merely that the woman, after so many years of patient conniving, felt the ache in her bones and the quickening of the months and, having tethered her lamb, as it were, could not resist a quick and sudden strike.

George Bolton was the first evidence of a deliberate maneuver on Miss Frampton's part to take command of the household.

Bolton presented to the world the countenance of a butler born; tall, broad, rubicund, refined in speech and manner, and as autocratic with underlings as it was possible to be without showing cruelty.

He came on the first day of the winter's frost, late, as it happened, into November. He came without preliminary warning and no advance notice, appearing one evening, in full regalia, in the doorway of the family parlor where Sophy and Leon were browsing over playhouse bills for the Christmas season and planning their engagements into the New Year.

Miss Frampton preceded him, and addressed herself to Leon.

"If I might have a moment of your time, sir?"

"Certainly, Miss Frampton."

"I have taken the liberty of inviting a Mr. George Bolton to present himself for interview in connection with the vacant post of butler to the household, sir."

"Have you, indeed!" said Leon, rising and peeping past the governess towards the figure who stood rigidly to attention in the open doorway. "Why?"

"Why?" The pointed question caught Miss Frampton a little off guard. "With a busy Christmas season almost upon us, sir, I felt that the vacancy should be filled."

"Did you advertise the post?"

"No, sir; George Bolton is known to me."

"That is advertisement enough, Miss Frampton," said Leon, without a smile. "As housekeeper you feel it incumbent upon us to acquire the services of a butler?"

"I do, sir."

"Why did you not inform me, Miss Frampton?" asked Sophy.

"The . . . ah, opportunity to avail ourselves of Mr. Bolton's services has only just arisen."

"Bring the gentleman in, then, Miss Frampton, and leave us to conduct the preliminary interview," said Leon.

As the governess made her way to the door, Sophy murmured to her husband, "Do we need a butler, Leon?"

"If he's a good one, then we may take him on."

But there was no meekness in Leon's expression, rather the shrewdness that caused him to veil his eyes into the slumbrousness that told Sophy her husband's agile mind was operating at the peak of its efficiency.

Miss Frampton closed the door, leaving the imposing George Bolton, white gloves, tailcoat and all, upon the carpet.

For a moment Leon kept the man waiting. Sophy noticed how Bolton's eyes flicked sullenly from their fixed point upon the pelmet rail to survey her husband and then herself. Somehow that quick, flickering glance unnerved her and only Leon's relaxed and easy manner gave her enough confidence to stay in the room during the interview.

"Former employer?" Leon asked abruptly.

"Lord McKinnell."

"In London?"

"Scotland, sir. Perth."

"Why did you leave his employ?"

"M'lord died, sir."

"And who took over the household?"

"Son."

"And he didn't care to retain your services?"

"No, sir."

"Why not?"

"Had been too strict with his young Lordship, sir."

"When he was a boy, you mean?"

"Still only a boy."

"You came to London?"

"Home, sir."

"I see. And Miss Frampton, is she a relative?"

"I know her sister, sir, that lady with whom the mistress has an acquaintance, sir."

"Yes, the Cornish sister," said Leon.

Sophy held her breath. Bolton now was no longer simply a butler on trial. He was a fuse that might explode the dream world in which she had been living these past months. The subterfuge became vivid and close. It would be from such a source as this that Leon might eventually learn of her faithlessness and folly.

The butler's eyes flickered and met her own. She glanced nervously away.

Leon said, "You have references?"

"Sir." Bolton reached into his inner pocket and produced a bulky cream-inlaid envelope sealed with a massive wax intaglio.

Though the fire was not high, perspiration dewed Sophy's brow and made her undergarments stick to her skin. The letter itself seemed threatening, like a summons or a confession. She gave a little gasp as Leon accepted the missive and, with his thumbnail, picked off the sealing.

"I see that we are your first choice," Leon said.

"Sir?"

"The seal is intact."

"Yes, sir; fust choice."

Nodding, Leon slid out the letter. It was written on a huge sheet of parchmentlike paper bearing the crest of the McKinnell family, daggers, a fist and a falcon's wings. The writing was flowing copperplate and, to judge from Leon's nods, the recommendations of the worthiness of the servant were glowing.

Bolton watched impassively as Leon read and digested the reference. The butler, Sophy judged, would be in his middle forties. His hair was still dark and thick, trimmed down in a mutton-chop style that seemed more becoming to a gentleman than to a butler in however high a post in however aristocratic a household. Customs in Scotland might be different, of course; she thought she recalled seeing such a fashion on members of the Queen's entourage who were of Scots descent. It was Bolton's mouth, however, that marked him, for Sophy, as a man not to be trusted. It was, she imagined, a slack mouth held constantly firm; the underlip red and full, like that of a compulsive wine-drinker, puckered up and compressed against the long upper lip that jutted below an aquiline nose.

She realized two things at that moment: the first was that she did not want this man in her household; the second, that she might have no choice in the matter.

Leon folded the letter, slipped it neatly into the envelope again and returned it to the butler.

"That," Leon said, "seems to be in order."

"Am I to be employed, sir?"

"Tomorrow," Leon said. "Please call here at this hour tomorrow and I will give you my answer then."

"As you wish, sir," Bolton said. With a stiff-backed bow he dismissed himself from the parlor and closed the door soundlessly behind him.

Hands behind his back, Leon took a turn towards the window then, head cocked, looked round.

"What is your opinion of the fellow, darling?" he asked. "Shall we take him on?"

"Do we . . . do we require a butler, Leon?"

Her husband shrugged. "Yes, I believe we do."

Sophy struggled to keep the conversation going a moment longer. Her instinct was to reject Bolton out of hand. But she was wary, even afraid, of what Miss Frampton would say to that.

"Does he . . . know wine, Leon?"

"According to the letter," Leon answered, "the fellow does everything in the cellar except trample grapes."

"Then," said Sophy, "we should have him."

Leon smiled. "Very well, dearest; if that is what you wish."

Jinny was lady's maid now, though Miss Frampton "when she had time" still attended to Sophy's clothes and her hair. There was less and less communication between the young wife and her housekeeper who, with a bedroom parlor of her own on the upper floor, limited her contact with the de Nervals to a minimum. There were, of course, accounts to go over, a detailing of domestic expenses, which occupied a whole afternoon each week. The figures were meticulously documented in Miss Frampton's own hand and Sophy could find no fault with them. Menus were planned; wholesalers and retailers tested and selected, and the whole administration of the house in Damaris Square generally put into smooth working order within a month—after which, it sailed along placidly enough with the housekeeper at the helm. Jinny, a solemn sixteen-year-old, was being groomed by Miss Frampton to take over the management of the mistress's wardrobe and accessories. Though the girl still had many other chores to attend to, it was not uncommon to find Eunice Frampton and the taciturn Jinny in conference in Sophy's dressing room or the master bedroom. Jinny Malone, of course, was another of the housekeeper's "finds."

In the last week of November, Leon de Nerval was obliged to make a week-long trip to Brussels to attend personally to the purchase of gold stocks from the reserve of a Belgian trader who had sponsored an ill-fated expedition to the South Seas and had lost cargoes and ships in a storm off the Cape Verde Islands.

Gold, Leon explained, would become a trader's last resort; the more of it an international house possessed in private security, the more stable would the business be in the aftermath of war. Gold was the language that every merchant and government spoke, a coin that lost nothing in frontier crossings and that could not be corrupted by the vagaries of weather, strife and man's low cunning.

He left London on a Friday and promised to be home again in eight days.

The Lloyds included Sophy in a theater party that evening, and treated her to a lavish supper afterwards, to ease the loneliness of her first long parting from Leon since her marriage. It was after midnight when the Lloyds' carriage dropped her at the door of the mansion in Damaris Square and, following a cheerful goodnight and promises to call for her tomorrow afternoon, the Welsh couple clopped off into the night for the drive back to Hampstead.

Suddenly lonely and depressed, Sophy rang the doorbell and was admitted to the house by George Bolton. Grave and courteous as always, the man relieved her of her cloak, gloves and bonnet, which he passed to a sleepy-looking Jinny who carried them upstairs. Bolton informed the mistress that he had left a little supper in the parlor should she wish to partake of it before retiring. He then asked permission to dismiss the servants, received it, and, having been given instructions to make the house secure for the night, locked and bolted all the doors and windows and retired, Sophy supposed, to his lair below stairs.

Seated alone in the parlor in all her finery, the young woman drank a last glass of wine. From time to time, she glanced at the clock and at the Dresden finch close by it, thought of her husband rattling across Europe, and wished that she had insisted on making the trip with him.

There was in her now a devotion to Leon de Nerval that was strengthened by his trust in her.

At one o'clock, in a melancholy mood, she made her way upstairs, disrobed and put herself into the large double bed. The warming pan was no consoling deputy for Leon's arms, and she lay for an hour, sleepless and restless, in the darkness. Outside the clocks chimed two, and then the half, and still Sophy lay awake.

At length, shaking aside her troubled mood, she rose on her elbow and prepared to light the lamp, to find a good racy novel to occupy her mind until sleep came. It was at that moment that she heard the stealthy creaking of the main stairs and, in the uncanny silence of the house that still and frosty night, there was no mistaking the footfall.

Catching her breath, Sophy listened intently.

She heard a muffled word, a masculine voice, then that quality of silence that seemed redolent of furtiveness.

Slipping from bed, she opened the door of her bedroom and peered along the corridor.

A lamp strengthened the wan pool of gaslight that bathed the main staircase, its wick rippling color upon the balustrade. Across it, like a shadow, moved the figures. It took Sophy only a moment to recognize the heavy set of Bolton, chest and belly bared, snug black trousers held about his middle with a leather belt, stockings and shoes discarded. He looked younger, less sedate, and his authority was rawer, a male dominance disconnected from his butler's garb and badge of station. Miss Frampton was dressed only in a flimsy frippery of a shift, yoke neckline draped low over her breasts, shoulders exposed. The portrait was flattering; the woman's figure was not revealed as gaunt but as rapaciously womanly. Her hair, unloosed, swamped her back, a thick, musky cascade to her waist. Bolton had one hand about her body, the other fist knotted in her hair, steering her, even as Sophy watched, along the short end of the corridor to the back stairs.

It would not have occurred to Sophy that the governess was a willing victim of the butler's assault if she had not heard low, husky laughter coming from the woman's throat and seen, as the gloom of the corridor's fork absorbed the couple, how Eunice Frampton wriggled coquettishly and drew the nails of her free hand down Bolton's chest.

Then they were gone, the lamplight fading as they descended the stairs to the back room in the basement where the butler had his pantry and his closetlike bed.

Appointed in the neat tweed suit she would wear out that day for her shopping trip with Gwen, Sophy sat rigidly at her dressing table. She had even had Jinny put on the bonnet and tie the ribbons into neat bows under her hair at the nape of her neck. She wore her kidskin gloves, ready to descend to the door to greet Gwen when her friend arrived with the cab. But Gwen was not due for a quarter of an hour and in that time she must perform the impossible task of acting as mistress of the mansion and undertake the beginnings of the campaign that would end in Miss Frampton's departure.

Jinny carried a message to the governess.

A minute later the woman presented herself in the bedroom.

Sophy studied her in the mirror, not daring, for the moment, to confront her directly.

"I . . . I saw you last night, Miss Frampton."

"Saw me, madam?"

"Come now, Miss Frampton, we have known each other too long to mince words. George Bolton is your lover?"

"George Bolton?" repeated Miss Frampton, as if recalling some long-dead king whose name had lodged in her memory. "Our butler, do you mean?"

"Is there another George Bolton of your acquaintance?" snapped Sophy, wheeling round on the velvet stool. "I will not have the moral status of my house lowered in such a way."

"You talk to me of moral status," said the woman, curtly. "How dare you castigate me for caring for a gentleman."

"It's bad for the servants' welfare," said Sophy.

"The servants know nothing," said Miss Frampton. "At least, I am discreet."

"I see. You don't then deny that Bolton is . . ."

"What did you take me for, my dear?" the governess asked, smirking. "Did you suppose that I was made of whalebone and canvas and had starch in my veins? Yes, child; yes, George Bolton is a *comfort* to me. He *is* my lover."

"Miss Frampton, I think the time has come for you to look around for another position. M. de Nerval and I will do everything we can to insure that you find something to suit your talents, a post that pays well. You will not find us niggardly in disbursing thanks in monetary terms for all that you have done for us."

"Will you tell your gentle husband, Sophy, just *what* I've done for you?"

"I . . . Miss Frampton, you put me in an impossible position. If Leon discovered that you were consorting with a butler, he would . . ." Sophy did not complete the threat.

Eunice Frampton had come closer. She reached out a hand. Sophy, in spite of herself, flinched. The strong fingers tweaked out one of the bonnet's bows and dexterously refastened it. Sophy sat motionless as the governess, head cocked, admired her former protégée.

"You haven't really changed, my dear," said the woman, wistfully. "For all the fine dresses and the jewels, you are still my Sophy, my little impulsive child. I've no desire to leave you, or this house. I am happy here, and here I feel secure. I wish to remain, to watch you grow into a mature woman, succeeding as a wife, a mother. I ask it, Sophy, as a favor and not because I feel you to be in my debt. You must, under the circumstances, allow me to remain."

"Very well, then," said Sophy, angrily. "I will ask Leon to dismiss Bolton."

"How unjust that would be," said Miss Frampton, lightly. "Poor Bolton; his only fault has been to . . . ah, become enamored of me. I'm sure you appreciate how that can happen. What am I to do, Sophy—rebuff the poor fellow?"

"I do not trust him."

Miss Frampton laughed at such nonsense.

"You will say next that you do not trust me," she said.

"I *don't*," Sophy blurted out.

The governess's eyes were like pebbles in clay. Her mouth closed to a severe, hard line as she caught Sophy's wrist and, dragging the girl from the chair, held her close.

"You *must* trust me, Sophy. You have no other *real* friend in this house, you know. You might *suppose* yourself too grand for the likes of me now, but I remember you as a distraught, sniveling thing. I remember you fat as a sow in childbearing. And I, and only I, know where the results of your silly folly can be found."

"Then tell me. Tell me where he is!"

Miss Frampton released her.

"What purpose would that serve? Do you intend to give up all this?" she asked.

"I feel that I should be told," said Sophy.

"I take it that you mean your love child and not your lover?"

"Yes, damn you."

"He is safe," said Miss Frampton. "That is all you need know."

"No, it is not all I need know, Miss Frampton. I must know where my son has been . . ."

"Not," the woman said, "while I am in your house, my dear. It is enough for one of us to carry that knowledge."

"What do you want from me?"

"Only what I have already: security of tenure. And perhaps some additional and tangible assurance that you are still my friend."

"Tangible assurance?"

"An occasional little gift, Sophy, would not be out of keeping with the close bond between us. Oh, I may pretend to be housekeeper here—every woman likes to keep herself occupied and I am not one of your snobs who looks down her nose at the domestic servant class—but it *is* pretense. I am your friend; I am, I flatter myself, as close to you as a mother, or, shall we say, a maiden aunt."

"What sort of gifts?"

"Whatever seems fitting."

"Is this blackmail?"

Miss Frampton screwed up her nose in distaste. "Such an ugly word, masking an ugly thought, Sophy."

"You are well paid."

"I don't deny it; but George, *our* butler, does like a woman to look her best."

Outside in the street the rattle of the hackney cab's harness sounded, jolly and sharp in the cold morning air. The hoofs of the horse clattered on cobbles and the driver's cry of "*Heigh-up thar*" penetrated the bedroom.

"Miss Lloyd, I believe," said the governess, turning towards the door.

"Wait," Sophy said. "What will you take to tell me where my baby is lodged, then to leave my house forever?"

Miss Frampton tutted her tongue against her upper lip, and looked slightly pained at the obviousness of the girl's rejection.

"Well?"

The governess smiled. "More than you can afford, my dear," she said.

Sophy settled herself into the corner of the cab and drew up the rough woolen rug that Gwen had provided. The Welsh girl followed her, having come down from the cab and entered the mansion with the express intention of hurrying her friend along.

The sun lit London's pavements prettily, and the morning was crisp and exhilarating.

As the cab lurched and started off round Damaris Square in the direction of the Opal Gardens and Tearooms, Gwen Lloyd broke into Sophy's brooding reverie.

"That man," the Welsh girl said. "Your butler?"

"Bolton? What of him?"

"I am sure that I have seen that face before. I thought so the other evening at dinner, now I am certain of it."

"He was formerly employed by Lord McKinnell in Perthshire in Scotland. Have you ever been to Scotland?"

"Never," said Gwen, frowning. "And yet . . ."

"Perhaps you confuse him with some other man, some person who resembles him."

"Yes, that must be it," Gwen agreed. "According to David there is a manufactory tucked away in the Romney marshes that turns out an endless supply of servants— cooks, maids, butlers—all to a regular pattern."

"And housekeepers?"

"Without doubt," said Gwen. "But not, alas, like your dear, solemn Miss Frampton. She must be a considerable help to you."

"Yes, indeed," said Sophy. "Miss Frampton and I are bound by more than friendship."

And, she was tempted to add, Miss Frampton is a leech who, in time, will surely bleed me dry.

# *Eleven*

Setting aside the mysterious George Bolton, Eunice Frampton was not the only exponent of cunning and contrivance to live under de Nerval's roof. The owner and overlord of the Damaris Square residence was not entirely free of a shady early career, nor wholly scrupulous in the handling of his professional affairs.

Though Sophy had no inkling of the extent and direction of his business interests or of the more nefarious "paper" transactions that Leon, as an adopted Englishman, undertook without a qualm of conscience, the truth was that the Breton trader had been moving for several years towards ascendancy out of the arena of crude commodity purchase and sale and into the circus of high finance.

Like many an immigrant, he had equipped himself well for his new career, setting his sights on secure and settled office backed by wealth and power. With David Lloyd's financial wizardry behind him, Leon had been gathering bills of exchange and establishing a groundwork of valuable contacts in the main cities of Europe and America. In recent months he had concentrated his energies on the acquisition of solid capital—gold.

Locked in his private safe in the study of Damaris Square was enough of the metal to keep the mint in production for half a week. Also locked in that safe was a portfolio of investments into which Leon had seeded his profits through a string of discount houses and infant banks. Of late, de Nerval had grown muscular enough soon to topple the least of these merchant banks, to absorb it, paint his name boldly above its doors and thus establish himself in that complicated circle of gentlemen who controlled the finances of half the world, old and new, and silently steered the destiny of international development.

Duplicates of all root documents, duly witnessed by a reliable amanuensis, were housed in Lloyd's private library in Hampstead and in the files of the deceptively shabby firm of Snodgrass, Morgan and Hare, lawyers to the City.

The premises of Snodgrass, Morgan and Hare were a pace beyond that territory generally recognized as the nub of the empire. Their offices crowded the second and third floors of a sooty commercial block in Farringdon Street, with a salutatory view of the gateway of what had once been the Fleet Prison.

The constant clamor of associated newsmen in and around the Fleet's courts and closes, and the hubbub of flanking tenements contrasted with the arctic silences of the tanks in which upwards of twenty clerks, isolated like tiny wooden monks in a Chinese puzzle, scribbled with muffled nibs in smooth ledgers or apologetically clicked their abacus beads along the frames. The street's endless fuss gave cover for visiting financiers who wished to remain anonymous, all those debtors and creditors, beggars, misers and thieves-out-of-law who earned their daily bread without visible skills.

It was not Leon's first visit. On this occasion, however, he did not pause at the galley rail of the open tank on the second floor, proffer the Snodgrass card and await mute admission to the inner sanctum. This time he climbed on, past floors two and three, high into the attic region where a certain Alfred Dawlish lived and worked, the two things being one and the same to that gentleman.

Pushing sixty, Alfred Dawlish was small, hale, and stocky, possessed of all his hair, most of his teeth, two good eyes and a pair of ears whose sharpness would have shamed a bat.

His one-roomed domicile-cum-office was hidden behind an unvarnished door off the landing at the very top of a corkscrew staircase. Leon's morning messenger had ascertained that Mr. Dawlish would be home that afternoon; consequently, Leon was expected.

In the heronry of clerks below, four or five seniors knew of Dawlish's function. But even they had held the little man in such awe that they steadfastly refused to trade information with their comrades and never bandied about the Dawlish name, referring, when absolutely necessary, only to "him upstairs" or, reverently, to "ol' eyes 'n' ears himself." Not Hare, not Snodgrass, and certainly not Morgan could put a label on Dawlish's profession. And if Alfred had a title for his trade, he kept it, as he kept all things, strictly to himself.

In his youth he had fought the hordes of Napoleon, survived five campaigns without a scratch. In middle life he had worn blue cloth, a chimney-pot hat and drawn fifty annual pounds as a Peeler. When a nervous burglar shot off his left kneecap in a house in Chiswick Mall, however, Alfred Dawlish, being a prudent man, had sought a livelihood less likely to lead him to the knackers' yard.

For fifteen years now Alfred Dawlish had made his living by inquiring with the utmost discretion into the affairs of certain gentlemen and ladies, their standing in society, their resources, their amorous adventures and their general proclivities and characteristics. Most, though not all, of his clients came to him, unknown to themselves, through the offices of Snodgrass, Morgan and Hare. Though Dawlish was not officially employed by the lawyers, rent was free and a "draw" on the block's coal

cellar without limit. For each piece of information duly
collected and copperplated in the form of a confidential
report, he was paid a fee according to the difficulty
involved and the length of time taken to acquire the facts
contained therein. Of those clients with whom Dawlish
worked independently of the parent firm, all were known
to him in advance: Leon de Nerval fell into that category.

Dressed in a neat jacket and fawn waistcoat, Alfred
Dawlish sat behind a small ink-stained desk in the center
of the room. A faded green curtain cut off light from the
street window and hid a quilted cot, chair, table, and
stove. In the part of the room where the interview was
conducted there was nothing at all to distract the appel-
lants' minds from Alfred's questions; no impedimenta on
the desk, no filing cabinets by the wall or grateful
references in ebon frames upon the skirting. Two chairs,
one desk, and a single unlit nickel lamp were all the
properties that Dawlish needed to begin his business with
de Nerval.

Without preliminaries Leon outlined the nature of his
suspicions against certain members of his domestic staff.

"The butler?" Dawlish said.

"Yes, the fellow who calls himself Bolton."

"Who worked in Scotland?"

"Ah, but he did *not* work in Scotland; at least he did
not work for Lord McKinnell as he claimed, nor was the
letter of reference which he presented authentic."

"Might 'ave been," mused Dawlish. "Letter authentic;
butler inauthentic."

"An assumed name?" said Leon.

"Hmm!" said Dawlish.

Leon said, "The man in question is tall . . ."

Dawlish held up one hand, palm uppermost, and closed
his fist. "See 'im for myself, sir: best plan."

"But how?"

"At your house. He's the butler, ain't he?"

Leon nodded. He knew enough of Dawlish's methods not to argue with them. "The housekeeper, too, while you're at it. Her name is Frampton, Eunice Frampton."

A strange faraway look came into Dawlish's hazel eyes. "Frampton, you say, sir?"

"Eunice Frampton."

"Used to be a whole gaggle of Framptons downriver a ways. Nasty lot they was, an' mostly girls if I recalls."

"It's not a rare name, of course," said Leon.

"True, sir," Dawlish admitted. "What's on with that lady?"

"Nothing," said Leon. "Except that she introduced Bolton to my household."

"Must be more, sir, wiff respect."

Leon hesitated. "My wife . . ."

Dawlish sighed, inaudibly. "Your wife, sir?"

"She seems to be under this Frampton woman's sway. Miss Frampton was her governess, I do admit. But . . ."

"But?"

"Find out what you can."

Alfred Dawlish put his hands upon the desk and stirred a dry inkblot with his forefinger, circling it round and round as if to erase evidence of some long-forgotten crime. "Who *am* I to inquire after, sir?"

"This George Bolton—and Eunice Frampton," said Leon, testily.

"And Madame?"

"Madame de Nerval has nothing to do with it."

"Not what yer said just a moment gone."

"Mr. Dawlish, do you imagine that I came here to invite you to spy on my wife?" Leon protested. "That is not only ungallant, but . . . but heinous. I have no reason to suspect Madame de Nerval of *anything*, do you understand me?"

"Perfectly, sir," Dawlish said. He looked Leon straight in the eye. "The lady is in danger, ain't she?"

"I . . . I don't know."

"You're not bein' quite frank an' 'onest, sir, are you now?"

"I don't quite know *what* I want from you, Mr. Dawlish," said Leon, uneasily. "And that is the truth. My wife is much attached to Miss Frampton; yet she seems afraid of her. I fear that there might be a hold there."

"And Bolton?"

"An accomplice?" said Leon.

"And Madame their victim." Dawlish nodded. "Why don't you dismiss them from your service, send the pair packing?"

"My wife would . . ."

Dawlish shifted, leaning his weight on his elbows. "Sir, let's clear the decks and make a-way for the powder monkey, to coin a phrase. You feel that Madame might be under a debt to this pair of codgers. You want me to find out if they're capable of it?"

"In a nutshell, that's it."

"Then I can't do it, sir."

"But why not?"

"Cos it'd mean findin' out what the debt is, and you may not like that, sir."

"If it . . . if it happens," said Leon, very slowly, "then, I will not hold you responsible."

"How long you bin married, sir?"

"Four months."

Dawlish nodded sagely. "Madame has no . . . hm, past?"

"None."

"You wants her protected, not spied upon?"

"Yes."

"Then I'll protect her. How would that do?"

"A verbal nicety, surely."

"Im-per-a-tive," said Dawlish.

"Ah, I see. You want a free hand?"

"Can't work otherwise."

Leon sat back and rubbed his brow with his knuckle. The inquiry agent's insistence on a definition of employment and a detailed brief had more to it than met the eye. Dawlish would watch, listen, sift and sort, and would release only what he, Leon, needed to know to settle or confirm the phantoms of suspicion that had haunted him since his odd conversation with Gwen Lloyd the day after his return from Brussels. Then, too, Sophy's behavior had been . . . strange. He did not care to define it more accurately; indeed, he could not. He had accepted her without question, and he must stand by that pledge. For all that, he believed her to be unhappy and, so instinct warned him, in some kind of danger. He could not challenge her, lest he drive her from him and, if the risk were grave, cause her to lose faith in him.

On the other hand, to put an inquiry agent on to her! No, Dawlish was an old hand. He had given him a ready-made excuse. The inquiry was into Bolton; Miss Frampton was a bonus. And Sophy—well, she would be treated with the utmost respect.

Besides, it was possible that his fears were groundless. The man calling himself Bolton could have drawn the wool over Eunice Frampton's eyes, too. He was, if only he had the gumption to admit it, a shade jealous of the governess's hold over Sophy. He wanted Sophy to himself, to carry into their new life without luggage from the past. But he was also a cautious man who could not bring himself to jettison cargo before he knew what it contained.

Dawlish would solve all that.

"Well, sir, does I 'ave me free hand—or not?"

"Yes, Mr. Dawlish," Leon said. "You have it."

"Reports, verbal?"

"Yes."

"Payment, how?"

"Draw from my account with Snodgrass and let him have the itemization."

Mr. Dawlish stood up and shook Leon's hand.

It seemed an unpleasant contract; for a split second Leon de Nerval was tempted to go back on it, cancel and erase it and let events take their course. But he was curious, and, in the midst of his own financial coups, naturally wary of all small sour notes in the harmony of his life.

Mr. Dawlish said, "By the way, sir, if you happens to see me round Damaris Square, I'd be obliged if you'd refrain from raisin' yer 'at."

"Very well," said Leon. "I won't acknowledge you at all."

"Best not, sir," Dawlish said.

Dr. Blancombe, a paternal general practitioner to middle-class wives, frowned at the lady who perched on the edge of the black leather chair in his consulting rooms in Seton Street.

"No, there should be no difficulty with the birth," he said.

The patient was neither joyful nor afraid. He would have marked her down as hard-bitten except that her soft, pretty features would have belied his theory that upbringing and life's knocks leave indelible traces even on the youngest complexion. She was exceedingly well dressed, was well spoken and well fed. She was also, according to the ring on her finger, married.

Dr. Blancombe said, "Which of my colleagues attended the birth of your first child, Madame de Nerval?"

The young wife licked her underlip. "None of your colleagues, sir. My first child was born out of wedlock to a gentleman other than my husband—a gentleman with whom I have now no acquaintance."

Dr. Blancombe had seen too much of the underside of matrimony to be astonished. He said, "Your husband knows, of course?"

"My husband does not know."

"I . . . see."

"Will you, under the circumstances, attend me?"

"Madame de Nerval, is *this* child fathered by your husband?"

"Yes, without doubt."

"Then," said Dr. Blancombe, "I will attend you."

"When will the birth take place?" Sophy asked.

"June, late in the month."

"It is, I assume, too early to guess of the sex of the infant?"

"Far too early," said Dr. Blancombe.

The woman smiled fleetingly. "It will be a boy, no doubt."

"Is it important?"

"No," Sophy replied. "It has no importance at all."

"Madame de Nerval . . ."

"Thank you, Dr. Blancombe. Good day."

"Good day, madame," the doctor said, and opened the door with no less courtesy than he would have shown to any of his more respectable patients.

George Bolton—formerly George Reginald Odell—stripped back the covers with arrogant haste and motioned Eunice Frampton to climb into the cot. By candlelight a half bottle of Chablis and a quart of milk stout, together with appropriate glasses, waited on the dresser. On the shelf above, away from the waxy smoke, stood a plate of boiled ham and buttered bread.

"Now, my love," George said, "we'll have a liddle diversion 'fore supper, shall we? And you be a good girl or old George'll spank."

"Lay a hand on me in anger or in threat," Eunice Frampton said, snapping the coverlet over her limbs and snaring it around her waist, "and I'll take a flat iron to more than your trousers."

Bolton thrust his hand out and clasped the woman's breast. He would have swarmed upon her there and then with an eagerness that most women over thirty would have found highly flattering. But the Frampton woman was more than meat for the mincer and, that night at least, seemed to need softening before she would yield. He shifted his hand to her throat to pin her—then yelped, stifling the sound, as her teeth sank into the pad of his hand.

"Godstrewth! You bitch!"

"Sit down, George; sit there on the bed end away from me."

Bolton lifted his arm to clout the biter but her expression, like sandblasted granite, stayed him.

She said, "You are careless. You went out today."

"Course I went out. Can't stay cooped up here *all* the bleedin' time. I *am* a butler, you knows."

"You were once a footman, a bad footman," Eunice Frampton reminded him. "*I* made you a butler. Save for that spell of cellar work, and that retentive memory you're blessed with, the disguise would have deluded nobody."

"My talent's in them, though," Bolton smirked, holding up his hands, fingertips hooked forward. "That's the talent you needs, my sweetest."

"You must *not* risk being seen."

"Nobody knows me round these 'ere parts; is it likely, I asks yer."

"Speak decently, will you?"

"I'm sick of this billet t'tell the truth. When will we pull?"

"When I say so."

"What's *in* that bleedin' great brute of a safe?"

"Nothing."

"Nothin'l!" Bolton exploded; then hissed. "You told me . . ."

"Nothing to what may soon be in it if the rumors I hear about our dear employer are true."

"Is it gold?"

"It may be."

"Find out?"

"And how do you propose I do that?"

"Ask 'er ladyship; you can twist 'er round yer finger."

"Certainly, I can *persuade* her," Eunice Frampton said, with some pride. "But I've not set up this venture to have it blown, George, *blown* by impatience."

"Awright, Eunice, dearest heart; let's wait in comfort, though, in bed."

"I can't imagine what Cora ever saw in you."

"She weren't so dry as 'er sister," Bolton retorted.

Eunice Frampton's face bore no hurt at the insult. Even the pleasure she took from him, Bolton knew, was counted out and calculated and utterly selfish, commensurate with the bitch's character.

"What's on, then?" he asked.

"I agree that we must not tarry *too* long," Miss Frampton said. "I cannot quite trust Madam Sophy, cannot be *quite* so sure of her reactions as before."

"She's growed up on you."

"That's true," Eunice Frampton said. "Do you remember little Cloris Escott?"

"A peach; a jewel!" enthused Bolton.

"Whose 'innocence' almost got you caught, and caused my poor sister to retire into hiding."

Chastened by the reminder of that unlucky episode, George Bolton contented himself by nodding his head ruefully.

"Have you examined the safe?" the woman asked.

"I can crack it."

"Swiftly and noiselessly?"

"Easy as pie."

Eunice Frampton sniffed dubiously. "And the plate?"

"Vallable."

"The jewelry?"

"Likewise—what there is of it."

"You understand, George, that it's Ireland for you the hour the job is over?"

"Colleens and donkey races and all the frolics o' the Emerald Isle," said Bolton. "And how about yourself?"

"That's none of your business."

"Is it liable to be done this side o' Christmas?"

"No," Miss Frampton said. "But her dear husband is, I believe, planning a visit to Amsterdam in February."

"With her ladyship?"

"With or without, it hardly matters," Eunice Frampton said. "What *is* important is that I discover just what is within that safe and how much I can persuade Madam to part with by way of information *before* the trader departs."

"Then we bust and run."

"But *not* before I'm certain that the haul is worth it: not a *single moment* before, George."

"Knowin' you an' your ways, my witch, it'll be worth it."

"When I have dearest Sophy sufficiently unsettled, she will become our accomplice."

"Or peep the whistle," Bolton suggested.

"No," said Eunice Frampton. "Sophy will never do that."

Bolton looked from the quart bottle to the ham cuts and back at Eunice Frampton's bosom half-revealed by the drape of her shift.

"So, in the meantime, all I got to do is wait?"

"Keeping well out of sight," the woman said.

"Like, under them covers, Eunice, my love."

Suppressing a sigh, the governess nodded bleakly and, modestly closing her eyes, lay back against the pillow.


Balaclava, Inkerman, battles on the heights, reports of heavy loss of life, slaughter, sickness, and foul weather blotted the pages of the nation's journals in the early winter of 1854 and laid a shadow over Christmas that not even good harvests and home comforts could quite lift.

Sophy was aware of the Balkan war as a frieze on the edge of consciousness. She read the *Times*, the *London Illustrated News*, and glanced at the biting cartoons in *Punch*. Her own affairs, however, soon claimed her attention and she had little pity to spare for the Queen's soldiers in the far-off Crimea. She saw to it that Leon contributed to the *Times* Fund and the Patriotic Fund, and felt a little patriotic herself over the fact that the French and English were fighting together for once and not against each other. But there were too many matters to occupy the young wife in her immediate circle that December, a remorseless march of incidents and episodes whose dreadful accumulation brought on a crisis in her health and circumstances much sooner than even Miss Frampton could have surmised.

Leon was free from any part in these events, stood apart from them and was, at all times, a model husband to her. It was four days before Christmas that Sophy told her husband of her pregnancy. She had no real reason to delay; yet guilt, lying in her heart, made her wait until Leon was relaxed.

Miss Frampton caused Sophy much unrest in the latter days of December. The housekeeper had once more insinuated herself into a position of confidence and put to Sophy certain confidential questions in regard to Leon's business ventures which Sophy, in her ignorance, could not answer. Though Miss Frampton was subtle in her approach, there was no doubt of her intention. She wanted information on that mysterious, amorphous creature called The City, by which, so the governess explained, she meant the state of company stocks and bills.

Still in fear, Sophy had questioned Leon who, delighted that his wife was properly exercising her intelligence, had been at pains to detail his hopes, dreams and plans to her.

Some of this information Sophy had passed on, casually, to appease the housekeeper's curious demands. But Eunice Frampton wanted more—more details: names, dates, figures. For what purpose the former governess needed such facts, Sophy could not imagine; nor did she yield them up without pressure. Eunice Frampton, however, was skillful in manipulating her charge, and extracted much from Sophy that the young woman did not intentionally divulge. By making Sophy defend her husband and her husband's acumen in the City, the infant firm of Frampton & Bolton was soon in a small line of business for themselves, thus smoothing the way for their sudden, inevitable departure from domestic service.

Guilt compounded guilt, fear mingled with anxiety and an inexplicable feeling of doom. Sophy was more afraid for the safety of that infant than she had ever been of anything in her life before. It was illogical to suppose that her unborn baby was threatened with the same fate as her first, lost son, but with Eunice Frampton as a constant threat, Sophy's apprehension increased rapidly into panic.

Leon and Sophy returned late from an evening at the Albany Street Cyclorama with a group of Leon's friends. They had found the scenes stimulating, particularly that of the Lisbon earthquake. A gay supper was taken in rooms near the Albany; convivial company, and champagne, put Leon into a talkative mood. All the way home to Damaris Square the trader talked of his plans for the coming year, and prophesied success piled on success. He was, thought Sophy, more than ebullient—he was arrogant and full of justifiable pride in his accomplishments, as ambitious as any man in London to crown his struggles with secure wealth.

Relieved of their hats and cloaks, the couple wandered into the back parlor where a fire was burning and Bolton had left out wine and cake for supper.

"I am glad, my finch, that you are not like other wives

—interested only in the *proceeds* of their husband's skill. It is a joy to me to realize how interested you are in the mechanics of making money. I do not have to sit at home behind my newspaper, or listen to gossip of nothing but bonnets and hoops and town tittle-tattle. That has its place. But it pleases me that you are versed enough in City matters to question me and understand my answers."

Seated on the ottoman, Sophy said, "In banking, Leon, will you require to travel as much as you do now?"

"Absolutely not, darling," Leon said. "In a year's time—less if all goes well—I will be able to sit in my office in Lombard Street and build up my portfolios of better-quality bills without budging an inch. Not for me a discount sharing with some upstart middleman or the need to kowtow to the Old Lady of Threadneedle Street. I will be my own lender of last resort."

"And come home each evening?"

"Dinner at eight, without fail."

"Not seven, Leon?"

"Seven if you wish, love."

"In time," said Sophy, "to kiss your little son good-night?"

Leon smiled, not grasping the point. "Of course."

"We must look out for a suitable nanny: a kindly one," said Sophy.

In an instant Leon was beside her. He did not know whether to smile or frown, whether to be filled with delight at her news or stricken with paternal responsibility.

"Do you m—mean . . . ?" he stammered.

"Yes, Leon."

"But . . . how did you . . . ?"

"I have attended a doctor; a good doctor . . ."

"We must, must have the best: *oui*, only the best."

"A glass of wine to steady yourself, Leon."

"*Oui*: yes, wine." Obediently and at great speed, the Breton trader decanted a glass of Madeira for himself and, spilling it over the rim, rushed back to his seat on the ottoman. He stared at her, gaping in boyish awe, all trace of sophistication erased from him. "See: I have my wine, Sophy. Now, tell me what the doctor . . ."

"I'm with child, of that there's no doubt. I'm also healthy, and the babe appears healthy and . . ."

"Take care! You must take care. Boil the water. Eat sparingly. Drain the vegetables."

"Leon, Leon, my darling!" said Sophy, laughing.

"He must have . . . have things: suitable warm clothing; a cot; a nursery; the room on the first landing, is it dry enough for . . . ?"

"Not until June, Leon."

The trader's head turned to the front again and he stared vacantly into space, as if the force and magnitude of her announcement had stunned him. "I am to be a father; in June; *Mon Dieu!* Leon de Nerval—a father!"

With a sudden loud whoop, the City gentleman leapt to his feet, reached out his arms for his wife, then hesitated, appalled at his own energetic enthusiasm.

Sophy said, "I may be your finch, Leon, but I'm *not* made of porcelain."

Laughing, Leon swept her into his arms and, hugging her, danced about the parlor.

Neither one noticed the door opening, nor, for a minute or two, saw Miss Frampton's gaunt form framed against the yellow gaslight of the hallway.

Breathless, Leon stopped and set Sophy down.

The housekeeper cleared her throat.

"Ah, Miss Frampton," said Leon, with unusual warmth to the woman. "I'm sorry if we disturbed you. You may as well be the first to know that Madame is about to become a mother."

Miss Frampton's mouth inched upwards, hooking into a smile.

"That *is* good news, sir," she said.

Sophy looked past her husband, waiting.

"Come, we must celebrate," said Leon. "Is there in the cellars a magnum of champagne, do you know?"

"Leon, it is late," murmured Sophy; her protest went unheard.

Eunice Frampton stepped into the room.

In her hand was a silver salver; on it a letter.

"This letter arrived by evening delivery," the housekeeper announced. "It is addressed to Madam."

"Can't it wait?" said de Nerval. "We have enough invitations . . ."

It was the trader's turn to pause. Visibly the exuberance drained out of him as he caught sight of the envelope's black border.

Lifting it, he carried it to his wife who had seated herself once more on the ottoman.

By the door Miss Frampton waited. Sophy slit the fastening and read the curt note within.

"Bad news, Sophy?" said Miss Frampton.

"My father," Sophy said in a small, timid voice. "My father died three days ago. He is to be buried tomorrow."

At once the boyishness was gone from Leon de Nerval. Pivoting, he demanded, "*When* did the letter arrive?"

"Tonight, sir; at six."

"Waken Miller," Leon said. "Send him at once to Fox's Hirings. I want a closed two-horse coach here within the hour."

"Why, Leon; why?" said Sophy.

"In spite of your stepmother, Sophy, we will pay our last respects," Leon said. "Miss Frampton, make ready our warmest clothes."

"Yes, sir," Miss Frampton said.

The housekeeper hurried into the kitchen, and through it. Shooting back the latch-bolt, she burst in upon George Bolton so abruptly that the butler started from his chair and spilled stout all over his nightshirt.

"Where's Miller?"

"In his attic, I suppose. What's amiss? Are we rumbled?" Bolton asked in a shrill voice.

"No." Miss Frampton paused long enough to close the pantry door with her elbow. Drawing the butler close to her, she put one hand around the nape of his thick neck and, grinning, told him the news. "Her father's snuffed it. And, what's more, my little Sophy's in calf again."

"So?" said Bolton, bemused.

"It's perfect, George. Don't you see, you lumpkin? Now we can make her pay."

Bolton's scowl changed gradually to a grin and the grin to a throttled laugh.

"So we can; so we can. Gawdstrewth! And 'er in calf."

"Yes, George, by Derby Day you'll be snug in Ireland."

"Rich," Bolton said. "Rich!" And he executed a heavy-footed polka round his room until Miss Frampton put a stop to the celebration and sent him packing to rouse the Boots.

# Twelve

Snow swathed the high passes through the dales and banked up the railway lines, blocking the tunnels. In the lower falls of land the ground stood burned by frost, iron hard, and cloud cover, like tinplate, lidded the sky from Sheffield northwards. By train and coach the de Nervals struggled through a twilit countryside, emerging only imperceptibly from night into a darkened day and back once more into dusk.

By noon, it was apparent that all hope of reaching Huffton before nightfall had gone. Not all Leon's lavish expenditure or planning of routes, not all his bullying of guards and coachmen could breach the wintry defenses of the Yorkshire Ridings.

Huddled in corners under rugs, Sophy nursed her feelings of isolation, cherishing the one small ludicrous hope that Agatha had played a cruel trick on her and that her father was not dead at all but merely ailing. Love had restored itself too late.

Leon's arm about her, his subdued concern for her welfare, and his occasional vain attempts to talk her out of her depression, all served no purpose. She wanted her father: not Agatha's husband, not the old fool who had allowed himself, in his gentleness, to be pulled down into premature senility by the woman's cunning. She wanted the man who had walked with her on the crest of Huffton Pike and talked with her in the quiet lamplit rooms of the mansion. She wanted the memory of her father, to be again as she remembered herself, young, virginal, and protected.

The irony of Christmas signs in the towns they passed through, the bustle of markets wrapped against the weather, brought up deep memories in Sophy. She remembered how, on Christmas morning, she had walked round the barns and cattle sheds with her father, how he had made a ritual of feeding his stock—oats for the cows, mangers of hay for pastured sheep. And she looked up out of the window of the crawling railway carriage and saw a village clock tower and the hands at two and she knew that, long before she reached home, her father would be interred in the graveyard under the church wall by her mother's side.

She wept, softly. Leon rested her head against his chest, saying nothing.

In a state of tension and fatigue the couple reached Huffton House at a quarter after four. The carriages of the mourners and those commercial friends of Thomas Richmond's who had poured from the surrounding towns had gone, rolling off quickly after the service to avoid becoming snowbound in the depths of the countryside. The scores of the wheels had fretted the thin icy snow-coat on the driveway. On the plateau before the mansion's doors, there remained only the lawyer's brisk chaise, isolated and horseless, shafts leaning as if it had been abandoned in flight. The whole façade of the mansion was in shadow. No lights showed. Skeletal trees crowded behind it, dykes and fences of the pastures like mounds of coal dross against the sprinkled snow. Sheep nosed disconsolately around the mangers. Two stooped and anonymous figures carted bows of hay from the barn.

Leon helped Sophy from the coach, escorted her up the shallow steps and rang the bell.

A strange servant opened inquiringly, took Sophy's name and that of her husband and disappeared into the nook by the dining-room door. Sophy, unfastening cloak and gloves, looked all around. The mansion had no smell today, and no unfamiliar sounds. She noticed one new piece of furniture in the hall, a massive carved dresser decorated with four branches of staghorn—ugly and useless.

The servant returned with Mr. Cairncross, her father's lawyer. He was a lean, bearded Scotsman in his early sixties, his sandy complexion reflected in hair like bleached barley and spectacles rimmed in brass wire. He held out his hand, drily offering commiserations to Sophy, and, as an afterthought, to Leon; then he ushered the couple without further ado into the dining room where, to an audience of one, the clauses of the will were being duly read.

Her long face hidden by a veil of freckled black lace, Agatha Richmond started at the sight of her stepdaughter. It had obviously been her intention to have this day, this particular hour to herself. That she had deliberately delayed in sending the news went without saying. Sophy had no heart to charge the woman with the deception at that moment.

Lawyer Cairncross pulled out a chair for Sophy, then awkwardly resumed his seat at the window end of the table. He cleared his throat. "I . . . ah, I'd almost finished. Shall I begin again?"

"Tell us," said Leon sharply, "the essence of the legacies."

Ill at ease, Cairncross prodded his spectacles onto his nose and rummaged among his papers as if in search of inspiration.

"Sophy: Madame de Nerval," he began.

Agatha interrupted. "There is nothing."

"Nothing for my wife?" Leon said. "Or nothing at all?"

"Nothing for any of us," said Agatha. "Your . . . your father . . ." The woman controlled herself with great effort. "He left debts, many debts. I can hardly bear to face the shame of it."

To Cairncross, Leon said, "How serious?"

Cairncross shook his head, and riffled his papers again.

"Poor Thomas wasn't himself lately. His judgment, I fear, was unsound," the lawyer said.

"Where is the documentation?" asked Leon.

"It is confused, sir," said Cairncross.

"But is it available?"

"Indeed, I have it."

Sophy hardly heard the voices. Waves of weariness swept over her, brushing away animosity, nostalgia and even grief. She thought of her father, safe now, with her mother in Heaven, far from the turmoil of this house and the evil calumnies of this woman. Safe: at rest.

"Leon?" she whimpered. "*Leon?*"

Cairncross, relieved perhaps, was on his feet in the instant. But it was her husband who reached her first and supported her as she slumped from the chair.

Leon lifted her and carried her; she felt as light as thistledown. Once, when she had had a childhood fever, her father had carried her so; she had clung to him and felt not ill, only weak, and in her weakness comforted and utterly secure.

It was the same that evening and throughout that night as she lay in the bed in the upstairs room in the house in which she had been born. Waking intermittently, she found Leon there. He wore his brown wool dressing gown and his hair was tousled, yet he did not seem harassed or concerned. He smiled at her gently, touched her brow and told her to sleep. His voice was a murmur, unbelievably soothing. "Sleep, little finch. Sleep." Like a bear, a guardian bear. "Sleep."

It was two nights and a day before Leon allowed Sophy to rise from bed; Christmas Eve, in fact. Sophy had no true awareness of time, only of season, and the solidity of the mansion around her, and its emptiness.

"Your stepmother has taken the children to Manchester

to spend Christmas with a friend," said Leon as Sophy, still shaky, sat by the fire in the upstairs parlor and ate soup from the bowl that Leon had brought her. "She felt that, under the circumstances, her duty was to her sons."

"A strange duty, Leon."

Leon smiled and shrugged. "She is a strange woman, after a fashion, though I have met several of that selfish bent. Are you concerned about her?"

Sophy shook her head. "I had hoped that we would be home again for Christmas. We will miss so many dinner parties and suppers, and the Lloyds are expecting us on . . ."

"Hush, finch!" Leon told her. "You have had a slight fever, that's all. If the climate remains kind, we will travel home again the day after tomorrow."

Sophy looked round the room, then out across the snow-laced fields, visible through the parted curtain. "Christmas here," she said. "How odd it will seem."

Leon stretched, and scratched his chest with his knuckles under the opening of the dressing gown. He did not, Sophy thought, seem at all distressed by the confusion of events.

"A breath of country air will do us good," Leon said. "I grow tired of London at times. It is my peasant blood, I suppose. I'm sorry, however, that the circumstances could not have been more congenial."

"Have you visited the grave?"

"Yes," Leon said. "It is like all graves—not much of anything."

Sophy nodded. Her father seemed remote from her, and yet, consolingly, closer than for many years. The relief of not having to face Agatha at this time was vast. She suspected that, somehow, Leon was behind her step-mother's abrupt departure.

The larders were well stocked, the cellar not quite empty. With the servants who lived in the region dismissed to their homes, Leon and Sophy spent the Christmas season alone together in Huffton House. In the ending of another phase of the mansion's history, Sophy discovered a fresh beginning.

As to the debts and muddled affairs of business that her father had left in his wake, Sophy was happy to leave their settlement to Leon. The one true moment of sadness came when she stood by the raw earth of Thomas Richmond's grave under the stunted alder tree by the churchyard wall. It looked so cheerless in the wintry gloom, undefended by shrubs and flowers. But she took some consolation from the weathered lettering on the headstone that, for twenty years, had waited for its concluding lines and that said man and wife were at last together and could not by any interloper be put apart for all eternity.

On Boxing Day, the de Nervals returned to London.

By that time, though she was only dimly aware of it, a new complication had entered Sophy's troubled life. She had fallen completely in love with her husband.


Though he was not a superstitious man, Leon de Nerval harbored forebodings about his imminent journey to Amsterdam. The meetings there would bring about the final coup in the series of maneuvers that had occupied him for four years. Three Dutch gold merchants had acquired a large collection of pure plate that had come, piecemeal, from Russia. It now awaited a purchaser who would exchange good English stocks for it, not inquire too thoroughly into the plate's origin and arrange to have it shipped secretly from Le Havre to Port of London in a manner that would not bring a gleam to the eyes of the Queen's excisemen or harbor authorities.

Paper money and bills of hand were all very well, but the backing of bullion, Leon judged, would set his future on a pinnacle of security from which he could view and select the best of the government contracts that were going a-begging in that first full year of war. In addition, following Nathan Rothschild's lead, Leon had set trap-lines for reliable foreign trade, much of it in America. The goods would never come within a thousand miles of the Dover coast, yet he would insure that the transactions left substantial percentage deposits in his coffers in London.

Few City men were aware of the extent of de Nerval's stratagems, or the depth of his financial resources. In fact, it was rumored here and there in Westminster that de Nerval was only an upstart "bubble-merchant" who would pop in the first wind to blow chill from the credit depositories.

David Lloyd, architect of de Nerval's master plan, kept his mouth shut and, with his usual effusion, parried all inquiries. Snodgrass, Morgan and Hare, though *au fait* with Leon's designs, would have downed a bumper of hem-lock before they so much as twitched an eyebrow in acknowledgment of their client's true standing. Let the City wait for its small sensation, the roaring of a new lion in the jungle.

There was no avoiding it, however, the last run to Holland had to be made personally. Weather, war, and unusual domestic affairs must be put aside until this final piece of business was concluded.

Sophy worried him. She had been more melancholy than ever since her father's death. Leon had taken on the onus of the legal complications and, through Cairncross, had delved into Thomas Richmond's commercial indiscretions with patience and thoroughness. He communicated little to Sophy who, quiet and grave, had sunk into herself in the month after Christmas. Leon even had a meeting with Agatha, in an unfashionable hotel in Chiswick; the woman had returned to her former haunts in search, he suspected, of yet another husband to be a father to her sons. The upshot of that meeting was comforting for Agatha Richmond and beneficial to Leon de Nerval, though he also kept this secret to himself, guarding it as jealously as he guarded his portfolios.

In this time of great activity, he was careful to present a calm, unruffled appearance in Damaris Square. Sophy, he realized, was in need of consolation; strength, not pampering. He gave this to her as best he could in the intervals between his business jaunts. But as the day of his departure for Holland came closer, Sophy's withdrawn condition became more and more distressing to her husband. He imagined that she was pining; pining for her father, or Huffton House, or for—for what he could not fathom.

It occurred to him that the child in her womb might be a factor in her morbid mental state. Several doctors assured him that this was improbable; Gwen Lloyd, when taken into his confidence, also did her best to quash that notion. Gwen promised that, in his absence, she would make herself a permanent guest in Damaris Square, and "camp" on the doorstep if Sophy would not cooperate.

Two days before embarking on the Channel packet, Leon once more took a cab to Farringdon Street and toiled up the high staircase to the attic level to keep an appointment with Alfred Dawlish.

"I expected to hear from you before now," were Leon's first words.

Seated in his round chair behind the desk, Dawlish said, "Been confirmin' certain facts."

"And are they confirmed?"

"Up to a point; only up to a point."

"Tell me what you have discovered."

"Bolton's a rogue sure as eggs," said Dawlish. "He served the Queen on the oakum bench and the rockpile in Coldbath Fields."

"For what crime?"

"Assault and robbery."

"How long ago?"

"He took six, served four and seems to 'ave been out for eight or more."

"What's the villain been up to in the interim?"

"Not certain yet."

"And the woman—Eunice Frampton?"

"Ah, now there's a pee-culler case," said Dawlish.

"Is she too a felon?"

"No, sir, not her; but she comes from a fam'bly that had a reputation for all sorts of tricks."

"I'm not interested in her family," snapped Leon. "Heaven knows, my own genealogy won't bear much looking into."

Smiling, as if the narrative amused him, Dawlish told his client several pertinent facts concerning the Framptons. He did not mention Kate Dreyer, but came quickly to Cora. "Sister Cora had a close-run thing with the force of law 'n' order. Noffink proved, though. She took orf like a rabbit for its burrow."

"She's in Cornwall now," said Leon. "My wife . . ."

Dawlish studied him, waiting.

"Your good lady *knows* Cora Frampton?"

"Yes."

"I see."

"Are you being straight with me, Mr. Dawlish?"

"Straight as I can be, sir," Dawlish replied. "Cora Frampton's mate in the close-run thing was George Bolton; different name, o' course, but the same gent without doubt."

"What was the nature of this 'close-run thing,' Dawlish?"

"Can't say yet, sir."

"Can't or won't?" Leon demanded; convinced that Dawlish was treading round and round the subject like a nervous cat.

"Can't; not yet."

"How soon will you have the information?"

"A week I hopes; takes time, you know, sir. Isn't done open or above boards."

"No, no, I appreciate that," said Leon.

"Madame de Nerval, sir . . . ?"

"My wife? What about my wife?"

"Does she need protection?"

"Dawlish, if you mean . . ."

Dawlish licked his upper lip without wetting it. He was relaxed, not nervous in any way, merely reticent, careful of the effect that his revelations might have on the gentleman. He knew only too well that Leon de Nerval was a powerful man. Powerful men, of all persuasions, had to be treated with caution, the more so when Snodgrass, Morgan and Hare had given the nod that even *they* held this Frog in considerable esteem. It was not de Nerval's rank, however, that the little investigator respected so much as the flaw in his character which might make him vengeful —the flaw, as any fool could see, being his missus.

Gruffly, Dawlish cleared his throat.

"Does Madame know, sir? That's the rub."

"Does Madame know what?" asked Leon, warily.

" 'Bout her housekeeper. You say she's been with the lady many a year now, as governess."

"You've proved nothing against Eunice Frampton."

"That's true."

"You have only hearsay evidence against Cora Frampton?"

"Yus."

"And nothing, I take it, against my wife?"

"Oh, no; dear me, no."

"Bolton, however, is worth the watching?"

"In my 'umble opinion," said Dawlish, "the redoubtable George ain't reformed; he's only lying doggo. He may mean no 'arm, o' course, but . . ."

Leon got to his feet. He was more confused than ever and his apprehension had increased. He had anticipated some sort of comfort from Dawlish's report, at least a few truths. But all he had to carry away were vague stories of criminal happenings a decade ago, and a garbled tale of a "close-run thing," which could be any scrape from padding the household accounts to murder.

"I'll be leaving London for ten days or a fortnight, Mr. Dawlish," Leon said, stiffly. "In that time, I would be grateful if you would continue your inquiries."

"In any partic-u-lar direction, sir?"

"No, that's up to you."

"Will Madame de Nerval be accompanyin' you?"

"No, Mr. Dawlish; my wife will remain in Damaris Square."

Alfred Dawlish grunted.

"Does that not meet with your approval, Mr. Dawlish?"

Dawlish rose and offered his hand again; in his experience gentlemen liked shaking hands. It also signified that he had no more to say and would not be baited for simply doing his job with tact and diplomacy.

"*Bon voyage*, sir," he said. "I 'ope the Channel's kind to you."

"Thank you," Leon said curtly, and went out.

Alfred Dawlish stepped through the curtain. Standing by the side of the little window, he craned his neck to look down into the street. Should take about four minutes for a spry youngish man to make the descent—unless he called in on old Snodgrass on the way. In three minutes, Leon de Nerval debouched into the street.

Dawlish sighed, and watched.

De Nerval did not summon a cab. He crossed the road and headed back on foot towards the City at a high rate of knots, his arms swinging and his chest thrust out under his overcoat. He looked like a little pugilist spoiling for a fight, thought Dawlish; a bantam in search of a heavy-weight to tame.

If only the poor Frog knew the whole sorry story, he

would not, thought Alfred Dawlish, charge at the world
with quite so much authority.

Still, it wasn't up to him to question, only to unearth
facts. He would have his chance at that game over the
next couple of weeks, when the client was in Holland, and
he, a nondescript spectator, had a clear field to spy on the
client's wife.

"Why do you question me, Leon? Do you doubt me?"

"No," Leon said. "I am merely curious."

"Curious," said Sophy, testily. "Suddenly, now, you
are curious."

Leon lay back against the huge soft pillow of the
double bed. Sophy, in the anteroom, changing into her
night clothes, said, "Why do you ask me these questions
tonight; is it because you are leaving tomorrow?"

"Partly," Leon admitted. "But I always did think it
strange that, when I called on you first in London, you
were living in the house of a notorious rake."

"*I* didn't know that."

"Miss Frampton . . ."

"Miss Frampton did not know it either, I'm sure."

"Are you certain, Sophy?"

"Quite certain."

Sophy appeared from behind the embroidered screen
that guarded the entrance to her sanctuary. She wore a
long flowing robe over her shift and her hair, loosened,
fell about her shoulders. She looked, Leon thought, darkly
tragic now, with smudged shadows under her eyes. She
gave him not so much as a glance as she turned out the
lamp, snuffed the bedside candle and, in darkness, slipped
out of her robe and entered the bed.

She lay on her back, tense.

Leon turned on his side and groped for her hand. She
allowed him to touch it, clasp it, but did not yield to him
or return his fond gesture.

"I worry," said Leon. "I worry about you, my love."

"About your child."

"Ah, yes, about him too."

"Only about him."

"That is unjust, Sophy."

"If you worried about me, as much as you say, you would not badger me with such questions."

Leon turned away from her. "I do not trust the Frampton woman."

Sophy was silent for a moment, then said, "Well, Leon, I trust her implicitly, and I know her a good deal better than you do. You have been put off by her strictness of manner. That is only her way."

"Yes," Leon capitulated. "I daresay you are right, darling. I am naturally suspicious of anyone close to you."

"Good night, Leon."

"Good night, Sophy."

Even now she did not unbend, drawing herself away a little as he sought to kiss her.

Leon lay quiet for some minutes, then asked, "Do you like living here?"

Sophy pretended not to hear.

Leon put his hand on her shoulder. "Sophy, do you enjoy London life?"

"Have I any choice?" she said.

The retort was uncharacteristically shrewish. Leon ignored it. He did not wish to fight with her on his last night at home—yet he was troubled, unhappy at this state of suspicion between them. All his fault, of course; he should never have embarked on the inquiry in the first place.

"No," Leon said, lightly. "No choice, Sophy. You must do as your husband wills—is that not the law in England?"

"And what *do* you will, Leon?"

"I wish you to be happy."

"I am . . . happy."

"Good," he said. "Then kiss me, finch, before I trudge off into the wilderness."

"Holland is a most civilized country."

"You *are* out of humor."

Sophy relented; she shifted against him and put her arm across his chest. A less sensitive man might have taken advantage, have pushed on with his questioning. But Leon de Nerval was too astute, and, at that time, too uncertain of himself to seize the chance.

He covered her arm with his hands, holding her to him. "Sophy," he said. "I love you very dearly."

In a small, shy voice, Sophy said, "I know."

She kissed him then, lovingly, and in his arms eventually fell asleep.

The cab rolled across the cobbles, drawing away from the house, from his home. Never before, had Leon de Nerval, that seasoned traveler, felt so torn at the prospect of leaving one place for another. There was a faint gilding of sun on the façades of the mansions in Damaris Square, though mist lay on the grass of the little park and, in adjacent narrow lanes, thickened into a still, yellowish fog. All along the railings rugs and carpets were already hung out, servants were busily sweeping the area courts and, here and there, knelt to freshen steps with chalkwash from wooden buckets.

The cab swung round the corner of the square heading up towards New Road. On impulse, Leon lowered the window and, leaning out, looked back at his property.

The front door still stood open.

It was not Sophy, however, who lingered on the threshold to watch him out of sight, but Eunice Frampton. Even as a clump of evergreens interrupted his view, he saw the butler, Bolton, step behind the woman and lay a hand on her shoulder. Leon craned to see more of that strange, brief intimate scene but the shrubs impeded him;

then his attention was caught by a slight figure strolling casually out of Wisden Street into Damaris Square.

The figure was dressed in a heavy black overcoat, like a mariner's pea jacket, and a squashed old-fashioned beaver hat. He carried a stick under his arm, not malacca but ash, and had the air of a would-be gentleman passing the time until luncheon. Then Alfred Dawlish, too, was gone and the gables of Woodigate Road blocked any further observations.

Wondering, Leon sat back against the leather bench.

The cab was picking up speed, swaying, weaving among stationary drays and tradesmen's carts.

Amsterdam seemed a million miles away. Perplexed, Leon consoled himself with the thought that Gwen Lloyd would arrive before luncheon and, welcomed or not, would stay over until his return. Dear bright trustworthy Gwen: he could surely depend on her to keep order until his return. Settling, he tried to turn his mind to enthusiasm for his Dutch purchases, his ultimate trading venture. But anxiety about Sophy still hung over him like a cloud.

If he had known that Gwen Lloyd was, at that very moment, attending her feverish brother in their house in Hampstead and would not, for over a week, be free of the chore of nursing David through a severe bout of influenza, then Leon de Nerval's concern would have known no bounds.

George Bolton slowly closed the door. He turned, pursed his slack lips and raised an eyebrow questioningly.

Eunice Frampton nodded.

"When?" Bolton asked.

"Tomorrow night."

# *Thirteen*

The governess came to her that night. Lonely and disconsolate, Sophy sat by the parlor fire, nursing remorse at the deceptions she had been forced to play upon her kind and loving husband. She had even sent him off without much show of love. How would it be with them in ten years if she permitted her marriage to descend into emotional estrangement? She would be no better then than Agatha. The baby would not bring them closer. On the contrary, in her present mood, she felt that the baby, whether boy or girl, would only serve as a living reminder of her infidelity.

For weeks she had surrendered to Miss Frampton like a weak and frightened child. She had sold her husband's secrets to placate the woman without knowing what she hoped to gain from the payments. Did she buy silence, or did she bid for pity? Decisions confused her and increased her misery.

It had come as a blow to Eunice Frampton that the Yorkshire estate was bound up in litigation, and that Sophy's share would amount to very little. Becoming careless in her power, Miss Frampton had allowed her frustration to show, and Sophy, though dunned by deceit, was not slow in interpreting the woman's reaction. Miss Frampton, and probably that butler too, had many plans laid, many profitable avenues open, and had thought so far ahead that she, without Leon's strength, quailed before their deviousness and complexity.

The yielding up of a few scraps of information on Leon's plans was as nothing compared to her willingness to barter security for information on her first child's whereabouts. In holding that secret to herself, Eunice Frampton retained control. Sophy could not determine whether she wanted the woman to vanish—would *pay* her to disappear from her life—or whether, in so doing, she would relinquish her one faint hope of redeeming her firstborn son.

Where was he? Was he safe, comfortable, well cared for, as Miss Frampton assured her? Or was the infant already dead? In Sophy, instincts of motherhood, as raw and fierce as those of a threatened animal, stirred. What hope was there for her, and for her marriage to Leon, when she could commit herself now to an unnatural crime of such enormity? It would be better to give up everything —even Leon's love—than to draw him unwittingly into this web of lies.

That night, that quiet, foggy night, in her elegant home in Damaris Square, Sophy edged herself towards decision. Fear and self-disgust were strong in her. Only Eunice Frampton, and a chance discovery, altered her destructive emotions, whetted them instead into a dreadful burning anger.

She had expected Gwen Lloyd. But David was ill, a note delivered by hand had told her. Now, late into the night, she realized that she would not have welcomed Gwen Lloyd's company. The events of the past year had streamed down into the pool of loneliness and silence in the parlor of the house in Damaris Square. She had to be alone, to be at the mercy of her governess who, it seemed, was the tangible embodiment of her past and the configuration of all her foolishness and greed.

Caught between her instinctive desire to buy back her

son, and to preserve Leon's love, she had reached a pitch of indecision that caused her physically to tremble. Every nerve, every muscle in her body quivered with the sensation of entrapment. When the parlor door creaked and softly opened, she spun round with a cry as if she had been attacked.

"It is late, Sophy, my dear," Miss Frampton said, unctuously.

Sophy regarded the woman malevolently. Hatred was diluted by envy of her forthrightness and her power. Always she had succumbed to that force—in Agatha, in Eunice Frampton, even, too, in Edmund Sutton, she supposed. She had no direction, meekly followed the example of women whom she did not admire, men whose fire stemmed from selfishness. Only in her meeting with Leon had she been fortunate; more than fortunate, blessed. Was it some sad strain in the Richmonds that they should be victims of the world's schemers, unable to defend themselves?

Look how the housekeeper appeared before her: the provocative gown, bought and worn for her lover's benefit, was a mockery of love, symbol of that lurking sensuality which Eunice Frampton had hidden so well. She could reveal it now, however, flaunt it. Her utter disregard for Sophy's authority could be quite openly displayed in this house without a heart. She seemed to shout out that *she*, not Sophy, was mistress of the property.

"Should you not retire?" asked the governess.

"I will retire when I wish, not before."

"I put the warming pan in your bed an hour ago."

That she could have allowed herself to be led by this woman, to envy her—Sophy got to her feet, pivoting away from the hearth.

Out of the corner of her eye she saw the Dresden finch upon its perch on a corner of the mantelshelf. The Dresden finch: even Leon, her husband, thought of her as a piece of delicate, fragile porcelain. How she appeared to Eunice Frampton, to Bolton, to the gaggle of servants whom the woman had vetted and employed, could only be guessed at.

Sophy said, "My husband does not trust you, Miss Frampton."

Impassively, the governess said, "I have long been aware of that."

"That lodging in Pelican Lane, for instance; M. de Nerval informs me that it was rented from a man of very low character and repute."

"Most suitable, I thought," said Eunice Frampton.

"You knew of it?"

"Of course: I made the arrangement with the gentleman," the governess confessed, with a smile. "How naive of you, Sophy, to scorn my methods."

"Who is he?"

"His name is unimportant," said Miss Frampton. "He kept his mistress there—until he tired of her. He was not in London when we 'borrowed' the house."

"I take it that he is a friend of yours."

"Of my dear sister Cora's," said Eunice Frampton. "But what's the point of this, my dear. You are as much a hypocrite as I am, you know. You made yourself blind to consequences, and cannot now cry innocence. We English are a nation of blind men and women, born deceivers. We have raised self-deception to a high art. If you do not believe me, or if you think me cynical, I ask you to consider what your husband is about at this very time."

"That is business," said Sophy.

"It is all business, Sophy. We women are traders, too. We must make what we can before our stock ages. Have you, for example, not capitalized on your beauty?"

"Miss Frampton," said Sophy, ignoring that taunt, "what do you intend to do?"

"Do?" The governess spread her hands in incomprehension. "I intend to serve you for many years yet, my dear."

"And bleed me dry in the process?"

"Favors deserve favors, do they not?"

"For the love of God," said Sophy, "do not play this game any longer. Tell me—what will you take to reveal the whereabouts of my baby?"

"More than you can presently afford, my dear."

"I have . . . I have jewels."

"Not enough."

"I can . . . get money," said Sophy; "if that's what you wish."

"I am happy here; I feel secure; why should I wish to move?"

"Because," said Sophy, "you know full well that, in time, you will be caught."

"Caught?" Miss Frampton repeated. "How can I be caught when I have not 'escaped'?"

"Where is my baby?"

"Safe and sound."

"If I told my husband . . ."

"Hah! Told him of your bastard son while you carry another in your belly," said the governess. "To what purpose? To cleanse your soul, perhaps? He would toss you into the gutter."

"No. Leon would not be so cruel!"

"Are you sure? He is French; he is proud, and will not appreciate being palmed off with secondhand goods, Sophy. Which child do you wish to lose, the one born in wedlock, or the love child?"

Sophy could not feign calmness. There was too much of the truth in the governess's assessment of the situation. That was the crux of it: Leon could rob her of the baby in her womb. Legally, she had no prop, no hope of justice in a system constructed by men for the protection of man's property. She was a wife, and wives were without stature in the eyes of the law. Leon could take the child from her and cast her off from him, throw her, as Miss Frampton said, into the gutter; no one in society would so much as murmur a protest or think her husband harsh in his treatment. She began to weep, very quietly, her fists pressed into her sides.

"Go to bed, Sophy," the governess said. "There is nothing you can do."

"If only . . . you would tell me your price?"

"I cannot be bought."

"You have no heart."

"Who put you here? Who arranged everything? Without me, Sophy, where would you be? In a workhouse, I'll wager, or selling your pretty body for the price of a loaf. Remember who it was that protected you—I did; your old governess, Eunice Frampton. But you do not own me, Sophy. Even kindness, generosity and affection have their prices, fixed by the market."

"*Then what is yours?*" Sophy cried, in desperate confusion.

"I told you: I cannot be bought."

"All the . . . the information I obtained for you . . ."

"Passed on to friends."

"Merchants and bankers, no doubt."

"They pay well for such tidbits."

"I will pay well, too."

"You cannot, Sophy; you have nothing of your own to give yet."

"Leon will . . ."

"Leon: M. de Nerval—what is he but a trader? I question if he has anything of real value. I mean, child, what use could I make of a warehouse full of corn or a tun of wine in some Marseilles cellar?"

"Leon has money: gold."

"Perhaps he has," said the governess scornfully, "but it will be salted away in some bank vault . . ."

"Here!" said Sophy.

Miss Frampton paused, then softly repeated, "Here?"

Sense caused Sophy to bite her lip and remain silent.

Eunice Frampton did not press for further information; but her eyes gleamed with avarice. She placed one hand across her bosom as if the debate had made her breathless, though her face was wreathed in smiles.

"I will find money," said Sophy, at length. "If it is hard cash that you want."

"No, my dear," said Miss Frampton, still beaming. "I want no more than I have. We have reached a zenith together, have we not? Look how your stepmother's empire crumbled under her and left her penniless again. That will not happen here. I will protect you."

"You are determined that I shall have no right of choice."

"There is nothing to choose, Sophy. You have it all now, everything you ever dreamed of. I cannot understand why you turn on me with such ingratitude. The master will soften in time, I promise you."

Sophy knew that the woman was endeavoring to lead the conversation away from that moment of admission. She was content now to let it go. It was only talk, so many meaningless words poured one on top of the other. Resolution would come from her heart—if it ever came at all.

She dismissed the housekeeper, and indicated that she would retire to her room very soon.

"May I instruct Bolton to lock up then, Sophy?"

"If you wish."

"And may I . . ."

"Yes," said Sophy, curtly. "You may go to bed."

Fog held London fast in furry yellow fists. All day long it swirled and sucked through the portals of Belgravia, the narrow streets of Marylebone, the gilded arcades of Bond Street, and the markets of the sprawling East End. It stretched downriver, past Blackwall and Charlton, on over the estuary and out into the Channel. It quilted ports

and harbors and smothered the winds that filled the sails
of the colliers' barges along the French coast. Little boats
and sleek ships crept into refuge and anchored, slack on
their chains and hawsers, riding lights blurred, lachrymose
at the loss of trade incurred by the unexpected February
fog.

In Amsterdam the air tasted of copper and dross; in
London of iron and coke. In both those cities the traffic
stood embedded in ochre banks and drifts of harsh mist,
brought to a prolonged halt and held, it seemed, in a static
state outside time and season.

Sophy remained in her bedroom most of the morning.
Queenie brought her chocolate and toast. Priss flirted
round the room, cleaning the grate and building up a
bright fresh fire. And Jinny, having laid out clothing for
her mistress to wear, lingered only long enough to com-
miserate on the shame of being made a prisoner by the
climate. No mail arrived; no newspapers were delivered.
Milk cart and bakers' drays failed to nose through the
fog. Servants, lit like goblins by old bull's-eye lamps,
groped along the pavements in search of provender to
sweeten the boredom of their housebound employers.
Even the cafés and public houses had few customers.
Cabbies and horse-hirers shut up shop before two o'clock,
leaving the streets of the city not only shrouded but
almost deserted. Dusk came with the striking of three on
the borough clocks; an abrupt darkening of the fog among
the tenements and terraces.

Sophy had lunched alone in the dining room and then,
miserable and unwell, had repaired once more to her room
to hide her weakness from the prying eyes with which the
house seemed full. She heard Miller laughing. She heard
the clank of a cart, isolated and funereal, making a pass
round the square. She heard Bolton in the cellar, three
floors below, the thud of ale kegs and the faint, elfin
clink of bottles as he took one of his many tallies. Of

Eunice Frampton, however, Sophy heard nothing, saw nothing, not even at luncheon.

It was six o'clock before she felt strong enough to rise once more and, with Jinny's help, put on her dress.

"Where is Miss Frampton?" she asked the girl.

Jinny shook her head.

"Is she in the kitchen?"

"No, mum."

"Has she gone out?"

"Can't say, mum."

"Find her," said Sophy. "Tell her that I wish to discuss dinner with her."

"Dinner's 'alf prepared, mum."

"Without consulting me?"

"I'll tell Miss Frampton."

"I shall be in the drawing room," Sophy said.

Miller was sent to placate her. They had dressed him to resemble a footman, and had even scrubbed his face and hands. He came in shyly with a tray of wine and cakes and, tucked under his arm, the daily copy of the *Times* which some courageous newsboy had finally managed to deliver.

"Where is Bolton?"

"Dunno, mistress," said Miller, in a hoarse whisper.

"Is he gone out, too?"

"Dunno, mistress."

"Who decanted the wine?"

"Cook, mistress."

"I see."

Out of sympathy for the boy's awkwardness, Sophy allowed him to pour her a glass of wine, then instructed him to place the tray and the newspaper on the table by her chair.

Miller gave her a deep bow and, like an ambassador leaving a throne, backed through the doors and closed them loudly behind him.

Sophy sipped wine and lifted the copy of the *Times*.

Its pages smelled of fog. She scanned the front page and, without interest in the political brayings that filled the main columns, turned to the gazette section.

Captain Edmund Sutton's name occurred in bold type in a cemetery of lesser officers. He had died of an illness in Scutari almost two weeks ago. He was mourned by his mother and father.

Stunned, Sophy laid the paper on her lap. Edmund was dead. The handsome, golden hussar who had tutored her in love was dead. He had not given his life on the battle-field, gloriously, colorfully, but had eked out his last hours in the mess of the cramped wards of Scutari. She had read of the horrors of that place, the pain and suffering of the men who had been there. It was ignoble and ugly, a sad irony on her cherished memory of the hussar.

She did not weep, however, but sat for some minutes in motionless silence staring into the fire; then, puzzled, she lifted the newspaper again and ran her eyes down the other memoriams. *Beloved husband of . . . Father to . . . Mourned by his wife and son . . .* Under Edmund Sutton's name was no such epitaph. It said only that he was the son of James and Edwina Sutton, making no mention of a wife or children.

Sophy rose and tossed the newspaper aside.

She reached for the tasseled end of the bellpull, groping, yanked it once and flung it from her. She turned a circle, her wide skirts billowing, then furious, headed towards the door before any of the servants could answer her summons.

She rushed into the hallway.

Eunice Frampton, flushed and a little bedraggled, had, at that moment, emerged from the door at the top of the servants' stairs. She lifted her hand to tidy her hair. In an instant Sophy had reached her and, taking the woman by surprise, caught her upraised arm and twisted it pain-fully, bringing the governess almost to her knees.

"Have you gone mad?" Miss Frampton cried.

"*You lied,*" Sophy shouted. "You told me he was married."

"What? Who?"

"*Edmund.*"

"Now, my dear; you're hysterical. Tell me what's hap . . ."

Sophy levered on the woman's arm and threw her over so that she staggered and fell against the doorpost.

"*Edmund is dead,*" she screamed. "And there is no widow to grieve for him. No widow, because he never had a wife. You *lied,* you *lied.*"

The maids and the cook poked their noses from out of the stairs. George Bolton, still with a shabby brown overcoat over his blacks, pushed past them.

"She—Madame—has had a brainstorm," declared Miss Frampton, hauling herself to her feet. "Restrain her."

Sophy whirled round, and pointed her finger directly into the butler's face, jabbing as if with a knife or a pistol. "Lay a hand on me, Bolton, and you will spend years in prison: I warn you."

" 'Ere," said Bolton to the governess, " 'ere what's amiss with 'er?"

But Miss Frampton was less than sure of herself. Warily she pressed back against the doorpost. She knew that ill luck had robbed her of control over the girl. Only a cool head and quick thinking might redeem the situation.

Sophy stepped close to her. The woman cocked her forearm to ward off the possibility of another assault.

Sophy pressed on, "Tell me the truth now, you vixen. *Did you lie?*"

"Sutton . . . Sutton was not for you."

"You *did* lie."

"I . . . ah, embellished the truth a little, my dear, that's all."

"And how many other truths have you 'embellished'?"

demanded Sophy. "How many other lies have you told me? Where is my child? Is he dead, too? What did you do with him?"

"I told you, he's . . ."

"Did you *murder* him?"

"Murder!" Bolton exclaimed in alarm. "Wot's all this? Murder? You didn't say noffink about . . ."

"Shut up, you fool," muttered the governess.

"But, Eunice, what's she . . .?"

Eunice Frampton smirked. She had regained most of her composure after the unexpected blow to her plans. She drew herself up, primped her hair and arranged the lace at the throat of her dress, superciliously ignoring Sophy.

"After all I've done for you," the governess said. "To think that it would come to this."

"It will come to imprisonment," said Sophy. "I intend to summon the police."

"Here, now, hold on!" said Bolton.

The cook and maids vanished at the mere mention of the constabulary; Bolton, too, seemed half inclined to project himself backwards down the servants' stairs out of sight. He might have done so, if Eunice had not pinned his arm in a viselike grip.

"This fine young bride," she said, "had a baby to a soldier."

Bolton's face was moonlike; he smiled, panic easing out of him. "You don't say now, Eunice; had a brat to a uniform, did she?"

"I mean it, Miss Frampton," said Sophy. "I *will* fetch the police."

"I question if you will, Sophy," the governess said. "You have no charge to lay against me: I have done nothing wrong in the eyes of the law."

"You stole my baby."

"Stole? My dear child, I acted only on your instructions," Eunice Frampton said. "However, it seems that our relationship is at an end. I take it that you are dismissing me?"

"Both of you: I wish you out of this house tonight."

"*Tut-tut!*" Miss Frampton said. "I thought you had learned the penalty of rashness, my dear. However—as you wish. George, it seems that we have been sent packing."

Bolton frowned; his glee had diminished. Eunice Frampton's manipulation of the accident of the newspaper report and its effect on her mistress were beyond him. He had sense enough to say nothing, however. The effect of Eunice's words on the girl was interesting and unexpected. All the temper went out of her.

"But my . . . my baby?"

"Ah, yes, your baby," said Miss Frampton. "Well, why should I carry responsibility for the brat's welfare any longer?"

"Tell me, please, Miss Frampton."

Sighing, the governess said, "What will you do with the information?"

"I will . . . I will claim my son and acknowledge him as mine."

"M. de Nerval *will* be pleased."

"That is no longer your concern," said Sophy. "You will be gone, and no blame will attach itself to you."

"Think carefully, Sophy, my dear."

"*Where is my baby?*"

"You will find him in the care of a . . . a Mistress Farmer, in Pikeman Street, Whitechapel. I would not advise you to go there tonight."

"I have heeded your advice too often," said Sophy. "Bolton, tell Jinny to fetch my cloak, bonnet and gloves."

Bolton stuck his tongue in his cheek, then nodded.

His pompous, deferential manners had been sloughed off like a snake's skin and a coarse kind of arrogance

showed in his gesture. He leaned round the doorpost and
bawled down into the stairwell. "Jinny, git up 'ere."

The maid scrambled obediently upstairs and, instructed
by the butler, ran on up the main staircase to return in a
moment with the garments.

Sophy said, "You will wait until I return, both of you."

Miss Frampton dropped a brief curtsey. "Very good,
madam," she said, with an irony that, in the stress of
that half hour, was quite lost on the younger woman.

Bolton opened the outside door.

The square was lost in thick fog, like a soiled flannel
curtain drawn close over the iron railings. Sophy hesitated.
Out in the murk, in the slums and stews of the Whitechapel area, her lost child waited.

She looked back into the warm hallway with its ornate
gas fittings and solid furniture. Bolton and Eunice Frampton flanked the door, watching her, saying nothing.

Moving carefully, Sophy dipped down the steps onto
the invisible pavement and turned left. In Bond Street she
might find a cabdriver willing to coax his horse through
the fog. She took her bearings by the portal lights of the
houses in that arc of the square and, at the corner, left
their security and crossed to the railings of the park.

Behind her the faded postcard of light that marked
her home narrowed and vanished. But she did not notice
it. Within her now was a fierce determination to find her
firstborn son. Not fog, not darkness, not Eunice Frampton,
nor the thought of her husband's anguish would stop her
now. She would find Pikeman Street in Whitechapel if she
had to crawl there on her hands and knees.

For an hour Sophy crept through the secret streets of
London, groping her way from one familiar landmark to
another. There were no cabs to be found in Bond Street,
and she picked her way uphill, keeping to the shopping
arcades until, at length, she reached the delta of Regent
Street and Oxford Street. Here there was light and noise,

a ghostly crowd spilling back across the pavements, lit by flares and coal-oil cans. A horse had fallen and lay still in the shafts of the upturned cart snorting and heaving pitifully. Cabbages and purple rutabagas, like decapitated heads, were strewn across the cobbles, and gleeful boys scuttered out of their holes to pluck up the vegetables and make off with them, jeering and ducking past the costermongers.

Pedestrians, coaxed out of hiding by the diversion, choked the corners, and a multitude of carriages and carts stretched a half mile east and west. The animals' nostrils puffed out steam, and the coiling fumes of the tar-brands added texture to the swirling fog. A couple of laconic Peelers in banded hats and oilskin coats, each with a carbide lamp clipped to his belt, struggled to restore order, have the maimed horse lugged off and the thorough-fare reopened. A gentleman in a topper and opera cape craned out of his private carriage, craking imperiously at the constables and thumping his gold-knobbed cane on the panel, demanding that his coachman, in defiance of the congestion, make way at once for Mayfair.

Finding her direction, Sophy hurried past the back of the crowd and along the straits of Oxford Street towards High Holborn. At the tail of the queue, which seemed to contain every hackney carriage abroad that night, she found a two-wheeler discharging a brace of irate young rakehells whose West End rendezvous, she gathered, had been scotched by the cabdriver's indolence and ignorance and who would not pay a jot in spite of having occupied the hack for an hour.

The driver was an elderly, bent man with a Somerset accent. He put up little enough argument with the spoiled young fellows who, still yawping insults, high-stepped it out of sight down Poland Street. He had lifted his whip to give the nag a touch round, when Sophy desperately clutched the heel of his boot.

He looked down at her wearily.

She took two crowns from her purse and held them up to him in the palm of her hand. The driver had her summed up in a trice. She was no doxy on the spree.

"Nay, miss, ah'm a-goin' east agin: home."

"Take me east then," said Sophy.

"Two crowns'll carry 'ee further than ah wants t' go."

"Whitechapel?"

Glancing behind him, the driver saw no shadows in the fog. With a shrug he mittened the crowns and, stooping, graciously handed the young woman into the cab. He could hardly see the nag's ears, but he had been navigating London's streets for a decade now and frequently boasted that he could follow any route blindfold. Besides, for two crowns in advance he would take the lady on a pleasure jaunt round the Plaistow Marshes if that was what she wanted.

"Pikeman Street," said Sophy. "Do you know it?"

"Ah knows it."

"Will you take me there?"

"Aye, miss, ah will."

He nudged his horse into a slow walk, made a roundabout turn, brought his near-side wheel rim against the curb and struck off east into the fog.

An hour, two hours passed. From time to time the driver sang out a street name as his old horse triumphantly hauled itself through the enshrouding murk without straying from the route. The cab moved so sluggishly that walkers occasionally passed them and one gentleman, obviously lost, trailed along only a few yards behind, sticking to the red lantern's glow like a moth.

It was after ten o'clock before the driver finally chucked his rein and brought the cab to a halt. Here the streets were so narrow that Sophy, peering from the window, could see both sides at once. The pallid glow of gin shops and doorways and tiny windows in the acres of brick gave added illumination. The fog here was even thicker, yet it had a clotted quality and there were regions where it thinned to sulphurous mist, allowing glimpses of people lounging under gas mantels at the mouths of drinking dens or of women, ragged and recalcitrant, hovering on the pavement edge in the hope of picking up a drunk to wring for a night's lodging or another jug of grog.

"How long is Pikeman Street?" she asked.

"Short."

"Thank you," Sophy said. "You may put me down here."

The cab stole off into the gloom, leaving Sophy on the narrow, broken pavement.

She consulted a door and found no name upon it.

She walked a few paces, found another door, also blank.

She moved on, reluctantly, towards the spot where she had noticed a woman before a fog bank absorbed all that end of the street once more.

The woman was not much older than she was. She stood in the gutter, peering out of red-rimmed eyes this way and that, tense as a hunting cat. Sophy was reminded of Cora Frampton's two wild felines, sly and opportunistic, giving no affection for their food and full of a proud and isolated hatred.

The woman stared at her.

Sophy said, "I am looking for Mrs. Farmer's house?"

The woman gave no answer, still scrutinizing the well-dressed, well-heeled apparition who had swum into her fuddled vision.

"Mrs. Farmer?" said Sophy. "She lives in this street?"

The woman grinned ferociously. "Whatcher got in that bag, dearie?"

Sophy took a pace backwards.

"I have money," she said. "I will give you one crown to tell me where Mrs. Farmer lives."

The woman surveyed the street in both directions, then held out a clawlike hand. "Give."

Sophy took a coin from her purse and held it in her closed fist. She swung the purse warningly by its ribbon.

"The dollar fust," said the woman.

Sophy dropped the coin onto the pavement between them and let the woman scramble for it. Still on her knees, the woman cackled gleefully and shouted, "Ain't no Farmer 'ere. You bin 'ad, dearie. No Farmer rand 'ere."

Swinging the purse in rage, Sophy stumbled after the prostitute. But the woman was too quick for her. Shrieking out malicious laughter she pranced away into the fog in the direction of a skirl of fiddle music from one of the nether-end public houses.

Confused and afraid now, Sophy turned and ran across the cobbles and, in a kind of terror, skirts in her fists, scampered up and down peering at the blank and blistered doors.

A man, indistinct under the cone of gaslight by the street's open end, turned his face to the wall as she came abreast of him. She glanced at him then, afraid of making contact with another of the savage, heartless creatures of this place, ran back across the street, darting from house to house, from window to window in hopeless confusion.

It was the gable house from which the noise emerged, the wailing cry of a child, and an abrupt burst of shouting. Sophy stopped in her tracks; listened, head cocked. More wailing, thin and piping, pierced the fog, then a babble of oaths and shouting more barbarous than before—a female voice.

Before she quite understood her own motive, Sophy crashed her body against the door. Her fists beat upon the woodwork and her shoes drummed upon the flaking post.

Within the hovel, silence came down like a guillotine.

Eyes squeezed shut, Sophy continued her barrage of blows.

A baby whined weakly and, quite distinctly now, she heard a woman's rolling tones cajoling the infant to keep silent. Relentlessly, and, at that instant, quite losing her reason, Sophy battered upon the door until it opened a half inch to show a line of eyes tack up the strip of darkness like studs on a leather strap. With all her weight, Sophy thrust herself against the children and pushed them ahead of her into the low room.

The floor was bare, and the walls were patched with buckram torn from sacks. The fireplace was no more than a hole in the wall with a handful of ashes in its throat. A table, a bench; a half a dozen children aged from two to five, sexless, crop-headed, in filthy smocks. The opposite wall—eight boxes stuffed with rags on a trestle of brick and greasy planks. Light from an oilcan with a shredded wick; smell; canvas wafting on the broken window pane through which the secrets of the nest had escaped to the heedless street.

Fine woman, fine clothes; a blossom of rich fabrics: Sophy in the center of the apartment. A fat slattern, broad-hipped, broad-cheeked, and steeped in gin. The pair confronted each other, each astonished and utterly dismayed.

"My baby?" Sophy declared. "I believe you have my baby."

"Gawd Almighty!" the fat woman exclaimed.

"I want him back."

"Take yer bleedin' pick; take all the liddle monsters."

"*Mine! I want mine!*"

"Well, lissen 'ere, I ain't got yours."

"Mrs. Farmer, I was told."

"Me name's Goldseye, not bleedin' Farmer," the fat woman bellowed. "Farmer: Yer tryin' ter be funny."

She stood with her massive back to the cribs, hands on hips, ponderous belly and breasts thrust out like buffers.

"Out of my way," shouted Sophy.

"I tells yer I ain't *got* your bleedin' kid."

"Shall I return with the constables?"

The woman caught at the collar of Sophy's coat and hauled her forward. The stench of liquor was sour about her. Behind the couple the children were utterly motionless.

"Constables, eh? Awright!" the woman wheezed. "Yer wants one, take that 'un."

Leaning to one side she allowed Sophy to look past her into the nearest of the box-cribs. In it, half covered with a cotton sheet, was a wasted little body, still and voiceless. The woman was laughing now, enjoying her macabre joke.

"Lissen: yer can't tell what's yours, can yer? That 'un's a girl, any roads. An' dead."

"Oh, God!"

"I ain't got no ladies' bastards 'ere; never 'ave 'ad. Your kid ain't 'ere; dead or alive." She laughed; then with an unexpected sigh, added, "But if you're keen, take 'er."

Clinging to the slattern's fat arm Sophy reared back and, thrashing her head from side to side, screamed loudly and without halt until the woman struck her down.

The small, broad-shouldered man in the pilot's coat supported her with one arm and, politely, lifted his squashed old-fashioned beaver.

"Alfred Dawlish, Madame de Nerval," he announced.

"Where . . . am I?"

"In the street, takin' a breath of air, if you can call this air," the man said. "I think we should be seein' about getting you home."

"My baby?"

"Warn't your baby," said Alfred Dawlish. "Rest assured on that. That hag there knows nothin' about you."

"But Miss Frampton?"

"A natural-borned liar."

"Yes," Sophy whispered. She was still propped against Dawlish's shoulder. She looked round, her head clearing. She was, as the gentleman had informed her, in the street a few yards from the closed door of the hellish apartment where babies were boxed, alive and dead, like fish in a market. She shuddered and closed her eyes and permitted the stranger to assist her round the gable out of Pikeman Street and into a wider roadway where, she was relieved to note, some traffic still rumbled and the fog was not quite so dense. "Who . . . who are you?"

"An employee of your husband's." The gentleman lifted his hat again. "Employee of Snodgrass, Morgan and Hare to be accurate."

"How did you . . . ?"

"Employed by your husband ter protect you, madam."

"Leon employed . . ." Sophy shook her head in bewilderment. "Why? Why did my husband do that?"

"Thought you were in danger."

"No," said Sophy, quickly. "I'm in no danger. I'm perfectly well, thank you."

"Perfectly awful, if you'll pardon me, madam," said Dawlish. "Perfectly tricky to foller too, 'specially in this pea-souper."

"Do you know why I went to that place?"

"Yes."

"And now, I suppose, you'll tell my husband all that you have learned?"

"Best get you home, madam," said Dawlish, frowning. "Can you walk unaided?"

"I can do without *your* aid, sir."

"Now, now, Madame de Nerval: Let's 'ave none of that talk," Dawlish said. "We'll find ourselves a hack and make fuller investigation when we're on the road back to your house."

"Perhaps it would be better if you left me here; it's where I belong."

"Damaris Square's where you belongs, madam," Alfred Dawlish said. "And the quicker we gets you there, the better."

"Why do you say that, Mr. Dawlish?"

"'Cause your Miss Eunice Frampton's not ter be trusted," said Dawlish, apologetically. "Fogs like this bring out the worst in felons."

"Felons?"

"A feeling in my bones," Dawlish said, then suddenly stepped to the curb and, raising his stick, barked out a demand for a trolling cab to halt.

The feeling in Alfred Dawlish's bones proved more accurate than Sophy would have imagined possible. The hack crawled into Damaris Square shortly before midnight. The mansion door was open, Miller hopping agitatedly on the step, peering into the fog. A bandage swathed his head, and a tracery of dried blood still marked his cheek.

Before Dawlish had properly helped Sophy to the pavement, Miller was at her side.

"It's Miss Frampton and Mr. Bolton, mistress," the boy blurted out. "Gone. Took all the val'ables, they did. Knocked me down, mistress, when I tried ter stop them. Locked me in the cellar till they was cleared and away."

Trembling, Sophy rushed up the steps and into the hallway. All the doors stood open, carpets wrinkled and askew. She looked, hesitantly, into the dining room. One glance was sufficient to indicate that Miller spoke the truth. As housekeeper, Miss Frampton had keys to all the cabinets. The gridded diamond-paned doors of the display case stood wide open, shelves empty, the handsome silver plate missing.

Behind her, Sophy heard Dawlish say, "When did it happen?"

And Miller answered: "Mistress warn't gone but ten minutes when they started. Had it all planned, sir, I'd say."

"You tried to stop them?"

"I did, sir; warn't right."

"And the rest of the servants?"

"I reckon they was too scared, sir. Bolton's no man ter cross."

"Who released you?"

"Cook."

"How long ago?"

"'Bout nine, sir. Him an' Miss Frampton didn't rush things. Left in a chaise wiff bags full of stuff. Cook told me."

"Why didn't you summon the constables?"

"I . . . I . . ."

Sophy paused by the couple. She patted Miller's shoulder and, in a strained and husky voice, told him that he had done well, and behaved bravely. She went on, numbly, into Leon's study.

The mahogany desk had been heaved onto its side. Books, papers, inkpots and files were scattered over the floor. The cornerpiece, too, had been prized from its place and jacked forward, tipping more books and documents across the room. The iron safe behind it had been levered several feet from its brick recess, far enough to allow George Bolton to work on it with his metalsmith's crab-like pincers, ripping a hole in its side. Jagged edges of metal protruded and the door lock, smashed from its vulnerable inner clasp, dangled loose. The safe, of course, was empty. The gold coins, gold plate, reels of thin gold wire and cigar-shaped nuggets in which Leon had invested were all gone.

Sophy pivoted round and, walking jerkily, went upstairs.

In her bedroom, cases and boxes lay about. A few valueless items of jewelry, pinchbeck mementos of childhood, had been discarded upon the counterpane as not worth the effort of haulage. In Leon's dressing chamber the scene was the same: his links, his pins, his watches and rings—all stolen.

It was in the parlor, however, that Sophy discovered that act that set the seal on the theft. Nothing had been taken from that room. But all the fine ornaments and fabrics, down to the very cushions on the chairs, had been torn and broken in a cold-blooded frenzy of wanton destruction. Theft was explicable, motivated by greed and gain—but the havoc wrought in the homely parlor was a gesture of unalloyed maliciousness, a sign of many years of suppressed contempt and, perhaps, of hatred.

Stooping by the hearth, Sophy lifted the shards of the Dresden finch. It had been dashed down upon the tiles and the parts attacked with the brass poker, beaten into powder. She dabbed at a few crumbs of colored glaze and stared in stunned disbelief at her fingertips then, still crouched, flinched as a hand lightly touched her shoulder.

She whipped round, expecting to see Alfred Dawlish. Leon stood above her.

"I should have heeded Dawlish," he growled. "He warned me about Bolton and Miss Eunice Frampton."

Holding her husband's hand, Sophy got to her feet.

"No, Leon," she said quietly. "There is more to this than you know: much, much more. I ask only that you hear me out and do as you see fit. I ask only this of you, and nothing more, ever again."

The trader's eyes were slumbrous, solemn brown and gave no hint of the depths of his feeling. Without another word he followed his wife upstairs into the privacy of their bedroom.

# Fourteen

Leon still wore the heavy ulster cape, for the chamber was cold. He stripped off his hat and gloves and threw them onto the bed. He looked round, found a chair and slumped into it.

"I should not have gone to Amsterdam," he said, more to himself than to Sophy. "Still, I bless the fog which closed the Channel shipping lanes and brought me back tonight."

Sophy was calm now: she had reached that inevitable moment of crisis. Issues that had been muddled before were clear-cut and precise. It would be possible, even now, to lay the blame squarely on Eunice Frampton's shoulders and to divert Leon's thoughts from her complicity. Only Alfred Dawlish knew the truth. Somehow, she assumed that he would remain silent and would not betray her. But the lie had to be exposed. She needed Leon, needed from him one final act of strength and composure —to find Eunice Frampton, and wring from the woman the whereabouts of her child.

Now that it had come to it, Sophy understood that love was no mere word to be frittered away on casual declarations. She had married Leon for what he could give her, had renounced her child to gain wealth, comfort and a modicum of standing in society. All that was dross compared to the issues now at stake. In loving Leon she had created for herself the most selfish of all choices—her son, or her husband.

"They have taken everything," Sophy said. "In a sense, Leon, I aided them in their purpose. I have been under Miss Frampton's sway for many years, too many years; yet I should not have betrayed you, not even carelessly. That was dishonorable of me, and less—much, much less —than you deserved."

"Gold cannot be disposed of easily," Leon said. "Do not distress yourself unduly on that score, Sophy. I am confident that we will run the villains to earth."

"Yes," said Sophy. "That is what I wish, too, Leon. I want her found. I want Eunice Frampton found—not for revenge, not even to retrieve your gold. I want her to . . . to return my baby."

Save for a slight start, and a stiffening of his hands into fists, Leon gave no sign of comprehension.

"I had a baby, Leon," Sophy said, unchecked. "A son. He was born to me last spring in secrecy while I was hidden away in Cornwall."

"That is the reason you would not marry me and go with me to America?"

"Yes, Leon, that is the reason."

"In spring?" Leon closed his eyes. "I have no right to ask you, Sophy, but was the child's father one of the Redfords?"

"No. I had an . . . an *affaire de coeur*. It began shortly after you left Switzerland, and was over before you returned. My child's father was a hussar. He . . . he died in Scutari last month. I learned of his death only this evening."

"Did you . . . did you love him, Sophy?"

"Yes, I loved him. I loved him for a little while. But it did not last, Leon, because I loved him for the wrong reasons."

"He would not marry you?"

"I . . ." Sophy hesitated. "I would not marry him."

"Because you hoped to marry me?"

"Not out of love for you, Leon. Out of greed, out of . . . selfishness."

"And now?"

"You may have this child, Leon: your child." She placed her hand on her stomach. "I have no right to it. But—but I must find my firstborn. That is all I ask you to do for me now, to help me find my firstborn son."

"The Frampton woman put you up to it?"

"I knew what she was doing, Leon," Sophy said. "I cannot escape responsibility for my actions. No matter how much I want to." She shook her head. Even the truth sounded now like a lie, a convenient excuse. Everything had become tainted, fouled by evil scheming and by selfishness. "I must have him back, Leon."

"I take it that the Frampton woman 'disposed' of him for you?"

"Yes. I saw him only once, fleetingly."

"The rest was blackmail: simple blackmail," said Leon.

"I . . . I gave in to her," Sophy confessed. "She asked about your business, and I told her. She even discovered that you had gold in your safe. Now, she has brought you to ruin."

Leon de Nerval smiled sardonically.

"Sophy," he said. "Was that the price of silence, or the tithings of hope?"

"I cannot be sure. I could never be sure."

"If she had asked you directly, would you have paid that price for your son?"

"Yes."

"And lost me?"

"Yes."

"And, Sophy, what price would you have paid to *keep* me?"

"Any price, Leon, any price in the world—except my child."

The trader sighed and pushed himself out of the chair.

For a moment he studied Sophy carefully, then, without a single gesture of comfort, walked out of the room.

The stricken girl ran after him and, clinging to the doorpost, cried out, "Leon, please help me."

Framed against the porous glow of the gas-mantel, the Breton trader paused.

"You must tell Dawlish everything," he declared. "If we ever want to see Eunice Frampton again we must track her down quickly, before this fog lifts and she escapes out of England."

"Leon?"

"We have one chance, Sophy, and we must take it. Dawlish will know how."

"I thought," said Alfred Dawlish, "that something was in the wind."

The little investigator sipped tea and helped himself to another slice of ham. He rolled the meat carefully, minding his manners, laid it on a piece of bread and took a mouthful.

Sitting apart from his wife in the long dining room, Leon was drinking coffee and smoking a cigar. Miller had relighted the fire and Leon had locked up the display case, though its empty shelves still seemed to glare rebuke at Sophy. The servants were still awake; Dawlish had insisted on questioning them individually while the memory of the theft was still fresh. It was imperative to glean every available scrap of information on Bolton and Eunice Frampton, and domestics, if Dawlish was any judge, were seldom innocent as to the schemes of their superiors. As the governess had employed them, had "found" them, they must surely know something of her habits and possible plans.

Midnight was long past, the clocks close to chiming one. Outside the fog was thicker than ever, yellowly clotting, blotting out even the area railings. Come morning, however, it might clear. Even now, it might be dispersing from the Channel ports, giving the steamers and ferries a bearing on France, or Holland.

"I'll be wanting a list of the stolen goods, sir," Dawlish said. "Detailed and itemized. I take it that the law will not be called upon to 'ave an 'and in the matter yet awhile?"

"Not until we catch the Frampton woman, and reach an agreement with her," Leon said. "They may not be involved at all."

Dawlish was relieved that Madame de Nerval had made a clean breast of the business of the farmed-out baby. He did not care to be hampered by that particular secret. Though he went about the process of eliciting information warily, his method of using the information gained was often too unorthodox to explain in courts of law. He would not willingly have betrayed the wife to the husband, yet, in tracking down Eunice Frampton, betrayal would have been inevitable. Thank God, he had no spouse to lead him such a dance. He had known the moment the Frog descended the stairs that she had broken the news to him; de Nerval, though, was too much of a gentleman to let it show much. He looked a touch stunned and acted reticent, and that was all—aside from the fact that he did not meet his young wife's eyes.

The tea revived Dawlish's spirits and gave him back that enthusiasm for pursuit that his odyssey through Whitechapel's fog had sadly diminished.

Leon said, "How will you go about it, Mr. Dawlish?"

Dawlish said, "I got certain facts already, sir. For one thing, you wouldn't 'ave no need to rattle off down to that Cornish village. Cora Frampton, the sister, has decamped. Cottage sold."

"How do you know that?" asked Sophy in surprise.

"Friends in all sorts of places." Dawlish, with a show of modesty, finished his tea, put the cup on the trolley and took from his inner fob pocket a small square of card. Reading from it, he recited, "Rose Cottage, offered for sale locally, wiff all possessions, November twenty-fourth. Bill of sale posted first December; gone to Sir Rupert Egg of Penzance."

Irrelevantly, Sophy wondered if the cats were classed among "all possessions." She said, "Where has Cora Frampton gone, Mr. Dawlish; do you know that?"

"Resetting."

"I don't understand."

"No, madam," said Dawlish, patiently. "She's gone a-fencing for her sister and her paramour, that's where she's gone. I found out about Cora 'fore I found out about Eunice. Cora 'ad quite a reputation as a settler of other folks' property. I even knows some of 'er haunts and contacts."

"Can you predict what the sisters will do?" asked Leon.

Dawlish shrugged. "Split. Bolton'll go his merry way with a sheaf of banknotes or a grip full of sovereigns to keep him hush. Cora an' Eunice will work a quick transaction on the portables and set sail for foreign climes, I reckon, together or apart."

"But my gold?"

"Ah, now, that's a bonus—for us, not them," said Dawlish. "As you knows, sir, gold's not so easy ter shift on the gray market, not in quantity. If anything trips the trap it'll be the shiny stuff, mark my words."

"How soon will the sisters depart?"

"Soon as they hive off the swag. And that, sir, is how we'll nab them."

"What of the gold?" said Leon. "The Framptons will know better than to try to sell it in London, will they not?"

"I feel they'll take it along. Gold is currency in any country in the world," said Dawlish.

"Very well," said Leon. "You will begin your tour of the rogues' rendezvous tomorrow morning, first thing."

"Right! Get them at breakfast, sir, I will."

"I want one thing made quite clear," said Leon. "The Framptons must be brought to me. Whatever happens, Mr. Dawlish, I must have the Framptons caught. The gold is less important now than certain information which only the sisters possess."

"Could it be, sir, that you intend to trade them a free pass for that . . . ah, information?"

"It could be, Mr. Dawlish."

Dawlish slid a glance at the young woman. Just what sort of bargain had she struck, what sort of trade made between husband and wife? The redemption of that babe might cost de Nerval a raw fortune. What did the mistress have worth that price to give in return?

Dawlish did not know the answer. But Dawlish had never been in love, as far as he could remember.

Instinct, experience, or a blend of the two shot Alfred Dawlish like a dart straight into that area contained by the loop of the Thames. Pelican Lane, Tobacco Street, Fastnet Road, the Barnacles, and all the joy shops, pawn-brokers, public houses, and market meeting places in and around that region of riverside London. There the Frampton family had had its fair run two decades ago; the district provided him with occupation enough for a dozen agents.

Hindered by the fog, and—though he would not admit it—feeling his years just a little, it was after seven o'clock in the morning before he set himself up at the first sleazy counter and forthwith began casual inquiries into what had popped the night before. He knew the techniques and methods of thieves well enough to wager that Bolton, at least, would hold hot property removed from Damaris Square not one moment longer than he had to. He knew too that the old-fashioned contact system worked for vil-lains as well as gentlemen.

As he had memorized the items on the list that Leon de Nerval had compiled in the small hours of that morning, Dawlish had no occasion to produce the foolscap sheets and dangle them before the queer fish he interviewed. Instead he dropped hints, invented plausible lies, prevaricated when pressed, flashed a gaudy banknote or two, clinked a half sovereign in the right places, stood a quart of ale in the wrong 'un, chatted with a woman whose seedy empire had tentacles throughout the whole East End, and, when nothing but frankness would serve, reported himself as a Lloyd's agent and rhymed off the list verbatim—pair of silver serving dishes, silver cruets, silver salver, chafing dish, engraved tray; French clock, filigree bon-bon; onyx cufflinks in gold setting, monogrammed, Taraman watch with heavy chain in gold and French fob; et cetera. The litany, short or long, was greeted with glinting eyes and gleams of greedy interest, but no telltale rises to the bait.

Night mists, loath to quit the caverns and lanes that riddled the decrepit buildings, rebuffed the rays of the sun and held the fog trapped. Anxiously scanning the sky between ports of call, Alfred Dawlish picked his way down the routes of perdition and graft, eyes bright under his hat brim and his nose pinkly embedded in the folds of his woolen scarf. Now noon, when the creatures of the night were stirring from late sleep, he had bored down into the lowest depths and traded now in coppers, cups of hot pea soup, and a mug of sour wine spiced with cinnamon. It was the purchase of this last libation that brought him his first clue.

His informant was a prostitute who had nothing to inform with, except the fact that she was starved for a sup of somefink 'ot and substantial. The mug of sour wine and cinnamon, warmed by a poker from the publican's grate, served a treat and loosened the woman's tongue. Among the gossip and meaningless rumors she gave out,

in hope of another tipple, was the plain, unadorned fact
that she had seen a "nob" with a big, black bag hoppin'
into Prater Williams's shop at the ungodly hour of one
o'clock the previous night.

"What sort of a 'nob' would that be now?" asked
Dawlish, paying for a second drink.

"Wiff a stiff starch collar an' gloves: proper gloves, I
asks yer!"

"Like . . . ah, like a butler, you mean?"

"Yer, like opens the door in posh 'ouses."

"How big, with the hat, would he be?"

"What 'at?"

"Thought you said an 'at?"

"No 'at; but big."

Piece by piece, Dawlish portrayed George Bolton;
Bolton burdened with a bag, which did not contain
"feathers," for sure. Nodding, Dawlish set up a third mug
of wine, a "tater pie" to go with it and, quelling the
whore's inventive eagerness, asked her curtly, "Where's
Prater Williams's shop?"

"Be'ind the chapel in Lighterman's Alley: three windows
painted green an' a brown door."

Dawlish lifted his hat a half inch from his head, grinned,
and was gone before the woman could embark on more
tales for more "tater pies."

Lighterman's Alley, a quarter of a mile away, was a
dipping chasm of broken cobbles in which fog swirled up
from the Thames like smoke, masking the bent houses and
shanties that nodded over the gap. The chapel was a
squalid timber mission, long abandoned, lying on its beam
end behind a stave paling. Prater Williams's shop, anonymous and too coy even to display a hoarding or a symbol
of its trade, snuggled up to the chapel wall in a lean-to
fashion, story piled on wooden story like tattered playing
cards glued together with moss and grime.

The windows showed nothing, nor the door.

Alfred Dawlish did not care. He was sure enough of his information to lift his boot, kick the lock, and follow on in the wake of the almighty thud through the low opening into the heart of the pawnbroker's nest.

The broker was a large, shambling figure of a man, with a head as bald as a bowl of lard and sharp little eyes set in mushrooms of fat. At the moment of Dawlish's unannounced entry he had been rummaging in a large tin box, one of many that crammed the shelves all round the room. While Prater Williams was not unaccustomed to receiving calls from unwelcome members of the society of law and order, he had certainly never been ambushed on his premises before by a person of such aggressive bearing.

"Last night," Dawlish said, without any preamble, "big feller in butler's duds; bag; in the bag family plate, nice an' shiny; ladies' ornaments, too, probably."

Prater Williams tracked along his shelves, smiling unctuously. "Closed last night, guv," he declared. "Closed, we was, on account of the bleedin' fog."

Alfred Dawlish had no time to spare for argument. He crabbed round the edge of the heavy counter and, before Williams could escape, caught a handful of shirting and one strap of the pawnbroker's canvas apron, yanked the large man up on tiptoe and slammed him back against the wall of boxes.

"Where's the swag, Williams?"

"Swag? I swear 'fore God I don't play that game!"

"Bolton," Dawlish reminded him. "George Bolton, butler ter the gentry. He brought you a haul, an' you bought it—by prior arrangement, I suspect. Now where's the loot?"

Williams opened his mouth to gasp out another protest and a denial of all knowledge of illegal purchases. But the gasp changed to a whinny of pain as Dawlish cracked the ash stick across his shins and then, as if the stick was a rapier, prodded it hard into the broker's bulging paunch.

"Got no time to spare, Williams. Where is it?"

"Cellar; didn't know it were stole, though. I swear 'fore Gawd!"

"Where's the cellar door?"

"There."

"Show me."

"Light . . . light . . . light the candle, then."

By the guttering flame of the tallow, Williams led Dawlish down three or four worn wooden steps into a half basement where, amid a conglomeration of furniture and old clothing, trunks, packing cases, and boxes, a green tarpaulin, folded over from corner to corner, shrouded the collection of smaller items from the de Nervals' house —the plate, the cruet, the silver dishes, some of it monogrammed.

"And the jewels?"

Stammering, and shaking his head furiously, Williams protested that he knew nothing about jewelry; indeed, he hardly seemed to know anything about the silverware in his cellar and, listening to him, Dawlish might have been asked to believe that the collection had appeared there by magic, as a fairy gift.

"Now, Prater, old friend," Dawlish said. "You're in deep, very deep."

"I got noffink to do wiff this."

"Yes, yes, you have, Prater," Dawlish said. "And I'm the lad who'll make the report."

"You ain't a copper."

"I'm a copper's nark—paid and in good standing," Dawlish said. "It's up to me, you know. How do you fancy a new life in Australia, a servant of Her Majesty's Government?"

"Transportation?" said Prater Williams. "They don't transport for . . ."

"They transport for anything," said Dawlish. "Even if they don't give you an ocean voyage, Prater, it'll be ten years 'ard in Pentonville."

" 'Fore Gawd, I'm innocent!"

"But," said Dawlish, prodding the Williams paunch with his stick again, "I'll deal, if you're willing."

"Talk," said Prater Williams, hastily.

"You talk, Prater," Dawlish said. "You'll lose yer money, like as not, but you'll still have your liberty."

"Right!" said Williams, nodding disconsolately. "What d'yer want ter know?"

They were like strangers; not enemies, but a couple thrown together by chance, passengers on the same small ferry or the sole occupants of a carriage on an interminably long journey. They were polite to each other, perfectly mannered, yet distant, in that cautious state that came uncomfortably close to hostility.

Sophy would not excuse herself from blame, nor compound her guilt by pleading for Leon's forgiveness. He had agreed to act for her, to obtain that which she most wanted in all the world, and that, at least for the time, must be enough for her. In all reason, she could expect no more.

If he had been an Englishman in the same situation any capitulation at all would have been an act of charity or the most self-sacrificing philanthropy. But Leon was French and the French were less prone to the hypocrisy of a male-dominated society. It was, after all, no peccadillo, no subterfuge, no illicit *liaison* that had been uncovered. Sophy's confession was one of love, of love lost, love found, and of a love stronger than that which any man had a right to expect from any woman.

Broodingly, Leon held himself apart from her. He was no longer a carefree and boyish humorist. No more, however, was he the strong, enigmatic person that she had first met in the Schneegarten twenty long months ago. They had both changed, in process, like two metals in a crucible. What would eventually become of her, Sophy dared not predict. She was willing, at last, to accept her husband's judgment and his decisions without protest.

With Miss Frampton gone, Sophy filled her time with the trivialities of management, ordering meats and puddings and, in the state of emergency that fog induced in thousands of middle-class homes, checking stocks in pantry, larders and cellar. Miller was dispatched to find his way to the grocery stores, an adventure he enjoyed, embarking from the house like a Greenland explorer who might never be seen again. Sophy immediately estranged herself from Jinny. She felt sure that the girl had been Miss Frampton's accomplice and, in due course, she would be dispensed with.

In midmorning, with the fog clearing just a little, Leon ordered a carriage and left the house. He gave Sophy no indication as to his destination, though she guessed that he intended to forge through to Hampstead and seek comfort from Gwen Lloyd and give comfort in turn to her ailing brother.

She had no right to complain.

Leon returned at three o'clock. At five past three, Alfred Dawlish was shown into the parlor. As he unwound the long scarf from about his face, Sophy saw that he was smiling triumphantly.

"Traced the plate, sir," he announced.

"And Miss Frampton?" Sophy blurted out.

"Traced 'er too."


The lodging was shabby but not without a certain jaded air of refinement, a repository of gentlemen fallen from positions of trust, of ladies run aground on the reefs of widowhood or impecunity. The carpets, like the tenants, were threadbare, and the whole establishment impregnated with the odor of boiled fish and cabbage soup. One cracked gas-mantel, in an ornamental flue, lit the staircase. The proprietress, who had been previously bribed by

Dawlish, led the way upstairs in a halo of light from a coal-oil lamp.

She knocked gingerly on a door off the first floor landing.

"Miss Frampton? Miss Frampton, are you there?"

A scuffling sound came from behind the wood, then a prolonged bout of harsh coughing.

"Miss Frampton, may I 'ave a word, please?" the proprietress insisted.

The coughing continued, muffled. The woman glanced over her shoulder at Alfred Dawlish. Crowded behind Dawlish, Sophy and Leon waited anxiously. Along the gloomy corridor a door opened a crack, and an eye watched the proceedings curiously.

Dawlish held out his hand. "The key, please, ma'am."

"Are you sure that the Misses Frampton are the ladies you require?"

"Yes, ma'am," said Dawlish drily, inserting the key into the lock. Behind the door, the occupant's key, nudged out, fell to the floor with a clink. "Now, if you'd just leave the rest to us. No fuss, ma'am. No disturbance."

The proprietress sidled anxiously away, carrying the lamp with her. She paused at the head of the stairs, then, shaking her head, descended out of earshot.

Dawlish turned the key and the handle, pushing the door open so that he could peer inside the apartment.

He let out a low whistle of astonishment then, beckoning the de Nervals to follow, stepped into the room.

There was no sign of Eunice Frampton. It took Sophy a moment to recognize the woman who lay slumped across the mattress. The truckle bed dominated the setting. For the rest there was little enough by way of furnishing, a chair, a table, and a dressing cabinet. On the floor, partly covered by trailing sheets, was a case untidily packed with clothing and personal items.

Hair unloosened, dressed only in a shift and one

tangled black stocking, Cora Frampton slumped face downward upon the bed, coughing and croaking, tears streaming down her shrunken cheeks.

Leon leaned over her and, with great caution, lifted and turned her face from the pillow. Her lips pulled back in a hideous spasm of fury, and, for an instant, her red-rimmed eyes blazed. Then coughing overwhelmed her once more, so violently that she tossed and writhed and, when the bout had eased, lay limp as a scarecrow on the floor, shoulders propped against the mattress.

Between them Leon and Dawlish lifted her onto the bed and Sophy covered her with the bedclothes. Fever racked her, two spots of vivid color on the ashen cheeks. A blood-speckled handkerchief was balled into her fist, and sweat glistened on her brow and bosom. She looked old, very old, and close to death.

"Is this Cora Frampton?" asked Leon, in a whisper.

Sophy nodded.

"We must fetch a doctor at once," said Leon.

Struggling for breath, Cora Frampton levered herself into a sitting position, her head propped against the wooden headboard. A flicker of rage twisted her face for an instant, then was gone. She stared at Sophy, unblinking.

"Cora," Sophy said. "Where is your sister?"

"Eunice?"

"Yes, where is Eunice?"

"Left . . . me: gone."

Dawlish was picking over the contents of the case.

"Sophy, this woman is dying," Leon said.

Dawlish moved quietly to the dressing cabinet and slid open the drawers. His examination of the room continued discreetly.

Bending over the woman, Sophy murmured, "How long have you been ill?"

"Week."

"And Eunice knew of it?"

"She . . . she . . . left me."

"When?"

The voice was the merest whisper, clogged and choked: "Hours . . . hours ago."

"Today?" prompted Sophy.

"I . . . I think so."

"Cora, where is my baby? Where did your sister leave my baby?"

"She left *me*; she . . . she . . . knew I was . . . going. They both . . . left me."

"Miss Frampton," Leon intervened. "You must tell us where the baby is lodged. We can help you; we *will* help you. But you must tell us the address in return—now."

The mouth slackened, then spread into a leer. "I dunno. That's the truth. She . . . never . . . told me where she left him."

Sophy whimpered and moved back, covering her face with her hand. Leon too stood back, long enough for Dawlish to touch his elbow and declare, "Nothing here: not a single thing."

Leon leaned forward. Hands on each side of Cora Frampton's head, he stared down into her face. "There was a plan, was there not?"

"*Her* . . . plan."

"Very well," Leon said. "I will make you a promise: Tell me all that you know, and I will see to it that you have the best medical attention."

"Prison?"

"No, not prison," Leon said. "A hospital. You must trust my word."

Cora swallowed painfully, and coughed again. But she had all the will of the Framptons behind her and fought hard against the fever that threatened to snuff out her life. Hatred was the mainspring of her strength now, hatred of her sister's final betrayal. Her lips were flecked with blood, tiny bright pinpricks of it, but her eyes were alive and through the feverish dreams that clouded her mind some of her former cunning was restored.

"Took . . . took advantage of the situation," she gasped. "Waited near ten years for it. Sophy—you—she planned it, most of it. Patient, my sister. Patient. Big haul. Wanted that."

"Where has she gone?" said Sophy. "We *must* find her."

"France. Dover . . . Calais: France. Got all the money. Got gold. Left . . . none for me."

"And Bolton?"

"Sold . . . his share. Went last night. She . . . she wouldn't have him, see."

"When did she leave, Cora?" Sophy said. "Think; please, think."

"Hour . . . hours ago; both of us; money . . . set up in France."

"Dover?" Leon said. He stood up.

"That's London Bridge station," said Dawlish, crisply. "Shall I be on my way, sir?"

"No," said Leon. "I'll go there. I can identify her more readily than you."

"You want me to . . ." Dawlish wagged his finger expressively at the prone figure in the bed. "See to 'er?"

"A doctor; fetch a doctor," said Leon de Nerval. "If she can be moved, take her to a hospital. If not—do what you can."

Dawlish nodded; he knew by the very look of her that nobody could do much for Cora Frampton now.

Sophy said, "Leon, take me with you."

For a moment the trader seemed about to refuse.

"Please."

"Very well, Sophy," he said. "But we must go at once."

While she appeared to be calm and in complete control of her emotions, inwardly Sophy seethed with impatience and the chill fear that the retribution that the Fates had designed as her punishment was the irrevocable loss of her child at the very moment when she seemed most close to discovering him again. Still Leon offered her no physical comfort as they swayed and jolted inside the fast chaise through the broad streets between the Ludgate lodging-house and the new railway terminus at London Bridge.

A final urgency was imparted to the journey by a change in the weather. With the first approach of dusk the fog had hardened into a slate-hued cloud out of which spots of rain fell, loud as pennies, onto the vehicle's proofed canopy.

By the time the de Nervals emerged from the chaise under the long glass-roofed promenade at the station's western flank, it was raining heavily and the last of the fog had been sluiced away.

Travelers, held prisoners for two or three days, had emerged *en masse* to throng the covered ways and wooden platforms, the concourses and shopping arcades under the Italian cornices. Long queues of none-too-orderly citizens snaked round the ticket booths and fed into the doors of the refreshment rooms.

Above the heads of the crowds the butts of the railway carriages could be seen, porters hurriedly strapping luggage to roof rails and racking mailboxes tightly into their allotted slots. Three locomotives steamed, hissed and shunted their pistons thunderously, belching tarry smoke through their tall stacks. Their brasswork was dulled and smeared by navigations through a fogbound countryside and the last sluggish haul into London's rain.

The span of the station roof seemed to stretch away into a murky tunnel no larger than a soup dish a thousand feet away. The plate glass was rivered with rain. A rush of water added to the deafening din of engines and passengers, and the sibilant *whish* of the huge conical gas lamps that hung in regular lanes under the arches and iron pillars.

The possibility of finding one lone woman in that bustling mass of folk struck Sophy as hopeless. She faltered and caught Leon's arm, supporting herself against him.

The noises; the jostling of so many bodies; the cloying sweetness of spilled engine oil; the sourness of chickens crated in wicker baskets awaiting dispatch; the acrid rasping smoke, all combined to remind her that she was pregnant and to bring a wave of nausea over her. Fear, too, lay cold and hard in the pit of her stomach. Her head reeled.

A rough laborer, holding a canvas roll in front of him like a weapon, all but knocked her down.

Leon held her, steadied her, but gave her no attention.

Head weaving and ducking, he scouted the shifting tides of passengers who streamed onto the platforms or dithered outside the carriage doors to attend the safe placement of their luggage.

With a sudden lunge, the trader collared a tiny impish man dressed in the uniform of a South-East official.

Holding the imp still, Leon bellowed: "The Dover train?"

"Yer lookin' at it," said the imp, indignantly wrenching himself free and making off under the clock at the double.

A salvo of closing doors announced the train's imminent departure. A trumpeting blast of steam jetted into the vaulted arch far overhead. The truckful of third-class citizens sent up a cheer.

Leon caught at her. "Sophy, you must hold on."

The third class, sprawling out of the shutters, had formed an impromptu choral society, and were rendering "Ben Battle" with gusto. Further along, second-class gentlemen were rioting politely for the best seats, and at the end of the line of carriages, two first-class coaches were sedately taking on the last of their booked passengers.

Running now, dragging Sophy behind him, Leon fixed

upon one compartment in the first-class section. Three uniformed porters, with stovepipe hats tipped back on their heads, were struggling manfully to hoist a wooden box, fastened with a huge padlock, onto the roof. To judge by their efforts and the strength required, the box was no ordinary piece of luggage.

Top-hatted personages and the neatly bonneted wives and daughters who accompanied them watched the proceedings with faintly amused interest, ignoring a fourth representative of the South-Eastern Railway Company who was endeavoring to persuade them to board.

For a second, Sophy had a clear view of the casual array of gentlefolk, the end boards of the platform feathered with steam and glossy with rain where the arc of the roof cut off. Under it was a veil of murk out of which a lambent red eye formed and grew. Sophy cried out and reached again for Leon's arm. But her husband had not noticed the incoming locomotive. His gaze was riveted on the loading scene, on the massively heavy box and, then, abruptly, upon the figure of the woman below.

"Sophy: there!"

In a rook-black traveling dress, hood folded down, Eunice Frampton stood transfixed, her arms raised to direct the positioning of her precious cargo. Slowly her head turned, cranking round as if on a cog. She appeared not to see Leon at all, only Sophy.

The wooden box creaked on its ropes, slipping on the knots and causing the porter to curse, then, without sincerity, to apologize.

All around, it seemed, the commotion became still, hubbub dying, the push and thrust of passengers of all classes frozen into a tableau of attention. Sounds isolated themselves in Sophy's mind and merged into sharp, snorting noise, which quickly rose in pitch and volume. The red eye, a brakeman's lantern, centered a dim planet of brass and iron that loomed closer out of the rainswept darkness in the spaces beyond the rails' end. Eunice Frampton was freakishly silhouetted against it, poised in a position of surrender. But surrender was far from her thoughts.

"Please, Miss Frampton; please," Sophy called out.

Eunice Frampton heard, and responded.

She lowered her arms, cast one last despairing glance at the chest slung from the rail-rack then, with a darting motion, plucked up a bulky leather portmanteau from the carriage step and, girding her skirts, ran.

There was nowhere to go; no escape, encumbered as the woman was by the bag and by the many layers of cloth she had donned to be stylish and protected against the sea air of the Channel. In the rook-black garb she looked strangely old-fashioned, like an acolyte of some forgotten order; the portmanteau, now no longer in her hand, clasped in her arms like a child. It seemed as if she were drawn towards the gloom at the station's end, rushing inexorably into the welcoming darkness, away from the palaces of glass and iron, from boilers, smokestacks, and the thrusting pistons that drove on the wheels of progress.

It was all over before Sophy could stir, before Leon could take more than a single pace towards the fugitive.

In running, Eunice Frampton was compelled to glance behind her. She seemed to hover, then to be sucked along like a skater on a long graceful slide off the wet boards, into the center of the gilded shield. She hung on it, pasted flat like a gigantic leaf, then vanished.

Sounds, screams and urgent shouts swarmed into Sophy's consciousness. She felt herself lifted and carried towards the monster, which, spewing sparks from its brakes and steam from its cylinders, shrieked to a grinding halt not five yards from the flock of spectators.

Gaping down, Sophy saw a tattered bundle cradled on the locomotive's buffers.

If she had been arranged there like a model on a

podium, Eunice Frampton could not have contrived a more pathetic yet decorous position. Her skirts were draped over her limbs, left arm hooked on the chains of the buffer junction. Her spine was supported by the metal bases and her thighs by the spring-pods. The hood had slipped round her throat, and her hair, though stained with blood, was still coiled tightly at the nape of her neck. Her right arm was twisted under her body, the portmanteau handle rigidly gripped in her closed fist.

Leon leapt down onto the track. He was bathed in a seepage of steam, a cloud of it swirling around him; he stepped back and beckoned Sophy, cupping his hands to take her weight as he lifted her down from the platform's edge and placed her on the track between the rails. The monster sighed; and was still.

"Is she . . . ?"

"Miraculously, she's still alive," Leon said.

Stepping close between the buffers, Sophy stared curiously at the woman. Her skin was bone-white, the shape of her face more delicate than Sophy had ever seen it before, almost beautiful. All the gauntness was gone, the stiffness. She lay like a chaste queen upon a metal divan, eyes wide open staring up at the rain rivering the glass high overhead. But the black fabric of the traveling dress was mottled with blood, a subtle scarlet flowering on the bodice and, soon, upon the skirts.

"I . . . can't . . . see you," Eunice Frampton whispered. "Who is it? Cora? Cora, is it you?"

"It's Sophy, Miss Frampton: your Sophy."

There were men behind her, officials of the railway, the locomotive driver, the brakeman, a young man claiming to be a medical student. Leon held them back.

Tenderly, Sophy gathered the woman to her.

They could feel life ebbing away, not noisily, as with Cora, not dramatically; yet Eunice Frampton was passing swiftly into the darkness that she had strived so desperately to reach. There was no selfish thought in Sophy's mind now, only overwhelming sorrow and resurgent memories of the woman's kindness and strength in girlhood days, of her companionship.

"My . . . dear?"

"I'm here, Miss Frampton. I'm here."

"Your little boy . . . in Horners' . . . Tobacco . . . Tobacco Street."

Lifting the woman, Sophy rocked gently, very gently, weeping with grief and a fearful kind of relief.

"Sophy, I . . . lied . . . before . . . but not . . . not . . . now." The words had no shape, dovetailed one into the other and faded; the eyes were sightless, the lips slack.

The canvas portmanteau dropped to the cinder track.

Leon lifted Sophy away. Scooping her into his arms, he carried her the length of the platform, across the astonished concourse and into the waiting chaise.

Only when his wife was safe, did he hurry back to the Dover train to answer questions and stake a claim to his gold.

# *Fifteen*

In spite of Sophy's pleading, Leon would not permit her to venture that night down into the Limehouse slums. Instead, he confined her to bed, summoned a doctor and, on that gentleman's advice, engaged an experienced nurse to look after his wife's health during the course of her recovery. Sophy could not be sure that Leon did not delay the last act of the drama that had marred their lives out of a conscious need to add punishment of his own to the suffering she had already undergone. She argued and begged hysterically, but found him adamant. At length, she capitulated and, soothed by a sleeping draught, sobbed herself to sleep.

Leon glanced at the nurse, a heavyset woman with a plain, kindly face. She nodded, signifying that Sophy was in good hands, and Leon returned to the study below.

The inquisition at the railway station had lasted an hour and had been continued, under the leadership of a policeman, in the drawing room at Damaris Square. Subterfuge of that sort was familiar ground for the trader, however, and, at length, he had satisfied the authorities that the gold, and the banknotes in the portmanteau, were his rightful property and should be given back to him as soon as the Board of Enquiry into Eunice Frampton's accident returned its verdict of death by misadventure.

Cora Frampton was in St. Olwen's Hospital and,

according to Dawlish, "like to pull through, after all."
A man of his word, Leon would not press charges against
her. When she was well again, he would allow her to slink
into hiding once more. It appeared that Cora was not
entirely without funds on her own account, though how
her savings had been acquired was a matter best left
dormant.

George Bolton had made good his escape. Of the three
conspirators, only Bolton had cleared a tidy profit on the
sale of his share of the swag—a sum lost not by Leon but
by the mysterious Prater Williams. This bit of business
seemed to amuse Alfred Dawlish considerably; the inquiry
agent was still hopeful that Bolton would surface again
in the near future and be brought to book, if not by the
law then by underworld vigilantes. Personal jewelry and
other items still missing from the house would, Dawlish
surmised, turn up on the illicit market and might be
bought back, if not actually retrieved *gratis*. To this end
Dawlish was commissioned to continue in Leon's employ
for a while longer.

It was midnight before Dawlish left for his lodging
and Leon de Nerval found himself alone. The servants
had cleared the debris from the parlor and tidied the
rooms as best they could. But the missing items seemed to
glare out at the Breton and made him acutely aware of
the perilousness of his domestic fortress, and of his own
position in regard to Sophy.

The Dresden finch was gone, shattered, its crumbs
swept into a dustpan and discarded; the symbolic nature
of the delicate ornament's destruction made itself felt in
the trader's heart. It was part of the romance of youth;
Sophy's youth, not his own. It was wrong of him to
regard her as a chattel—and the reality of her affair with
a captain of hussars did not fill him with morbid depression. The hussar was dead. For all his charitableness,
Leon could not regret that one fact. What remained of

Sophy's passionate and ill-guarded girlhood romance was a baby, a child. By any natural law, he would have been better with the soldier as competitor. He could not challenge the unsentimental love that his wife had for her son.

Come the fall of the year, he too would have a child, would have fathered a son or daughter; the pride and excitement he had felt already at the prospect was not to be denied. How much pride would he sacrifice, *could* he sacrifice to be rid of the phantoms of the past? Perhaps, after all, he should have chosen the easy path into matrimony and should have wedded Gwen Lloyd. He had always enjoyed her company and had great respect for her. But he did not love her; several years ago he had reconciled himself to a belief in love, in the need for love. He had loved Sophy; did he love Sophy still?

He drank coffee from the pot that Miller had left by the hearth, and warmed his hands at the fire. An ache of weariness was in him, and a fretful agitation whose source was no mystery. For a short while he tried to pretend that he was concerned for his business house and the Amsterdam agreement. But that illusion did not endure. He had driven himself ruthlessly all his life, climbing out of abject poverty, in search of . . . of what? He could count and have accounted all that he had gained in his struggles. But where was the tally of what he had lost? Pride was the spur: could pride also be the drag-rein?

Pushing himself to his feet, Leon de Nerval set out for Tobacco Street, alone.

It was not the squalor that disgusted him—he had seen his share of that in his time—but the unctuousness of the couple and the contrasting passivity of the children. He could see how they had been broken, not by circumstance but by deliberate punishment and by the total withholding of love.

The Horners admitted him reluctantly, after he had

thundered on the door for a quarter of an hour and threatened to summon the constables unless they gave him entry.

They had given him entry in barking bad temper, which, when they saw his fine clothes and the gold ring on his finger, changed at once to a simpering desire to please.

"You do us a 'onor, sir," the man said.

" 'Scuse us bein' dressed so informally," the woman said. "But we had a hard day wiff the liddle 'uns."

A barred door, and a curtained alcove: Leon surveyed the hovel-like kitchen in search of some evidence of "liddle 'uns": ale and gin bottles, glasses, a pipe still reeking smoke, a hambone set high on a shelf where no child could reach it.

The woman was blowsy and fat and smelled of grease. She had thrown a robe over her night clothing and bagged her hair in a cotton cloth. The man had thrown on a shirt over a pair of filthy moleskin trousers, and stuck his naked feet into boots.

The ache, which he had mistaken for weariness, changed in Leon, and he was suddenly impatient with the couple. He extracted two Bank of England notes, each valued at ten pounds, from his fob pocket and held them like calling cards between finger and thumb. In that way, he gained the couple's full attention.

" 'Doption, is it?" the woman asked.

"Good 'ome for a liddle 'un?" Horner said. "Brought up in the bosom of our fam'bly, like one of our own."

"Baby, is it?" the woman said. "Gotter a wet nurse; though 'er services cost . . ."

"I wish to buy a child," de Nerval said, evenly.

"*Buy* a child!" Horner and his wife exchanged a sly glance. "Buy one of our liddle fam'bly?"

Cautiously, the woman said, "We . . . er, don't trade in liddle souls, sir."

"Do you take me for the law?" said Leon. "When did

the law ever brandish money? I want a boychild; one year old. He was brought to you as a newborn infant last March, brought by a tall, gaunt woman."

Horner and his wife exchanged another glance, speculative and not without apprehension.

"I don't seem to recall . . ." Horner began.

Leon tossed the money onto the table.

"Find him, and it's yours."

"Find 'im?" said the woman. "We ain't lost him. He was never brought 'ere."

Was it possible that Eunice Frampton, with her dying breath, had lied once more? Leon's heart thudded in his chest, and a sudden sharp pang of fear gripped his midriff.

The inner door beckoned him. He knew already what scenes of horror he would find there; he could hear the scuffling, mouselike sounds; he could smell the sourness. He wanted no responsibility for the other poor mites— only for Sophy's child. It no longer mattered that he was not the father. If it had been within his power at that moment he would have swept up all the children and carried them off with him. But that was impossible; one would have to serve, to be a token of the whole emotion.

"A boy; one year old," he repeated.

The curtain moved an inch, no more: a draught from the broken windows, or a rat scuttering back into its hole in the wainscot? Leon darted to the curtain and tore it open.

In the filthy bed, three babies lay, naked and as motionless as clay dolls. The only light came from the kitchen; a wan shaft that lit up the figure of the tall girl in the corner, her knuckles in her mouth and her eyes full of dread.

Below her, in a tier of boxes and drawers, four other children slept. They were a little older, though hardly larger or more robust than the infants on the bedding. He could smell in the air the sweetish, sickly odor of the opiate medicine with which the children were kept drugged and passive.

Rage surged in him: a frightening explosion of raw fury such as he had never experienced before. He fought against it, released it only in one backward slash of his left arm as Horner sought to draw him back from the hellish alcove. He heard the man cry out and the tumble of a chair as he fell; then Leon slipped into the alcove and drew the curtain behind him. He struck a match and lit the wick of the candle in the jar on the shelf. The medicines stood in rows along the shelf and it was only by a supreme effort of will that he stopped himself from sweeping them to the floor.

It was the girl who fascinated him; the girl must not be frightened.

Thickly, Leon de Nerval said, "I have come to take my . . . my son home."

"Daddy?" The girl took her knuckles from her mouth and cocked her head. She was broad-shouldered, full-breasted, and young, very young. "You, Daddy?"

Leon nodded, and looked down at the sleeping children.

Pinched, tight-lidded faces in swaddles of rags: he felt as if his heart would break.

"Which . . . which one is mine?" he whispered. He knew that the girl had heard every word spoken in the kitchen, but could not be sure that she had understood.

She was smiling, fat cheeks split and eyes merry. "Daddy! He's come. Daddy's come."

Unerringly, she lifted one infant from a drawer, spilling away the rags. The child, a boy, whimpered and closed his tiny fists upon her hair. She held him up, like a rabbit.

"He'll take you 'ome," she said, delightedly. "Told yer you wasn't forgot."

She held the little boy out and Leon, wonderingly, touched the cap of flaxen hair, struggling against the belief that he could see some resemblance to Sophy in the sleeping face.

The child whimpered again. On impulse, Leon caught him and pressed him against the nap of his overcoat, wrapping his arms protectively around him, giving him warmth.

He studied the girl. Her hands were clasped to her breast and, for an instant, her blue eyes were piercingly vital and alive.

"Woman brought 'im; saw 'er through the curtain," she said. "Woman in a black dress. Near . . . near a year ago, when I 'ad milk. He were mine for a six month." She cocked her head once more and looked on the child with such fondness that Leon's last doubts were dispelled. "Now he's got 'is daddy, like I told 'im he would."

Turning, Leon carried the child through the curtain. The Horners sulked and glared at him.

"This is the one, is it not?"

Horner growled, "Yus, that's 'im."

"What's his name?" Leon asked.

Horner shrugged and snorted derisively, "Ain't got no name, has 'e! Never got round to it, like."

"For Gawd's sake, take 'im," the fat woman said. "That's what yer came 'ere for, ain't it? Take 'im an leave us be."

"Yes," Leon said and, without another word, carried the child out into Tobacco Street and into the waiting chaise.

In the leathery darkness of the carriage's interior, he unbuttoned his overcoat and wrapped the sleeping child close against his chest. Only then did the trader let tears well up and trickle down his cheeks and, clasping the little boy more tightly still, carried him safely home.

At last the winter was over. Spring spread north through Yorkshire, coaxing out green buds and sprigs of new grass. The pastures were lively with sturdy lambs and along the ridge of Huffton Pike the flocks of hill ewes trailed with their young deeper into the dales.

Seated in the broad closed four-wheeler, behind a pair of strong little horses, Sophy delighted in the open countryside. Leon sat opposite her, the little boy on his knee— Thomas de Nerval, an heir adopted and made fast to the family by every legal contrivance that money could buy.

In the ten weeks since that incredible night when Leon had restored her son, Sophy had seen very little of her husband. Her joy in her child, and in the baby now making its presence known inside her, had been dimmed by Leon's change in manner. He was not cold nor hostile, merely preoccupied, exercising that part of his character that blotted all trivial and irrelevant things from his mind, to concentrate on matters of great complexity. For a week or two Sophy had been glad to allow the wounds to heal, to recover her health and her interest in the future. It appeared that Leon had no intention of seeking divorce, or of casting her from him. For all that he had become more than preoccupied: almost secretive. Sophy debated with herself whether Leon had taken a mistress to console himself in the period of hurt that followed inexorably in the wake of the fogbound days of February.

It was Gwen Lloyd, a kind friend indeed, who put Sophy's mind at rest, assuring her that Leon was merely engaged in several complicated business deals—"a kind of winding up of his affairs"—and in reshaping the design of his plans for the future of the House of de Nerval.

Sophy had no right to question her husband; he, in turn, volunteered no information. His golden nest egg was returned intact by the authorities. Most, though not all, of the jewelry and trinkets removed by Eunice Frampton and George Bolton was redeemed. In mid-March, Leon finally found time to visit Amsterdam, with David Lloyd as a traveling advisor, and conclude the purchase of even more gold. He journeyed, too, to other places in England, of which Sophy knew nothing.

Building up the strength of her son was Sophy's main

concern. She also reestablished the domestic routine of Damaris Square with a full complement of new servants. Jinny, the maids, the cook and even the loyal Miller had been given notice; Leon would brook no arguments on the subject. It was Leon who interviewed and engaged the domestics, including Nurse Harrison and a youngish, sprightly butler called Wellwind upon whom the duties of housekeeping fell. Leon also chose the child's name, arranged baptism, and the technicalities of adoption.

For all his activity, the atmosphere of secrecy increased; with it Sophy's fears that social pressure would be brought to bear to which her husband would eventually yield. It occurred to her that Leon was already seeking refuge in his profession, that, even if he did not sue for divorcement, he would drift away from her over the course of the years and she would find herself, though still a wife, estranged and alone.

Leon would not speak of the events that led to the recovery of her son, nor would he discuss details of his business. Life in Damaris Square, however, soon settled to an even keel, though there was no real contentment now that the communion between husband and wife had dwindled.

It surprised Sophy when Leon proposed a trip to Yorkshire, explaining that he had some final items of business with Cairncross to settle before her father's debts were put to rest at last. Though Sophy had no wish to meet with her stepmother again, spring had brought a longing for the countryside, for the Riding in particular; she readily agreed. How she would explain her year-old son to Agatha was a problem that concerned her greatly for a day or two, but it gradually paled into unimportance as the sunshine increased and the trees in the park put out their tender leaves. London, the house, became a prison, stifling and confining. She wanted to enjoy the sight of her son crawling among the flowers of the meadows and to introduce him to the land in which she had been born and where, once, she had been happy.

Thomas de Nerval had recovered quickly from his drugged, half-starved condition. He had put on weight and soon developed his mother's robustness and his father's strength. He was alert, lively, and full of fun and, during the train journey to Manchester, slept not at all, badgering Leon incessantly with gurgling noises and expressions of amazement at the wonders that unreeled beyond the carriage windows. The bond between Leon and his adopted son puzzled Sophy: it seemed deep, enduring and natural, as if they were related by the ties of flesh and blood. With humor and a whole orchestra of assorted sounds, Leon was at pains to explain the sights of the countryside to little Thomas, already beginning that invaluable education that only a loving father can give to his son.

For a moment, seated in the swaying four-wheeler as it rounded the curve and approached the Huffton policies, Sophy felt a wave of happiness at the sight of the child on her husband's lap, at the baby in her womb and the freshness of the landscape around her. Sternly, she told herself, it must be an illusion, another dream, as dangerous perhaps as the dream she had had of romance, the mirage of adventure that her affair with Edmund had shattered. But the desire for a home and a husband, for the continuity of love through children, that was the true reality. If only the foolishness of her pursuit of freedom, and her stepmother's vindictive examples had not wormed its root. The irony of it all was that she loved Leon more than ever before.

It was not until the carriage halted at the door of Huffton House that Sophy had an inkling that she was unwittingly involved in a ceremony of forgiveness. The face of the young man who opened the door was familiar, though the good rustic tweeds and the banded cloth cap were not.

She looked again; then, inquiringly, up at Leon.

"That . . . that was Miller?"

"Why, so it was!" said Leon, making the child ready to step down onto his grandfather's estate.

"Leon, why is Miller here?" Sophy paused, still within the carriage. Another kind of anxiety possessed her at the unexpected occurrence.

Leon said, "I felt the lad would be happier in Yorkshire. I employed him to serve in Huffton."

"*You* employed him? Did Agatha agree?"

"Come, let me help you down, Sophy."

Leon handed Thomas to Miller who wrapped the little boy securely in his arms and, with much mutual clucking and chucking, held him up to stare at the sheep and horses and the benign green pastures.

Leon stepped onto the gravel and, turning, lifted his arms to Sophy. Carefully, he swung her to the ground, but he did not release her.

"Leon? What's . . . what's happening?"

"We're coming home, Sophy: that's all."

The carriage moved off towards the stables and, swinging round, Sophy looked up at the open door of the mansion.

"Where is Agatha?"

"Agatha is no longer mistress of this estate," said Leon.

"She sold it?"

"To me," said Leon. "It's our house now, our land."

"But . . . but Leon, you are a trader."

"The railway runs to Liverpool, and to Manchester," said Leon. "I will continue to trade. And we will still have Damaris Square for the London season. But this, Sophy, is our home."

"I don't . . . understand."

"Your stepmother preferred capital to property; she preferred the city of London to the wilds of Yorkshire. I took purchase. It's as simple as that."